A thriller loaded with mystery and suspense!

SAVING NEW YORK

ROBERT E. B. WRIGHT

Saving New York **is a work of fiction.**
Characters, places, names, businesses,
organizations, incidents and events are products of the
author's imagination. They are used fictitiously
and not to be regarded as real. Any resemblance
to persons, living or dead, or to actual events
or locations, is coincidental.

Copyright © 2017 by Robert E. B. Wright

ISBN: 978-1-950312-04-7

Cover design by Hilton Graphics, Lindy Leftwich, Robert E. B. Wright and Valerie Cardarelli-Wright. Stock photography from the author and various sources, rights obtained.

Manuscript typing, all editing, interior book design and formatting by Valerie Cardarelli-Wright.

For Val.
One hundred lifetimes together would not be enough.

ALSO BY ROBERT E. B. WRIGHT

Saving an Innocent Man

Saving Kenya

A special thank you from Robert:

Thank you for buying this book.
I hope you enjoy it.
If you do, please go to my website at
RobertWrightThrillers.com
and let's get to know each other better.

*Who is this man called Chance?
And why is the Mayor of New York
willing to pay him almost anything?*

ONE

In Bayside, Queens, NYPD patrolman, Brian O'Neill woke up at 6:00 this Monday morning with no inkling he would be murdered today.

The love of his life since high school, Beth, had no fears today either. But foreboding thoughts did cross her mind now and then. When they did, it was usually as soon as Brian walked out the door.

Brian's bare feet hit the carpeted floor as Beth got up and put a quick breakfast on the table. They shared a few minutes together over coffee and they planned their week: a lecture on perennials at the garden club Wednesday night, dinner at her parent's house in Smithtown on Saturday night, the farmer's market on Sunday after church.

Five-year-old, blonde-haired Savannah shuffled up to the kitchen table rubbing the sleep out of her blue eyes. A daily ritual.

But this morning, she started to cry.

"Sweetie, what's wrong? Why are you crying?" Brian asked with a sad face.

"I had a bad dream."

"What kind of dream? What did you dream about, honey?" Beth said sweetly.

Savannah couldn't get the words out.

"What was it?" Beth asked again.

"I dreamed Daddy got hurt."

Brian's and Beth's eyes flashed to each other.

"Oh, honey," Brian said as he hugged his little girl,

"don't worry. It's just a dream. A bad dream. Everything's fine. Mommy and Daddy are here to love you and hug you every day."

Beth's face gave her away. She wasn't a superstitious woman, but her child's dream gave her an uneasy feeling. She comforted her little girl. "Daddy's strong and he's smart. He'll be back before you know it, just like always. Now, you come up here on my lap and keep me company while Daddy's at work."

Brian got up from the table and walked into another room. In the crib, sleeping, was his three-month-old son, Brennan. He leaned into the crib and kissed his son's head. He paused and took a lingering look at his baby boy. At the kitchen table, Brian kissed Savannah and Beth goodbye.

"You're still the prettiest girl I ever saw," he said to Beth.

"Oh, your eyes are going. Not good for a policeman."

Brian, dressed in his blue uniform, gave her a loving smile. "See y'all later. Love you."

"Love you, too."

As he closed the door behind him, Snoozer, the family's little Cairn terrier, walked to the closed door, sat down and just looked at it for a while. A long while.

Beth looked at Snoozer, looked at the closed door, then looked at Savannah.

. . .

In Manhattan, on the fourth-floor of an apartment building on the corner of Murray and Broadway, an ominous looking black rifle lay on a frayed, white bedspread. In the dim light, a dark silhouette raised the rifle and sighted through the scope, aiming through a sun-bright window. Fingers dialed the knurled knob on the scope and the brass ball on top of a distant flag pole changed from blurry to sharp focus.

. . .

The gray metal door clanged open to the bright sunlight and an elderly man in a loose-fitting black suit closed it behind him. He walked across the black surface of the flat roof to the flagpole. He squinted in the sunlight as he grabbed the ropes and looked up at the American flag hanging at half-staff. Pulling on the white ropes, he began to raise the flag, bending his neck back to get a better look. Satisfied it had reached the top, he turned, head down, slightly blinded by the bright sun. He took a step forward toward the metal door but his foot kicked something that rolled away from him in a zigzag motion. Then he saw something else. He picked them both up, one in each hand, and continued to the door.

. . .

Police officer, Brian O'Neill, in full gear, walked out of the deli on Chambers Street carrying two cups of coffee. He walked over to the police car and handed his partner one of the cups through the passenger's open window. Brian carefully removed the plastic lid and brought the cup to his lips.

The view through the riflescope showed steam. Steam from a coffee cup. The sight picture moved slightly up and to the left. The chest of the silhouette holding the rifle inhaled deeply, let out a little breath slowly, then held it in.

. . .

In the walnut paneled room, in front of an antique leather-topped desk, stood two women speaking with a distinguished-looking 63-year-old man in a tailored suit and a shiny blue tie. "Thank you, Mr. Mayor," one of the women said as she took the Mayor's hand in a feminine handshake.

"Yes, thank you so much, Mayor Wertz," the other woman said. "We appreciate your time and consideration of our organization. A speech from you would do so much to give us the credibility we need to raise funds this year."

"Happy to help, ladies, happy to help. Patty here," his head nodded to the short woman standing to the side, "and Tom Elliott, my Press Secretary," he nodded toward Tom, "will check my schedule, pencil you in and confirm two weeks before the event."

The three expressed final pleasantries and the women departed, ushered out by Patty Bromstad, Mayor Wertz's dedicated Secretary. Tom stayed in the room.

The Mayor took off his jacket and took his seat. "OK, Tom, let's go over today's media."

An elderly man in a loose-fitting black suit, walked in and put something on the Mayor's desk.

"What's that, Andy?"

"The top of the flagpole. The ball on top."

"It broke into two pieces? Lightning?"

"Don't know, Mr. Mayor. Must have been something pretty powerful to split that metal ball apart."

Patty Bromstad poked her head through the open door. "The Police Commissioner is on his way over. He said it's an emerg…" Patty couldn't finish her words. The Commissioner burst in.

"Another one! There's been another one! On Chambers Street. Two blocks away," the Commissioner raised his arm and pointed toward the wall.

The Mayor and old man Andy looked stunned. Frozen.

Commissioner Brix couldn't get the words out fast enough. "One shot. A bus is on the way. But he's gone. We're swarming all over it."

You could hear the sirens now. Many of them.

Brix throttled on, frustrated. "Poor kid!" He paused for a breath. "Gonzalez was riding shotgun. He's fine. They stopped for coffee. O'Neill brought it back to the car and boom! Actually, no boom! No boom! Nothing! Nobody heard anything!" The Commissioner stopped, as if running out of gas.

The Mayor sat down. Andy held his hand to his face. He had seen a lot in his time, but nothing like this. Two officers gunned down in a week. Tom Elliott sat down.

Commissioner Brix continued, "Stevens was on a Monday, too."

The Mayor said, "I hope we don't have what we're all afraid of here."

"Gotta check ballistics ASAP," Brix said. "We already called everybody in to start pulling everything together."

The Mayor spoke with surprising calmness, voice low. No screaming from the Mayor. "Press conference, two hours."

"Ed, I don't know if we're going to know much in two hours." The Commissioner worried the words.

The Mayor ignored him and continued, "Informative. Concise. Make it clear we're on top of this. We can't let this get in front of us. Get any and all info you can. Who, where, when, and what we're doing next. Two dead cops, assassinated cops, within one week. We've got to say something. Two hours! Get on it, Elliott!"

Tom Elliott spoke up. "Who do you want there?"

"The usual cast of characters. But let's hope this doesn't become a habit."

The Mayor nervously massaged his temples. "I want hard copies of everything you have in one hour."

As they all filed out of the room, Patty sat down in a chair in front of the Mayor's desk, dutifully waiting to help her boss.

He didn't say anything.

He just looked at the broken gold-colored objects on his desk.

. . .

The moss-green door with the brass knocker opened slowly. Beth O'Neill had her three-month-old in her arms. Little five-year-old Savannah stood at her side, whimpering. When Beth saw the tears in the eyes of the two silent police officers, her knees gave way and she sank to the floor. She knew that her life had changed forever.

. . .

"We're waiting for Mayor Wertz to start the press conference scheduled for 3:30 P.M. As soon as he…" the young man was speaking into a microphone in his hand. Behind him was a podium in front of a blue wall with a repeating NYC logo pattern. The American flag was on the left, the New York State flag on the right. In the middle, on the podium, were a half dozen microphones waiting for the words of Mayor Wertz and his cadre.

Eight feet away from the young reporter, an older man was speaking in front of a shoulder-mounted TV camera. "We're expecting Mayor Wertz to address the shooting of a second New York City policeman and take questions. It's unknown…"

On the side of the room was another TV reporter. An attractive young woman in a dark purple blouse and white skirt. Her blonde hair fell below her shoulders and glowed against her blouse. She, too, looked into the camera and spoke into her mic: "… this is the second police officer shot in a week. Last Monday officer Richard Stevens was gunned down as he walked his beat on East 13th Street." She noticed people moving to the podium behind her. She turned back to the camera. "Let's listen to Mayor Wertz."

The Mayor shuffled some papers on the podium. He looked up at the camera and at the reporters that filled the room. Three of his people stood on his left, four on his right, everyone somber.

"We're here today to report the tragic and brutal shooting of a young police officer that occurred at 1:32 P.M., approximately two hours ago. The officer's name is Brian O'Neill, on the force for seven years. Officer O'Neill leaves behind his wife, a five-year-old daughter and a three-month-old son."

If there is a sound to sadness, empathy, sympathy, heartbreak, it was heard at that moment. The Mayor took a breath and continued.

"As you know, or should know, in another unrelated incident, we think unrelated, officer Richard Stevens was shot last Monday. A week ago. The entire New York Police Department, every patrolman, every detective, our special investigative unit, are all working one-hundred-percent on both cases to get answers to questions that we all have. In addition, the FBI has stepped in to help, even though this investigation remains under the jurisdiction and authority of the NYPD. We will try to answer all of your questions based on the information and leads we have at this time. But, first, let me ask Police Commissioner Brix to provide some more details."

Brix took the Mayor's place at the microphone.

"Officer O'Neill was working the day shift out of precinct…" his voice droned on above the silent audience.

· · ·

The picture was of officer Brian O'Neill in uniform, taken the day he graduated from the police academy. The picture was on a TV monitor, one of a dozen, each showing different images and video at the production studios of WPIC TV–10. Sitting behind a control console was Video Editor, Ramon Sanchez and an attractive blonde reporter in a dark purple blouse.

"He looks so young," Nicole Jensen said.

"He *is* young. What, maybe thirty?"

"Maybe thirty. Maybe younger. I'll have to find out." She made a note on a yellow pad.

"Let's see the footage of his house," Nicole requested.

Ramon entered some numbers into the keyboard and a gray, two-story house with a moss green door replaced the flutter on the screen. The camera pushed toward the door.

"Great. That's perfect," Nicole said. "We can do a soft-cut to the still of his wedding picture and then to the kids."

"You're going to rip my heart out."

"I want to rip everyone's heart out. I want to make them feel what she's feeling." The wedding picture was on the screen. A cross-dissolve revealed a picture of the kids. A portrait type shot. It dissolved into a shot of the family sharing an afternoon at the playground, then the backyard and kiddy pool.

"What a shame," Ramon said, almost to himself. No response from Nicole. He looked up and saw her eyes filling up.

"Why?" she asked rhetorically. "Why do so many good people die and the bad ones live. Get away with murder. You see it every day in this business. Sometimes I think I have to change careers." But she knew she didn't mean it. She always felt born for this business. She graduated Summa Cum Laude from prestigious Bolingbrook College with a degree in journalism. But pure academics, as good as they were, were not her most impressive strength. She was fearless, putting herself in dangerous situations, one after another, to make a point – to teach people how to survive, to live better lives, to stay healthy and get more out of life. To Nicole Jensen, parachuting out of planes, escaping from burning buildings, demonstrating how to stop a rapist...these on-air reports were as trite as teaching CPR.

At 24, she had already done pretty well for herself. Three years ago, fresh out of college, a small local station in Miami gave her a chance to test her wings. And she flew. Then she flew all the way to New York City, to a new job, carrying with her the dream of making it to the top. But in New York, WPIC TV–10 was closer to the bottom. So, for two years now, she worked doubly hard as much as she could. She was thrilled to do on-location shots and fill-in for other reporters and anchors when she had the chance. She even got to anchor her own half-hour morning show on Saturdays. One day, somehow, someone from a major would take notice. Somehow she would get that scoop that would put her on top.

But when?

"Looking good, Ramon."

"Yeah, I think it's coming out good, but it's going to make a lot of people feel pretty bad."

"Yeah, it will. A lot of people except one. The killer."

TWO

"Two days! Two days since O'Neill! Nine days since Stevens, and what do we know?" The Mayor was frustrated. Sitting in a circle in the Mayor's office was Commissioner Brix, Deputy Police Chief Wilcox, Press Secretary Tom Elliott, Director of the IT and Digital Department Robert Knickerbocker, two detectives from the Special Investigations Unit, one from the city's Terrorism Task Force and two doctors.

Brix was the first to respond. "We know the bullet came from a rifle, probably shot at a long distance, maybe as much as, say, a thousand yards."

"One shot?"

"One shot. Had to be a scope. A powerful scope. Sniper level skill."

Deputy Commissioner Wilcox interjected, "Ballistics matched everything from both shootings. Same barrel. Same ammo. Same entry into the body. I mean *exactly* the same." He turned his attention to an older man in a dark gray suit. It was Doctor Grinell, M.E., Forensic Pathologist. The M.E. spoke up. "In both cases, the bullet entered the base of the skull at the back of the neck. The bullet severed the spine, obliterated it actually, continued through the neck and out the throat area leaving practically nothing. Nothing except some flaps of skin."

Another man spoke up now. It was Crime Scene Investigator Mike Mankowitz: "Bone fragments and blood were sprayed over the top of the cruiser and in the face of officer Gonzalez sitting in the passenger seat."

"Jeez!" the Mayor said aloud to himself.

"It was instant. Painless, if that makes it any easier to take," Dr. Grinell offered.

"No. No, it doesn't," said Commissioner Brix.

"Terrorists?" the Mayor asked. "Lone wolf? Whacko? Cop hater? Both these officers are white. Is this a racial thing? Is this guy, I assume it's a guy, this killer, is he black? What?"

Psychiatrist Gloria Mahaffey took the floor. She was the only African American in the room. And the only woman. She sat next to Dr. Grinell and they traded knowing glances as Dr. Mahaffey explained. "All logic says it's a man. The size of the person required to handle the weight, the heft of such a powerful weapon, would suggest a male rather than a female." Heads nodded. She continued. "As far as black against white, who knows at this point. Nothing indicates that at all."

Brix cut in. "The first thing we should do is to list the most common motives and go from there when we have more facts."

Detective Julio Morales spoke up. "With all due respect to my fellow officers," he spoke with a distinct Brooklyn accent, "is it plausible, at all, that these two dead officers were banging this killer's wife and he took them both out?"

"We said common motives, Morales. Common," the Deputy Commissioner said, annoyed.

"Well, then it would qualify," Morales insisted. Some in the group looked at the ceiling and shook their heads.

Brix said, "We should look at everybody these two guys put away, or even arrested, over the past two to five years. Maybe there's a common thread."

Another detective interjected, "We'll comb through the latest bulletins from Homeland Security. Maybe there's a clue in there."

"And we'll stop anybody we see, on the street, in the subway, in a store, carrying a case that could conceal a rifle," added Deputy Commissioner Wilcox.

The Mayor jumped in. "Better check legal on that first. Make sure we're on solid ground before we stop half the people in Manhattan and all we find are golf clubs, telescopes and fishing rods." There was a slight pause as everybody caught their breath.

"OK, let's get on it everybody," the Mayor instructed.

As they all left the Mayor's office, Patty walked in, "It's Sheamus O'Neill on the phone, father of Brian O'Neill. He's been waiting quite a while."

The Mayor had a 'deer-in-the-headlights' look for a few seconds. Quite a few seconds. He just looked at Patty. This was not the phone call he wanted.

Finally, "Yeah. Yeah, OK, I'll take it."

Wertz took a breath and reached for the desk phone. He picked it up, but before he could say anything Sheamus O'Neill let him have it. "You son-of-a-bitch. My son! My *son*!"

"I'm sorry," Wertz said genuinely.

Sheamus O'Neill had a shock of thick red hair and his freckled face was just as red with rage. "You call yourself a Mayor! You're no fucking Mayor, you dip-shit! People are going to find out some day what you're all about!"

"I'm...I'm sorry."

"More of your shenanigans! Look what you've done! Look what you've fucking done! For what, Mr.

Fucking Mayor?"

There was a short lull in Sheamus' tirade.

Then he released another barrage: "You'd better take care of whoever did this, you hear me!"

"I have no idea who…"

"Then you'd better find out! And fast! Or else!"

"Or else what?"

"Or I'll start talkin'!"

"You wouldn't be that stupid."

"Oh, yeah! Watch me, Mr. Fucking Mayor!"

Sheamus slammed the phone down so hard it hurt the Mayor's ear. Wertz swiveled in his chair and stared out the window for, what seemed like, at least two minutes.

"Mr. Mayor?" It was Patty again. "Sorry. The father of Richard Stevens, Arthur Stevens, is on the phone now."

The Mayor's shoulders dropped. His mouth opened slightly. His eyes searched the floor for something invisible.

"Put him on."

• • •

"Excuse me, Ma'am. You're probably aware that the police department is doing everything possible to find the killer of the two policemen."

The young, gypsy-looking woman standing on the subway platform looked both confused and skeptical at the same time. Her one-word answer came out as a question. "Yeah?"

"So do I have your consent to let me see what's in the case you're carrying?" the police officer asked.

"My case?"

"Yes, this guitar case."

"I, ah, I guess so, yeah."

She opened the clips on the case and rumpled clothes fell out onto the shoes of the police officer. He looked at her. She looked at him.

"I'm moving," she said.

In another part of the city, a policewoman was asking a well-dressed older man to open a long case. He did. No rifle. Trombone. It was right in front of Carnegie Hall.

On a side street, next to some black and white sawhorse barricades – the kind with round, blinking, orange lights – a man held a long case about five feet long and about four inches in diameter. He popped off the end-cap for the police officer and something long and black slid all the way onto the ground.

"What is that?" the officer asked.

There was a pause, and a quizzical look at the officer.

"I'm a surveyor."

· · ·

On the cheap white bedspread, the huge, black .50 caliber sniper rifle lay beside boxes of ammo. Some of the shiny brass cartridges had spilled out in a pile next to the odd-looking hollowed butt of the weapon. They were large, five and a half inches long, and pointed, like mini-missiles. Next to the large rifle, was a small black pistol, so small it could be concealed totally in the palm of your hand. Next to it were tiny .22 caliber cartridges, not much bigger than the eraser on the end of a pencil.

· · ·

Fingers were tapping on desktops. Hands were pulling on

mustaches and beards. Pencils were knocking on pursed lips.

It was Monday morning. It was 11:15. And, so far, nothing. Just a normal Monday morning of the usual school stabbings, laundromat robberies, domestic disturbances and, of course, illegal drug sales outside the Port Authority Transit Station on 34th Street.

This was good. Really good.

"I'm going to lunch," said Bob Knickerbocker.

"Lunch? It's only 11:15. You must be really hungry."

"I want to get an hour in at the gym before I eat. I have some time coming to me anyway. Use it or lose it, Phil."

"Hmmm. Use it or lose it. I don't have anything left to lose," said the older, gray-haired man in the small office next to Knickerbocker's. His phone rang, "Hell-o. Yeah, he's here. He's standing right in front of me."

"Bob, it's Patty. Says your phone didn't answer."

"Oh, I had it on mute. I had to concentrate on a report."

"Patty says Wertz wants you in his office ASAP."

"ASAP. Does that mean before lunch or after lunch," Knickerbocker said, knowing the answer.

"Message delivered, Patty. OK, see 'ya."

. . .

"Have a seat, Bob," Mayor Wertz said with just a glance from the papers on his desk. "How many in the rank and file, Bob?"

"You mean in uniform? Detectives? Undercover?"

"Yeah, everybody on the force."

"Grand total is around 34,450. But, that's not

including 4,500 auxiliary, 5,000 school-safety and 2,300 traffic. Robert Knickerbocker, 34, was Director of Digital Communications in charge of IT and Social Media. He often worked closely with Press Secretary Tom Elliott. These were both appointee positions, which meant that both men served at the pleasure of the Mayor. Elliott, 32, was chosen by the Mayor because of a long alma mater relationship he had with Tom Elliott's father, Jim. Besides, Tom was qualified, having been in the public relations business right out of college. Knickerbocker, on the other hand, didn't have any family or social ties to the Mayor. Knickerbocker made a cold-call to the Mayor's office almost-four-years-ago, persuading Patty to just show the Mayor his resume. He told Patty he admired the Mayor and would consider it an honor to serve in any way, shape or form. Mayor Wertz came up the hard way, too. It was always his intent to remain accessible. That's why he never closed his office door. And, having just returned from his nephew's wedding (his brother's son) in San Francisco, the mood was conducive to helping another young man take some positive steps in his life. Knickerbocker's experience in social media and advertising agencies was good groundwork for a position that needed to be filled; Karen Albright, the city's first Digital Director, had to leave the job due to her husband's transfer. The timing was right.

"Bob, how many uniform and detective openings do we have to fill in a given month, on average?"

"I'd say, in the neighborhood of three hundred or so. The NYPD can give us a more accurate figure."

"Three hundred or so? Sounds like a lot"

"That's about one percent per month."

"Yeah, but that's about twelve percent a year. Isn't that a lot?"

"Not really. Even at companies that people are dying to work for, like tech companies, there's a higher turnover factor. The average turnover rate for all businesses is about fifteen percent."

The Mayor thought for a second and continued. "Well, the thing is, people are dying to get in at those places and, I hate to say it, our people are dying here. Two of our guys going down in a week has me worried. For a lot of reasons. One of them is that people are afraid to work for the city and the NYPD."

"We did have twelve applicants telling us to remove their names from the hiring list this week," Knickerbocker said.

"See! That's what I mean. They got spooked."

Knickerbocker just sat there, expressionless.

"Here's what I want you to do. Write up a report. Historical numbers, averages, say the last three years. How many on, how many off. And a projection of what we'll need for the next five years. Will we need a hiring campaign? Do we need to sweeten the deal? Offer more? Do we need to reach into different sectors to find people?"

"Got it. I'll get on it right after lunch."

"Sorry. Can't wait that long. I have a budget meeting at three. I'd like to have it for that meeting."

There was a pause. Again, Knickerbocker was expressionless. Obviously thinking about his position. How hard it was to get it. And that he could lose it just by hearing two words from Wertz.

"You got it. I'll put together whatever I can in the next two hours."

"Good man!"

. . .

The sound was deafening. Fifteen bagpipers, left arms pumping, blew into their instruments with vigor and out came the almost crying, sobbing sound that had marshalled courageous heroes into wars hundreds of years ago. And today, that same sound would carry heroes into heaven. The bagpipers, in red kilts and full regalia, were flanked by no less than one hundred men in blue, regimented into lines ten-by-ten. On either side of a make-shift stage were the families of the fallen – the Stevens family on the left, the O'Neill's on the right. A large picture of each man was displayed proudly above each family group.

When the bagpipes stopped, Police Commissioner Brix stepped up to the microphone.

"We're here today to honor and say farewell to two of New York's finest. Two of America's best. Officer Richard Stevens and Officer Brian O'Neill."

Sobs were heard. Sniffles were intermittent in the crowd. Tissues went to women's faces. Men wiped away tears with their hands.

"Officer Stevens leaves behind…" As the Commissioner eulogized both men, Nicole Jensen and her TV crew recorded the service for editing and air later in the day. Her biographical program of both slain men would air tonight in a special presentation after *News at 10.*

"Officer Stevens and Officer O'Neill will be missed by every man and woman on the NYPD team. And now, I'd like to introduce Mayor Wertz who would like to say a few words."

Mayor Wertz walked up to the microphone.

"Yes, I'd like to say a few words. But a few words could never express the sadness we all feel at the loss of these two great men. Selfless men. Giving of themselves each and every day. Putting their lives at risk. Their own lives on the line, for me and for you. For all of us. Yes, I'm sad. As you are. But I'm also angry. Angry that someone with a warped mind ..." As he spoke from the podium, Wertz noticed a man he recognized. A red-haired man with a ruddy complexion. Sheamus O'Neill. And on the other side of the ensemble, Arthur Stevens. The Mayor made a point to make eye contact with each of them when he said the following words:

"...with no regard for life...took these beautiful God-loving, family-loving men from us." Sobs and sniffles erupted again. "You have my word that we will not stop, we will not lose our energy, we will not waver in our mission, in our duty, in our passion to find whoever did this and bring them to justice. So help me God."

With that, Mayor Wertz walked away from the microphone. Commissioner Brix took his place.

"And now, Susan Stevens, sister of officer Richard Stevens, would like to sing a song of remembrance."

To the side of the stage, a young woman played the guitar on her lap and sang a beautiful song that touched the hearts of everyone there. Susan fought the tears that came. As did everyone gathered.

As two flags were folded in the honors ceremony, Mayor Wertz made his way to the rear of the crowd toward his waiting limousine. He was stopped suddenly, quietly, by Nicole Jensen.

"Mayor! Mayor Wertz, please excuse me. Would you like to say anything to PIC-10 viewers before you leave?"

"I would love to, but I have an important three o'clock meeting to get to. I would just like to say to everyone out there, New Yorkers work together when things get tough. Let's work together now to catch whoever did these heinous acts of savagery."

The bagpipes started again.

• • •

"It's Monday and it looks like we dodged a bullet today, no pun intended." Detective Morales was speaking to Detective Bixby, both of them getting up from their facing desks.

"Don't speak too soon," Bixby said, grabbing his jacket.

"Why? You think it's bad luck?"

"I don't know. But don't bad things come in three's? Adios, amigo."

• • •

"Good night, Mr. Mayor," Patty said.

"Thanks, Patty. Let's hope it continues to be."

• • •

"See 'ya Phil," Knickerbocker said.

"Yeah, man. Watchin' the game?"

"Nah. Got somethin' else to do tonight."

"Catch 'ya tomorrow," Phil said.

• • •

William 'Will' Harrison was a fairly large African American man. Six feet tall with a strong body for a 46-year-old with a wife of eighteen years and six kids from two marriages on both sides. He worked hard to be able to stand in the driveway of the two-story house he and Lily bought seven years ago in Floral Park. Keeping with her namesake, and the town in which they choose to live, the yard was full of flowering bushes, leafy trees and fragrant flowerbeds. Overgrown, some might say. It wasn't easy for Will to negotiate his way under and around the abundant summer foliage of a prized magnolia tree. Especially in the dark. It was 10:30 at night and he had just come home from his side job as a maintenance man at the hospital. He could hardly wait to get out of his dirty overalls and wet shoes.

Will had a bag in his hands. His clothes from his day job.

Ducking under a tree limb, he rose up to see someone standing in front of him. A shadowy figure wearing a full-face ski mask. Before Will could even drop or swing the bag, the killer raised a gun to Will's forehead and a rapid '*pop-pop-pop-pop-pop-pop*' was heard. Not big pops, but a sound similar to when a bird flies into a window. Six .22 caliber hollow-point bullets penetrated Will's eyes, forehead and brain.

When he fell into the flowerbed, he was twitching and kicking at the tulips. Thrashing, disturbing the mulch and roses.

Reggie, Will's 13-year-old son, looked out the window but saw nothing.

Will stopped twitching.

• • •

The cell phone rang in the total blackness, lighting up the side table next to the bed. Mayor Wertz got up with a start, as if shocked by electricity. He was at the edge of the bed, feet on the floor.

"Hello," said the Mayor.

He was silent.

Then…a sigh. A very big sigh.

. . .

It was dark and drizzling outside City Hall. The antique gold clock on the fireplace mantel of the conference room read 12:42. A dozen people were gathered around the table this Monday night, actually Tuesday morning. People trickled in. It was noisy. The mood was agitated. Worried. The discussion was already heated. Detective Morales spoke over the din, "Thank God it wasn't a cop that was killed this time."

"What makes you say that, Morales?" the Mayor asked.

Morales answered: "No police uniform, no police car. Just another random murder."

Everyone who worked with Julio Morales had the same opinion of him. Not the sharpest knife in the drawer. But, nevertheless, he was part of the team. And he felt completely at home with his NYPD family. It was the only family he had.

"Maybe you got here late, Morales," said Commissioner Brix with obvious impatience. "Or maybe you need to have your hearing checked." Brix paused, then continued. "He was off duty."

. . .

The words across the TV screen said BREAKING NEWS. The anchor read his lines:

"A third New York City police officer has been shot. It happened last night at approximately 10:30 P.M."

A different TV screen said ALERT in a streaming banner moving from right to left.

"… the slain Officer is William Harrison, the third to be gunned down in cold blood. Ambushed and shot at point-blank range. Officer Harrison was off-duty when he was shot and killed in his front yard in Floral Park."

Another TV monitor said NEWS RIGHT NOW. The reporter said, "Harrison' body was discovered by his 13-year-old son. It's thought that Harrison died instantly from gun shot wounds to his head fired at point-blank range. It is not known at this time…"

Nicole Jensen watched all three news reports simultaneously in the production room at the PIC TV–10 station. The room was dim. The moving light from the images played against her face, flashes of them in her eyes. She picked up her cell phone.

"Tom, here." It was Tom Elliott, Director of Communications. He looked at the big round clock on the wall. 8:10 A.M.

"Hi, Tom. It's Nicole."

"Ahh, I was wondering when I'd hear from you. You held out as long as you could, huh?"

"Why do you always have to start in? Can't you let it go? It's been more than a year, for God's sake."

"Wow! Testy in the morning. Like always."

Nicole, knowing this was going nowhere, changed the subject. "I thought I'd take a shot and see if you came in early today."

"Yeah. Lots to do. And no, I can't get you an interview with the Mayor. He's overloaded."

"I think he's about to get even more overloaded. Have you watched the morning news yet?"

"No. I literally just walked in. I got up late. Had a

meeting with the Mayor in the middle of the night." Elliott flicked the remote and the TV set lit up in his office. It was one of three. He clicked the others on now.

"Shot at close range," Nicole said. "And, he was off duty. The killer knew he was a cop."

"Oh, is that right?" Elliott said, indignant. Who's saying it was the same killer? Can't this be just another random killing? It just happened to be a cop," Elliott said, annoyed.

"Oh," she said, skeptical. "A coincidence?"

"Happens every day, Nicole."

"Right," like yeah, sure, "one cop a week, every Monday, and this is a coincidence."

"Maybe you know something we don't know," Elliott retorted, sarcastically. "You're assuming. You know what they say about people who assume?"

"Well, at least that's true for one of us."

"Gotta go, Nicole."

"Hey, see if you can get me in with Wertz!"

"No can do. Unless you've got something really important to say."

"I'll work on it."

. . .

The newspaper hit the chair with a slap in the strong morning light.

"Son of a bitch!" Commissioner Brix was pissed. "I got three hours of sleep after our meeting last night..." He looked exhausted. The bottom button on his dress shirt was undone. His tie was loose, neck button open. "...and I have to wake up to this shit!" His hand motioned to the newspaper.

"That's nothing, did you watch the news?" the Mayor asked.

"Yeah, I watched it. What's wrong with these people? These damn news reporters. They've gotta dig, dig, dig. We decided last night not to let all this out. But no, they've gotta…" He thought about not saying it, but he said it anyway. "…they gotta fuck things up at the worst possible time. We don't need anybody knowing that the killer didn't use a rifle, used a small caliber handgun, snuck up on Harrison knowing he was a police officer, knowing his home address, for God's sake!"

The Mayor cut in: "The question is, how did the reporters find all of this out? We told our people to keep quiet on the details. Don't say too much. But maybe it's our own people."

"Nahh. It's not my guys. They listen and they do what they're told." Brix thought for a moment. Then whined, "His home address, Ed. In front of his house!"

"It's a different world today," the Mayor said. "Nothin's private or secret anymore. You can find out anything about anybody in seconds. Like somebody's address."

Brix was steaming. Blood pressure high. Face red. He sat down heavily. He said, "All of these reporters have police scanners. Sometimes they're on the scene before we are. Maybe they told our guys what happened."

"Maybe. But…and I hate to think this…" the Mayor added.

"What?" Brix said.

"We have a leaker."

• • •

The gray metal door opened and old man Andy walked out into the morning sunlight. It was time to lower the flag to half-staff again. Like a lot of older folks, he had a habit of muttering to himself as he went about his daily chores. "I've been up on this roof more in these past three weeks than in my twenty-one years here. Up with the flag, down with the flag, up with the flag. They may as well leave it at half-staff until…" He was at the base of the flagpole when he noticed the first one. It was hard to tell what it was at first. A rag? A Christmas tree ornament? No. Neither. It was a dead bird. Then he saw the other one.

Andy walked down the hall a little faster than usual. He carried a broom and a dustpan. He walked into the Mayor's office.

"Not now, Andy, please. It's clean enough in here and I have a meeting in …"

As Andy walked closer, Mayor Wertz could see what was in the dustpan. Patty followed Andy into the room and stood beside him with a pained look on her face.

"I found these on the roof. I thought you should know right away."

The Mayor's face was puzzled, "Andy, why do you think I need to be concerned about two sick parakeets that died on the roof?"

"They're not parakeets," Patty said.

Andy added, "And they've been shot."

. . .

Thirteen people were once again gathered around the conference table, from Commissioner Brix to Detective Morales and Tom Elliott to Robert Knickerbocker.

"Do you know what this is?" the Mayor asked all present. The dustpan with the two dead birds was in the middle of the table.

"Two dead birds," said Morales.

"That's right, Morales. Very good," said the Mayor, trying not to sound too condescending.

"Now, we have to figure out what it means. Before Monday."

THREE

The priest was radiant in his colorful robes this Sunday morning as he looked down from the pulpit at the flock of loyal parishioners. The fingertips of each hand touched in front of him before he spoke. Then his hands parted. "We're gathered together this morning to count our blessings. To show our love to God and each other…and to pray for His help in healing the wounds of the world… and the wounds, the fresh, painful wounds, of our city. God knows, yes, God knows how much we need His help. We all know of the senseless tragedy that has befallen our blessed place, the city we love. The city we cherish. We ask God's intervention. Please, God, heal the sick mind of the person causing this pain, this carnage, these senseless horrific deeds of violence. God, guide our police in their efforts to stop these senseless acts."

As Reverend Patrick Regan preached, Detective Morales listened intently. Fervently. Looking up, something caught his eye to the left of the pulpit. A stained-glass window, bright light shining through, projecting colors on the parishioners in the pews near it.

Near the base of the leaded window were two birds of colored glass. Doves facing each other. Like lovebirds. Morales stared at them intently. Thinking deeply.

. . .

It was 7:30 A.M. on the kitchen microwave when NYPD Police Officer Tyler Jackson put his service cap on his head.

He was already dressed, his ammo belt, cuffs, service pistol, radio, all in place. He straightened his hat in front of a wall mirror. Next to the mirror was a wedding picture of himself and his wife of ten years. They made a beautiful, happy African American couple, for sure.

He called out to his wife, "You 'bout ready, woman? We gotta get to work."

The bathroom door was slightly open, the light was on. "I'm ready. I'm ready," she called out.

Juliette Jackson walked out of the bathroom in her NYPD blues.

Tyler said: "I'm going to be late getting to my house." House meaning his station house.

"And I'm going to be late getting to mine, too. I don't want to listen to Sergeant Ryan ragging on me." She grabbed her hat and they walked out of their apartment together, stepping down the steps and onto the sidewalk.

"See 'ya later, babe," Ty said to Juliette.

"Love you," Juliette said to Ty.

Ty gave Juliette a goodbye kiss.

Then they died together on the sidewalk this Monday morning.

• • •

Detective Morales burst through the front door of City Hall at 8:16 this Monday morning and rushed down the hall. He saw Patty coming the opposite way.

"Is the Mayor in yet? Is the Mayor in?" He was a little frantic.

"In his office, what's the …"

Mayor Wertz looked up to see Morales, out of breath, blurting out …

"I know what it means! The birds! I know what it means!"

. . .

Nicole Jensen stood on the sidewalk where Tyler and Juliette Jackson died, "Two people. One bullet," she said to the camera. The camera pulled back and showed the four steps and the front door of the apartment building. It pulled back farther and showed the entire building. It panned and showed other buildings on the block, down the street and on the next block.

"Somewhere, probably in one of these buildings, the killer, the sniper, raised a powerful rifle, took careful aim with two people in the crosshairs, and fired." Their wedding picture appeared on the screen. "Both officers were with the NYPD. They were probably kissing goodbye as they left their home, each going in different directions to two different precincts when the single bullet passed through both of them. The couple were the fourth and fifth police officers who have been gunned down by what is now being called a serial cop killer."

The Mayor clicked off the TV report from Nicole Jensen. "You're a little late Morales. If you had figured this out last night we might have been able to trace married officers, or relationships, and stopped this." The Mayor looked perturbed. All of a sudden it was Morales' fault, or so it seemed. Morales looked dumbfounded.

The Mayor now turned to Tom Elliott, Commissioner Brix and Bob Knickerbocker.

The Mayor said to Commissioner Brix, "These reporters always seem to know more than we do. How does this reporter, ahh…." He pointed to the screen, not knowing her name.

Tom Elliott jumped in. "Nicole Jensen."

"Yeah, Nicole Jensen. Where does she come off saying it was one bullet? What the hell! We haven't even done ballistics yet, but, I suppose, she has. Is that it? She's dangerous! Misinformation. Maybe that's her real name. Miss Information!"

"Drives me crazy," the Commissioner added, sympathizing. "I'm sick of it! It's making our job harder and harder. They're so desperate to dramatize everything. They're going to beat the drum until we have a feeding frenzy on our hands."

"Tom," the Mayor turned, "I want you to go talk to this… 'Miss Information'. Not an email, not a phone call. Go see her. Keep it verbal. I don't want to be accused of trying to control the press, God forbid! Understand?" Tom nodded. "Try to explain that some of the information she's telling people might not be good for the investigation, for the city…or for her, because the Mayor will not grant her interviews, or even admission to the press conferences and events, until she understands and cooperates."

Tom made his lips disappear, like he had no teeth, stopping words that his mind wanted to say but he didn't want his lips to speak. He hoped the Mayor didn't pick up on it. He just nodded. He knew that this was the worst news that Nicole could hear. How would he tell her?

"Now, Bob," the Mayor said to Knickerbocker, "our hiring is going to go from slow to nothing. Come up with some ideas on how we're going to attract new people to the last job they want. Other than going to Afghanistan."

Knickerbocker nodded also.

"Work with Tom to identify where we run ads, hold job fairs, that kind of thing. We can't run a police force with no police. Let's get ready for the worst."

That's exactly what Tom was saying to himself, thinking about his talk with Nicole.

. . .

"This is Nicole Jensen, reporting on the streets of the West Village to find out how the community feels about police officers being gunned down. Street-savvy New Yorkers might give us some answers." Nicole had attracted a small crowd around her. She turned to the man closest to her.

"Sir, are you worried for your own safety?"

"Why should I be? I'm not a cop."

"Yes, but aren't you afraid that the killer could miss and maybe hit you or somebody else?"

"Let's hope the sniper's a good shot."

Nicole raised her eyebrows at the camera.

"Sir!" It was a Rastafarian dude. "What do you make of the recent increased violence in the city and the serial killing of cops?"

"It don't bother me. I'm a mellow fellow. I don't worry 'bout nothin'." He took a toke.

"Ma'am. Ma'am. How about you? Do you have any advice for the police or Mayor Wertz?"

"Are you kiddin'? Wertz is the worst. I mean, things are going one way. Downhill! Fast! Get rid of Wertz, get rid of the problem!"

She turned to a young man to her left. "Sir, do you have any advice for Mayor Wertz?"

"Take the first bus outta town!"

To her right, Nicole spotted a distinguished looking man walking by carrying a leather briefcase. He wore a classic, perfectly-fitted dark blue suit, a striped hand-knotted silk bow tie crowning a bright white dress shirt. Glancing down, she noticed that his cordovan wingtips were burnished to a high sheen. His hair was cut very short. His eyeglasses were round frames...made of dark wood. She anticipated an insightful, intelligent response.

"Sir, sir, can you just take a minute to give us your thoughts on what more Mayor Wertz could be doing to stop the cop killings in our city?"

"Well, I'm probably not the best person to ask. I don't have any experience in law enforcement. But I would imagine that better communication with our citizens would be a good first step to ease tensions and fears. Secondly, bring in more outside help from sources like the FBI and terrorism experts. And thirdly, we just don't know what the motivation is. What we do know is that anger, resentment, frustration and vengeance can exist in all people."

"Very well said. Sounds like you're a college professor."

"No. I'm a psychotherapist."

"Maybe you should be working for Mayor Wertz?"

"Did you say working *for* Mayor Wertz or working *on* Mayor Wertz?"

The man smiled and walked away.

Nicole's face was full frame now.

"Well, that's what some New Yorkers think in this West Village neighborhood. On other nights, we'll be interviewing on the streets from one end of the city to the other, to bring you a cross-section of opinions and ideas that might help this city. And might help catch this cop killer. This is Nicole Jensen for PIC-10."

Watching all of this take place in front of him was Tom Elliott. Nicole didn't see him. Until now. "Tom, what are you doing here?"

"I came to see you. To talk to you."

"Well, how did you know where I was?"

"I called the station and Ramon told me."

"And you came all the way up here to talk with me? Don't tell me that Wertz agreed to an interview. That would make my whole night."

"No, not quite. Want to grab some coffee?"

"Ummm, sure. How about we catch a cab and go to Roxy's, my favorite old-fashioned coffee shop?"

"Ready when you are."

"Are you sure? It's all the way in Brooklyn, by my apartment."

"Lead the way. The Mayor's picking up the cab fare."

In the back seat of the taxi the conversation was light. "So how's the job," Nicole asked.

"Great! Great! Going well. Busy."

"We're all really busy right now. And stressed to the max," she said.

The taxi made its way south on this long drive. Dusk had arrived quickly. They passed a billion lights on the way; headlights, taillights, neon lights, streetlights, window lights. The conversation made the time go fast.

"And I heard you're seeing someone," Nicole said.

"Yeah, yeah. Nice girl. Attorney. Got together about a month after we broke up."

"Wow, that was quick."

"Well, yeah, I guess. But, you know, it just kinda happened."

Nicole knew she couldn't have a life with Tom for a host of reasons. But every girl appreciates just a glimmer of sadness from the guy she broke up with. Even if she called that one. But she was happy, nonetheless. It made the conversation a whole lot easier. It started to rain lightly.

Tom said, "I'm planning a trip to Hawaii. That's if I can get away. Not sure with all the chaos going on right now. I can't wait until they catch this maniac."

"You and everybody else."

Before they knew it they were at Roxy's in the trendy section of Brooklyn called DUMBO. Tom paid the fare and they hurried inside. The cordial conversation continued at a red, pleated, faux-leather booth. Two cappuccinos were on the way. Nicole had been patient. Now she was busting. "So, tell me, you have a special assignment for me? A one-on-one with the Mayor? Whatcha got?"

"Well, no, not exactly, but I do have a special request from the Mayor himself. He needs your help."

"My help?"

He nodded yes.

"From *me*?"

He continued to nod.

"Like…?"

"Well, ah, he's trying to maintain some control over this whole cop killer problem and…"

She cut in. "Control? He wants control? Control of what? The media?" It didn't take Nicole long to catch onto things. Perceptive was her middle name.

"Ahh…" Tom was flustered. "Poor choice of words, sorry." His face was red from his faux pas.

Her face was red from being pissed off. *This is why I could never have a life with Tom.*

"Let me start over, please," Tom said.

"Yes, please!"

"Let me see how I can say this…" Tom searched the ceiling for the right words.

Nicole made a funny mouth, like *this had better be*

good.

"You're a very dedicated woman and…"

"Ah huh," she said, skeptical, waiting to pounce.

"You're smart…"

He's so transparent.

"And you always find a way to get your story. To dramatize it. To milk it so you get every drop of, of, ahh, emotion out of it."

She made another face, like *he's getting really deep now. Does he really think I fall for this shit?*

"And the Mayor, while he loves your reporting, your digging deep and presenting insights missed by other, lazy journalists…"

Let me gag!

"…and he thinks your talents would be better spent at one of the majors…"

Aha! He finally said something I can believe!

"… at this particular time, when tensions are escalating on the streets, if you could just tone it down a notch or two, help us turn down the heat out there on the streets…"

She had heard more than enough. "I get it! I get it!" she finally said. And she took over. "I'm a journalist, not just a reporter." His eyes said he understood. He also understood that he was about to lose. He was already writing his report to the Mayor.

Nicole was fired up: "Anybody can be a reporter. Yes, I dig deep. Yes, I look to present insights others miss. Yes, I don't shrink from hard news, from hard facts, from disgusting facts and stats, from the truth!" She emphasized truth.

"At any cost!" he said. That stopped her, but only momentarily.

She went on: "If I'm going to make a name for myself I have to be…"

He jumped in, "Ruthless!"

She stopped again, her eyes getting bigger but her pupils getting smaller.

He decided to push harder. "Nicole, I know you. And you'll stop at nothing to get the story you want. I know your career means everything to you. But where do you stop?"

"Tom," *you asshole*! "I'm going to present the news in my own words, in my own pictures, in my own style, in my own way. And there's nothing you, the Mayor, or anybody is going to do about it."

"How 'bout Eric Jacoby," Tom countered. That was Nicole's boss. She let out a breath and pursed her lips.

"Look," Tom implored, "all we're saying is please consider taking some of the edge off for a while." He actually said this to a woman who spent her life looking for an edge. But she let him continue.

"Just think before you show or say something that might encourage a demonstration, a riot, racial tensions, whatever. That's all we're asking."

She wasn't happy. He knew she wasn't buying any of this. So he sweetened the deal. "Tell you what. I'll get you that interview with the Mayor." She poked her lips to the side in a sideways pucker, thinking. Tom motioned with his shoulders and his arms as if to say, 'Well'?

"A two-hour-long interview," she demanded.

"Two hours? That's way too long."

"I need two hours to do a one-hour show."

"Uhh, well, OK. I'll see if I can get him to sit for that long. I don't know, but I'll try."

There was a pause. A pause uncomfortably longer

than usual.

"Gotta go," Nicole said suddenly. She started to get up.

"Hey," he said, "I could talk for another hour or so, that is, if you're up for it. Maybe someplace nearby?"

Meaning what? My apartment, of course! Would Tom never grow up?

"No thanks, Tom. I have to spend the night with another man." She turned and left him with the bill. *Jerk!*

· · ·

Nicole was wearing her cozy flannel pajamas as she walked from the small kitchen in her apartment to her comfy brown leather couch. She curled up Indian-style sipping a glass of ice water. She was about to spend a part of the night with an important man in her life.

She tapped her phone and a number appeared with a 307 area code.

"Nikki!"

"Hi, Dad."

"What a nice surprise. I didn't expect you to call until Sunday. Is everything OK?"

"Yeah, everything's fine. Just a little homesick."

"Big-city-girl missing Wyoming?"

Nicole was born and raised in Cody, birthplace of Buffalo Bill Cody, population 9,520.

"'Ya might say that."

"Well, things are pretty much the same as when you left. 'Cept Carlson's" (that's what you might call the general store), "did a little remodeling."

"Oh, man, I hope they didn't change much. I liked it just the way it was."

"That's what lots of folks said. But it's not too bad. More products."

"And higher prices."

"Everything seems to go up and nothing seems to come down. How's the job?"

"Well, speaking of ups and downs, it's just like that."

"Is it kind of down right now?"

"Kind of, yeah."

"Well, are you still there at PIC-10?"

"Oh, yeah. I'm really there. *So* there that the Mayor had Tom, you remember Tom don't you, find me on location and read me the riot act. No pun intended."

"Yeah, I remember Tom, but what do you mean riot act?"

"He basically told me I was reporting a little too much. Saying things I didn't have to say. Making it harder for him to keep a lid on things."

"You mean that you should not report on all the facts? Keep some things hidden?"

"Exactly."

"I know he's the Mayor, but can he do that? Is that legal?"

"I'm not really sure, there are a lot of gray areas. He would need good reasons. And things can't be swept under the rug for too long. It goes against everything I believe."

"Well, think about it. Sometimes you have to push a little bit to see where the real boundaries are. And sometimes you just have to sit back and see if the weather is going to be stormy or nice."

"'Ya know what bothers me the most, Dad? Back home, we killed animals to eat. Here the 'animals' kill people for sport. It's a way of life that I'm not used to.

Makes me wonder what's happening to the world."

"Nikki, if you study history, you'll find that it's been the same for thousands of years. And we're all still here because there's a lot more of us good folks than there are of the bad. And in your job, you get a real good look at the bad."

"You're right about that."

"Do your best to report on the bad, but encourage the good. That's how you can justify what you do and make the most of your voice."

"Thanks, Dad." Nikki thought her Dad always had a sensible point of view on just about everything. Good advice. Wisdom. The kind of down home, salt-of-the-earth wisdom that comes from a hardworking rancher in God's country. Nicole always felt better after talking with her Dad. Especially after her Mom died just last year.

The water in her glass was gone. So were a lot of her doubts and fears.

"Well, you know, honey, it just all comes with the territory."

"Thanks, Dad. I feel a lot better now."

"OK, honey, give me a call soon and let me know how things are going." There was no question that Joshua Jensen would do anything to protect his only daughter. His only child.

"OK, Dad. Love you."

"I love you too, sweetie. I know you'll do what's right."

"Bye, Dad."

"Bye, honey."

Nicole hung up missing home more than ever. She walked over to the bookshelf and retrieved an old-fashioned photo album. Curled up again, she flipped through the pages of her life. There she was, at five, on a rope swing. Then she was nine, pulling back the taught string of a bow, sighting along the arrow. Then a picture when she was 12, tossing hay at the back of a tractor, feeding twenty-two head of Black and Red Angus cattle. There she was at 17, going to the prom with her date, a local rancher's boy. She was 19, next to her old hand-me-down pickup, washing pail and sponge in her hands. There was her Mom, in the purple sweater she loved. Nicole's eyes filled up now. There was Nicole with her Dad, both holding rifles, both dressed in camo hunting outfits, about to get on the ATV and head for Big Horn Basin. There was a picture of her kneeling on the ground next to the six-point white-tailed buck she brought down.

Nicole turned the page and some old DVDs fell out of the back of the photo album. She inserted them into the disc player and a video appeared on her TV; there she was at her birthday party when she was 11. There was Thanksgiving dinner, two big tables put together, fifteen people raising their glasses for the camera. Her Dad gave her Mom a great big hug and a kiss on the cheek. There was the video clip she remembered vividly. She was with her Dad getting on the ATV, heading out on the hunt. Then the scene of her raising her rifle, higher and higher, then taking in a big breath, letting out about half and then holding the rest in. The duck, flying high, folded and flipped and fell out of the frame. Then another duck, blasted out of its flight. And another. The picture cut to a wire stretched between two trees. Twelve birds hung from the wire, limp wings hanging down like rags. Father and daughter stood proudly.

Joshua Jensen was a damn good shot.

So was Nicole Jensen.

FOUR

The six-story yellow brick building stood abandoned for more than five years on the corner of Grand and Hester in the Lower East Side. Shards of dirty glass clung to the edges of empty windows. Crumpled cigarette packs were strewn on the chipped stone steps. The front door teetered at an angle from broken hinges. The chain-link fence that long ago lost its tightness did nothing to keep vagrants out. It had been slit open halfway up its height. The NO TRESPASSING signs and CONDEMNED signs were barely readable now. The buildings around it were not much better.

It was 3:28 on a quiet Sunday afternoon. The sky was overcast and a light rain was falling, so there was virtually no foot traffic outside the building.

In the dimly lit room, the black rectangular electric guitar case opened. Inside, in protective hollowed-out insets, were the separated sections of the .50 caliber sniper rifle: stock, receiver, barrel, flash and sound suppressor and scope.

Hands, sheathed in black latex gloves, carefully removed the sections and slowly assembled the weapon. From the backpack, the hands removed a folded black tripod and set it up in front of the open window. The hands mounted the rifle on the sturdy tripod. Looking up at the second floor window from the street below, no part of the rifle was visible.

The target was directly across the street.

The blurry view through the scope came into sharp focus. The sign on the building said, CITY OF NEW YORK POLICE DEPARTMENT – 64th PRECINCT. The field-of-view widened and moved to the right. There were two cavernous openings protected by sliding security gates. One was an entry, one an exit from the underground parking garage. This was home to the precinct motor pool.

It was 3:42 P.M. Police cruisers were arriving to close out their eight-to-four shifts, entering the opening to the right. Fresh cruisers were pulling up into the opening on the left, ready for their shifts to begin, waiting for the security gate to open. They were sitting ducks. The shooter, dressed in total black, put an eye to the scope. The blurry view behind the crosshairs came into focus. It was the chest of an officer in the driver's seat. The sight picture moved to the throat.

The car entering descended into the lower level of the garage. The car leaving, pulled out, turned right into the intersection.

The shooter moved away from the window as more police cars entered and more left.

Not a shot was fired on this peaceful Sunday.

The shooter checked the time. 4:34 P.M. A long wait was ahead.

From a large, deep pocket, came a whole wheat and tuna sandwich in plastic wrap. The killer threw a scrap of bread to a rat in the corner.

The digital watch displayed 11:48 P.M. Again, the police cars began pulling into the right side of the motor pool. Stopping. Waiting. Fresh cruisers were driven up to the left side, ready to start the midnight to 8 A.M. shift. The cars would not leave until just after midnight. Monday morning.

Fluorescent lights on the ceiling of the garage and sodium vapor streetlights lit the area like daytime.

The rifle was ready to fire.

The scope was calibrated for a perfect hit.

The shooter was stropped.

The watch changed. 12:00. Midnight.

Two officers drove their car up the ramp from the underground garage. They stopped at the exit gate. They waited. They were clearly visible through the windshield.

From the street, a police cruiser pulled in at the entry gate. The two officers waited for the gate to open.

The shooter was at the scope.

The shooter inhaled deeply. Then let out half.

Hold. Hold. Don't shake.

Both gates slid open.

The trigger finger hesitated. Just for a moment.

Then! *PING!* The shot hit the driver of the car on the left.

Quickly! Another *PING!* The bullet hit the driver's partner. No flash. No loud bang. Just the roar of the police car as the driver's leg straightened, rigid, pressing the accelerator, sending the cruiser smashing into a parked car across the street, horn blaring on impact.

Then! *Quickly!* A third *PING!* The driver of the car entering was hit in the back of the neck. The bullet shattered the rear window of the car. It penetrated the unprotected neck of the driver, severed his spine, exploded out the front of his neck and shattered the front window. The officer in the passenger seat opened his door and dove to the concrete as the car moved slowly forward down the ramp.

Alarms sounded inside the precinct. Security gates closed.

The shooter urgently broke down the weapon. *Now, get out of here!*

Sneakered feet flew down the rickety old steps to the first floor. The feet splashed into a puddle from a leak in the roof and...

Stop! Stand still! It's a man!

He was barely visible, standing in the dark corner.
He shuffled forward slowly, sheepishly, his hands out in
front of him, his palms upward. He had a large shaggy gray
beard, messy hair, dirty skin. His clothes hung like rags. He
had no shoes. He spoke softly, almost pleading, "I ain't seen
nothin'. I ain't heard nothin'."

He continued, "I don't know noth..." Before he
could finish his brief sentence the shooter reached into a
deep pocket. The little .22 caliber gas-operated pistol blasted
a shot into the forehead of the homeless man. The shooter
tried to take another shot but the jamb-resistant little gun
jammed. The shooter pulled on the slide, but it wouldn't
budge. The wounded man dropped to the filthy wooden floor
on his back. But he refused to die. He was moaning and
moving slowly, face up, blood dripping from his eyes.

Suddenly, the sniper's sneaker was on the man's
throat, pressing down mightily, full force, as the homeless
man tried to raise his arms. He fell silent. Unmoving. Still.

The killer grabbed up the case and dashed to the
back of the building.

The dead man stirred.

Car horn blaring, alarm bell ringing, two-dozen
policemen in full riot gear streamed from both sides of the
station house. Half the men on the left flank sprinted across
the street to the crashed police car, while the other half
covered them. The right flank poured into the motor pool
behind the closed gates and ran to the crashed car inside. The
police medical emergency vehicle arrived, lights spinning
and flashing. Ten more cops in riot gear flowed into the
street and immediately ran into alleys. *Run, duck, cover, run,
duck, cover...*

The Precinct Commander dialed his cell phone:

Commissioner Brix's home.

A SWAT team arrived from another precinct. Their large military-style vehicle was dark and imposing on the street. Barricades went up on all streets within a four-square-block area. Police cars arrived, sirens blaring, lights flashing.

In the middle of the southbound lane, an officer saw something on the ground. Something crawling. A man trailing a line of blood. A homeless man with bloody eyes. He was gasping for air. A dozen boots ran to him, surrounded him, guns drawn. They wondered: *Is he the killer? Or did the killer try to kill him? What happened to him?*

With the last bit of strength he had in him, the bloody man raised his right arm. He pointed with a crooked finger. He pointed to the abandoned yellow brick building.

The street was lit up like an amusement park. Police were swarming everywhere. Bright red and blue lights were flashing on buildings, cars, trucks and people. A public address system told residents to stay in their homes. Strong searchlights illuminated the yellow building so it glared and reflected back. The chain-link fence had been torn down in front to allow access. A SWAT team swarmed into the building.

Standing in front of the building, as if protected by some invisible shield, was Police Commissioner Brix speaking with the Precinct Commander. A black limo arrived next to them, waved in by the police at the barricade. The Mayor stepped out. No time for small talk.

"The guy who was shot, the homeless man, did he tell you anything," the Mayor asked.

"No. He pointed at the building and dropped dead,"

the Commissioner responded.

The Mayor's body slumped. "Shit! The fucker couldn't stay alive for another minute?"

The Precinct Commander cut in: "They just found somebody else inside, hiding." The Commander pressed his earpiece into his ear. Brix and the Mayor just looked, waiting for more. The Commander listened intently to his earpiece.

"He's alive! They're taking him out."

"Holy shit," the Mayor said, "this could be over. This could be the guy!"

All eyes were on the door at the top of the stone steps. Including the eyes of the few TV news people who were on the opposite sidewalk from the building. One of them, Nicole Jensen, had her microphone out. Her cameraman hoisted his camera to his shoulder.

There was movement at the door. Two police officers came out first. Then the man-of-the-hour stepped into the blinding spotlight.

There was absolute focused attention.

The homeless man was about four-feet-eleven, had a big, round belly, was missing his left eye, missing his right arm and missing four teeth. He smiled for everyone.

The Mayor, stunned, threw something invisible on the ground, like a big-league baseball pitcher, and yelled out a very loud "Shiiiit!" That's when he noticed the TV camera and Nicole Jensen behind him.

"Get that fuckin' TV camera and the press outta here!"

Unfortunately for the Mayor, he was on live TV.

The searchlights on the building were shut off, the yellow tape went up and many of the vehicles were driving away.

The Mayor was still there in front speaking with Police Commissioner Brix. Nicole Jensen walked up but kept a respectful distance from the two. The Mayor noticed her standing there.

"Ms. Jensen," the Mayor said. The Commissioner walked away.

Nicole said, "One of the officers told me you wanted to speak with me."

"Yes, yes, I do." He didn't realize that Nicole Jensen looked so sweet up-close. And he didn't realize that this was exactly the affect that Nicole Jensen wanted to have over him. After all, this was the Mayor and he could make her life hell if he really wanted to. She considered him the one with the leverage, until...

"Ms. Jensen..."

"Call me Nicole."

"Nicole, I'm sorry for blurting out profanity at you and your crew before."

Aha!

"Were we, ah, were we..."

"Yes."

"Yes, what?"

"On live TV."

"Shh..." he started to say shit but changed it to shoot. "That's what I thought. Nothing I, or anybody else can do about that now, right?"

"Well, no, not the live broadcast, but there's only one live broadcast. All the rest would be just playing the recorded tape over and over...." She paused for emphasis. "...and over."

"Yes, but we all know you can't air what I said, you'd have to bleep it out."

"Correct. But, honestly, people will have no problem knowing what your lips are saying."

The Mayor was getting frustrated, he took in a deep breath and she didn't want to hear what he was about to say.

"Mr. Mayor, I'll edit out the whole line. No one will hear it after tonight's live feed. And there aren't a lot of people watching PIC TV–10 at 1:30 A.M. So I wouldn't worry about it."

"Thank you! Thank you! You're actually a lot nicer than I ever thought."

Was that a compliment? She had some leverage over him now. "No problem," she said generously.

"Tom mentioned that you would like to do an interview," the Mayor said.

"Yes, I would love to, if you have time. I know you're busy."

"Well, I would like to negotiate. You're a young reporter…"

"Journalist."

"Ah, journalist, trying to make a name for herself. You've been working extra hard, staying up late, like tonight, putting a hard edge on the news. A no-holds-barred, take-no- prisoners approach. Do I have that right?"

"I do work hard, yes. And I know where you're going, Mr. Mayor."

"Then what do you say we have a little understanding. Just go a little easy for a while. I can't have an uprising in the streets. Things are bad enough. Over the top, right now."

"Mr. Mayor, I respect the job you have to do. It can be impossible at times. If I can help you in some way, I will, but you can't suppress the press!"

"I'm not trying to suppress the press! I'm trying to

suppress a civil war in the streets!"

"If I can help in some way, I will."

"Promise?"

"Promise. But I have to be true to myself, too. I want to do just as good a job at what I do… as you do at your job."

"Well, think about it. And if you think of something that will help, I'm all ears."

"I'll remember that, Mr. Mayor."

"Safe home," he said.

Wertz thought: *That bitch!*

Nicole thought: *That bastard!*

FIVE

A brilliant sun was rising over the Verrazano-Narrows Bridge beaming 'God rays' from the span. It was a glorious morning to be alive in New York.

The strong voice coming over the airwaves was a familiar one.

"This is Paul Nelson with breaking news on Good Morning New York. Unfortunately, it's not good news for New York this morning. Just after midnight last night, three of New York's finest were killed by the New York Sniper. The names of the officers are not being…"

Mayor Wertz turned away from the TV screen for just a moment to bark an instruction to the group of fourteen gathered around the conference table. "Make damn sure the names of these officers are not released before the press conference."

• • •

On the screen was a brightly lit yellow brick building. Two police officers walked out of the entry, sidestepping a door barely attached to its hinges. Then a little man stepped out the same door. Not in handcuffs, because he only had one arm. One eye was a closed socket. He smiled when he saw the spotlights on him. The brightness only emphasized the black spaces where there were missing teeth.

Nicole Jensen spoke. "This is the man, homeless and nameless, at least for now, until police give us more information as to who he is…and why he was inside the building that police believe is where the sniper fired his weapon, killing three NYPD Officers."

The picture widened. "As you can see, Police Commissioner Brix and Mayor Wertz were discussing the capture."

Nicole was sitting at the editing console with Ramon Sanchez watching herself on the screen. She instructed, "Let's cut out the Mayor saying shit, or almost shit. That whole part. And cut just before he turns and says: 'Get that fucking TV camera and press out of here!'"

"OK," Ramon replied.

Nicole also instructed, "And let's put up a graphic of a scoreboard showing eight police shields and a score of eight, then the logo for the Mayor's office showing a score of zero. Wertz will hate that, but if I give the Mayor one, I get one. That's the way it's going to be."

. . .

Mayor Wertz was standing behind a podium with six microphones sticking out the top. The media presser it was already in progress. Pictures of the three slain officers were on easels at the front of the room. One was white, one was African American and one was Japanese. He pointed to someone in the audience.

"John."

"Mr. Mayor," John stood, notepad in hand and said, "I know you can't do ballistics without a bullet. Were any bullets found, and if so, where?"

The Mayor answered. "We did find bullets, in fact. They were found on the floor and on the back wall of the garage. There were a total of three bullets."

John pitched a follow-up. "Well, sir, is there any

indication that there was more than one shooter?"

"That's quite possible." The room lit up with murmuring. The Mayor pointed to someone else.

"Alice."

"This took place at the 64th Precinct. Why do you think the sniper, or snipers, chose that particular location? And, as a follow-up, I see that you and Commissioner Brix were on the scene at the same time. How is it that you were both there at that time?"

"I'll answer the last question first. Gracie Mansion is just six miles away. When Commissioner Brix called, I went right over. I was there in ten minutes. As to why the killer chose that location, I guess because it has a motor pool entrance and exit visible from the street."

The Mayor continued. "Yes, you in the back." The Mayor pointed.

"Mr. Mayor, was Officer Daniels shot at?"

"Officer Daniels could have been targeted. He probably was. But when he heard the shots…remember, the shooter started on the left and moved to the right…it gave Daniels time to open the door of his car and, basically, fall to the pavement, hiding behind the car. He then reached into the car, putting himself at risk, and turned on the alarm. So, although only officers Tate, Jefferson and Takahashi were hit, it doesn't mean that officer Daniels wasn't meant to be next."

A different voice in the crowd said, "Mr. Mayor!"

"Yes, in the back."

It was Nicole Jensen. "Mr. Mayor, three police officers were shot and killed last night." The Mayor had a blank, poker face on. He was trying to hide his *Oh, oh, here we go again!* expression. *What's going to come out of her mouth now?*

Nicole continued, "And two officers were shot and killed last week. And one officer the week before that. And one the week before that. And another the week before that."

"That's right, unfortunately."

"Do you think it will be four officers next week?"

The room erupted into unintelligible murmurs.

"What kind of a question is that?" the Mayor said, clearly annoyed. "Don't even think that way. With good police work and a little luck, there won't be anyone dying next Monday."

The Mayor pointed to someone else.

"Yes, you."

A reporter stood up. "A lot of people in the streets are saying that you are not doing enough to catch the cop killer. That you have a press conference every time there's a shooting and you tell us who was killed and when and where, but you don't tell us what you are doing about it."

"That's right! That's exactly right! Because if we tell you, we tell the sniper. Look, we're doing everything we can, using every department we have, working on this every day. In fact, day and night. The FBI has been involved and is working as hard as we are. When there is more to report, we'll let you know. We'll take one last question."

There was a slight pause.

"Yes."

"As we speak, there is a demonstration forming at Times Square. Are you worried about this getting out of control? What are you doing about possible violence?"

"Violence? We've had violence for the past four weeks. I'd call eight police officers shot and killed in a month extreme violence. We don't need any more. I think the people of New York City know that. What we need is help, not hindrance. A small demonstration by a few

concerned citizens is a good thing. I'm not worried about it."
The Mayor folded a small book on the top of the podium.

"Thank you." He and his people walked off.

. . .

The handmade cardboard signs were on sticks held above the heads of the crowd. They were in stark contrast to the iconic neon signs that rose above them in Times Square.

STOP THE KILLING NOW

WERTZ IS WORTHLESS

The demonstrators were well behaved, but not well organized. They just milled about in no specific pattern, hoisting their signs above their heads. This was an ad-hoc rally. A few small simpatico groups networked through social media and gathered together with no official thought-out plan. This was seventy-three mothers, wives, husbands and teenagers of all colors, sizes and ethnicity. All of them concerned citizens doing their civic duty. Conscientious in their endeavor to make the city a better, safer place.

Within forty-five minutes, the crowd grew in size from seventy-three to one hundred and three. Then to two hundred and three. There were those who wanted to become part of the 'event'. Those that wanted to add their voices to a good cause. Those who wanted to make history.

And then, there were those who wanted to cause trouble. The rabble-rousers, the inciters, the igniters.

Police arrived in cars and on foot. Barricades were set up to contain the swarm. Mobile TV news crews arrived, cameras perched atop white vans with big logos painted on their sides. They recorded the chant that was promulgated by one of the agitators. "They protect us, whose protecting them?" More and more people picked up the chant. Amazing

how a little poem set to an incessant beat can become
hypnotic, mesmerizing, can generate steam and power. It
grew louder. The signs now rose higher. The crowd larger.
The mounted police rode up, two on each side of the throng.
Nicole Jensen was on the street, microphone in hand. She
was somewhere at the edge of the crowd, struggling to be
heard over the din.

"Sir! Sir! Tell me, what do you think it will take to
catch this cop killer?"

It was a middle-age man wearing a sport coat and
shirt opened at the collar. "How many have been killed so
far? It's eight, I believe. This killer is elusive. He hasn't been
caught yet. And he may never get caught. The question is,
how many more men in blue will die before the killer
disappears?"

Nicole moved on.

"Ma'am! Ma'am! What do you think it will take to
catch this killer, bringing such fear and frustration to the
city?" She was a very old black woman; small, fragile,
stooped over from age. She wore an antique, tasseled satin
shawl around her head that framed her deeply wrinkled face.
Her slightly-yellowed, cataract-fogged, blood-vesseled eyes
gave the impression that they had witnessed many things
over many lifetimes. And, when she spoke, her voice rasped
with the wisdom of the ages. The old woman's eyes seemed
to lose focus on anything in front of her. It was as if she were
seeing something, a memory, from the distant past. She
spoke: "Girlie… (she sighed) this is about good and evil. Do
you believe in good versus evil?" The old woman paused to
give Nicole a chance to answer. But Nicole did not speak.
No one did. It was as if all sound was silenced.

The old woman spoke again. "This will be an
outcome determined by chance. A chance for good to win."

She paused again.

"A chance will come. But when?"

The old woman's words, the way she said them, had a mysterious, haunting aura. The kind of goose-bumpy feeling you can't ignore. Words you can never forget.

Nicole turned to the camera. Her face was full screen. She spoke, surprised. "In all the interviews I've done, I've never heard it put quite that way. Tell me…" she turned back to the old woman. But the woman was gone.

Nicole turned back to the camera again, "If I ask a thousand people, and there are certainly a thousand here tonight, we'll hear a thousand answers. But a couple of things seem to be common threads from all. Not enough is being done. This is Nicole Jensen in Times Square for PIC TV–10."

• • •

The digital clock on the sofa end table said 1:03 A.M. Nicole Jensen was in her flannel pajamas, sitting Indian style on her couch, eating Chinese takeout with a fork. Her TV lit up the room and her face. She pushed a button on her remote and the playback started. She saw herself interviewing people on the street. The headline at the top left of the screen said RECORDED EARLIER.

It was the man in the sport jacket. "…how many more men in blue will die before the killer disappears?"

Nicole, with mouth chewing, watched herself move to the little old black woman. The one who had the aura of a soothsayer.

"Ma'am! Ma'am! What do you think it will take to catch this killer, bringing such fear and frustration to the city?"

"Girlie…(she sighed) this is about good and evil. Do you believe in good versus evil?" The old woman paused.

The old woman spoke again. "This will be an outcome determined by chance. A chance for good to win. A chance will come. But when?"

Nicole's mouth stopped chewing. The old woman's words echoed in her mind. They descended deep into her soul like the chill of an evening on a dark night. She repeated them in her mind with her mouth closed. *This will be an outcome determined by chance.*

Nicole's head turned slightly to the left. Her eyes searched the ceiling for something. A memory. A visual. She got up from the couch, went to a drawer in her computer desk, and rummaged around until she found something. A thumb drive. She clicked off the TV and started up her sleeping computer. She inserted the drive. A few clicks and the video started. It was a two-lane black-top rushing toward the cell phone camera on the dashboard of a car traveling fast. It was a sunny day. Palm trees blurred by on both sides. Music from the radio fought the sound of wind blasting in from open car windows. The camera panned left. A twenty-something woman was driving, her brunette hair whipping around wildly, beating against her turquoise top. She was laughing hysterically.

"Don't take my picture, I'm a mess!" Giggles could be heard from off-camera.

"Give me that phone!" The driver said as her hand loomed large in the lens. The picture tilted to bare legs and pink shorts, then a blur across the dashboard at a dizzying speed, then it swept up to another young woman sitting in the passenger seat. She had blonde hair up in a ponytail. Lipstick pink lips were smiling. It was Nicole; white blouse, robin's-egg-blue shorts.

"Payback!" Maggie shouted against the ambient noise.

"Don't do that," Nicole said, laughing and chiding Maggie. "You're driving, you're going to get us killed and we'll never get to Jen's wedding."

"We'd better make it to Jen's wedding. I bought a new dress just for this."

"How far is Bonita Springs from here?"

"I don't know. Maybe two hours? Never been there."

The picture suddenly changed to Nicole painting her toenails.

The picture changed again. Nicole was driving now, singing a song with the radio.

The picture changed again. Maggie was driving again. Through the open right window they could see a column of smoke in the near distance. No, it was steam. It was billowing up into the clear blue sky. As their car got closer, a huge dust cloud made the air brown for at least fifty feet long and eighteen feet high on the side of the road. People were gathered, maybe thirty of them, at the edge of a black-water canal. Fishing poles were scattered helter-skelter on the embankment.

"My God!" Nicole exclaimed. There was a car, a station wagon barely floating in the middle of the thirty-five-foot-wide drainage canal – a canal that ran the entire length of the Tamiami Trail that traversed the Everglades from Miami to Naples.

"This just happened! Minutes ago! Stop the car! Stop!" Nicole yelled.

The picture lurched to and fro. A car door opened and legs and blue shorts got out and ran toward the steam, the dust and the crowd. The video was jiggly and blurry.

The camera ran into the middle of a frantic crowd of mostly Hispanics and African Americans. It appeared that they had all been fishing along the bank.

The shrieking was hair-raising.

"Jesus Christ!" was heard from many. "Holy shit!" was heard from most.

The jumpy picture settled down now. Bubbles were rising to the surface all around the floating car. People, a family, could be seen gasping for air behind the glass.

There was a man in the water near the sinking car. He did a surface dive and disappeared.

The phone captured the sounds of the onlookers.

"My God, hurry!"

"There's too many of them."

"Those poor people."

A whole minute went by.

A black man blessed himself with the sign of the cross.

The picture panned to a froth of sizzling bubbles. From the middle of them, up popped a six-year-old boy. The crowd was joyous. Some of the men extended arms and helped the boy to shore.

The camera now panned back to the sinking car. Ten seconds later a 15-year-old boy coughed and flailed his way to safety. Another fifteen seconds and an old man and a middle-age woman popped to the surface simultaneously.

Ten seconds after that, a 10-year-old girl appeared.

The crowd cheered each time. Arms raised toward heaven. Signs of the cross.

Then, another middle-age woman emerged. Fishing poles extended to reach her and ropes were tossed to her.

The crowd cheered ever louder.

Then there was a long pause.

The drenched mother who had just been saved screamed.

"Ana! Ana! Mi nina! Ana!" She started for the water but the crowd stopped her.

Then, a few bubbles.

They waited.

More bubbles.

"Ana! Save my Ana!"

More bubbles.

The crowd muttered. Prayed. Blessed themselves and whispered prayers. The car was still floating, but barely.

Suddenly, a little Chihuahua popped to the surface and doggie-paddled over to the group.

The mother was screaming through her tears.

The father tried to break free from the men holding him back.

Like a geyser, the man, the lifesaver who had rescued the rest of the family, burst to the surface holding 14-month-old Ana. He swam the baby to her family and the crowd went wild with joy.

But the baby wasn't breathing.

The unknown lifesaver laid the baby down on the ground and began breathing air, gently, into the baby's lungs.

No one said a word.

The mother wept. One-by-one each person descended to their knees and bowed their heads. All you could hear were voices whispering prayers. Then! Little Ana coughed! She began to breath! Then cry!

The crowd went wild with delight!

The lifesaver stood up, well above the heads of the people gathered there. Tears streamed down the faces of the family in front of him.

As he stood there, Nicole's voice said, "My God!" Maggie's voice said, "Holy Shh!" Because this man, this lifesaver, this incredibly brave person was what could be called a gorgeous man. Accentuated by the fact that he had a dream body and a skimpy, skimpy, skimpy, Indian style breechcloth. This was not the kind of man a woman saw every day. Or any day. Somehow the cell phone camera drifted slowly down, and then up.

The nearly-naked man turned and jogged to the edge of the canal.

"Wait! Wait!" the mother yelled. "What can we give you? How can we thank you?"

He thought for a moment and said: "Just remember what I did here today."

"But…but…who are you? What is your name?"

"My name is…Chance."

He turned and dove in. They all watched. But they never saw him again.

"Holy freakin' shit!" was about all Nicole could get out.

"Fuck me!" came out of Maggie's mouth.

"Well, yeah, duhh!" Nicole said.

Her thumb drive ended and the picture stopped. Nicole, still curled up on her couch, closed her eyes and could see that day like yesterday. The memory played in her mind. She could see herself there again. "Do you believe what we just saw," she was saying to Maggie as they drove away that day.

"It was like, like a movie," Maggie said. "Did we get it all on the phone?"

"Man, I hope so," Nicole said. "I'm sending this to the station, like right now."

"Nah, nah, nah, nah! Hold it! Not so fast!" Maggie

insisted. "Didn't you hear what I said? Like fuuu…"

"Oh, yeah, don't worry, we'll edit that out before it airs."

"You'd better. I don't want to see myself saying that on the Community Connection Channel in Miami," Maggie insisted.

Nicole assured her, "OK, don't worry, I'll fix it. Now put the pedal-to-the-metal and let's get our asses to that wedding. Or we're going to lose a friend."

As they drove, they talked.

"Did he just come out of nowhere?" Nicole said.

"That's what they said."

"Where did he go?" Nicole asked.

"I'd love to know."

"Did we dream all that?" Nicole asked.

"No, but I will tonight," Maggie said.

Nicole, still curled up on her couch, smiled with her eyes closed. She opened them and the memory was gone. For now at least. She removed the thumb drive and hit the playback button of her DVD. On the screen was the interview of the old black woman at the protest. The sage. The oracle…or whatever she was.

"…this will be an outcome determined by chance. A chance for good to win. A chance will come. But when?"

Nicole pressed stop. She just said one word: "Chance!"

SIX

A man's hand took a phone out of his jacket pocket and tapped the keypad. His starched white shirt had French cuffs and jade cufflinks. He was sitting at a large modern chrome and glass desk. Outside his window was the Washington Monument.

At the other end of the line, a tough looking man answered the call. He had a tattoo of a black teardrop running out of his left eye onto his cheek. He was immersed in a crowd of demonstrators.

"Yeah!"

"How's it looking?" Cufflinks asked.

"Ripe."

"I'll have fifty G's in the box for you by tomorrow. Get what you need. You have the key I sent?"

"Around my neck."

• • •

The sign on the wall said WSGN-Miami. The beige desk phone rang with a trill in the office cubicle. The young woman answered. "Maggie Van Buren."

"Hey, girl!"

"Nikki! I was just thinking about you!"

"Oh, am I in trouble for not calling enough?" Nikki said.

"Hey, I could have called you, too. It works two ways, right?"

"Right. How's SGN treating you?"

"Lots better than when you were at Community Connection TV in Miami, that's for sure."

"Hey, speaking of that," Nikki said, "remember Jen's wedding and that guy we saw?"

"You mean that guy who wouldn't leave me alone and asked me to dance every dance?"

"No, not him. Another guy."

"Who?" Maggie was clueless.

"That guy who saved the people in the canal."

A slight pause. "Oh, yeah, that hunky naked guy. Yeah, who could forget?"

"Ahh, yeah, him. I have to get a hold of him."

Maggie was incredulous, "It took you this long to come to that conclusion? It's been two years."

"Yeah, I mean, no, it's not that. It's this New York cop killer thing. I don't know, maybe it's a long shot, but they can't get a handle on this for anything and it's getting pretty scary up here. And…"

"And you think this guy can help? How?"

"Well, I remember reading some newspaper articles after we were there that day."

"Yeah, I remember reading them, too." As Maggie talked she punched some keys on her keyboard. "I'm going on the newspaper archive right now. That was on June 7th, two days after my birthday, two years ago."

Nicole grabbed her laptop from her bag and opened it up. "Good idea."

Maggie found a page in the archive. "Hey, got something, look at this!"

Nicole was getting there, scrolling through pages quickly, trying to catch up with Maggie.

"There's a picture of him. He's diving into the canal." Maggie turned her head at an angle.

"Yeah, I'm there," Nicole said. "But it doesn't say much about the guy because he disappeared so fast. I remember seeing something else about this guy. Something about hiding and tracking and surviving in the Everglades."

"Ahh, this might help you," Maggie said. "Here's a pic from the Governor's Award Ceremony about a year later. Looks handsome. Let's see…says he spent almost two years evading police in a case of mistaken identity…blah, blah, blah…and survived by tracking, stalking and catching animals."

"Found it. I'm with you. He is handsome," Nikki confirmed. "Better than I remember!"

Maggie continued: "…he had to act like an animal himself…has eyes like a hawk, can run like a gazelle and hold his breath underwater for…"

"It just has three dots and a question mark." Nikki said. "Must be a long time. Remember how long it took to get all those people out of the car just before it sank?"

"Yeah. Then he dove in and never came up for air. He just disappeared!" Maggie kept talking. "This says the Governor gave him a special State Award for helping to capture a secret foreign military group training in the Everglades. The Governor also said that he reserves the right to call on Chance in the future if the safety and security of Florida requires it."

"That's good enough for me," Nikki concluded. "I'm thinking this guy could help catch this cop killer up here. Now, we have to get a hold of him."

"I could make some calls to some people who might be able to find something out," Maggie offered.

"Anything you can do since you're still in Miami, Mag. If you know somebody, I'd really appreciate it."

"OK, let me see what I can do and I'll give you a

text or a call ASAP."

"Great. Love 'ya Mag."

"Love you, too, Nikki."

"Later."

"Ciao for now."

Nicole hung up but kept her hand on the receiver. She took a breath, looked toward the bank of editing machines without really seeing them, and turned to the big round clock on the wall. She drummed the fingers of her other hand on the control console. There was no one else in the room at the time. She looked around quickly. She dialed the phone.

The voice answered. "Tom Elliott."

"Hi, Tom, it's Nicole."

"The girl of the hour."

"What does that mean?"

"It means that you managed to make it to the top of the Mayor's list."

"You mean, he wants to do the interview."

"No, not that list."

"Oh, *that* list. What a distinction. I must be doing my job."

"Ahh...a little too well, per his Honor."

"Well, that's too bad, because I just might be in a position to help his Honor."

"How so?"

"We need to catch this guy."

"That would be nice."

"And nobody has been able to do anything except guess at a profile, let alone, where, why...we just know when. Mondays."

"I'd say you're right on track."

"Ahh, on track, that's just what I was thinking. On

track. Tracking."

"You were doing good until now. You lost me."

"Tracking. We need a tracker."

"Tracker? Like big game hunter tracker?"

"Exactly."

"And?"

"And, I know where we can get one. A good one. He got a big important award from the Governor of Florida."

"New York City is not Florida. We don't have alligators. Well, we might. In the sewer system. At least, that's what I've heard."

"Yeah, yeah, yeah, I know, it sounds far-fetched but in…"

"Far-fetched? Like, you mean, ridiculous? Sorry, I don't mean to sound mean, but…I want to keep my job."

"Tom, just get me in to see Wertz and I'll handle the rest." *He always was a pussy!*

"Nah, nah, I can't do that."

"Why? Why not?"

"The NYPD hired a psychic once to find a missing kid. Do you know what the papers said?"

"That was different. With this guy, there's a basis of proof. It makes sense. Think about it."

"I'll think about it. But things would have to get a lot worse before any of us would stoop…I mean, go to that extreme."

"They just might. They just might."

SEVEN

The crowd was growing quickly at Times Square. People
kept coming. A mix of African Americans, whites, Asians,
Hispanics and other minorities. The crowd had ballooned
from fifty to two hundred-fifty to eight hundred. Half of
Broadway was now blocked by cars, cabs, trucks and busses
stacking up on one side of the street. More police arrived on
the scene, trying to keep at least one lane open so cars could
pass. Six mounted police came from nowhere, no doubt
dispatched from their posts at Central Park. Sitting high on
their mounts, they lorded over the crowd. But the crowd
grew even larger now, closing off Broadway entirely despite
police presence. Police megaphones came out. But the
instructions, the demands, were muffled by the noise, the
voices, the shuffling of what could now be called a mob.

A middle-age woman climbed to the roof of a car.
She had a bullhorn. "The Mayor is doing nothing to help us.
Is he? Tell me!"

The crowd was unified. Instead of a voice from here
and a voice from there, they now answered as one. One
large, angry, frustrated, powerful organism. A dangerous
organism.

"No!" Came the same answer from twelve hundred
people. "No!" Again. Then louder. "No!"

"We need the Mayor to take action."

The crowd went into a chant. "Action, action, action,
action…"

Times Square's famous neon signs were lit up,
moving, spinning, blinking above the mass of people below.

Now more than eighteen hundred. Arms were raised. Fists were in the air. And one person in the crowd had a black teardrop tattoo under his left eye.

The woman with the bullhorn yelled, "What do we want?"

"Action!" the voices echoed for blocks.

"What will we take?"

"Action!" The answer was deafening.

"What will we show them?"

"Action!" It was one thunderous voice reaching the tops of the skyscrapers, reaching throughout the city.

A helicopter buzzed the top of a skyscraper as it peered down into the Grand Canyon that was Times Square. It wasn't alone. There were two more up there swirling around in an aerial ballet. How they did not crash into each other, and to the throng below, was a miracle. TV news cameras were mounted on moveable eyeball pods attached to the bottoms of the choppers, each giving a similar view of the melee blocking the entire Y-shaped intersection of Times Square.

It was a spectacle to behold. With the incessant, pulsating, heartbeat-sounds of the three news choppers, and the prattling on of the onboard reporters, police bullhorns could barely be heard far below on the streets awash in bright spotlights and colorful neon. The echoing, conflicting voices became distorted to almost unintelligible levels. In a sea of confusion, the crowd responded with raised fists. A mob on the verge of chaos. A bull elephant, that could, at any moment, break loose from its chains and thrash about uncontrolled. This was the potential. The powder keg. This was the fear.

At this very moment, hundreds of policemen in six of the city's precincts were picking up riot gear – helmets, face protectors, shields, body armor, assault rifles and ammunition. In motor pools, armored vehicles were moved into position outside police stations. SWAT teams were loading their pistols, shotguns and sniper rifles.

In Times Square and surrounding streets, shopkeepers closed doors and pulled floor-to-ceiling security gates across storefronts. Merchandise was removed from windows. Metal storm shutters were put up.

Suddenly! A swell of commotion erupted in the crowd!

About thirty yards away, three teenagers were on top of a police cruiser, jumping up and down with all their might. One dented the roof. One stomped and stomped and stomped on the windshield until it cracked in a million lines and caved in. Another jumped on the hood and held his arms up to the sky in victory.

The crowd cheered. It sounded like a football game.

SMASH!

Glass shattered. Twenty-five people stormed through the obliterated window of a retail-clothing store, walking over thousands of pieces of broken glass fragments. In minutes dozens of looters were making their exits, arms so full of dresses, blouses, skirts, handbags, shoes, and whatever, that the clothes were falling from their arms. So heavy was the loot that some women couldn't make it across the street. Odd thing was, nobody stole the stolen goods from the stealers. There was, as they say, honor among thieves.

Then, two hundred feet away!

FIRE!

A police car was ablaze! The crowd backed away, faces reflecting red. Eyebrows were singed. An older man was tripping backwards. Some of the young were trampled by the stronger and bigger.

The flames shot up higher! Some screamed, "Get back! Get back! It might blow!" As if on cue, a blast from the gas tank made the streets look like Iraq or Afghanistan.

Terror, from America's own, had come to the civilized streets of New York City.

And it was just getting started.

A platoon of police, sixty strong, in full riot gear, amassed on the north side of Broadway. A 'DO-NOT-CROSS' line four-men-deep and fifteen men wide formed quickly. They were positioned about one hundred feet away from the crowd. Another platoon moved into position on the south side. A third line of riot police were in single file directly across the street from the rioters. Six mounted police appeared and pinched the mob against the buildings so they were trapped. But not for long.

Two more windows were smashed!

Alarms were screaming!

Looters were rampaging – blacks, whites, Hispanics, Asians...police and news helicopters hovered above, searchlights illuminating the scene like a sports event. All the news channels were there, including PIC TV–10. News reporters were on foot, crews following closely – cameras, lights, action...lots of action! There...it was that famous news reporter everyone knows elbowing his way through the boisterous crowd. All the while talking non-stop into his mic.

A different reporter was speaking on camera: "The fire department arrived a few minutes ago...and they've already got this car fire under control. If you look over there to my left..." The camera panned "...you'll see that the retail store is still being ransacked. The liquor store, a few doors down, just about emptied."

Then!

A fiery blast!

A concussion!

A bomb!

Across the street, clear across Broadway! So powerful, shards of glass became killer shrapnel flying toward the line of police. Glass penetrated! Blood let from cuts on faces and necks! Horses went down with policemen under them! Shields went up! Helmets were blown off! The concussion of the blast knocked some officers off balance. They fell to the pavement. Many in the crowd, in wild-eyed frenzy, adrenaline taking over mind and body, attacked the police ferociously. Bats from the pillaged sporting goods store pummeled officers. Police fired their handguns. Pointed tent poles speared policemen's eyes. Police fired weapons. Stolen hunting knives sliced policemen's legs. Police shot their guns.

Fire raged at the blast site across the street. Fire trucks arrived. Hoses were pulled. Water was pumping. Steam was rising.

Tear gas was fired into the crowd. Many were choking, tears flowing, hands to faces. Many were now in handcuffs, led to paddy wagons.

Within twenty minutes the streets were empty.

Empty except for policemen, police cars, fire trucks and two SWAT vehicles.

Empty except for three rioters, lying dead on the sidewalk.

Empty except for four police officers lying dead on the pavement.

Each one shot the exact same way.

Through the back of the neck with a large caliber bullet.

And it wasn't even Monday.

EIGHT

In the morning light of this beautiful summer day, the historic landmark of City Hall, the oldest one in America, was stunning. It is a brilliant white limestone architectural jewel set among the green grass and mature trees at City Hall Park. It was built between 1810 and 1812 in a French Renaissance style with a central dome and flanking wings, magnificent in its detail and rich appointments. It represents a time of delicate civility and artistic expression. Something to be revered by the citizenry. Its imagery suggests a genteel, sophisticated, diplomatic approach to managing mankind. It stands today in a very different world. Yet its wide stone steps still welcome the people of the city for tours, discussions, debates and, yes, demonstrations. There were no demonstrations taking place here this morning on its broad imposing entrance. But it was still early. No doubt, demonstrators were sleeping in this morning, exhausted from the previous night's terror at Times Square.

There was one person up and about this morning, however. Mayor Wertz. As he stepped into his car outside City Hall, smoke from the Times Square riots still rose up in the air six miles away. He drove around the front of City Hall on a small road and headed for a building practically next door. A building with a totally different bearing – 1 Police Plaza, known as 1PP. The NYPD Headquarters. Wertz, a long-time enthusiast of history and the arts, found it amusing that the building, finished in 1973, was of the architectural style called Brutalist. This is a fact. Fourteen stories tall and your basic box fortress. Wertz had often wondered if the architects, playing a sarcastic game, were trying to make a point. An inside joke to be revealed long after the building was erected, hoping some trade book would expose their 'genius' eliciting kudos from their peers.

The car made its way to the entrance. The Mayor, tireless, was wearing a suit jacket that looked like it had been slept in. He walked into the building, through security and entered the elevator. He pushed 14. He was alone.

BING! He walked down the carpeted hall, past a few desks, and into the corner office of Police Commissioner Brix. He saw no one. It was 6:10 A.M. Brix was asleep on the couch.

The Mayor played Revelry through tightened trumpet-lips when he saw Brix.

"Geez! What the hell," Brix said, irritated, groggy, as he rolled on the couch and sat at the edge. "Don't we have people to stop you, for Christ's sake!" He yawned.

"How much sleep did you get?" Wertz asked, not really caring.

"Not enough, thanks to you." He put on his shoes and straightened his shirt.

"Me too. I'm exhausted. But we've gotta talk before our press briefing in a couple of hours." The Mayor sat down.

"Why didn't you just call me," Brix said, annoyed.

"Nah, nah, nah! I don't even trust the security of our own lines anymore. Or emails. No, we need to talk face-to-face. This is just between me and you." The Mayor closed the office door. "I think we would be out of our minds to let it be known that the sniper got four more last night."

"What are you smokin', Ed? The reporters, TV cameras, and number one PITA, Jensen, were swarming all over the scene."

"Not behind the crime tape, they weren't. They saw the cops down and all the rest, but they don't know how the cops died. They could have been trampled by the crowd. I'm just saying we don't tell 'em it was the sniper."

"What do we say then? We don't know?" Brix thought Wertz had lost it.

"We say it's unclear. We're investigating. A lot was going on last night. The fog of war. How's that?"

"The fog of war? That makes it sound worse! War?"

"Well, never mind that phrase then. We say that we need to examine everything. Then we'll give a formal report later," Wertz said.

"And what about the bomb blast across the street?"

"Truth is, we don't know who did that. Could have been a rioter who set off a gas explosion. Do we know yet? No, we don't. We've gotta play this down, not up for God's sake. It could have been an accident. I don't know and you don't know. That's our story," Wertz insisted.

"And what happens later when they all find out that we withheld information?" Brix said.

"We have to present it the right way now, so we are not trapped later. Protection. That's what this is all about. Protecting the people. We want to throw the sniper off. Not tip our hand. Not give him credit. That's what the fucker wants. Another notch in his belt. Four more notches? We don't give it to him, that bastard!"

"That might make him more angry."

"Then he'll make a mistake. They always make a mistake. This can't go on forever."

"I don't know, that TV reporter, Jensen, she has a big mouth. She's everywhere, getting her hands into everything. She's trouble. What if she gets a hold of this?" Brix asked.

"I'll take care of her," Wertz insisted.

"How?"

Wertz hesitated for a second.

"I'll think of something."

. . .

On the screen, the TV anchor was giving her 8 AM news report. "…and there's more bad news for the city. Four more NYPD officers were killed in last night's Times Square rioting." Pictures of the four officers appeared side-by-side on the screen. "Officers James Lucius Brown, Terrel Williams, Sean Kelly and Carlos Rivera lost their lives, but the Mayor's office is saying that it is unclear at this time exactly how their lives were taken. In other news…"

. . .

The digital clock on the side table said 7:56 A.M. Nicole Jensen, dressed for work, was just about to put her lipstick on when she heard a furious knocking on her apartment door. She hurriedly stroked the lipstick on her upper lip. The knocking started again, this time louder and longer. She padded to the door shoeless, lipstick tube in her right hand, and looked through the peephole.

"Nicole, it's Tom," the voice said.

She saw Tom standing close to the lens. She opened the door, quizzical.

"Tom! How did you get in the front entrance door?"

Tom stepped into the doorway and Nicole saw a uniformed policeman behind him. She took two steps back and froze. "The Mayor wants to talk with you," Tom said matter-of-factly.

She thought for a moment.

"I can't do the interview today," she quipped.

Tom just looked at her as if to say, *Now is not the time for jokes.*

"About what?" Nicole said reluctantly.

"He wants to know everything you know."

"Everything I know? Know about what?"

"About everything. The riots, who you know, what you know, when you knew it, what's going to happen next…"

"Sounds like he thinks I'm the cause of it."

Tom shrugged his shoulders and made an I don't know face. Nicole sighed as if exhausted.

"Where?"

"City Hall."

"When?"

"Now."

"Now? I have a press conference to get to or did you forget about that. I'm sure you're going. And so am I."

"He wants to talk to you before the press conference."

"Before the conference? That doesn't leave us much time."

"That's why he sent us to get you. To get you through rush hour traffic."

Nicole thought about this for a moment. Was it truth? Or lie?

"OK, fine. Can I put the rest of my lipstick on?"

. . .

Nicole sat at a small conference table. Her back was to the only door. The door was open. Her purse and phone were placed neatly in front of her on the table. Tom Elliott sat opposite her. She was clearly annoyed and running out of patience.

"Look, we've been here for ten minutes now. It's 8:50 and I have to get to the press conference in the Blue Room.

"The press conference was...delayed."

"Delayed?"

"Yes, until ten."

"I didn't know about that. When did they delay it?"

"Just now."

Nicole sighed.

"The Mayor gave me a list of questions to ask you about in case he was held up." Tom pulled three sheets of paper out of his briefcase. "How much footage did your crew shoot last night?"

"I don't know. We were there for two hours. I won't know how much we got until we start to edit."

The clock on the wall moved from 8:55 to 9:20 as Tom asked question after question. Nicole changed positions a few times during the Q & A session. She finally ran out of patience.

"Look, these questions are inane. You're just wasting my time."

"Sorry, Nikki, I'm just doing what I've been asked...told to do."

"This is an important news day for me. You'd be smarter if you asked me what I know after today, not before it."

"You have a point."

"I have a point? You're just stalling."

No answer from Tom.

Nikki lost it: "I'm getting the hell out of here. I'm

going to the press conference."

"The press conference is over!" It was Mayor Wertz, standing behind her.

"Over? Over?" Nicole was irate. "You deliberately kept me out of the press conference? Oh, I can't wait to get this one on the air." She stood up.

"I wouldn't leave right now if I were you," the Mayor snarled.

"Oh, yeah? Watch me! Or arrest me!"

"Maybe we will."

Mayor Wertz sat down at the table next to Tom Elliott.

Nicole was fuming. "On what grounds? You don't like my style? Or is this a male feminist thing?"

"How about aiding and abetting civil disorder. Disobedience," the Mayor said.

Nicole cocked her head like a dog in disbelief.

"Helping to incite riots," the Mayor continued. "Fomenting hate. Agitating nice law-abiding citizens to turn against authority, the police, the government. It wouldn't be the first time a reporter crossed over to the other side."

"You're crazy!"

"Yeah, crazy enough to put you out of business for a few days. Or a few weeks. Want to be on the news? What will everyone think of you when *you're* the news?"

Nicole made a hidden fist like she wanted to punch the Mayor.

"Why don't you sit down, Ms. Jensen? I'd hate to see you stand for another twenty minutes while we go over all the possible charges that we could hold you on, under suspicion, until we get to the bottom of all this."

Nicole was seething! Steaming! Her brain was working overtime, ready to unleash a barrage of stinging words at the Mayor. But she had to figure out what was behind this weird, corrupt behavior. He had a city percolating, about to boil over worse than last night, and here he was wasting time with her. Why? Obvious, she decided. *She's a big mouth. Shut her up. At least until he has a chance to control what happens next.* Nicole sat down.

"You want to keep me here to shut me up. What are you hiding?"

"Now, now, Ms. Jensen. You just made a big mistake hurling accusations at a Mayor. Do you know that I'm the Mayor? Do you know what I can do? So don't be so aggressive, Nicole."

"Or what? Or what?" Nicole blurted, almost spitting the words out, veins in her forehead ready to burst!

"We're getting nowhere." Wertz said calmly. "You're wasting my time, so I'm going to waste yours."

Tom was shrinking, knowing that the Mayor was on very dangerous ground. This was clearly dubious, Banana Republic tactics. He had never seen this before.

"Officer Thomkins," the Mayor commanded, "read the charges against Nicole Jensen. Mirandize and book and hold her for twenty-four hours until we…"

Nicole's phone vibrated on the table. Nicole's eyes snapped to the screen. A text from Maggie. Nicole's finger punched a button and the message appeared as officer Thomkins droned on.

Got it, had to pull teeth and…you don't want to know. Contact Chance at 555-642-1345. Good luck. Stay out of trouble. Maggie.

Nicole didn't even hear what officer Thomkins was saying. It didn't matter right now. As Mayor Wertz stood up to leave, Nicole stood up, too. Right in the doorway.

"Wait," she insisted, "you're desperate."

"Of course, I'm desperate. Can't you see desperate written on my forehead?" He motioned with his hand.

"Desperate people do desperate things," Nicole said. "I think I can help you, the city… everyone."

Wertz's face said, *yeah, sure, tell me another story.*

"I have an idea I've been working on for more than a week. It's a long shot that might be your best bet. You may not believe this, but I'm on your side."

"I gotta go. I've got a lot to do." Wertz made a movement to leave.

Nicole went for the finish line: "This will only take fifteen minutes and maybe you'll have something worthwhile to tell people instead of the same-old, same-old. Something that can work for a change. If you don't like it, don't do it. If you think it's a crazy idea, don't tell anybody. You can't lose by listening."

Mayor Wertz stopped but his mind was working. Thinking. Analyzing. What to do next.

"Tell you what," Nicole continued, "I'll work with you to prove I'm on your side. I'll work with you every day to prove that. I won't be your puppet, but I'll help get the word out. The words you want to get out."

The Mayor sat down, reluctantly, and folded his hands on the table. He stared at Nicole.

Nicole sat down across from him. "How would you describe this cop killer?" Nicole asked the Mayor.

"That's what we're trying to figure out," he answered sarcastically.

"He's an animal." *You idiot.*

"Yes, he's an animal." The Mayor looked bored already.

"He hides in the shadows. No one has seen him. He strikes unexpectedly. Even when we know that he strikes on a Monday. We know his prey. But we can't hide his prey away in a closet. We need police officers on the streets. They're sitting ducks."

The Mayor just stared at Nicole blankly.

"He has powerful weapons, but he knows when not to use them."

She continued: "He's stealthy, attacking from high places, low places. We never know where he is. He's like a leopard. Quiet. Secretive. Powerful. Crafty. He leaves no trace…no trace that we have found, even with hi-tech tools and systems. But we all know that there's always a trace. Always a sign. Always a remnant of something."

The Mayor, against his will, was falling into her web.

"Maybe we forget the hi-tech toys. Forget the computer-generated graphs and charts, the endless profiling, digging into statistical files and we forget the FBI. They haven't come up with anything. Because they are so bureaucratic they just keep doing things by rote. The same systematic, analytical path every time. Takes forever."

She paused to let it all sink in.

"Maybe what we need to do is break out of the box. Get back to basics. Primitive basics. Become a leopard ourselves."

The Mayor sat back in his chair. Silent. Absorbing every word.

"Maybe what we need is not ten thousand of New York's finest and an army of G men thrashing about in the thickets, signaling our every move. Maybe what we need is just one man. The right man. A leopard himself."

The Mayor was puzzled. Waiting. Skeptical. He looked at the clock on the wall. He breathed heavily. She was losing him.

"There's a guy in Florida. In the Everglades."

"Oh, geez!" The Mayor groaned, turning his head.

"No, wait. Wait until you hear the whole story."

"Yeah, fiction."

"The Governor of Florida gave this guy an award for tracking and helping to capture a Central American paramilitary group training secretly in the Everglades. He saved a family that crashed their car into a canal. He held his breath for something like, I don't know, a half hour."

The Mayor's eyebrows went up. "Please! Please! Please!"

Nicole pressed on. "He has vision like a hawk. And he survived almost two years in the Everglades evading the police."

"Evading the…that does it! This farce is over." The Mayor stood up.

"Mayor Wertz, this may be the simplest, smartest, fastest way to catch this killer. It's worth a call to the Governor of Florida, at least."

"You're a journalist alright. Full of tall tales that have no basis of truth."

"It's all true, Mayor."

"Holds his breath for half an hour! Preposterous!" The Mayor bristled.

"I can prove it!"

"If you can prove that, then I'll call the Governor, how's that?"

A light went off in Nicole's head, she reached for her phone and held it up.

"I have the proof right here, Mr. Mayor. Right in the palm of my hand. A video of the man himself!"

"Thanks for taking the call Bill, we haven't talked

since the conference in DC. So how have you been?" The Mayor was talking into a speakerphone in the 14th floor conference room at 1PP.

"I'm great, Ed. Especially since the fine people of Florida were smart enough to re-elect me Governor. Things couldn't be better. But I know you've got a mess on your hands. How can I help you, Ed?"

"Bill, I have with me, on speaker, my Communications Director, Tom Elliott and ahh, ahh, an…. associate, Nicole Jensen."

"Hi, everybody," said the Governor.

"Hi, Governor!" They both said in unison."

"Bill, I'm calling to pick your brain and get some background on a fellow you may know. A man that could possibly help us. But please keep this conversation in the strictest of confidence, Bill."

"Goes without saying, Ed. Anything to help."

"It's about a guy named Chance."

"Know him well. Great guy. Unusual guy. And speaking of confidentiality, please keep anything I say completely between us. I have to admit, the speakerphone makes me nervous. Chance is a very private guy and there are things about him that I think I need to protect."

"I understand, Bill. You can trust everyone listening." The Mayor held up his index finger and shook it at Nicole, as if to scold her and warn her.

"So why don't you ask me what you want to know and if I feel I can answer, I will," the Governor said.

"Fair enough. Some here think this guy Chance might be able to track the sniper. With what you know of him, do you think he could?"

"That's easy to answer and hard to answer. If you have a jungle in Manhattan, or woods, without a doubt. But last time I checked, Manhattan isn't built that way. Except for Central Park. So, I don't know. I do know he has acute senses. Hearing. Sight. Smell. Breathing control. Strength. Endurance. He sees things other people don't see or can't see. He's proven that many times over in work, secret work, that he's done for us. There's a lot that goes on in the Everglades that most people never hear about, and frankly, we don't want them to."

"Like finding those Central American military guys with a secret training camp?"

"Yes, like that. Unfortunately, that got out into the press. Since then, Chance has done other things to help the state and nation, but it's all below the radar."

"Then why did you have a press conference and give him your Governor's Award if you want to downplay this guy?"

"Because the report got out through a leak and I wanted to control it. It would have been worse if we said we had no knowledge. So we went the other way with it. Since then there has been very little press on Chance."

"And what about these far-fetched claims I hear about this guy having eyes like a hawk and being able to hold his breath underwater for half an hour? Things like that?"

"Remember, I said there are things about Chance that I don't want to be revealed. Certain unique advantages that have to be protected. Things that we don't want the bad guys to know about. Let me ask you, Ed, from what I told you so far, do you think that you will decide to work with Chance?"

"At this point, quite possibly, yes," the Mayor confided.

"Then let me get to the bottom line. He's the most

unique human being that I've ever met. With abilities that are astonishing. Unbelievable. Until you see it for yourself. Yes, eyes like a hawk. Literally. Yes, he can, let's say, breathe underwater. Yes, he can run like a racehorse, think like a computer, track anything that breaths. He's pretty amazing."

"Well, Bill…" said the Mayor, disbelieving what he just heard, "I'm not doubting what you're saying, but how is any of that possible?"

"You'll have to ask Chance that question."

"And just one more thing, Bill, out of curiosity, I heard that you arranged for this guy Chance to use some acreage within Everglades National Park for his own use, as a kind of reward."

"Yes, true. I had to pull some strings with the National Park Service, but yeah. It's not technically his, but he can use this land, ten acres, as steward over it, and basically to do whatever he wants – build a house, boat dock, gardens. Have the life he wants as long as he's on call for the State's needs. The smartest thing I've ever done. He keeps a good watch over the Everglades."

"Think he'd be interested in a nice apartment in New York?"

"I don't know. I think he's happy right where he is. But money talks. Big money talks louder."

"Thanks a lot, Bill. We appreciate your time."

"Good luck, Ed. Stay safe. Let me know if I can help in any way."

Nicole's eyes were as big as saucers when she made eye contact with the Mayor.

Tom Elliott was at the water cooler in the corner as the Mayor finished up his call with Governor Wilkinson. Tom pushed the blue lever to fill his cup. A stream of

bubbles rushed to the surface inside the large water bottle
with the sound effects from a scuba diving adventure movie.

NINE

A silvery shaft of sunlight penetrated deep into clear turquoise water illuminating the coral reef below. Rising in the shaft of light was the silhouetted form of a man with long flowing hair. Chance broke the surface and flashed a magazine-cover-smile as he hefted a 20-pound black grouper with his muscular right arm. The grouper, thrashing, was still on the end of a long spear.

"Dinner!" Chance shouted looking up. The stern of the blindingly white yacht looked huge from the blue-green water. The name of the yacht, written in gold leaf on the stern, was Coralina. The gold lettering glinted like treasure in the bright sun.

"Good thing! I really didn't want hot dogs tonight." It was Chance's first-mate, Cha-ley, shouting as he made his way down to the swim platform. His job right now was to grab the heavy fish - almost half his size - and get it to the ice locker built into the deck of the boat. Charles Devon Hastings was affectionately called Cha-ley because of the way he pronounced his own name. He was from the city of Cambridge. Not the Cambridge in England, but the one in New Zealand. Many people mistook his accent for British, which, in fact, it was derived from. But Cha-ley was a Kiwi. The five-foot-five 54-year-old Cha-ley was a vision of a first-mate: wiry, tanned body, stubby salt & pepper beard, a receding hairline, ponytail, a tattoo on both arms and both legs, white baseball cap, azure tank top stained by the blood of many a pelagic monster, thready blue shorts and bare feet. Cha-ley had a space between his two front teeth that gave him an adorably cartoonish, comic look.

"Ouch!" Cha-ley, pricked by the spines of the fish as it slid onto the ice, shook the pain out of his hand. As Cha-ley worked, Chance did a quick gymnast move and was standing on the swim platform in a blink. Curiously, there was no mask, fins or snorkel. Just the man himself. Naked except for a skimpy purple swimsuit. Chance's left arm reached up and caught a towel pitched at him from above. "Thanks," he said, as he dried his mane and swept the towel over his deeply tanned, muscular, six-foot-five body. He was the picture of a 26-year-old movie star in the prime of his life.

"Thought you'd want to get the saltwater off before having a drink. I put out some cheese and crackers." It was the lilting voice of Addie Mae, not tall but a large 42-year-old, dark-skinned, Seminole Indian woman who moved with the grace of a cat. She dressed in colorful skirts, blouses and dresses, even on Chance's boat, true to the traditional Seminole culture she grew up in. Chance thought the world of Addie Mae. Totally understandable, since she helped save his life. Chance met her at the Indian Village on the Tamiami Trail about two years ago. The Tribe took Chance in and nursed him back to health. Addie Mae was the cook who nourished Chance with food he had never tasted before. He grew to love the food and the Tribe that helped save him. And he grew fond of Addie Mae. After a short time, Chance had to leave the Tribe. But later, when he needed help around the big house he built in the Everglades, he thought of Addie Mae and the food she cooked up in big black pots on an open fire.

Chance leaped over the thick transom with the lightness of a gazelle and plopped into a deck chair. Thirsty, he reached for the Margarita, rocks, no salt, that Addie Mae had poured for him and Cha-ley, too. He grabbed a hunk of Gouda and a cracker.

"Salud!" he said, repeated by Addie Mae and Cha-ley. As their lips got wet from the sweet and tangy drinks, the cell phone rang. It was a 212 area code. "Who do we know in New York," he asked. He picked it up, "It's a beautiful day where we are," he said, drawing smiles from Addie Mae and Cha-ley.

"I wish I could say the same here in New York," the voice said.

"Sorry to hear that."

"This is Ed Wertz, Mayor of New York City."

Chance's eyes riveted on Addie Mae and Cha-ley.

The Mayor said, "I think we need your help."

As the Mayor and Chance spoke, the forty-two-foot fishing boat drifted thirty feet to the left on the taut anchor line. The sun dropped just a little in the fifteen minutes that elapsed. The level of Chance's Margarita also dropped and was refilled by Addie Mae, still sitting next to him and Cha-ley.

"Mr. Mayor," Chance offered humbly, "I appreciate your confidence in me, but I don't know if I can get this done for you."

"I know it's incredibly dangerous," the Mayor said.

"It's not so much that, it's…"

The Mayor cut in abruptly "…and I know that this is not a slam-dunk, not guaranteed, that it may take a while and there may be more officers who will die before you can stop this madness but…"

"Man, talk about pressure," Chance interjected.

"Look, we're desperate. I admit it. Frankly, I don't know where to turn. I have *got* to fix this, like…*now*. People are dying. People are rioting. We're in trouble. Governor

Wilkinson says you're amazing. One of a kind. We need your help, and we're willing to make it worth your while. What will it take? Let's make a deal right now."

Chance put his drink to his lips and paused to think.

"Tell 'ya what," the Mayor said impatiently, "we'll pay you ten million if you catch or kill the sniper within the first week. Five million if it's within the *second* week. After the second week, it's one million. The clock starts the minute you land in New York."

The only sound was the slapping of the waves against the hull of the boat.

Chance gulped a slug of his Margarita. His eyes closed. Addie Mae waited. Cha-ley waited. The Mayor waited.

"I'm on my way."

The knife-edged bow of the boat parted the turquoise Gulf throwing white water to the left and right, leaving a sudsy wake a half-mile long. Chance was at the controls on the fly-bridge twelve-feet above the sea. The forty-two-foot yacht etched a path through a large tropical bay that grew more and more shallow as the Coralina neared the shoreline in water so clear the boat cast a shadow on the bottom.

The boat slowed to idle with a deep-throated gurgle of the inboard engines. Chance nursed the bow toward the T-dock, reversed the engines, and goosed the stern drive to bring the craft softly against the pilings. Cha-ley jumped to the dock with a line immediately and secured the bow to a cleat. Addie Mae was already tying up at the stern. The engines became silent. The only sound now was the stream of water pouring out on the side of the boat from the bilge pumps.

"Now we have some work to do to get ready,"

Chance said to Cha-ley. "Get the catch inside the house and I'll get The Beaver ready."

To the right side of the boat, about thirty feet away, was a fairly large, chunky, old-fashioned-looking, high-wing float plane – The Beaver. It had eight seats, a big radial engine, a red and white paint job and two pontoon floats almost as big as the plane itself. A bear to fly, but one of the most reliable and sturdy amphibious planes ever built. Which was in 1948. Chance liked his plane just like his wines: vintage.

Cha-ley pulled the wheeled ice chest down the dock toward the house. And what a house it was! A low, long, dream of white coral rock and glass. Inside, stained and polished multi-level concrete floors, natural log cathedral ceilings and walls of glass that presented a wondrous view of the Gulf of Mexico. Outside, an infinity-edge pool appeared at one with the bay, two hundred palm trees decorated the tranquil scene and tropical birds ornamented the trees. It was the picture of heaven. As Chance prepared to enter hell.

"I got some food together for you," Addie Mae called out. "Some of your favorites to take on The Beaver. Leftovers. No time to make anything fresh. Sorry 'bout that."

The combination of Addie Mae and Cha-ley was a deliberately created family of sorts, replacing the one Chance lost. It was a surrogate family that Chance grew to love. And they loved him in return. It wasn't easy for Addie Mae and Cha-ley to see Chance ready himself for the sudden assignment. To watch the warrior go off to war.

The huge 450-horsepower radial engine of The Beaver belched a cloud of smoke as the prop spun up and blew a chop in the water behind.

Cha-ley untied the holding lines and gave a big push

to the dockside pontoon. Chance stuck his head out the window and waved a cheerful goodbye. Cha-ley waved and forced a fearless smile. Addie Mae wiped away a tear, hoping Chance didn't see it. Chance thought, *Now, drift away from the dock, go over checklist, lock rudders, rev up, flip switches, check gauges, build manifold pressure, push throttle, get up on the step, increase speed…lift off!*

The Beaver banked to the north and disappeared over the palms.

As Chance flew, the sky to his left was a brilliant palette of red, orange and purple. At this altitude the sun had already set in the west and the kaleidoscopic show would end soon. The sky to the east was already dark. For the remainder of the trip it would be black Atlantic below, black sky above. The only sound was the droning of the engine and the groaning of his stomach. Chance opened the one-person cooler that Addie Mae had prepared. He happily bit into the grilled gator leg, toes and all.

The Beaver flew into the darkness.

. . .

Chance spoke into the headset: "New York Center, Delta Sierra 555."

"Go ahead Delta Sierra."

"Delta Sierra is twenty-five miles to the south, three thousand five-hundred, request permission to enter air space and water landing at 23rd Street Skyport."

"Yeah, we got a heads-up from the Mayor's office on your ETA. Due to heavy traffic, use Hudson River Corridor and cross over to East River. Maintain one thousand five hundred in Corridor. Landing at Skyport approved. Contact New York Center ATC upon landing."

"Affirmative."

"Oh, one more thing Delta Sierra. Good luck!"

As The Beaver descended into the ink approaching New York City's Class B airspace, twinkling lights began to emerge to the west. New Jersey. Then Staten Island. The bottoms of clouds ahead were lit in a reflective glow from Manhattan's lights below. It was always a thrill flying over the Big Apple, even for veteran airmen. But tonight held a sharp-edged, apprehensive excitement that would intensify with each nautical mile covered and with every two-hundred-feet-per-minute decent. As Chance passed parallel to the shoreline at Battery Park, he saw a fire below. Not a brush fire or oil barrel fire for the homeless. A building was ablaze. Black smoke poured out as if it were a smoke stack. The column of smoke rose high above Chance's altitude of fifteen hundred feet. Cars, trucks, taxies and buses were halted, chock-a-block, from river-to-river – strings of white lights, strings of red lights. Helicopters swarmed around the smoke.

As Chance made his way up the Hudson, vigilant for other aircraft, there were two more fires burning below. Two more buildings. One on the west side around 37th Street and another around 42nd Street. Big buildings. Big fires. Big smoke. Big traffic. More helicopters. 'Mercenary Soldier' Chance had entered the war zone.

Then!

It appeared out of nowhere!

It was there! In front of him!

Suddenly! "Jesus!" Out of the dark sky and haze of smoke, a news chopper, dead ahead! It twisted this way and that, out of control!

No time to think! No time to react! Yank the yoke to the right and descend! Now!

Dive! Dive!

In a severe sixty-degree bank, the left wingtip of The Beaver slipped, just barely, between the landing skids of the chopper. A near mid-air collision. The Beaver's engine roared as the plane dropped.

"Whew! I gotta land this bird!"

Righting the plane to straight and level, Chance was already headed toward the East River. He crossed over Central Park and banked to the right, base leg to final, skirting around the Queensborough Bridge…then over Roosevelt Island…past the United Nations…past the raging building fire near 42nd Street.

Chance set The Beaver down on a watery table of polluted blackness, hoping to avoid the expected array of floating debris: trashed refrigerators, rusted heating oil tanks, bloated corpses gassed up from the bottom. Thankfully, without incident, he idled his way to the sea plane dock. Landing time: eerily, 9:11 on a Friday night. An eight-hour flight including his fuel stop in Myrtle Beach. Chance thought: *The ten-million-dollar-clock starts now!*

There, on the dock, a backlit deckhand was waiting. At least, Chance hoped it was a deckhand. Chance, standing on the pontoon, tossed a line and the helper fastened it to a cleat. Then another line that Chance had tossed. Chance jumped from the pontoon to the dock and was greeted by the helper.

"Hi! I'm Nicole Jensen. Welcome to New York."

Even in the harshness of the sodium-vapor security lights of the Skyport, Nicole could see that Chance was very tall and handsome. Even more so than what she remembered.

He was clean-shaven. Neat. Not at all what one might expect of a jungle-tracker of animals and men.

"I have a taxi waiting on the other side of that gate." They talked as they walked.

"Sorry you had to come out here in the dark," Chance said.

"No problem at all. Security is pretty good here at the Skyport. I was working just before I got here and I have to go right back."

"Mayor's office?" Chance asked.

"No. I'm a...TV Reporter," *forget the journalist handle for now*, she thought. "I'm covering the fires, three of them, live on scene. I have to go right back to my crew."

"Then you broke away for me? You didn't have to do that."

"The Mayor wanted to make sure that you got to your hotel with no problems. Tom Elliott, the Mayor's Press Secretary, would have been here but, with the fires, he's working on putting together an early morning press conference for the Mayor. So I volunteered to take his place. I needed a break from the fires anyway."

"But...you're a TV Reporter."

She could tell that Chance was suspicious and confused. After all, why would independent media work for the government. There's something inherently wrong with that. "We're all working toward the same goal." Nicole said. "It's all hands-on deck. I'm happy to help out. No conflict of interest, I can assure you."

"Small city relationships in the big city. Who would have thought," Chance said with just a little skepticism.

They stopped at the taxi. "Here's an info sheet that will help you. The Mayor would like to meet with you at six in the morning in his office. It's all on the sheet. Just grab a cab outside your hotel. Should take about twenty minutes at that hour. Traffic backups tonight should be cleared up by then. If you have any questions, give Tom Elliott a call. His number is on the sheet."

This girl is buttoned-up. Doesn't miss a beat. As pretty as she is, not the kind of girl you want to tangle with. Well…maybe.

. . .

Chance tossed his khaki duffle bag on the king size bed in the spacious hotel room. He parted the drapes seventeen floors above the Avenue of the Americas and peered out the window. Dancing flames reflected on his face from the Grand Central Station fire eight blocks away. He splashed water on his face and the man in the mirror said, "What have you gotten yourself into now?" He flicked on the TV with the remote and plopped into the soft couch. A quick click of the channel button revealed a picture that made him stop. Nicole Jensen, full screen.

"…the fires have been raging since the 5 P.M. rush hour." The camera panned to the carnage. "Fire fighters are finally beginning to gain control of the rampaging flames. Sadly, nine people have lost their lives. Thirty-six are injured. The Mayor's office is planning a press conference at eight o'clock in the morning. Hopefully, the people of this city, already burned by frustration and fear, will get some answers…and solutions. Reporting from Grand Central Station, this is Nicole Jensen for PIC TV–10."

Chance clicked the TV off and went to the window again.

"What have I gotten myself into?"

TEN

Saturday Morning: Day One

"Right this way." Patty Bromstad led Chance down a hall past double walnut doors. As they passed by, he could easily hear a heated discussion from behind the doors. It was vociferous enough that he turned his head toward the hidden fracas as he walked by. Patty ushered him into a small meeting room right next to the noisy conference room. It was 6:00 A.M. sharp on the wall clock. Chance sat alone in the little room for three minutes listening to the muffled voices. Then, a door between the two rooms burst open and Mayor Wertz hurried through it. Chance could see a conference room table in the other room filled with men and a few women, some of them red faced, shaking fingers and pointing at each other. The blame-game.

"Chance, welcome! Welcome!" Wertz extended his hand. Chance stood up.

"Morning, Mr. Mayor."

"Ed. Call me Ed. We're going to be sweating this out together, crying together and…God willing, drinking champagne together, so call me Ed."

"Yes sir, Ed."

"Your hotel is OK?"

"Yes, perfect. Thanks."

"Sorry to rush but I have a press conference in less than two hours and, as you can tell, I have a mess on my hands. You need background: names, places, everything. Lots of stuff. I can't take you through it all so you're going to meet a few people who will spend time with you, as much as you need. You'll have access to everything, every piece of evidence, photos, files, people, departments, you name it. We'll provide you with a small office that you can use, down the hall from me. You can keep your notes, files, reports, pictures and anything else you need in there. We don't want anything to be kept at your hotel room for obvious reasons. If anybody gives you any trouble, resistance, you call me. The only people who will know about you, who you are, why you're here, will be those who need to know."

Chance jumped in, "And who are they?"

Wertz drew a breath and looked up at the corner of the room, "Let me see, how can I explain this?" He held up two fingers.

"One!" He bent down one of his fingers, "There are a few people who know your name, Chance, where you're from, why you're here and what your capabilities are. That would be me, Police Commissioner Brix, Tom Elliott, Nicole Jensen and my secretary, Patty.

"Then, two," he bent down the other finger, "is everybody else. The people who will only know what we want to tell them. We have to make up a bogus name for you and we'll say you're a special expert advisor. The fewer people who know the details, the better. We don't want information leaked out, at least for as long as we can prevent it. Especially to the media. If we tell the media, we tell the sniper. We tell the sniper and he'll be on the lookout for you. Your life will be in jeopardy every time you step outside. If he knows your identity, your name, what you look like, what you can do, we give him the upper hand...and you die, sorry to say. That's how it will go down. This guy is not your run-of-the-mill-killer. He knows the city. He picks his targets. And he doesn't miss."

The Mayor paused to let it all sink in. "Now, I've

told Tom Elliott, my Press Secretary, to clear the path for you. You'll need an I.D. badge with your picture on it. Tom will take you for that and handle any questions or snags. You'll also meet Nicole Jensen…"

"I, ahh…"

"Oh, yeah, you met her last night when you landed."

"Yes, very thoughtful of you. Thank you."

The Mayor continued, "She's a…reporter. She's done…a good job of covering this from top to bottom. She will show you TV reports since this killing spree started and give you inside information into locations, interviews, public attitudes, whatever."

The Mayor turned to a side table, grabbed a stack of papers ten inches thick and banged the stack on the table in front of Chance. "Now, here's some 'light reading' to bring you up to speed. Police reports and so on." Chance's eyes opened wider, but he remained remarkably silent, not that he could get a word in edgewise.

"Now, what name do you want to use?"

"Name?"

"Yeah, anything. Whatever," the Mayor said impatiently.

The light bulb went off in Chance's head. "Frank Stoneman," Chance said. "Yeah, Frank Stoneman, he repeated."

"Frank Stoneman." The Mayor seated the name in his brain.

"Sounds good. Gotta go." The Mayor's head nodded toward the room next door. "Let's touch base later today, Frank Stoneman." The Mayor already had his hand on the brass doorknob. He turned and was gone.

The black-and-white photocopy showed a dead body

on a sidewalk next to a parked police car. Even with the reduced resolution of a copy, you could see that the head of the deceased was only attached to the body by a flap of skin. The head had rolled into the gutter. It was Brian O'Neill. Chance, sitting at the table, shuffled through a stack of copies. He saw Ty and Juliette Jackson commingled in an almost sensual position. A last moment of love. In another, William Harrison appeared to smell the roses in the flowerbed one last time. There was a picture of Tate, Jefferson and Takahashi at the 64th Precinct motor pool. There was Richard Stevens, the first killed. They were all there. Chance wondered if the killer had pictures of his victims. A shrine to his skill. To his...power.

But there was another dead body. Not of a police officer, but one that interested Chance even more. The dead homeless man who crawled out of the deserted yellow brick building. The building across the street from the 64th Precinct. Chance studied this picture more than the others, even though he assumed the police and the FBI would have scrutinized the photos already. But, a fact of life, true even of the police and the FBI, who cares about a homeless man? Even if it is a homeless man, *the* homeless man, who stared right into the eyes of the killer. In the picture, the man was sprawled on the street, surrounded by the black shoes and boots of police officers who came to see him gasp his last breath and agonizingly point in the direction of the building. Chance peered at the man's baggy dark trousers, his torn shirt, his contorted face, the hole from a small-caliber bullet in his forehead. It was a clean, close-up wound, except for the gun powder residue around the hole. Something in the picture caught Chance's attention. He looked closer. It appeared to be a mark on the victim's neck. On his throat, to be more precise. Chance made a mental note to examine the actual digital photo file when he had access to it.

Suddenly, the door opened and a thirty-something man put out his hand.

"Hi! I'm Tom Elliott."

"Good morning. I'm, ah…" Chance started to say, still seated.

Elliott cut in and said, "Frank Stoneman! The Mayor just told everyone in our meeting." He nodded to the conference room next door. "I was on the call with the Mayor, Nicole Jensen and the Governor, so I know the real story. Chance is an interesting name. Family name?" Tom took a seat so Chance remained seated.

"No, actually. It's a name that kind of…fits me. It's a long story."

"Well, one of these days I'd love to hear about it. When we have more time. So," Tom continued, "I see you've made a dent in the pile."

"Yes, police reports are always fascinating reading," Chance said with more than a touch of sarcasm.

"Scintillating!" Tom added with a knowing smile.

"Say, Tom, I was going through the pictures and I would love to get a look at the actual digital files if I could."

"Absolutely. We can go over to Forensics after the press conference and go through anything and everything."

"Are you going to the press conference?" Chance asked.

"Yes. Right here." Tom clicked on a TV in the room. "It's about to start. I came in to answer any questions you might have."

The Blue Room, down the hall and to the right, was on the screen. It is where most of the press conferences are held. There, again, was the blue background with the repeated NYPD logo. There, again, was the American flag screen left and the New York State flag screen right. And there again, were the six microphones at the podium. Everyone was waiting for the Mayor and his cadre.

There was a double-knock on the door. The door opened slowly. A dark-haired man in a snug fitting gray suit and maroon tie poked his head in.

"I hope I'm not intruding."

"Not at all, Bob. Come in," Tom Elliott said.

"Hi, Frank, I'm Bob Knickerbocker. I'm the IT Digital Media guy." Chance stood up and Elliott followed.

Knickerbocker offered a handshake. Chance extended his hand in turn. It was about then that Elliott and Knickerbocker saw that Chance was about six inches taller than them. They were both about 5'11" and about the same age. But other than height and age, Elliott and Knickerbocker were quite different from each other. Elliott was on the thin side, wiry, possessing the frame of a long-distance runner. Yet, he had an almost bone-crushing handshake. Muscular strength came from genetics for Elliott. He was as strong as an ox in spite of being a bookworm. He looked older than 33. His early gray didn't help.

Knickerbocker, on the other hand, worked out every day and it showed. He had the blessings of thick, jet-black hair and rugged looks that some would call attractive, but he definitely wasn't your pretty boy type. Sizing up the two men before him, Chance realized that he was the only one in the room not dressed in a suit and tie. Oh, well. His purple knit pullover, cream colored casual pants and deck shoes would have to suffice. In Chance's world, this was formal wear.

"So," Chance said to Knickerbocker, "you're the unseen guy who's the cyber interface between the city and the rest of the world."

"Yup, that's me. And Tom here, he's the face between the Mayor and the city that everybody sees. We work together quite a bit."

They all seemed to know it was time to sit down and watch the TV. Especially since Nicole Jensen was full screen.

"The Mayor will be coming to the podium any minute. He'll be addressing the three buildings set ablaze simultaneously last night. Was it a terror attack? The work of three arsonists? Was it the work of the New York City sniper? The Mayor will shed light on…" Nicole was killing time until the Mayor appeared.

"Tom," Chance queried politely, "as Press Secretary, don't you have to be at the podium, too?"

"I rarely make an on-camera appearance at a press conference when the Mayor is present. He doesn't need me there. I do smaller press conferences, meetings, and my work is not just isolated to the media. No, this is his baby. People want to hear directly from him, not me. And…here he is."

The Mayor was at the podium.

"Ladies and gentlemen, yesterday, at approximately 5 P.M. fires were set simultaneously at three locations around Manhattan. The three locations were a building next to the very secure New York Stock Exchange, a building next to Grand Central Station and at Penn Station. The fires were all set on the tops of these buildings causing severe damage to the roofs, air conditioning systems and the upper floors. Unfortunately, nine people lost their lives and thirty-six were injured, including police and firemen. This morning it seems the worst is behind us. The fires are out, the damage is being repaired and the injured have been cared for. Sadly, for the families who lost loved ones, the pain will never go away. Our thoughts and prayers are with them today. We all owe a debt of thanks to the heroic, immediate action by our world-class fire department." There was spontaneous applause from everyone in the room except the cameramen.

The Mayor continued. "And to New York's finest, our men and women in blue." The applause erupted again. "The fires are out, but not our passion and determination to find out who did this heinous act and bring them to justice. Now, we face the difficult task of sifting through the debris for clues. Digging to find out who did this and why. We're working hard with the FBI. They are bringing in fifty additional agents to help with the investigation. The city's Counter Terrorism Task Force is gathering information and following up on leads as we speak. Our Arson Squad has been on the scene since last night before the fires were even put out. Our detectives are on increased duty to apply more man-hours.

In a moment, you will hear from Dean DiAmico, Director of our Counter Terrorism Task Force. You'll also hear from Bill Murphy, FBI Lead Investigator, Police Commissioner Brix and Battalion Chief Neal Waters of the FDNY."

Mayor Wertz started to turn away from the microphone. A voice from the crowd stopped him.

"Mayor Wertz, Sir! One question, please." It was a veteran TV reporter.

The Mayor turned back to the mic.

"Mr. Mayor, were any police officers killed in any of the fires last night?"

"No. No police officers lost their lives in the fires, I'm happy to say. However, three sustained life-threatening injuries and are being treated now, and six firemen suffered minor injuries but did not leave the scene."

The Mayor started to turn away again.

"But, Mr. Mayor!" It was a woman reporter from a major network. "Mr. Mayor, has the National Guard been called out to help?"

"The National Guard has not been called out. The National Guard is used for infrastructure control and to help with logistics, like handing out water or food and for aiding injured people or stranded people. None of these needs are occurring at this time. We have control of all locations, the fires are out, all injured people have obtained medical attention and properties are already being restored. So, no need for the National Guard at this time."

The Mayor began to turn away again, until a voice in the crowd repeated, "At this time."

The Mayor turned back and surveyed the audience but couldn't tell who spoke up. He decided to let it go.

The next speaker came to the podium.

"My name is Dean DiAmico, Head of the NYPD Counter Terrorism Task Force. As we speak, we are conducting a full-scale investigation into the possibility, I repeat, the possibility of terrorist related activity relative to the three building fires set yesterday afternoon at the three different locations in Manhattan. While these events may have nothing at all to do with any organized or lone wolf activity, the fact that they occurred at a building contiguous to the New York Stock Exchange on Wall Street, and at a part of the Grand Central Station building and at Penn Station, provokes immediate, complete and widespread investigation into that possibility. We will announce any new or relevant information as soon as it is deemed reliable and permissible for public dissemination without jeopardizing any aspect of the case. That's all we're going to say at this time."

"Mr. Director! Mr. DiAmico, Sir."

DiAmico paused at the mic.

"Sir, are there any indications that the fires are related to the recent sniper attacks?"

"No. There may be no connection at all. We are considering these as two different cases, but all possibilities are being considered."

"Mr. DiAmico, do you have any leads at this time?"

"That's all the questions for today." He walked away from the mic and the Fire Battalion Chief walked up.

"Hello, I'm Neal Waters, Battalion Chief, FDNY. As Mayor Wertz said, all three fires are out and a full-scale investigation is underway. We have three different forensic teams to speed up the process and collaborate on the investigation. We are working quickly so we can make temporary repairs to the roof structures so people can return to the buildings and businesses can get back to work. Happily, the Stock Exchange was not affected by the fire at the building next door. Transportation was not affected by the fires near Grand Central Station." The Battalion Chief started to walk away.

"Sir! Chief Waters! Why were the fires all at the top of the buildings?"

The Chief came back to the mic. "Fires draw a lot of attention. It could be that the person or persons who set the fires wanted to get a lot of attention, like national news coverage for whatever reason. When you have the tops of three tall buildings on fire, it looks like the whole city's on fire. But that's an answer we don't have right now. And it's probably a question best answered by the FBI. And, speaking of the FBI, here's Bill Murphy."

In the small meeting room, with the three men watching the closed-circuit TV, Robert Knickerbocker couldn't refrain from asking the question: "You sure you want this job, Frank?" Knickerbocker and Elliott looked at Chance intently, waiting for some kind of response.

Chance finally answered: "Time will tell."

Bill Murphy, FBI Investigator was at the microphone pledging his team's determination in catching and prosecuting the sniper and anyone connected to the three building fires.

"Frank, I have to handle a conference at one," Tom Elliott said, "so if you want to go over to Forensics and check out pictures and ballistics, we'd better get going. We'll have to get your I.D. badge first.

"I'm ready to go."

"Frank," Knickerbocker offered his hand again, "if you need anything in the digital world, I'm happy to help. Here's my card. Call or stop by anytime."

"Thanks a lot, Bob. Nice meeting you. I'm sure we'll see each other again."

"I'm sure we will."

· · ·

Against the black background, the head of the man looked ghostlike. The unblinking eyes were vacant. Zombieish. Chilling. The face was yellow-brown. Almost transparent. On the verge of glowing.

The eerie silence was shattered by the loud crack of a gunshot!

The fluorescent lights in the Ballistics Lab came on and the technician opened the chamber to examine the gelatin head that had just been shot by a high caliber pistol.

"I wouldn't want to be that guy," Tom said. The test bullet had removed a chunk from the back of the dummy's head, the entire right ear and the right eye.

"That represents an actual case. The exact weapon, ammo, trajectory and wound. Pretty much proves that the injury was inflicted with the weapon found at the crime scene." The man in the white lab coat, Bill Spencer, Director of the Ballistics Lab, was explaining to Chance and Tom Elliott what they just saw.

"How many times a day do you conduct tests like this one?" Chance asked.

"More times than I can count, Frank. That's why we all wear these ear protectors." All three of the men had them down around their necks. "Otherwise we'd all be deaf."

"Do you test all kinds of firearms here? I mean, handguns, rifles, shotguns…?" Chance asked.

Bill responded, "Pistols, revolvers, rifles, shotguns, BB guns, pellet guns, sling shots, spears…anything that is propelled in some way through the air in the commission of a crime to cause death or damage. That is, anything up to .50 caliber. Anything bigger than that, like artillery, grenade launchers and shoulder mounted rocket launchers, are tested at a different facility."

All interesting stuff, Chance thought, but he wanted to get on to what he was there for.

"What can you tell us about the sniper? Skill level? Intelligence? What kind of weapon, bullets used, range…?"

"We've been asking ourselves those same questions for more than a month now. We've conducted lots of tests. That's practically all we've been doing since the first shot was fired. And after, probably, two hundred tests, there are still some things we don't know. I can tell you this though, the shooter is very intelligent. I can't say academically educated, but tons of street smarts. He, or she, had to get that somewhere. The shooter is highly skilled. Sniper level.

Knows the weapon and ammunition intimately. Analyzes the best shooting position. Knows when to pull the trigger and has no hesitation doing so. No problem killing. But only wants to kill the specific target."

"Bill, I have to apologize in advance," Chance said, "I have a million questions, so I'll probably drive you crazy. I hope you don't mind and I hope you have the time."

"Fire away. No pun intended."

"The weapon. A rifle? What kind of rifle?"

".50 caliber. Long barrel for extreme range and accuracy. Probably hand-made, possibly in the U.S., maybe by a survivalist or white supremacist group with a member experienced in the tooling of weapons. Or, it could come from a country like the Czech Republic, Hungary or Slovenia. Or Russia. Or even a sub-culture workshop in Germany. The Germans have a long history of excellent gunsmithing."

"Not the kind of rifle you'd buy at your local big box store." Tom Elliott quipped.

"No, not at all," Spencer responded. "This would be a one-of-a-kind."

"What makes it so unusual?" Chance asked.

"Well, for one thing, it is extremely powerful for a quickly and easily transportable weapon. The sniper moves fast after a shot. So, it can't be too cumbersome or too heavy. It probably breaks down in pieces. However, it's extremely strong, sturdy, has to stand up to the ammunition and the rounds that come out of it. Bullets like this one here." Spencer grabbed a sample from a shelf with many bins full of shiny cartridges of all kinds. "Military ordinance. The biggest we can test at this facility." Spencer handed it to Chance. It was more than five inches long.

"Wouldn't that have quite a recoil and make a huge

sound," Elliott asked.

"It would indeed," Spencer confirmed.

Tom added, "So the shooter would have to be strong enough and experienced enough to absorb the recoil."

"I would imagine," Spencer agreed.

"Silencer?" Chance tossed out.

"I'm sure. But more than that, a silencer combined with flash suppressor so the fire that comes out of the muzzle doesn't attract attention at night. So far, we have no reports of anyone in the vicinity of the attacks hearing or seeing anything unusual at the times of the shootings," Spencer said.

"Wouldn't a silencer reduce the power of the bullet, robbing it of some of its energy?" Chance asked.

"Yes, it would. That's what makes this weapon even more remarkable. It's possible that the silencer is of a unique design that, in effect, lengthens the barrel of the rifle, thereby enhancing its accuracy. The extreme power of the cartridge itself would mitigate the relatively small loss of energy to the point it becomes inconsequential."

Chance summed it up: "So this rifle is probably made of extremely strong steel or an alloy or even titanium, it has a long barrel made even longer by the addition of a silencer and flash suppressor, but can be broken down into pieces quickly making it easy to disguise as something else."

"Don't forget the scope," Spencer instructed. "The sniper requires an extremely high-end scope, one that is used in military or police sniper ops. Or, in top level competition, like the Olympics. But that's not all. The sniper wants the rifle to be bolt action. One bullet at a time so there are no empty cartridges being ejected automatically to be picked up by police later. With bolt action, the empty cartridge stays inside the rifle until the shooter ejects it himself."

"Nothing to leave behind," Elliott said.

"Correct. And, this weapon has unusual rifling."

"Rifling?" Tom asked.

"Yeah, rifling." Spencer looked around left and right. "Look...look at this rifle." He picked up a totally black military rifle from a tabletop about eight feet away. He checked the chamber to make sure it was empty of any rounds and he opened the breech where the cartridge would reside, ready to be fired. In place of a cartridge, he inserted a white piece of paper. He held the entire weapon up to a light and he sighted down the inside of the barrel to demonstrate what he wanted Tom and Chance to do. "Take a look at this, at the inside of the barrel. Do you see the helical grooves inside the barrel?"

In a moment, Tom spoke, "Yeah. Yeah, I see them. Five or six. Like a spiral."

"That's rifling," Bill Spencer said. Chance took the weapon and looked through the barrel as Spencer explained.

"This is an M-16. Military issue. It has one full twist of rifling, or grooves, in seven inches of barrel length. The bullets propelled by this weapon fly fairly straight and true, give or take wind, temperature, altitude and so on.

"Like throwing a football," Tom said.

"Exactly. Put a little spin on it and it tends to fly through the air with less yaw and less tumbling in flight."

Spencer put the weapon back and picked up a different black rifle from another table. "This is your classic AR-15." He hefted it in front of the two men. He checked the chamber, inserted the white paper, and handed it to Tom.

"This weapon, as well as the Mini-14, a favorite of street gangs because of its small size, both have one complete twist in nine inches."

"Wouldn't that give the bullet a little more chance of

turning or tumbling in the air," Chance asked.

"Yes, it would. But these weapons are usually fired at relatively-close range, so that's not such an issue." Chance took a look now.

Spencer continued: "But we believe the weapon used by our sniper has a progressive twist ratio. It starts out at one-in-nine and then goes to one-in-five before the bullet leaves the barrel. It revs up the heavy bullet."

"That would give the bullet less chance of wobbling or tumbling on its long way to the target," Tom said.

"Bingo!" Spencer exclaimed. "That's exactly what the sniper wants. Look…" He picked up the round that he had held up before.

"Let me give you a quick primer on ballistics." He held the cartridge in his fingers horizontally at eye level. "When the round is in the chamber, ready to be fired, it's called internal ballistics. That involves many things, one of which is the rifling we talked about. When the firing pin ignites the gun powder inside the casing, the gases build up and propel the bullet out of the barrel. As soon as the bullet leaves the muzzle, the end of the barrel, it's in uncontrolled flight. This is called external ballistics. It's launched and on its own. It's subject to wind, humidity, temperature, altitude, etc. It's also affected by its shape, velocity, mass, weight and drag." Chance and Tom were engrossed in the lesson.

Spencer went on: "Our killer wants a number of things out of this rifle and bullet. The killer wants to be as far away from the target as possible. Hence, the need for a long barrel and a powerful projectile to travel a long distance. The killer wants to inflict one-hundred-percent assured killing power with only one shot, not a lot of penetration, doesn't want the bullet to pass through the target."

Chance jumped in, "So you're saying that the killer wants all the kinetic energy to be released at the target to do the most damage."

"Precisely. Well said. Textbook," Spencer confirmed and continued, "Therefore, the choice of a bullet shape that's not too pointed is important. The shooter wants more of a flat point, so it makes a big hole when it gets to the target causing massive permanent cavitation. High velocity is equally important. It causes shock waves to create what we call temporary cavitation. And, most gruesome and diabolical of all, our killer is using a unique bullet design, handmade, and carefully crafted. We call it the Blender Blade Bullet."

"The Blender Blade Bullet?" Chance and Tom said simultaneously.

"The Blender Blade Bullet," Spencer said somewhat theatrically.

"Do you have…" Chance started to ask.

"Well, we have the closest thing to it. We made a few here at the lab for testing. We got them as close as possible to what we think the killer is using and, of course, we have the actual spent slugs we found from the shootings. Let me show you. Come over here for a second." Spencer held up a long shiny missile-like round before their eyes.

"This is what we made here. It has a copper-alloy jacket so the lead core of the bullet doesn't deform too early. Lead melts at two thousand feet per second. It has a hollow point, see that hole? The lead mushrooms when it strikes the target."

Spencer paused so they could absorb what he said. Then he went on: "Muzzle velocity is 3,240 feet per second. At a distance of fifteen hundred to two thousand feet, it impacts the target at about 1,700 feet per second. To give you some idea of what that means, skin breaks at 163 feet per second. Bone breaks at 230 feet per second."

Spencer paused again to let that sink in.

"All that is bad enough…you might say 'bad to the bone…' but that's not the most deadly part. You see these little vertical lines or grooves here on the bullet part, the indentations on the copper part that covers the lead bullet?" They all squinted their eyes intently.

"Yeah, yeah, I see 'em, I see 'em," Tom almost whispered.

"This leads us to our final phase, terminal ballistics," Spencer said. "When the bullet hits, these indentations in the jacket, they split apart," Spencer held up specimen number two, "and they open up like five knife blades that slice through soft tissue. Like scalpels. At the same time, the lead inside fragments bone."

Spencer paused again and watched their faces, eyes still on the bullet. Now they understood the name.

"That, gentlemen, is the Blender Blade Bullet. Like the spinning blades in a blender, it cuts through everything."

"I could have used that a few years ago," Chance blurted out. "Would have made my life a whole lot easier."

Spencer and Tom looked at Chance wanting to ask about his statement, but decided against it. Better that they not know, they thought.

"That must leave a very big hole," Tom said.

"Our killer isn't happy with big holes. Let me show you," Spencer said.

Spencer called out to one of his assistants, "John, get Martin into the chamber, please." John went to fetch Martin. What he came back with was a full-size gelatin bust of a man.

"That's Martin," Spencer announced.

"Why do you call him Martin," Chance asked.

"He's named after the man who developed ballistic gelatin. It's basically swine muscle tissue replicating human soft tissue. But Martin is a special fellow because we've added cadaver bones in his neck and skull. This will give us a much more accurate picture of what the Blender Blade can do to a victim. Or should I say, what the Blender Blade has done to New York's finest. It's a damn shame. But that's why you're here, isn't it Frank?"

"I'll do my best, Bill."

"OK, let's get this set up. John, are the cameras ready?"

"Yes, sir! Ready!"

"You see those cameras over there on the tripods? Ultra-high speed. They can stop a bullet in flight. Even at two thousand feet per second."

Spencer called out again, "Is Martin ready?"

"Yes, sir! Martin is ready!"

Spencer spoke to Chance and Tom, "As you can see, we have Martin positioned with his back to the weapon because the victims were shot in the neck from behind."

"Pete, are we all set to fire?" Spencer asked another man.

"Yah vol!" Pete knew Spencer for years, so he could afford to be casual.

"OK, ear protectors on. This is going to be loud."

Half the lights were shut off. Pete was at the end of the large black test rifle, the closest thing they could find to the unconfirmed murder weapon. The twenty-foot-long glass and steal chamber was closed. Martin sat there. Waiting. The yellow-brown, semi-transparent gelatin of his head and shoulders took on a ghoulish glow against the black backdrop. Martin was oblivious to his imminent destruction.

"Fire!" Spencer ordered.

A fiery blast belched from the dragon!

A thunderous clap of ear-splitting sound!

It was instant death for Martin. Total decapitation. His head was on the floor of the chamber. Shoulders intact. But everything between the shoulders and chin, gone. Obliterated.

"Lights! Let's check the footage!" Spencer commanded.

On the large monitor, the bullet appeared as an illuminated mini-rocket in slow motion. It traveled through the darkness. No way to stop it. No way to avoid it. Spencer explained, "The bullet penetrates Martin's neck between the C4 and C7 vertebrae. The lead in the bullet mushrooms and expands upon striking the bone. The bone then fragments into many pieces becoming sharp projectiles themselves. At this point, the five sections in the copper bullet jacket split apart like the sharp fingers of a blender blade spinning through the soft tissue of the neck. Everything in its path is pulverized, almost atomized. All seven cervical vertebrae, tissue, muscle, bone, nerves, tendons, ligaments, the spinal cord…everything is turned into a bloody mist."

The picture reflected in the eyes of all three men.

Spencer continued. "The shock waves clean up the decapitation and sweep everything forward. Particles so fine they're practically irretrievable."

The screen went black and Bill Spencer turned away from the monitor as if it were just another day. Which is was. Chance and Tom Elliott turned away with the look of men wishing they could erase the images they just saw, in spite of the fact that Martin was just a dummy.

"That's it. That's about all I can tell you at this point."

"Just one more thing, Bill," Chance said. "Were there any additional spent bullets picked up at the scenes that I could take a closer look at?"

"Amazingly, all the bullets fired were picked up. Like I said, the shooter did an incredible job of making sure that the bullets got to the victims and no further. They were all found within twenty-five feet of the victims."

Tom said, "That seems almost impossible."

Chance said knowingly, "It's all mathematics."

Spencer said, "And computers."

They all thought for a moment.

Spencer continued, "If you want to see the bullets, you'll have to go to the Property Office."

"I can take you there right after this," Tom offered.

"Sounds good," Chance said. "Thanks a lot, Bill."

"Anytime, Frank. If you need anything else just give me a call."

"Thanks. Say goodbye to Martin for us."

. . .

It looked like a tiny mushroom. A mangled mushroom with sharp blades attached to the stem. The fingers that held it were inside latex gloves on the hands of Chance. He was examining the spent bullets under a bright lamp on a desk. He held the spent bullet very close to a magnifying glass he held in his other hand.

"Not too close!" the female Property Clerk cautioned. "If you touch that bullet with anything except your gloves, it's useless and I have to go crazy with paperwork explaining how it happened. And you will have to explain why you didn't deliberately destroy evidence. So be very, very careful."

Chance backed the magnifier away a bit, but not so far that he didn't notice something of interest. He looked a little closer.

"I see the rifling marks that Spencer showed us. There's not much of it because the bullet is so deformed and pushed down. But I also see…I also see something else…I think. Hard to make out."

Tom, sitting next to Chance, craned his neck toward the bullet in Chance's hands. Chance carefully handed the bullet to Tom who was also wearing latex gloves. Tom took the magnifier and stared into it. He turned the bullet this way and that.

"Right there! No, there!" Chance said. "Do you see it? Right under that part. That ridge that's sticking out."

"I see the rifling marks," Tom said.

"Turn it slightly to the left. About a sixteenth of an inch," Chance said.

Tom played the object in the lamplight. He turned it to and fro. Moved the magnifier in and out.

"I think I see…it looks like a tiny A and…P."

"That's what I saw. Does any ammunition come with a stamped A and a P on the bottom of the bullet?" Chance asked.

Both Tom and the Property Clerk shrugged their shoulders.

Tom gave the smushed bullet back to Chance. The magnifier, too. Chance took a closer look. He said quietly, "How do we know there's nothing before or after the A and the P? That bulbous ridge is in the way. I can't see under it." Chance turned and looked up at the Property Clerk, a short pudgy middle-age woman with kind eyes. She looked into Chance's blue-green eyes and turned away, walked to the corner and blew her nose into a tissue. Chance had just enough time to use his thumb to bend the lead up just a millimeter. Just enough so he could see if there was anything under the hard glob.

"Holy Sh…"

"What is it?" Tom's interest was piqued.

"It's something before the 'A'."

The Property Clerk lady was over Chance's shoulder, looking.

"It's a…" Chance wasn't sure.

"Yeah? It's a…what?" Tom asked. Waiting. Wanting to know.

"What?" the Property Clerk lady asked. She couldn't hold back.

"It's a…number four."

• • •

The images were a blur rolling up on the large monitor in front of a young man at the controls. He must have been all of eighteen. The image slowed and stopped on the screen. It was a picture of a policeman lying on a sidewalk, his dismembered head in the gutter near the police car. Chance and Tom sat behind the young video tech, all three heads silhouetted against the bright screen.

"Is that the picture you're looking for?" the young man asked.

"Yes, yes, that's the one I wanted to see. Thanks," Chance replied.

"Can you tell much from this?" Tom asked Chance.

"Only that the bullet came from down the street from O'Neill's right. It didn't come from directly behind."

"How can you tell that?"

"Because O'Neill's left leg is bent. See that?"

Tom looked intently at the large image. "The shot came a bit more to O'Neill's right side, making the left leg collapse first."

"Hmm," Tom uttered.

"And there's something a bit more-subtle," Chance said. Trevor, can you push in a bit on the head, please." Tom winced as the head and bloody scene loomed larger.

"If you look carefully, you'll see that there's a tell-tale flap of skin extending from the left shoulder to the head."

"Yeah…I see it," Tom grimaced.

"From what we learned from Spencer, the shot destroys everything in its path, so this path was just slightly to the right of the crosshairs. Which means it may have been aimed at an oblique angle, which will help in the search of the sniper's position."

"Hmm," Tom uttered again.

"Let's go to the next picture," Chance instructed. Trevor consulted a sheet of paper and punched some buttons on the keypad. The screen blurred again. The images came to rest on something Chance did not expect.

"What's that?" Chance asked.

Trevor blurted, "I made a mistake. Must have punched in the wrong numbers. Sorry."

"No, that's OK," Chance comforted. "Let's take a look at whatever this is. Looks like dead birds."

"It is," Tom said, "lovebirds to be exact. They were found by one of the Mayor's attendants on the roof of City Hall. He found them when he went up to put the flag at half-staff."

"I see blood. Were they shot?" Chance asked.

"Yep. Both of 'em. Just lying there."

"What time of day?"

"Morning."

"Exact time?"

"You'd have to check with Andy, the guy who found them."

"Were they cold, stiff, there for a while?" Chance asked.

"Again, I have no idea. Andy can probably tell you. But a few days later, two black officers, a married couple, were gunned down outside their apartment. Lovebirds."

Chance sat there thinking for a moment, trying to tie things together. So far, there were no knots forming. "Let's go on to the next shot, Trevor."

ZIP! BLUR! STOP!

The picture of the homeless man lying on the street was on the screen. The victim was lying on his side, the scene lit by streetlights. It was the image Chance had seen in the stack of files in the Mayor's small meeting room. It was the picture that Chance wanted to see enlarged. There was something about that picture that gnawed at him. Something that teased him. Something that was barely there. Or maybe, not there at all.

"Trevor, let's blow this up. Get in closer. Closer on the man's neck," Chance requested.

When Chance first saw the picture, just a low-res copy of the shot, he saw something that made him curious. As the image pushed in on the man's neck, the picture also lost resolution. The smudge, the bruise, the birthmark, whatever it was, was not in sharp focus. And the man's body was on its side. Difficult to get a distinct view of…whatever it was.

Chance, disappointed, thought deeply. His head turned and looked down to his left. The room was quiet. He turned and looked up to his right. He was searching for something. He didn't know what.

Then, Chance asked, "Tom, every murder victim gets an autopsy, right?"

"Yes, that's right."

"And every autopsy includes pictures taken by the M.E., is that right?"

"Yup."

"Trevor, do you have access to those images?" Chance asked.

"I have access to every image in the system."

"Do we need someone's approval to pull them up?"

"I'm already on it." Trevor's fingers were working the keypad.

Chance sat back in his seat waiting for the show to start. Tom glanced at Chance and subtly nodded his head, impressed with this 'special advisor'. Within three minutes there were images whirling on the screen. Trevor was taking some notes and punching buttons. If Chance were a nervous type, he would have been biting his nails. Tom Elliott was biting his nails.

The pictures stopped. It was the homeless man lying on the M.E.'s autopsy table, a cold slab of stainless steel, a bin at the end to collect blood and organs. The body was brightly lit by intense operating room lights. The man's greasy hair was a flattened mat of gray. His long beard smushed to the side. His face was ruddy, in spite of recent death, still presenting a roadmap of small red blood vessels across his face, nose and cheeks. The single bullet hole from the hollow-point .22 caliber bullet showed a star pattern at the entrance of the wound. Some black powder burns surrounded the hole. The man's eyes were still open. Vacant. Dull. Almost matte. Staring at the ceiling.

"There," Chance said. "Right there. Under his

jawbone. That mark, that smudge. Go in on that, Trevor."
The heads of all three men moved an inch closer to the
screen.

Chance's eyes were wide. Hopeful. "Can you
increase the sharpness at all, the resolution?"

The image grew in size. It sharpened. And there it
was. What Chance had suspected.

"What is it," Tom asked.

It was a design. A circle with lines radiating out
from it.

"A sneaker print," Chance announced. "A sneaker
print."

• • •

"Whew, it's been a long day already," Tom Elliott said. "But
a productive one." Chance and Elliott were riding in the back
seat of a car.

"And you still have that conference to go to in
fifteen minutes," Chance remembered.

"Yeah, and no lunch. My stomach will be doing as
much talking as I will. And you have to get over to the TV
studio. I told Nicole to expect you around one thirty. It's not
far from here. Just across the bridge in DUMBO."

"DUMBO?"

"Yeah. It's an acronym. Stands for Down Under the
Manhattan Bridge Overpass."

"I wonder how many people know that?"

"Only the people who live in DUMBO. Like Nicole.
And speaking of Nicole, everything go OK last night at the
seaplane base? I wanted to be there, but I was just
overloaded."

"Everything went fine. Nicole was right there

waiting. She even helped tie up the plane to a piling."

"That's Nicole. She jumps right in on everything. Not afraid a nothin'."

"Sounds like you know her well."

"Ahh…maybe a little too well." The black four-door stopped in front of City Hall. "Hey, we're here already. Benny here will drive you over to the studio but you'll have to get a taxi back to your hotel or wherever."

"Great. Thanks for all your help today, Tom."

"It was fun," Tom said, "if this stuff can be called fun. It's not every day I get to play detective. I'll give you a call in the morning and we can hook up."

"Thanks, Tom."

"Hope everything goes well with Nicole."

"We're about to find out."

. . .

Smoke poured out of the window as a blonde-haired woman made her escape down a dangling rope. She descended, hand-over-hand, until she reached the sidewalk two stories below the apartment building. Slightly out of breath, reporter Nicole Jensen turned to the camera: "Well, there you have it. As simple as that. Just remember, use fire resistant rope." She held the end of the rope up to the camera. "Tie knots every foot, be sure to secure the rope to something very strong and unmovable, like a steam radiator or door frame, not a door handle, and make sure the rope is long enough. Only do this if you are not higher than two or three stories and you're in good health. Smoke kills more people than flames. This simple and cheap rope, as well as rope ladders, can save your life. For PIC TV–10 News, this is Nicole Jensen."

The picture on the TV monitor froze.

"Impressive," Chance said.

Nicole turned and looked up from the controls of the editing console. She stood up to welcome Chance. "Oh, that's nothing. But thanks."

"Where'd you learn to do that?"

"From my Dad."

"Your Dad? Is he a fireman?"

"Nope. Rancher. It's the fastest way down from the hayloft."

"And all this time I thought you were a city girl."

"You mean all this time from last night?"

"Yeah!"

"Wyoming. Country girl. And from the sound of what you do, I guess you're a country boy?"

"Nope. City slicker," Chance said.

"Oh, what city?"

"This one."

"This one? And here I thought you needed someone to show you around."

"Well, I could always use that. A guy can't know everything now, can he?" Chance said playfully.

"That's what I've been saying my whole life," Nikki said just as playfully.

"So how'd it go with Tom?"

"Great! He'd be here but he had a conference."

The banter seemed to stop awkwardly about then. It was obvious that Chance was struck by this attractive young woman. Especially what he just saw on the screen and the words that came out of her mouth. A very pretty mouth, to be sure.

Nicole felt the same awkwardness and tried to break her stare at Chance. Tall. Very tall. Handsome. Very handsome. And flirty. Very flirty. At least she thought so.

"Oh, ahh…" Nicole stammered as she turned to the only other person in the room, the person who was totally forgotten about until this second… "this is Ramon. Ramon Sanchez, my editor."

"Hi, Ramon. Frank Stoneman."

"Hey, Frank. Nikki told me you might be stopping by. Pull up a seat and we'll show you what we've got."

The editing console was an array of buttons, switches, sliding controls, meters, knobs, speakers and a large specialized keypad. Covering a wall, about eight feet away, was a rack of a dozen TV monitors each playing different images. Below the monitors were racks and stacks of computers, recorders and dubbing machines. The room was all gray and softly lit. A quiet controlled chaos typical of a production studio where hundreds of pieces of news intersect, all of them racing toward deadlines.

"Frank," Nicole said, "why don't we start by showing you all the footage we have and if you want us to stop at any point just let us know."

"Sounds perfect."

"We already have the files organized chronologically so you can get a sense of the frustration and anger in the streets. The riots, the fires, up to where we are right now."

"OK," Ramon said, "here we go with the story after the first shooting of Richard Stevens."

The three of them sat at the console, minute-after-minute, hour-after-hour, three heads watching the monitor, with comments and explanations interjected now and then.

"Here's the report we did on Brian O'Neill," Ramon said.

"We put a lot into this one," Nicole added, "lots of

emotion, feelings. We made it personal. Touched a lot of people." There was the O'Neill's wedding picture. The kids playing with Dad on the swing set.

"It probably enraged a lot of people," Chance said.

"Funny, that's what the Mayor said," Nicole added.

Footage of the Mayor's press conference came onto the screen. Then Nicole's footage of policemen in various locations checking cases and long bags that could contain a rifle. Then Nicole saying the people of New York were quite understanding.

Then, it was the bagpipes blaring from the studio speakers. The O'Neill and Stevens joint funeral. Police Commissioner Brix was at the microphone. The usual obligatory words spilled out. Big on volume, little on emotion. It was Mayor Wertz's turn to speak. "...putting their lives on the line for you and me..." As he droned on, the camera panned the ranks of officers, the colorful bagpipers, the families and others in attendance.

"There!" Chance said suddenly, "Go back a little. Stop there, on the Mayor." The camera was on a close up of the Mayor's face as he spoke. "Yeah, start there and watch. Watch the Mayor's face. His eyes." The Mayor's words rang out over the crowd. "Yes, I'm sad, as you are. But I'm also angry. Angry that someone, someone with a warped mind..."

"Right there!" Chance exclaimed. "Right there. Roll it back just a few feet. Yes! There! You see his eyes when he said that?" Something caught his attention. Something he didn't like. "Look at his eyebrows. Now let it roll a little." The camera pulled back at that point and began a slow pan to the right. As it did, more and more of the crowd were in the frame, the people getting smaller and smaller. Chance saw something, although not sure if it was anything worth looking at.

"Stop! Now, go back just a little and slow-motion forward," Chance requested. "Can you push in now, Ramon? On the guy with the sunglasses? The red-haired guy."

"That's Officer O'Neill's father," Nicole said, very interested in why Chance was focused on him.

"A little tighter," Chance said. "Yes. Now, can you kind of go back and forth so we can get a look at what he's doing?"

"Yeah, I can rock back and forth like this."

"That's it! You see that? Why is he doing that?" Chance asked. They all watched intently as Sheamus O'Neill put two fingers of his right hand in a V formation, then put the two fingers up to his own eyes and then pointed his index finger at the Mayor. His signal to the Mayor was, 'I'm watching you.' Then his hand and index finger made the shape of a gun pointed at the Mayor.

"What do you make of that, Frank?" Nicole asked.

"Well, I don't know. It looks like he doesn't like the Mayor very much, doesn't it?"

"Well, don't forget, his son was just gunned down. His son was a cop. And he was a cop. He probably blames the Mayor, like a lot of people do."

"Maybe so. Maybe it's as simple as that," Chance said, not quite believing his own words.

The viewing went onward. More footage. Many more minutes. It was William Harrison's turn on the screen. There he was, sprawled out in the flower bed before a sheet was placed over his body.

"Of course," Ramon said, "we didn't show the uncovered body on TV." But there was Will's 13-year-old son and Will's wife sobbing so hard they couldn't speak. Chance recalled seeing the autopsy photos of Will's face, six small bullet holes in his forehead and eyes. The gunpowder residue left a distinct 'tattoo' all over his grimaced face.

"The sniper switched from a rifle to a small handgun for this man. Up close and personal. I wonder why," Nicole said to herself out loud.

The answer came from Chance. "The Mayor and the police, for all intents and purposes, told the sniper to change-up the game."

"How so?"

"Think about it. You did a report that aired all over New York showing police stopping people on the street, asking to look inside long cases that could conceal a rifle. So…if the police are looking for a rifle, the killer just does the opposite."

"The Mayor and the Commissioner thought it would slow down the killings. Even for a week. Make the sniper stop. At least for a while," Nicole said.

"Apparently, the killer has a schedule," Chance said.

The images rolled on the screen.

"Two people. One bullet." The screen showed Nicole in front of the apartment building, microphone in hand. "Somewhere, probably in one of these buildings, the killer, the sniper, raised the powerful rifle, took careful aim with two people in the crosshairs…and fired."

"The lovebirds," Chance said.

"Yes. Sad. Very sad," Nicole said quietly.

"You know about the lovebirds? I mean the actual birds?" Chance asked.

"Yes, but I didn't learn about them until much later. Too late. I missed the opportunity to enhance the story. Besides, the Mayor asked me to not report on that because they wanted to keep it hush-hush and not compromise the investigation."

"I guess, as a reporter…" Chance started to say…

"Journalist," Nicole corrected.

"Journalist, you wanted to dramatize the story as much as possible."

"Of course, wouldn't you?"

"I guess that's why you're a journalist and I'm not."

Nicole didn't know how to take that comment. She let it go deciding it could be an insult or a compliment.

And the footage streamed on.

It was the yellow brick building bathed with bright searchlights. The little homeless man walked out the front doors escorted by SWAT team officers. It wasn't the hoped-for vicious killer. The Mayor threw something invisible on the ground in a rage. "Shiiit!" He turned toward the camera and Nicole, "Get that fuckin' TV camera and press outta here!"

"That was a live TV shot," Nicole laughed.

"The Mayor has a way with words," Chance smiled.

"You don't know the half of it, believe me. He and I had quite a talk that night. And it only got worse since then."

The editing console whirred some more and demonstrators carrying signs were on the screen marching to and fro.

STOP THE KILLING NOW

WERTZ IS WORTHLESS

Nicole was on camera again, reporting from the scene. She was in the middle of hundreds, determined to ask questions and get some answers. She struggled to be heard above the chanting crowd.

"Sir! Sir, tell me, what do you think the Mayor should be doing to ease tensions in a city that's frustrated, as you can see right here?"

"We need more information about what he's doing

to find the killer."

"Hold it," Chance said, "can you push in on that person to Nicole's left? The white guy with the black skull cap." Ramon enlarged the screen and shifted it to the left. The white man with the skull cap grew larger in the frame. The movement continued but only on him. The man had a glass eye. It was obvious. His right eye moved around to constantly survey the crowd, but his left eye never moved. "He's like a chameleon," Chance said.

"A chameleon?" Ramon questioned.

"Yeah, chameleon's are one of the only animals in the world that can keep one eye straight and rotate their other eye."

"Ahh, I see," said Ramon. "I think I just made a pun."

Chance and Nikki just smiled.

Chameleon was talking into a baby-blue cell phone.

"OK, thanks. Ramon, you can go back to the full frame," Chance said.

"Stop right there, Ramon. 'Ya see that guy in the back on the right?" The picture enlarged and shifted to the right.

"That guy?" Ramon asked.

"No, not him. The guy way in the back. The guy who looks like he could be Hispanic or Middle Eastern, with the black wavy hair." The frame moved.

"Yeah, him. Tighten up on him." It was a man about five rows back. He was wearing a gray tank top.

"Can you get a little tighter? Right on the guy's face?" The picture enlarged. Ramon, Nicole and Chance could see something on his face. Under his left eye. A birthmark? No. It was a tattoo.

"It's a tear," Nicole said.

"Yeah. A black tear," Chance said.

Then, the man put his cell phone up to his left ear and spoke into it.

"Ramon, is it possible to isolate that guy's voice so we can hear what he's saying?"

"No way, Jose. That's only in the movies. He's probably calling his wife to say he'll be late getting home," Ramon said.

"OK, let's go back to full screen and move on," Chance said.

The screen now showed a pull back from a sign above people's heads. HOW MANY MORE? The pull-back revealed a middle-age woman with a bullhorn standing below the sign.

"How many have to die before we find out why?" she yelled.

"That was some anonymous woman in the crowd," Nicole said to Chance.

She kept speaking to a crowd of about fifty, but it grew quickly as she spoke from a flatbed trailer parked at Times Square. "How many more? How many more brave, courageous po-lice officers have to die, be gunned down like rabid dogs on the streets where they live and work and raise families?"

Voices in the crowd replied back, as if at a church rally. "Yeah, how many?" A voice said. The crowd grew larger. Perhaps eight-hundred now. The camera pulled back farther.

A voice in the crowd said, "If the Mayor cared, maybe we'd see somethin' happenin'!"

Another voice said, "Yeah, get a new Mayor. You be the Mayor."

The provocative voices became more intense,

eliciting a broader response from the burgeoning assembly now numbering over twelve hundred.

"We need the Mayor to take action," The woman with the bullhorn yelled emphatically.

"Action! Action! Action!" The words from the crowd become a chant, repeating and repeating.

"Hold it for a minute, Ramon," Chance said. The picture stopped. "There's someone in the crowd, hard to see, in the back on the right." Ramon enlarged the image and zoomed to the upper right of the frame. Even enlarged, there were still one hundred people in the shot. "Now, go in a little tighter to the upper right. Yeah, move to the right now." The image enlarged again and there were fewer people in the scene.

"OK. Now isolate the dark-haired guy down three people and to the left." The image moved like a microscope searching for something small.

"That's it! That's it! Now make that guy's head bigger, please."

The man's head grew in the frame. "You see it?" Chance asked Nicole and Ramon. Ramon's trained video eye saw it before Nicole.

"The teardrop tattoo," Ramon said. "How the hell did you see that?"

"Yeah," Nicole asked, "how in the hell did you see that in the wide shot?"

"Just a hunch," Chance said with humility.

"OK, Ramon, can you just release the still frame so we see movement now?" Chance asked. The picture rolled but stayed on Teardrop. The audio started up again.

The crowd yelling: "Action! Action! Action!" over and over. Teardrop moved. He left the frame to the right, walking behind dozens of people.

"Stay on him if you can," Chance requested. Ramon widened the shot a bit.

"There he is," said Nicole, pointing. "There!" Teardrop was moving faster now, looking behind him. Now, past a dozen more heads and bodies and signs. The audio rose dramatically in volume, the chanting was so loud in the studio the volume had to be reduced. It was deafening at the actual location. Now the sound of smashing glass filled the studio. Police bullhorns. Screaming. Cursing. A policeman on horseback trotted through the frame, making it black for a second.

Then! The flash of a fire! A car fire! Voices: "Get back! Get back!" Teardrop was captured on the video, his face turned toward the camera, erupting flames dancing on his face. Heads and bodies ran past the image of Teardrop. Teardrop put a cell phone up before his eyes. He tapped the screen. He disappeared into the throng.

Then a blast obliterated the scene! A yellow white-hot light blew out the image on the screen. It went dark.

"The explosion," Nicole said. "From across the street."

"You weren't hurt?" Chance asked incredulously.

"We had just moved, thank God! I wanted to get a closer shot of the looting, glass on the ground, people running, carrying stuff. We were walking way off to the side. The blast blew my hair right over my face. I couldn't see anything for a minute. Couldn't hear either. Thought I'd be deaf after that. Chaz, my cameraman, went down, scared to death. His camera hit the street pretty hard. Didn't break the lens, but it wouldn't work right after that. That's why I don't have shots of the carnage that was left. Two horses and a half dozen police officers down on the ground. Rioters were dead or wounded. Fires out of control. People running for their lives. Screaming! It was a war zone, for sure. It was chaos!"

"But, even with all the chaos, you got Teardrop!" Chance said.

"I got Teardrop?" She was mildly shocked. "*You* got Teardrop. I still don't know how you did that. Needle in a haystack!"

"Just needed a little help from Ramon here," Chance said generously. "The CIA could use a guy like him." Ramon had the biggest smile ever.

"But…" Chance said and then let the word hang.

"But?" Nicole said, waiting for the rest of it.

"But now it's the hard part. We don't know for sure what Teardrop was doing. Calling his wife…ordering takeout, or ordering an explosion."

"And we don't know if Teardrop has anything to do with the sniper," Nicole said.

"Exactly!" Chance confirmed.

"Remember, I was hired to find a sniper, not a bomber. And that's what I have to do. So…" Chance teased.

"OK. So?" Nicole raised her eyebrows.

"So, Mr. Teardrop lucked out. He's on the back burner. At least for a while. I have somebody else who's going to keep me busy for a while."

The screen on the TV monitor went black.

"Frank, great to meet you. I have to get to my son's softball game. But fortunately, we had enough time to get through all the footage."

"Thanks a lot, Ramon. It was great working with you."

"If you need anything that I can help you with, just give me a call and I'll set it up."

"Long day," Nicole said. "Can you believe it's six

o'clock already?"

"Time flies when you're chasing snipers," Chance replied.

"Well, if that's all you need right now I'm going to get going. I'm starving all of a sudden," Nicole said picking up her satchel.

"Need a lift home? I have to catch a cab anyway," Chance offered.

"Nah, I just live two blocks away. But thanks."

"Hey, I didn't have lunch today. As a matter of fact, didn't have breakfast either. If you want, we can get a quick bite and you can still get home by seven."

Nicole hesitated. Something inside her head said, *Ahh…I don't know. This might be a bad idea. Besides, I'm tired.*

"Don't even have to talk business." Chance's mind was working, too. *I'd rather look at a pretty face than a bowl of chili.*

"Why not?" came out of Nicole's mouth, whether she wanted it to or not. "We can go to my favorite Italian place. Not fancy. It's right down the street."

Pasquale's was small and cozy. Not fancy, but warm and inviting. The music of the "old country" played gently in the background. Flickering candles cast a romantic glow. A white tablecloth reflected a particular softness to Nicole's near-flawless skin. Not something that was lost on Chance as he sat across from her.

"This is perfect," he said.

"I like it," Nicole said.

"And the food smells sensational."

"Lino, that's Pasquale, makes everything himself," Nikki said proudly.

"Is Lino his nickname?"

"Lino is short for Pasqualino, or little Pasquale. But Lino is anything but little."

"I think that if I hung around here a lot, I wouldn't be little either."

"I like your shirt," Nicole blurted, regretting it as soon as she said it. Chance looked equally baffled by the statement.

"Purple," she said. He looked down at his shirt.

"My mother's favorite color." Nicole was sorry she brought it up.

"So your mother and I have something in common then."

Nicole remained silent. Holding her tongue for a change. Chance was different from the men she came across. And she really didn't know him at all. Although he seemed nice. Very, very nice.

The waiter poured water and asked about wine.

"Do you like red?" Chance asked.

"Love it."

"Do you mind if I…" Chance said, picking up the wine list.

"Please," she affirmed.

Chance looked at the brief wine list. All were the best quality Pasquale could offer for the price.

"Well, let's see. I know most of these. Nice selection. And…what the hell, I'll just order a bottle."

Nicole thought, *This is turning into a date for God's sake. Do I want that?*

Chance read her face. "Well, that's only two glasses each. And we worked hard today, don't you think?"

"Indeed," was her reply with a smile. *This guy has potential.*

Chance ordered the wine. Then he looked over the menu. Nicole didn't. "Already know what you want?" Chance asked.

"Yup! I knew before we got here. My favorite. Chicken Parmigiana. It's outta this world."

"Well, that's good enough for me. I'll have the same."

"I just want to warn you, it's loaded with garlic."

"Then our breath will smell the same." Now it was Chance's turn to ask himself why he said that. Nicole said nothing, but her head moved ever so slightly as she looked at him. Her mind started to work overtime. That's when the bottle of wine arrived. And the evening started right then and there.

"So, how did it go with Tom this morning?"

"Good, I think. Went to ballistics and got an education, examined some evidence and looked at autopsy pictures."

"Umm, just the kind of thing we want to talk about at dinner," Nicole said with some levity.

"We stopped before we got to the good stuff. These were just of a guy's face. Nothing too gruesome."

"Did you learn anything from it?"

"Well, it's hard to tell at this point, just like the footage we saw at your studio. What does it all mean? Is any of it connected? Did we see the face of the killer? Was it more than one guy? Pieces of a puzzle. Let's hope it all comes together and doesn't fall apart."

"A toast!" Nicole said, "To putting it all together before another 'piece' falls."

"What's today?" Chance asked rhetorically.

"Saturday."

"It's hard to believe I just got here last night."

"It is. And it's even harder to believe that another 'piece' may fall on Monday. Not much time to solve the crime and stop the killer," Nicole stated soberly.

"So we'd better enjoy tonight." Chance raised his glass. Nicole raised hers in silence, but her libido was starting to talk to her.

The plates of sinfully delicious food were placed before them.

"So you're a country girl."

"And you're a city boy."

"Well, there must be some common ground here somewhere."

"Only if you went to a dude ranch," Nicole said.

"Nope. Never left Manhattan 'til I was twenty-two."

"You never…wait a minute…you never left Manhattan…you mean literally?"

"Literally."

"Not Brooklyn?"

Chance shook his head.

"Not Queens? Not Staten Island?"

Chance continued to shake his head. "Nope."

"Then…" Nicole ventured incredulously, "how did you become this tracker, ahh, hunter? Did you go to survival school in the Everglades? Was this, like, no offense, a case of the city boy's bucket list?"

Chance replied. "Survival school? I suppose you could call it that, yes. But not one I signed up for, that's for sure. It was the last thing that I would ever want."

"Something happened? Something big?" Nicole asked.

"Something big, yes."

"Like?"

"Like…it's a long story."

Nicole let it go. Obviously Chance did not want to go into it right now. So, for the next twenty minutes, while they enjoyed their meals, the conversation took on a lighter tone. But, finally, Nicole couldn't resist the words she was about to say. She had been thinking about it since the Mayor's phone call to him.

" 'Ya know, last night isn't the first time we met."

"Oh? We met before?" Chance asked.

"Well, sort of met. I was there, at the canal in the Everglades two years ago, when you saved that family in the car."

"My God! That was a long time ago. A lot has happened since then."

"That was a very brave thing to do."

"Thanks, but it was easy for me. I'm glad I was there to help."

"Easy? It looked anything but easy! I was there! I saw! And I still don't know how you did it. No one does. How did you hold your breath for so long? Was there trapped air inside the roof of the car?"

"Yes, there was, but I didn't use any of it. The family was breathing that air and the car was sinking. Thank God it was sinking slowly. Just slow enough that they had enough air to make it."

"But how did you breathe? That was the amazing part. You didn't come up for air once!"

"Well…it's a long story."

"Another long story. How many long stories do you have?"

Chance thought for five seconds and searched the ceiling for an accurate answer. "Well, about a dozen, give or take a few hundred."

The candlelight glowed through the glasses of red

wine casting ruby colors on the white tablecloth.

"So, now that I've answered all of your questions," Chance said with a sly smirk, "how about you? Tell me about you."

Nicole took a sip and the colors wobbled and moved on the table when she put her glass down. She got lost for just a moment of reflection as her mind wandered back home.

"I grew up on a ranch in Wyoming. Cody. A town of about 9,500. A great way to grow up. Everyone knew each other. Still do. That's good and bad, but mostly good. God's country. The great outdoors. Do you know that Cody has the largest variety of wildlife in the continental U.S.?"

"I thought Miami Beach had that distinction."

"Very funny. But seriously, Cody does. Wolves, antelope, grizzly bears, deer…"

"But no alligators," Chance kidded.

"No alligators in Cody, no, but they say we have alligators right here in our sewer system."

"Then I should feel right at home."

"Speaking of home, I should get going. Is dinner on the Mayor or should I chip in?"

"Dinner is on me, not the Mayor."

"You're a gentleman. Thank you."

"We'll have to do it again."

"Yeah, and maybe I'll hear some of those…long stories." Nicole smiled.

"That means lots of dinners! Lucky for me," Chance replied.

"Lucky for *me*!" Nicole insisted. Chance paid the bill and they walked out to the street.

"Can I walk you home?"

"You don't need to do that, but thanks. It's only a

few blocks and it's safe here."

"I imagine it would be safe in a place called DUMBO," Chance smiled. Nicole smiled.

She thought, *This guy has a good sense of humor and he's a gentlemen.*

"Thanks again for all your help today, Nicole. I appreciate it."

"Oh, no problem. Happy to help. And thanks again for dinner."

Nice girl, Chance thought. *Gee, I didn't even ask if she has a husband or a boyfriend. What a dope!*

"Well, goodnight, Nicole."

"Goodnight, ahh…"

"You can call me Frank." Chance grinned.

They both walked in different directions. Then Nicole turned and called out to Chance, "You can call me Nikki."

ELEVEN

Sunday Morning: Day Two

The shiny brass elevator doors opened and Chance walked across the hotel lobby toward the revolving doors leading to the street. He had his backpack over his shoulder, laptop secured inside, and was just about to put his sunglasses on when something caught his eye. His name. Actually, his fictitious name, emblazoned across the top of a newspaper on a rack offering free copies of six big-city and national newspapers, including an alternative paper…the irreverent NYCritic. Above the headline was a black silhouette in the shape of a man, like a target.

NYCritic
All the news they don't want printed.

WHO IS FRANK STONEMAN?
AND WHY IS THE MAYOR KEEPING HIM A SECRET?

New York, NY: Shhh! This is a secret! Don't tell anyone! Mayor Wertz does it again. Puts an umbrella over the Sunshine Law. This is called going to the dark side. Well, how about it Mr. Mayor? Who is this guy you called in to help find the 'Manhattan Marauder', the 'Skyscraper Sniper', the

'Kop Killer'? What? The thirty-five thousand member police department not big enough? The three hundred member NYFBI Office not smart enough? All the geniuses in the Counter Terrorism Task Force not savvy enough? But, pray tell, this one man is! Lo and behold, Frank Stoneman. So you ask, how did we get this secret information? The NYCritic works in mysterious ways, fortunately for you, dear readers. Because there should be no secrets. No hidden agenda. So, let's have the skinny, Mr. Mayor. Exactly who is and what is Frank Stoneman? Psychic? Finder of lost souls? Super sleuth? And how about a picture? Does he glow in the dark? Have antennae coming out of his head? Does he come from another planet?

Tell you what, Mr. Mayor, your keister is on the line. So is Frank Stoneman's. And so are the lives of every police officer in New York City. Tomorrow is Murder Monday.

Chance walked out of the revolving door of the posh hotel to a taxi waiting at the curb. A light rain was falling.

"Morning, Mr. Stoneman," the doorman said as he held an umbrella over Chance and opened the taxi door. Knowing the names of VIP guests was customary at the best hotels, but, nevertheless, this put Chance off. Here is a man who knows what Frank Stoneman looks like. Now there's someone who could take a picture and send it to the NYCritic. Would they pay him for a picture? Who else knows what Frank Stoneman looks like besides the Mayor, Patty the secretary, Nicole, Tom Elliott and Knickerbocker. In the cab Chance closed his eyes and pictured who else knows his identity: Spencer in Ballistics, Pete the guy who fired the test gun in the Ballistics Lab, the hotel front desk clerk, the bellman, Trevor the autopsy picture kid, Benny the driver… the lady who issued his I.D. badge…then he thought, *I must be missing somebody.* Chance squinted his closed eyes. He pictured…the hotel cleaning lady. Could be her. She has a list of guests. *There's probably one more. There's always one more.*

• • •

The glass in the double-hung window was filthy, smudged with body grease, cracked from sordid activities in full view of tenants across the alley. The yellowed white paint flaked off the frame and sill. Dusty plastic blinds hung crooked, at a severe angle, the cords dangling all the way to the dirty bare wooden floorboards.

"Ahgh! Ahgh! Ahgh! Ahgh!" The guttural deep-throated gasps of the man sounded like murder. The ecstasy subsided quickly and Teardrop zipped up his khaki colored cargo pants, took twenty dollars out of his fat wallet and threw the bills on the disheveled single bed. An unattractive woman, some would say repulsive, wiped her mouth with the back of her hand and scooped up the money. Neither spoke. She left. Teardrop's pants pocket played music and vibrated.

"Sup?" he said into his cell phone.

"Congratulations!" It was Cufflinks. It was raining today in D.C. Out the window, a gray mist hung over the Washington Monument.

" 'Bout time you called. Where's my money?"

"I just want you to know how impressed I am that you pulled it off." An unknowingly appropriate comment, considering where Teardrop was at the moment.

"You mean pulled all four off," Teardrop corrected. "Three fires and one big bomb. On Times Square no less. So if you're so impressed, where's my fuckin' money?"

"You'll get it. Look, I don't have a lot of time for this call, it's running too long already. I need to talk about the next step in the plan, so…"

"The next step? I'll tell you what the next step is! You pay up! That's the next fuckin' step!"

"You'll get your money, don't worry."

"Look, you're there, I'm here. My money's there, I'm here. If you don't get my money from there to here, I'll come there and get it myself. Your choice."

Cufflinks took a second phone out of his jacket pocket and tapped the contacts key. A phone number popped on the screen. Then he went back to wrestling with Teardrop on the other cell phone. "I'll overnight twenty-five thousand tomorrow. Monday. You'll have it Tuesday."

"You know they won't overnight to a P.O. box. You know that! And I ain't givin' my address to nobody. I'll wind up dead. 'Ya think I'm an idiot? You're going to have to have somebody drive it here."

"Drive it there? Drive it there?" *Now this low life was calling the shots? Does this scumbag know who I am? What I can do to him?*

"Yeah, drive! Like, in a car! Takes like four hours. So make the trip worth it and bring fifty-thousand."

"Are you out of your mind? Fifty thousand! No way!"

"You say 'No way' and I say 'No way'. Now, who wins?"

Cufflinks picked up the other phone and eyed the name and phone number.

Teardrop was on a roll: "You owe me 25K for what I already did and 25K for the stuff I'm about to do."

Neither man said a word for a few seconds.

"OK. I'll have someone bring it to you. On Tuesday," Cufflinks said.

Teardrop barked out more commands: "The middle of Times Square. Where they sell tickets. 2 P.M. sharp. Khaki pants with a lot of pockets. Black tank top. No tricks or somebody winds up dead."

Teardrop hung up.

Cufflinks still held the phone to his ear and scowled at no one there.

Then he dialed the other phone.

• • •

Chance still had his eyes closed in the taxi. He went over the details again. Who else knows what Frank Stoneman looks like? *Ahh*, Chance thought to himself, the receptionist at the studio. He remembered that she waved when he and Nicole

left for dinner. But there has got to be one more. Got to be.
The name Martin comes to mind. But Martin was a test
dummy in Ballistics. Try free association. The alphabet: J…
James… John… John! Spencer's assistant!

*But there has to be one more, there's always one
more.* Chance realized that in today's world, he could only
keep his identity secret for so long.

The taxi drove through puddles filling potholes.

· · ·

"Yo!" Chameleon said answering the phone.

"I have a special job for you," Cufflinks said.

Chameleon's left eye stared straight ahead. His right
eye darted around the small room.

"Ahh, yeah?" The eye moved quickly now, nervous.

Chameleon was alone and scared to death of saying
the wrong thing. He knew who was on the other end of the
phone. His real eye could not stop moving.

But…Chameleon did something smart. He looked at
the screen and quickly scrolled to an app. He tapped the blue
voice memo icon, then tapped RECORD on the left side.

"It's time for you to step up," Cufflinks said.

"Ahh…step up?" Chameleon said, eye darting
wildly.

"Yes. Time for you to take over the operation. And
I'll pay you a lot of money to do it."

Chameleon's glass eye was locked in place. His real
eye stopped darting around and stared straight ahead, wide
open, red veins like a road map.

"Ahh, take over? A lot of money?" Chameleon said.

"Fifty thousand dollars."

"Fif..fifty…fifty thousand…ahh" Chameleon

stammered. "But what about...?"

Cufflinks cut him off. "He's going to waste you."

Cufflinks let the weight of that statement descend upon Chameleon. He didn't expect a response. "He's going to kill you and keep the money he was going to pay you. So you have to waste him." Cufflinks paused, but only briefly. "Now, you get to live, get fifty Gs, and change Ameerica forever." Cufflinks had a strange accent, an odd way of saying America. He couldn't say it any differently than...Ameerica. This didn't bother Chameleon at all.

"Kill me! Geez! How do you know that? Are you sure?"

"I have spies in all the teams. I know what's going on at all times." Cufflinks paused again. He knew Chameleon was a little slow. "I'll pay you cash. No one will know. You'll be rich. And a hero. Because *you* will be the one to change Ameerica forever."

"I never thought I could be a hero."

"You have to take him out."

"When?"

"As soon as possible. Today or tomorrow. He's going to pick up fifty thousand from my delivery guy at Times Square on Tuesday at two o'clock. He told me he'll be wearing a black tank top and khaki cargo pants. You take his place. Get the money and use it to get all the things you need to get the mission done. When the mission is complete, I'll pay you the additional fifty Gs that you can keep. Got it?"

"Got it."

"You can't call me, so I'll call you Tuesday night to make sure you have this done."

"I'll get 'er done."

"And remember our motto," Chameleon's good eye

started darting around the room again. His glass eye stared straight ahead.

Chameleon thought hard about what to say next: "Divide…and…"

"That's right, divide and conquer."

Cufflinks hung up.

Chameleon looked at the screen of his phone. He tapped the red STOP RECORDING icon.

. . .

"I thought we could use something nutritious to start our day off right, but I see you beat me to it." The hands deposited a white and pink box of cream donuts and two cups of coffee on the conference room table. It was Robert Knickerbocker in a blue T-shirt, black exercise shorts and sneakers.

"Right on brother. Nothin' like bagels and cream cheese to kick-start your day," Tom Elliott responded. He had already brought some breakfast goodies for both of them. Tom was also dressed casually on this dreary, compulsory, Sunday workday.

"Been here long?" Knickerbocker asked.

"Nahh. Just got here."

"This seven days a week crap's gotta stop," Knickerbocker groaned taking a seat.

"You can say that again," Elliott said as he swallowed and sipped. "Hopefully we get this killer so we can all get back to our lives." Knickerbocker didn't say anything in agreement. He just looked at Elliott, so Elliott felt compelled to add, "I know, I know, that sounds selfish, like I'm only thinking of myself, but this 24/7 workload is getting to me."

"You know what? It's getting to me too, Tom. More

than you can imagine. This can't go on forever. Something tells me it's gonna come to a head soon. One way or another."

"From your lips to God's ears."

"Oh, hey, speaking about God (sarcastic face) how did it go with Frank?"

"Frank? Oh, Frank, yeah. Went OK, I guess. Nothing concrete. Not yet anyway. We just went over evidence, pictures, reports. Lots of stuff."

"What kinda guy is he?"

"I really don't know much about him." Elliott was being guarded now. He was sworn to secrecy by the Mayor. All the things he heard on the phone with Governor Wilkinson could not be repeated. To anyone. But Tom felt like he had to give Bob Knickerbocker something. A tidbit. Something that wouldn't matter one way or another.

"I know he's a pilot."

"A pilot?" Knickerbocker said with some surprise. "He has his own plane?"

"Ah huh."

"Cool! Little plane, jet, what?"

"I don't know exactly. I know it's an amphibious type thing. Flew it into the seaplane port."

"Wow! How cool is that?" Knickerbocker said.

"I always wanted to learn to fly," Elliott lamented.

"Yeah, me too. Never got around to it. Maybe someday."

Elliott said, "I could never afford it. I doubt that I'll ever be able to. Not the way things are going."

Knickerbocker seemed to wake up to a sudden thought. "Hey, we'd better get busy with this hiring campaign for the Mayor so we're not here all day. Got a strategy in mind? Media? Message?" Knickerbocker asked.

"I have a few ideas that can work in print and can be converted into digital. Check it out." Elliott shifted some papers over to Knickerbocker as they both stuffed their faces with bagels and strawberry glazed donuts.

. . .

The yellow taxi pulled away from the wet entrance of City Hall as Chance clambered up the stone steps. As soon as his wet feet got to the dry surface, he stopped in mid-stride. He looked down intently, brow furrowed, eyes zeroing in on something. It was a wet footprint not yet dried. A number of them; left foot, right foot, leading to the doors. It was a footprint, a design, that looked ominously familiar. The same pattern, the same sole, the same deadly stamp on the throat of the homeless man who faced the killer. *Could it be? Could the killer be inside this building? In City Hall? Quick! Before the wet footprints dry up! Get through those heavy doors! Through security! Stare at the floor!*

There they are. Chance thought for a moment: *Am I sure? Do I remember correctly?* He searched his memory bank. He compared a mental picture to what he saw on the floor. In his mind they were side-by-side. The same. Exact.

Now, where do they lead?

Quick! Move fast!

Chance walked as if his legs were stiff. Step-by-step. He followed the prints but they were drying up way too fast.

Then! A rug!

Damn it! A rug to dry up wet shoes!

On the other side of the rug...nothing.

Eyes still searching for any tell-tale signs of a faint footprint, Chance passed a doorway and heard voices he recognized. He stopped. He looked in. The small meeting room was just next to the temporary office the Mayor told him to use the day he arrived at City Hall. There was Tom Elliott and Robert Knickerbocker sitting at a table. Beneath the table, two pairs of sneakers.

"Frank!" Tom blurted out.

"Tom!" Chance acknowledged.

"Hey, Frank," Knickerbocker added.

"Guys! Looks like you're working overtime."

"You, too."

"'Ya gotta do whatcha gotta do," Chance said in his best New York City accent. His eyes flashed to the sneakers beneath the table, wishing he could command them to magically rise up, revealing the bottoms.

"Guys, will you be here for a while? I have to meet with the Mayor. Maybe we can catch up later."

"Yeah, we'll be here for a couple of hours," Elliott said.

"At least," Knickerbocker added.

"Later," Chance said flatly.

"Later," both men replied.

Chance walked down the hall and turned right into an open door. The mayor had his feet up on his antique mahogany desk. He was wearing a velour jogging suit. And sneakers.

The soles matched the killer's.

"Morning, Frank."

"Morning…Ed."

"You'll be happy to know that your ten mil was approved by the Budget Committee, not that they had any choice."

"Any dissenters?"

"Oh, of course, there are always dissenters, no matter what's proposed. But, with what I know about them, like I said, they had no choice."

"Politics," Chance said.

"As usual. Most of 'em don't think we'll spend the
ten million anyway, so it wasn't too big a deal. If we spend a
million or even five, it's well worth it. When you have an
eighty-two billion budget to run the city, a few million is
chump change. But, you'd better perform. Or I'll have to
listen to their bullshit for the rest of my term and beyond. So,
let's not waste any of your...our valuable time. What do you
know so far? Where are we?"

"Too early to tell, Ed." Chance was playing it safe.
He was smart enough to know that he didn't know who he
could trust. So he trusted no one. Not even the Mayor. It
wasn't the ten million that was on the line, it was his life.
The Mayor was wearing sneakers with the same sole pattern
as the killer, for God's sake! Elliott and Knickerbocker are
both wearing sneakers. Gotta get a closer look at them. Who
made the prints at the entrance to the building?

"Been here long, Ed?"

"An hour or so. Got here early so I could get a
workout in the exercise room next to my office. Only way I
can stay in shape on this job."

"Do you have a gun, Ed?"

Wertz just looked at Chance. Glowered at him,
actually. "I beg your pardon?" Wertz said with indignation.

"What I mean to say, Ed, is that you're here alone,
early in the morning and..."

"Am I a suspect, Frank?" The Mayor's eyebrows
were both raised as high as they could go.

Chance paused. "Everyone's a suspect, Mr. Mayor,"
trying to show respect.

"Good answer, Frank. That makes me feel safer.
Knowing that you won't overlook...anyone. Not even me!"

"Looks like you work 24/7, Ed." Chance feigned concern.

"I do. Even when I'm not here, I'm here." The Mayor put his feet down and sat upright in his desk chair. "I suppose you'll want to keep some things close to the vest for a while, until you know more…trust more of us…but I'm having a meeting here in a little more than a half hour with my Counter Terrorism Task Force, FBI, Fire Department, Doctor Mahaffey and the Commissioner. And you're included. They'll share what they know as of now. And they'll want to know what you know. My advice? Keep it quick, keep it simple and keep 'em out of your way. They'll try to help with the best of intentions, but you know what they say about intentions and the road to hell."

"Understood, Ed."

"And, as much as I like these people, there may be a little competitive spirit going on here between the insiders and the outsider. So don't lay it on that you're better than them or that you pick up on things that they missed. They don't need to listen to bullshit."

"Are you sure you want me in this meeting, Ed?"

"No, I'm not. But we both have to be in it anyway. And," the Mayor continued, "tomorrow is Monday. The stress for all of us intensifies right now. Can you feel the pressure on you building?"

• • •

The hands on the round analog clock on the wall indicated exactly 12:00. Noon. The Mayor had the sleeves of his velour exercise outfit rolled up as he stood in front of the white flip chart mounted on the easel. He twiddled with the marker pen in his hands as he addressed the group before him, each dressed in similar Sunday casual attire.

"We've been here for more than two hours already, and I don't think we're much ahead of where we were when we started. No offense to anyone in this room," the Mayor said. "Maybe I missed something, so let me recap the meeting for all of us, OK?"

Heads nodded in agreement.

"Bill, the skinny is the FBI is still digging into national profiles, convicted and suspected bad guys with political agendas, ties to radical groups, hate groups and taking a hard look at dishonorably discharged military people who have qualified as sharpshooter or expert with weapons. Do I have that about right, Bill?"

"We've got more going on than that, but that's the bulk of it so far, yes."

"Dean, what you reported from the Counter Terrorism Task Force is that your group has found nothing that points to the building fires or the bomb at the Times Square riots having a link to foreign terrorism from a particular country or specific radical group. And you're thinking is that it is probably domestic in nature, perhaps the work of a small American hate group trying to take advantage of the disruption, while our security forces are distracted with a serial sniper. That right?"

"In a nut shell, yes."

"Now, Waters, the Fire Department's view is that the fires were the work of relative hacks who used common accelerants and some old, weakened jell explosives. They probably used a cell phone to trigger relatively modest and relatively unsuccessful fires compared to what a real professional, a serious arsonist group, could have done. In other words, they're a step up from common street thugs who tried to pull off a big event."

Waters responded, "Well, it was a big event. Could have been much worse, but yes, this was not September 11, no."

"Brix, your Special Investigative Unit has examined hundreds of police officer background files, complaints, reports, claims and cases. You've examined internet pages for any indication of traumatic stress syndrome, personality evaluations, and even comments from concerned cops about anyone on the force, God forbid it's one of us."

"That's right. We've dug deep. Some say too deep. But we stand strong. Stronger than ever, in fact."

"And you've interviewed our own SWAT and specially trained sniper guys for any insights that might help us understand this killer?"

"Yes, we have. But nothing to hang our hat on or help us move in a certain direction."

"Now, Gloria," Wertz continued, "your take on this whole citywide mass hysteria is for us to listen better. Talk nicer. That's it?" As Wertz addressed Gloria Mahaffey, the city's Psychiatrist and Social Behaviorist, an African American, his face involuntarily showed more than a trace of skepticism.

"First of all, this 'mass hysteria', as you call it, Ed, is not *hysteria*. It's citywide frustration."

"Frustration? You're telling me that these riots are because people are frustrated? With all due respect Dr. Mahaffey, that sounds like an overly simplistic rationale to me."

"Ed, if you want to listen to a professional opinion, that might help." Her face flared with irritation. There was a respectful pause from all in the room.

"Do any of you remember what happened in Chicago in November of 2016? There was mayhem in the streets because of a game that took place at a stadium. After the game, fans rioted in the streets. Not because their team lost, but because their team won!"

Gloria Mahaffey paused to let that bit of irony sink in. She looked at all in attendance around the table and continued.

"There are many reasons why people have a hard time containing the emotional energy that can build inside to a point where it bursts out in tears, laughter, happiness, sadness, despair or extreme joy. Even when their team wins. Yes, frustration is a powerful emotion. It often leads to anger. And anger often leads to violence. Domestic violence cases often start with frustration."

She paused again for reflection. Again, she looked at all gathered around the table.

"As a psychiatrist, trained to analyze faces and body language, I can see, Ed, that you are the only person in the room who doesn't believe any of what I said."

Wertz looked perturbed.

"Now," she offered, "there's fear across the whole city. And where there's fear there's a strong response for self-protection. There's a crying out to be listened to. And, yes, we're afraid, too. Ask any officer out there. Ask anyone in this room. One of the strongest weapons *we* have…" she motioned with her head and a flat wave to include all listening, "…is communication. Instead of just reporting, we need to *speak* to people. *Explain* to people. We need to *work* with people if we want to defuse what could be a worsening situation."

"Well, we'll have to work on that," Wertz said.

"You'd better work fast," Mahaffey concluded.

"Ok," Wertz continued, "last but not least, our special advisor on the sniper case. In a meeting I had with

Frank this morning, the nutshell is he's read through hundreds of reports, watched hours of TV footage, he's examined evidence, talked with ballistics, the ME…all in the thirty-six hours that he's been here. Bottom line: no solid conclusions yet. Still gathering info as quickly as possible. Do I have that right, Frank?"

"That's exactly right. I know every hour counts. The stakes are incredibly high. I'm just here to help in any way I can. And I'm proud to be part of such an amazing team."

Brix spoke up. He was holding his cell phone. "I just got a text that there will be three protests tomorrow at three different locations. Right here in front of City Hall at one o'clock, in front of the 64th Precinct at four o'clock, and at seven o'clock in front of the apartment where Tyler and Juliette Jackson were gunned down."

"Great!" The Mayor said sarcastically. "Now we have three times the likelihood that this could blow up in our faces again. Are we gonna be ready?" Wertz said to Brix.

"We'll be ready."

"Thank you everyone. Let's all hope and pray for the best."

Chance thanked the Mayor for a good meeting.

"Let me or Tom know if you need anything, Frank."

"As a matter of fact, I do, Ed. I need transportation. I want to visit each of the crime scenes to look for clues."

"Benny is off today, but you can take one of the cars in the motor pool. Right down that hall. Use it as long as you want. Parking won't be a problem as long as the OFFICIAL CITY BUSINESS sign is in the windshield. Oh, and when you go out to the crime scenes, be sure not to mess anything up. Don't disturb or move anything."

"Understood," Chance said and turned away.

"Oh, Frank!"

Chance turned back to face the Mayor.

"Good luck finding something three hundred other people couldn't."

Chance walked to the small meeting room where Tom Elliott and Robert Knickerbocker were working earlier. The room was empty. He hurried to the security guard at the entrance. He took note of the guard's name badge.

"Ah, Dan, did you see Tom Elliott or Bob Knickerbocker leave?"

"Yes, sir. You just missed them. They both just got into a taxi I called for them. Just pulled away."

"Oh, OK, thanks, Dan."

Chance didn't waste any time getting through the door and walking down the broad stone steps. The rain had stopped falling but the pavement was still a bit wet. Just enough wet and dry spots that Chance could make out the faint impression of a design. The same design on the sole of the Mayor's sneakers. The same design on the soles of the killer.

. . .

The bugle sounds came from a black purse. The sound of a fox hunt. One hand reached for the phone as the other held up a hanger holding a khaki safari coat, the kind with a million pockets of all sizes. The kind that TV journalists would need.

"Hello!" Nikki said as she appraised the coat.

"Hi, it's Frank. I hope I'm not disturbing you, I'm sure you're busy."

"Not at all. It's my day off. I'm just shopping for a

few things. What's up?"

Chance was sitting in his temporary office at City Hall inputting notes into his laptop. "I was thinking about all the footage you showed me of the protests and riots and I was wondering if I can get a still-shot of Teardrop, you know, the guy with the tattoo under his eye?"

"Oh, yeah, sure I remember."

"And also one of the guy with the glass eye?"

"I don't think that's a problem. Ramon's not there today, but we can get somebody else to pull it. Why don't we meet at the studio, let's say in forty-five minutes?"

"But, you said today is your day off. I don't want to…"

"Oh, 'phsssh', no problem. It's close by and I can't find anything I like here anyway. Besides, we have a killer to catch, don't we?"

. . .

The picture on the screen rocked back and forth, forward and reverse, trying to settle on exactly the right frame, the clearest shot of Teardrop.

"Right there!" Chance exclaimed. The picture froze. "That's good! That's what I'm looking for, Stan. Now, just one more and we're out of your hair. The one of the guy with the glass eye."

"That should be easy," Stan said, "I have Ramon's notes right here." The blur on the screen stopped suddenly and video appeared of the protesters. To the side, mostly hidden, was a man with an odd gaze.

"That's him. Right there. Just get a close up and we're all set."

"Bingo!" Stan whispered.

"Thanks, Stan. I appreciate your jumping in on this on a Sunday."

"I'm here anyway. Happy to help."

"That was painless," Nikki said. "What else can I help you with?"

"I think you've done enough for me on your day off."

"Where are you off to now," Nikki inquired.

"I want to go to all the locations of the shootings. Spend some time at each one. Maybe I'll pick up on something."

"Don't you think it would be helpful to go with someone who's already been to each location?" Nicole asked.

"Sure. Who would that be?"

"Me!"

. . .

The black four-door sedan with the OFFICIAL CITY BUSINESS sign on the windshield pulled up in front of the derelict yellow brick building. It had a chain-link fence in front ribboned by a day-glow yellow CRIME SCENE tape. A sign on the building said DO NOT ENTER – BY POLICE ORDER.

Chance and Nicole entered. "Shhhh!" Chance held his finger to his lips, "Don't tell anybody!" Nikki made a sign with her hand like zipping up her lips.

It was easy for Chance to pull up a corner of the fence that had been haphazardly wired to a rickety support pole the day of the shooting. They squeezed past the two front doors, one held by only one hinge. They tiptoed to a wooden staircase, testing their weight on each step. The thick banister swayed. Rats ran in the dark.

Light shafted in through the open second floor window facing the 64th Precinct. It was a straight enough angle to see that clear shots could be easily aimed at the police cars stopped at the security gates, waiting for them to open. Both Chance and Nikki, independently, without speaking, pictured what went on that horrific night. The filthy, decrepit sniper's perch seemed to warrant an ironic air of solemnity in honor of those slain.

"A shooting gallery," Chance said quietly with disgust.

"They didn't have a chance. Never knew what hit them." Nikki said.

"An ambush!" Chance added. Then he realized what he was there for. He turned from the window and began looking around, eyes adjusting to the darkness of the far reaches of the room. Searching for a clue, a tell-tale sign. No spent casings. Like Steve in Ballistics said, a bolt action. No cartridge cases spitting out onto the floor. Everything controlled. Planned. Steady. Calculated to the last detail. Unexpected emergencies anticipated.

Chance said, "There had to have been a steady platform. Nearly impossible to fire three powerful shots, rapidly, with such accuracy. Had to have a tri-pod or bi-pod, at least.

"Could it have been attached, clamped somehow to the window sill?" Nikki asked.

"Possibly. Let's take a look. I don't see any impression left by a clamp. Maybe it was handheld leaning against the window frame. See any fibers stuck on the peeling paint?"

"Nothing," Nikki responded.

"Any powder residue?"

"Not that I can see. There's filth everywhere."

Chance's eyes scoured every board on the floor. And then he saw something. Nikki noticed his stare. "What is it?" she asked.

"Not sure." He didn't know if he should tell her. He wanted to, but wasn't sure if he should. Finally, he said, "It looks like a muddy footprint. Actually, half a muddy footprint. Was it raining that day?"

"Yes."

"Not that that's a guarantee of anything. Not sure when this print was deposited here." Chance was not being completely open with Nikki, because part of the pattern matched the sneaker print he was looking for. But only a small part. And the print was smeared, distorted, stretched out, as if the person who left it was on-the-run.

"I don't think this will do us much good," he said.

"Do you know who owns this building?" Chance asked.

"No, I don't, but I can find out. Why do you ask?"

"I'm just trying to put two-and-two together. We're standing on the spot where the sniper fired the shots. It's an abandoned building. Maybe the other locations were abandoned buildings, too. It would be a definite advantage for the killer. Think about this. The killer wants privacy, plenty of room, a lofty perch, a good sight-picture available from a variety of windows, and multiple escape roots. And, if seen, it would probably be by a homeless person or drug addict. All of which could be dispatched quickly without anyone giving a rat's ass."

"Makes sense." Nikki said. Then tapped her phone requesting New York City Property Records. Within thirty-two seconds she was standing outside with Chance punching in the exact address. Six seconds after that, the answer appeared in digital file folders.

"The City of New York," Nikki reported.

"The City of New York," Chance repeated, wondering if this information would lead him anywhere.

. . .

The three gray stone steps led up to double French doors that had been painted many, many times in thick green enamel. In New York, these steps were commonly called a 'stoop' where raggedly clad teens would often sit, wondering what kind of trouble they could get into that day. Today, there were no hoodlums. There was no one. This was the scene of death.

"So this is where it happened? Right here?" Chance asked.

"It was over here," Nikki said, standing in a spot in the middle of the sidewalk. The spot where Tyler and Juliette Johnson said their last goodbye. Shared their last light kiss. Heads together...*BOOM!* It was all over. Two lovely people. One disastrous shot.

"Do you know exactly how they were standing," Chance asked.

"No one knows that. No witnesses at that exact moment."

"Which way was the husband going to walk?"

"That way."

"And the wife?"

"The opposite way, to her station house four blocks away."

"So the husband, Tyler, would probably have been on this side, right?" Chance said.

"More than likely, I would guess."

"And the wife, Juliette, on this side?"

"I would imagine, yes," Nikki agreed.

"Here," Chance said, "stand here like you're Juliette and I'll stand here like I'm Tyler." Chance held out his arm to put it around Nikki as she moved into position…a little awkwardly…a little reluctantly.

Chance and Nikki were now close, bodies together, Chance's arm lightly around Nikki.

"And then they kissed?" Chance asked.

"We think so. We don't know for sure." Nikki looked up at Chance.

"But probably," Chance insisted.

"Let's say…let's say they did," Nikki agreed.

"So, their heads would come together. Like this." Chance bent his knees a bit to lower his head to almost match the height of Nikki's. He put his head against her's. Nikki's eyes met Chance's eyes. Their faces turned ever so slightly toward each other. For Nikki, it was impossible not to dive into his ocean-blue-green eyes.

"And then?" Nikki asked softly.

"And then…well…" Chance thought, *This girl looks so beautiful right now*. He thought he'd better stop right there. "And then a bullet ended everything," Chance concluded.

Nikki exhaled.

"So," Chance forced himself to get back to business, "according to what we know from ballistics, the shot came from that direction."

"Yes, that's right," Nikki said getting herself back up to speed.

"And from a height of, maybe, fifteen to twenty feet."

"Yes, that's what the ballistics report said."

"So that's, once again, a second-floor perch. Looking in that direction, I see a couple of possibilities."

Nikki said, "They checked everything on this block. They came up with nothing."

Then Chance said, "The reason they came up with nothing is because they checked everything on this block."

Nikki looked puzzled. Chance explained: "The fronts of all the windows and doors of all the buildings on this block are at a ninety-degree angle to the trajectory. The shooter would have to lean out the window and twist his body in the direction of the target. The last thing the shooter wants to do is hang out of a window holding a very heavy weapon. Too easy for people to see and hear. The rifle has to be on a solid object and have a direct, straight ahead shot at the target. The sniper wants to take all the time necessary and not hurry the shot. There's only one chance to get it right. The police are used to the standard, same-old, same-old, day-after-day SOP. This is anything but SOP. This is a sniper using a weapon and ammunition that none of us have ever seen. A weapon designed to launch a projectile faster and farther than any other. To deliver one hundred percent of its kinetic force at the target and to go no farther. To start killing with shock waves before the bullet even gets to the victim. Then, to explode and vaporize the cavity so there is unbelievable destruction."

Nikki was still. Eyes wide. Impressed by Chance's dramatic description.

"I'm sorry," Chance said, "I didn't mean to go over the top like that."

Nikki gulped a little. "That's OK," she said, "I just never heard it put that way before."

"We have to understand what we're up against if we're going to overcome it," Chance said.

"Look," he said with a softer voice, "you see that building about four blocks away? The concrete gray one with the white trim and some broken windows?"

"Ah, yeah, I see it. It's pretty far away."

"That building is abandoned."

"How can you tell that from here?" Nikki asked.

"I can see into the rooms. They're empty."

"You can see that from here?" Nikki said, incredulous.

"Yes."

She looked at Chance as if to say *Sure. Right.* Chance countered her doubt. "I have very, very, good vision. Better vision than…well…almost like a hawk, actually."

"That's what I've heard. But how is that possible?" Nikki asked.

Chance drew in a breath and let it out, "It's a long story." *

"Another long story," Nikki said.

"We'll get to that later," Chance responded. "For right now let's concentrate on what we have to do to save lives tomorrow. Let's get the address of that building and find out who owns it."

Nikki thumbed her phone keypad. In moments, a map, and in a few more moments, a street view, and in a few more moments, a picture of the building and its address. Nikki's thumbs went to work again. Within seventy-two seconds, she had the answer.

"The City of New York," she said.

"The City of New York." Chance repeated. "Of course."

---

* To hear the 'long story', read SAVING AN INNOCENT MAN, the first of the SAVING SERIES of thrillers.

• • •

The black sedan was on the Verezzano-Narrows Bridge, linking Staten Island to Brooklyn. The sun was setting in the west. Chance was at the wheel.

Chance spoke up: "We had a busy day today. We visited every location. And what do we have? Twelve cops dead, six crime scenes and four out of the six have city owned vacant buildings within the trajectory of the kill shots."

"Coincidence or strategy, Frank?"

"That's the jackpot question, isn't it? But I would put money on strategy."

"We need to let everyone know ASAP," Nikki said.

"Don't act too fast, Ms. Jensen, crime sleuth. We need to be very careful who we tell about what we discovered. We jeopardize catching the killer...if the killer is on the inside."

"One of our own?" Nikki asked.

"Exactly."

"But not likely."

"Right. Not likely. But possible," Chance said. "We can't take that risk right now. Most people don't know that the City of New York owns over 1,300 empty buildings in the five boroughs and scores of occupied ones."

"But the killer would know," Nikki said.

"Yes, but we don't want the killer to know that *we* know. We have to keep this to only a few people."

The car pulled up to the curb in front of Nikki's apartment building in DUMBO. The engine kept running.

"Thanks for your help today, I really appreciate it. And on your day off, no less. I'll have to make it up to you,"

Chance said.

"When?"

"Well, I could buy you dinner tonight."

"I have leftovers in the fridge," Nikki said.

"From Pasquale's?"

"From Pasquale's."

"Well, I can see why you'd opt for leftovers from Pasquale's. Beats dinner from just about anywhere else."

"It's not that, Frank. I'm tired. Dog tired from all we did today and I have a super busy day tomorrow. You do, too. It's Monday."

Chance thought: *She's thinking it's only been two days that I've known this guy. I just had dinner with him last night, for crying out loud. Don't blow it. Wait a day or so. There's time.*

Nikki thought: *He probably thinks I'm a wild woman. Well, I am, but not after just two days. Slow down. Don't blow it!*

"You know, Frank, I would really love to have dinner with you, but I think if we do it another night we'll both have a better time."

"Wow! I've never been turned down so beautifully. And by someone so beautiful."

"I doubt that you've ever been turned down in your life, Frank."

Chance smiled.

Nikki smiled.

"Sweet dreams," Nikki said.

As the car pulled away Chance said aloud to himself, "I'm sure I will."

. . .

The Mayor was having dinner at a fancy restaurant with Police Commissioner Brix when he answered his ringing cell phone. "Wertz."

"Ed, it's Chance."

"What's the latest, Frank?"

Chance was driving as he spoke, "I think we can reduce the possibility of murder tomorrow if we take action on something right now."

"What?"

"Put a patrol car and a couple of officers outside every city owned vacant building. At least the ones in Manhattan."

"Why?" the Mayor looked at the Commissioner.

"I just visited the scenes of the shootings. Four out of the six locations were in New York City owned vacant buildings. The shooter found them by searching the city's online database and he uses them to setup, do dry-runs and wait. I don't have proof of this theory yet, but I have a strong belief that this is what's happening."

"Do you realize that it's already 6:15 on a Sunday night and there is less than six hours before midnight. Which is Monday!"

"I would have called you sooner, but I only got here Friday night."

"I don't know if we can pull that off that fast. That's a lot of buildings and a lot of men to move. And all on a hunch." The Commissioner, listening, put his fork down.

"I know it is," Chance said, "but do you know what it means if we don't have a murder tomorrow?"

"It means we win," the Mayor said.

"Yes. And the killer loses."

"I'm with the Commissioner right now. We'll see what we can do." The Mayor hung up and turned to Brix. "We'd better not order dessert."

TWELVE

Monday Morning: Day Three

The morning sun cast a shaft of light across the plush carpet as Chance drained his coffee cup from his room-service breakfast. He was at the computer early this morning. He had many questions before he could get to the final answer.

He closed his eyes and could see the video footage of Wertz speaking at the burial ceremony for officers O'Neill and Stevens. He couldn't get the image of Brian O'Neill's father, Sheamus, out of his mind. He kept seeing Sheamus bend his fingers into a gun shape and point at the Mayor. Was he just an angry father?

Chance went to the newspaper digital archive, 1981 to present, and combed through any and all articles related to Edward Wertz and or police officer Sheamus O'Neill. White squares and rectangles flashed in Chance's eyes from the computer screen as he shuffled through page-after-page of archived articles and crime stories from thirty years before.

There was a lot of information on District Attorney Edward Wertz, then a much younger man. And apparently, an aggressive DA. A man who dug in doggedly, not shying away from a fight even when there were only strands of evidence. However, he had his critics voicing claims of dubious dealings.

Police officer Sheamus O'Neill played a prominent role in some of the cases mentioned. O'Neill was known to be a fighter, too. Reinforced by a reputation for having a hot Irish temper.

Chance was engrossed, reading rapidly, when his

phone rang.

"Good morning," Chance said, knowing who was calling.

"Are you going to the rally?" Nicole asked.

"Yes, but right now I'm combing through the newspaper archives. I want to see if I can find a connection between Mr. Mayor and old-man O'Neill. See if there's something more there than just a pissed off father."

"Umm. Only thing I can think of is that Wertz was a Prosecutor back in the day. O'Neill's father was a cop around then. So maybe they go way back and O'Neill expects more help from an old associate to find his son's killer."

"Maybe there's no more to it than that," Chance said. "Could be a waste of valuable time."

"I know you're super busy and I have a few hours before the rallies. Is there anything I can do to help you?"

"How can you help me? Let's see." Chance thought for a second.

"OK, here's how."

There were four other people on the hotel elevator with Chance. A couple looked at him inquisitively, but Chance dismissed this as curiosity because of his six-foot-five height. He let all of them exit first. When Chance walked by the newspaper rack in the lobby, he knew why they showed such interest in him. There he was. On the front page. An actual picture of him, not a target-like black silhouette like the last time. He felt naked, exposed, even though he was dressed in pants and a pullover ready to go to City Hall. He took a minute to read the front page.

FRANK STONEMAN REVEALED!
THE MAYOR'S SECRET WEAPON!

New York, NY: Not many know about him. Few people have seen him. And no one knows what he does. He's a mystery. And so is the reason why our dull-usterous Mayor continues to keep us all dumbed-down. Perhaps this matches his level.

In keeping with our motto, 'all the news they don't want us to print', we're proud to be the first to reveal Mayor "Worst's" secret weapon. Frank Stoneman. The man brought in to do what the NYPD and FBI can't do. Find the killer who's been sniping and snuffing out the lives of our police officers one-by-one, two-by-two, three-by-three. We do know from our source that Mr. Stoneman, perhaps aptly named, is tall. About six-foot-four, five or six. But we do not yet know what unique capabilities said Stone Man brings to the table. Psychic powers? Metaphysical channeling? Forensic mastery?

> Diviner of dangerous minds?
> Maybe we'll all find out soon.
> After all, it's Murder Monday.
> Again! And again, we ask the
> Mayor what's happening?
> What's being done? What
> progress are we making? There
> has to be more to say to us
> than…nothing!

Chance turned the newspaper at a slight angle and looked more carefully at the picture. There, above his head, was the awning over the front doors: HOTEL EMBASSY.

On his way out of the hotel, the doorman hailed a taxi for him.

It wasn't the usual doorman.

. . .

The Beaver, Chance's float plane, bobbed gently up and down, to and fro, as commuter float planes took off and boats and barges plied the polluted river.

Near the seawall, next to two large trash barrels, eight black trash bags had been placed waiting for the normal Monday morning pickup. As usual, right on time, the grimy green garbage truck backed up to the pile, pneumatic brakes farting into the stench of the humid waterfront. Two 'sanitation engineers', clinging to either side of the business end in back, jumped off with some aplomb and started hefting the black bags into the gapping mouth of the crushing hopper. The younger of the two workers, Rodolfo, noticed a trash bag that appeared to be hung up on one of the pontoons of The Beaver. Someone must have hit it with a car and the bag found its way over the side of the seawall only to be snagged by a cleat or some sticking-out-part of the pontoon. Being a responsible sort, Rodolfo grabbed a handy boat hook, mounted on a piling nearby, to retrieve the snagged trash bag. It only took a minute. But Julio, the young man's superior, was bitching that it was slowing them down and he'd catch hell for it.

Cool your jets, Julio! It's already in the truck, Rodolfo thought. It would be far worse to leave a bag floating in the already odious, almost lethal river.

The truck pulled away briskly, the two men holding on for dear life, leaving only acrid plumes of exhaust behind.

• • •

The door of the pet shop opened with the sound of an old-fashioned ding-dong bell. A nostalgic remnant of the past. Nicole Jensen walked in straight to the proprietor, past cages of canaries, finches and tanks of tropical fish.

"Good morning!" the short, balding 50-year-old man said with a polished smile. "How can I help you?"

"Good morning. Do you have any lovebirds?"

"I did. About a week ago, I had two pair. They were b-utiful."

"Do you remember who you sold them to?"

"That's an odd question. Why do you ask? Are you with the police? The birds were legal, I assure you. Not on the endangered list. Not quarantined."

"No, no, I'm not here for that. I'm…working with the police and we're following up on a lead. I would really appreciate…"

"I sold the first pair to a woman from 57th Street. Came all the way down here for them."

"And the other pair?"

"Sold them to a man. Didn't say where he was from. A man about five-feet-eight or nine, black hair, darker skin, like a good tan. Maybe he just came back from vacation. That was my impression."

"Anything odd about him? Different?"

"Well, let me think. In all my twenty-two years here, more than half the time, people buy a birdcage when they buy birds. Or at least bird seed. But this fellow said he didn't need a birdcage. Or bird food. Walked out of here with the birds in a cardboard box with holes in it."

"Do you have a credit card receipt?"

"Paid cash."

"Do you have a security camera?"

"Lady, this is a pet shop, not a jewelry store."

. . .

Chance was in a taxi when he answered his cell phone.

"Got a minute," Nikki asked.

"Yeah, on my way to the rallies."

"So am I."

"Did you get anywhere with the pet shops?" Chance asked, curious.

"A guy five-foot-eight, black hair, bought two last week from a pet shop on Fulton Street. He didn't need a cage or food, just a box with holes in it. And he paid with cash."

"Good job," Chance said.

"Not much to go on."

"Every little bit helps," Chance comforted.

"See you at the protest," she said.

"Later gator."

Funny, Chance thought, he used to say those exact

words to gators.

. . .

The grimy green garbage truck, with the two men clinging to the sides in the back, roared its smoky, noisy way north on 1st Avenue. A frenetic swarm of flies buzzed busily at the ass-end of it.

Just as it was approaching the area of the Queens Midtown Tunnel, within sight of the United Nations...*KA-BOOM!* A bomb exploded inside the steel hopper! The sound was deafening – heard for blocks. Three thick metal access doors blew off, one hitting a young woman pushing a stroller. The two men holding onto the back were blown to the left and right, each landing on the pavement in loosely connected pieces. The cavernous mouth of the hopper belched dragon fire and smoke out the back. The steel top and sides of the hopper, reinforced by a thick cross member, bowed out, ballooned, became rounded in shape. The driver was crushed against the engine, now fully exposed. The truck's hood was on top of a mini-van half a block away. An investigation into workplace violence, possible terrorist behavior, or someone placing hazardous material into their trash would begin immediately.

The Beaver still bobbed in the choppy water of the East River.

Intact.

. . .

Looking at the fragility and beauty of the myriad colorful flowers of City Hall Park, the juxtaposition of an angry mob protesting right next to them would be impossible for anyone to ignore. But there are many of the opinion that a civil protest is a thing of beauty unto itself. The American way. Freedom of speech and self-expression. An open door to societal improvement. An uplifting of the downtrodden. Giving voice to the unheard. This is a concept that has been promulgated, encouraged even, as long ago as 1806 when City Hall opened on this location, the third City Hall location in the city. The one that endures to this day welcoming discourse, counter opinions and new ideas.

On this beautiful, hot, sunny, summer day, with flowers bursting from the soft, moist loam of the planted beds, and the cool silvery sprays of water from the large, extravagant Mould Fountain, the protestors started to gather. Their number increased rapidly on the hard pavement of the plaza in front of City Hall.

The first part of today's planned three-ring circus was about to begin. Handmade signs along with professionally made ones on sticks, were hoisted above heads in the expanding crowd. TV news reporters, microphones in hand, were already talking to shoulder mounted cameras stationed amid the growing throng. Polite police attempted to appear unobtrusive, non-threatening, hanging back at the periphery. Beyond them, but getting as close as they could get away with, was an assortment of vendors selling hot dogs, drinks, protest buttons and T-shirts, as well as black toy gun water pistols, targets and belts adorned with empty bullets.

Protest as spectacle.

Angst as entertainment.

There is a published limit of three hundred protestors at a time allowed on City Hall Plaza. The number present was now four hundred and growing. The central walkway from Broadway was becoming choked with people arriving.

One of them was Chance. Being so tall, he had to look down toward his feet every so often for fear of stepping on someone. There were small children in the crowd, easy to overlook. Some of the kids were off to the side, running into the sprinklers that watered the lawns from the northwest and northeast corners. That's when Chance noticed something at his feet. The sneaker print he had been hoping to find! There it was coming out of a puddle from the sprinklers. Chance kept his eyes on the print as he hurried forward, faster and faster. The wet prints would dry up fast in the afternoon heat. He rushed ahead much faster than the pace of the crowd, brushing past people, apologizing as he went.

Then he came upon the person leaving the tracks. A young girl with a limping left leg, doing her best to get to the Plaza to add her voice to the protest. Obviously, the sniper was not the only person in the city wearing these shoes. A dead end, Chance thought. Not the way to start his day at the protest. And there were still eleven hours left to Murder Monday.

Looking above the sea of heads, Chance spotted Nikki, microphone in hand. The cameraman was crouched down low, apparently trying to get Nikki and the front of City Hall in the same frame. Nikki was speaking, unheard by Chance, motioning with her hands and arms. The words and yells from the crowd were undistinguishable, the chatter blending into the deep-throated rumble similar to a train rolling through a small town. Chance was in the middle of it now, elbow-to-elbow, with what had to be six hundred strong. It would take a while to get to Nikki who, by that time, would probably have moved her location looking for the shot of the day. Chance didn't see Tom Elliott and Robert Knickerbocker. They were behind him, toward the back, opting for the nearby protection of the police. Mayor

Wertz and Police Commissioner Brix were not far away, either. They were inside City Hall, monitoring the event on a closed-circuit television system, toggling between security cameras mounted on poles around the plaza and the park.

Something caught Chance's eye! He did a double-take to his left! There! In the crowd, a long distance away. A man that stood about six-foot-one wearing a black wool ski hat. Chance zeroed in on him using his unusual hawk-like vision; a telescoping vision, racking an adjustable depth-of-field system of iris, retina and pupil. Chameleon came sharply into focus, his left eye unmoving, his right eye flitting this way and that. In what seemed to be an unshakeable habit shared by many others in the crowd, his phone was up to his ear. Slowly, persistently, Chance made his way toward him.

As Chance moved through the gathering, he was surprised to see that about half the people were white. Obviously, there was more unity here in New York City than one would have expected. And more than the national news had reported.

If Chance was going to make a move, now was the time. A few feet from Chameleon, approaching from behind him, Chance 'tripped' and fell into Chameleon from the side. A Hollywood stunt man could not have done a better job. They fell to the ground together in an awkward, stumbling, flailing sprawl as people stepped away, giving them room.

"I'm sorry! Oh, my God! Sorry! I tripped over someone. So sorry," Chance pleaded. Someone helped Chance to his feet. Someone grabbed Chameleon's arm to assist. Helpful New Yorkers, Chance thought. "Thank you! Thank you!" Chance said to them. "Sorry, man! Sorry," Chance said to the man he bumped into and knocked down.

"You'd better be more careful. Asshole! You're

gonna hurt somebody!" Chameleon gruffed, adjusting his ski hat on his head.

"Sorry, man, sorry!" Chance repeated as he made his way off into the crowd and quickly disappeared. Chameleon patted his pants pocket, looked around on the pavement urgently, but could not find his cell phone.

Chance got as far away from Chameleon as he could get. He made his way to the back, by the edge of the lawn at almost the same spot where Tom Elliott and Robert Knickerbocker had been observing the event. Chance could see Chameleon searching for him. Chance tried to make himself smaller. Something to Chance's right grabbed the attention of everyone in the crowd. It was a woman with a bullhorn, the same woman with the bullhorn at the previous rally. She was standing on the roof of a white box truck, standing next to her was a middle-age man and a young boy. "This is my husband," the man waived to the crowd. "And this is my son." The 8-year-old moved closer to his mother. "We live within two blocks of the last shooting. Now, what if…what if one of the shots was a stray shot? What if one of those stray shots hit my husband? What if one of those shots hit my son? This has to stop. And whose going to stop it? The Mayor? The Mayor is worthless!"

The crowd went wild! Signs were lifted high, rising up and down. Signs that said:

HE'S WERTZLESS
DUMP WERTZ
YOUR WERTZ DAY

"Stop the BS!" The words were almost ear shattering. It was a teenage boy standing on the top of a van to Chance's left. He was wearing a T-shirt with a huge BS on the front.

"BS!" he yelled into the bullhorn. The crowd settled

down. "BS!" he repeated. The crowd grew quiet. "BS is what we're gettin' from the Mayor. We're gettin' BS from City Hall!"

There was a slight pause for emphasis, setting up the next line.

"Because City Hall is full of bullshit! The Mayor is full of bullshit! And it's really starting to stink."

The crowd erupted in jeers and cheers.

"So…let's throw out the Mayor!"

The crowd cheered.

"What has he done for us?"

"Nothin'!" from the audience.

"What has he done to catch the killer?"

"Nothin'!"

"How long does it take? How long can this go on? Until there are no more police officers left in New York City? How much blood has to be spilled before it stops? White blood, black blood…it's all red blood! It's all American blood!"

The crowd went into pandemonium with hoots and hollers, signs gyrating, arms waving, fists in the air.

The chanting began:

"White blood, black blood, red blood, American blood, white blood, black blood, red blood, American blood…"

Then! A commotion over Chance's right shoulder! A man on stilts, lording over the crowd, smiling, holding a bucket. A bucket dripping red liquid. Was it red paint? Or red blood?

The chant was steady. Unending. Hypnotic. "White blood, black blood, red blood, American blood, white blood, black blood, red blood, American blood, white…"

With no hesitation, 'stilt man' tossed the contents of

his bucket into the crowd in a circular motion, all around him, hitting as many people as possible. Making an indelible point.

"...white blood, black blood, red blood, American blood..."

Five cops standing nearby sprang into action! They tackled the thin wooden legs of the interloper and slammed him to the ground! And who caught this power play in action? Nicole Jensen's cameraman, Chaz, climbing up on the low ledge of the fountain. Chance spotted Nicole running along Broadway trying to get in on the action. She arrived after the slam-down but she could add her on-camera report to the footage later. Her cameraman climbed down from the fountain appearing to have wet his pants. He set up to get some footage of Nicole.

"Frank!" It was Tom Elliott with Knickerbocker.

"Tom! Bob!"

"Looks like you got bombed." Chance was splattered.

"Geez! I didn't even notice. Too much going on."

"I think you need a couple of rolls of paper towels," Knickerbocker said.

"I think I need a change of clothes," Chance responded.

"I think you do, too." It was Nicole. "You're a bloody mess!"

"Let's hope it's not blood." Chance said. "Smells like paint to me."

"I don't think throwing them in the wash is going to work," Nicole said.

"Maybe a wash of paint thinner," Elliott suggested.

"Well, I gotta get changed. Gotta get back to my hotel."

"We can give you a ride in our van," Nicole offered. "We have paper we use for backgrounds. You can sit on that."

"Hey, thanks. Good idea. But what about the rest of the protest?"

"We have enough of this one. Besides, there are two others today."

"Sounds good. No rush." Chance said.

"And we have to get back to work," Elliott added. "See you later."

"White blood, black blood, red blood, American blood…"

In the van, Nikki sat next to Chance as Chaz drove. "Did you hear about the garbage truck that exploded today?" Nikki asked.

"No. Must have had some really old tomato sauce in there," Chance replied.

"Try C-4. It destroyed everything within a one-block radius and killed four people. One was a woman with a baby in a stroller. Fortunately, the baby's fine. The good news for you is that your baby is OK, too," Nicole said.

"My baby? What do you mean 'my baby'?" Chance asked.

"Would you say your plane is your baby?"

"Yes, I sure would."

"Turns out the garbage truck had just left the Skyport before the bomb exploded," Nicole said.

"Are you trying to say that they picked up trash that contained the bomb?"

"Looks that way. Looks like someone might have been trying to blow up your plane."

"But, what if they picked up the bomb somewhere

else?" Chance asked.

"It was their first stop."

The white PIC TV–10 van pulled into the valet lane of the Hotel Embassy. Chance, Nicole and Chaz got out. "Tell you what, why don't you guys wait down here for a few minutes and I'll run and get changed real quick. Then we can all go to the next protest rally."

"Perfect," Nicole said. "We'll get something to drink at the bar. So take your time."

"I'll be right back," Chance said. "I'll take a margarita, rocks, no salt."

Chance entered his hotel room, washed his hands and face, then removed his shirt and pants. He carefully hung both over the wastebasket, even though the paint was mostly dried by now. He walked to the closet and removed a fresh shirt and beige pants and placed them on the bed.

. . .

The backpacker walked briskly down the street. The black hood on the sweatshirt and dark sunglasses blocked the afternoon sun. The backpacker moved past some storefronts, popped into a deli, stood in the doorway and removed a small black pistol from a pocket. A teenage boy, sweeping the checkered linoleum floor, looked up to see the gun pointed at him. Before he could react, the teen was shot in the leg. He crumpled to the floor. Two young girls shrieked behind deli cases. One grabbed for a phone, crying.

. . .

The police cruiser was parked in front of the vacant twenty-story building. There were three officers assigned to this building on this Monday afternoon. The officers were enjoying the 'easy duty', not expecting anything unusual or urgent to disturb their conversation as they leaned against their car.

The radio crackled to life! "A shooting at a deli, East 54th and Sixth, EMS on the way, closest cars respond!"

"Car one-five-nine on the way!"

Two of the three officers jumped in the car and yelled instructions to the third. "You stay here and watch. Walk around the building a little. We'll be back ASAP."

The young rookie nodded his understanding. He was trained well. And his training was recent. He was on the job just a week.

The backpacker entered the vacant building swiftly and began a climb to the seventeenth floor. The backpacker set down the heavily laden pack, quickly assembled the .50 caliber rifle and pointed it out the window. In the scope, Chance's nearly-naked body came into sharp focus.

As Chance pulled the shirt over his head, the shooter, eyeball-to-scope, had a clear and accurate pinpoint shot at his chest.

The trigger finger squeezed!

The rifle fired a flash-less, smokeless, virtually soundless explosion and the bullet rocketed forward so fast, so hot, it left a vapor trail through the air. The Blender Blade Bullet shattered the hotel window and blasted into a floor-to-ceiling mirror. Tiny glass fragments rained into the room and littered the floor. The deathly missile struck, literally, a mirror image of Frank Stoneman.

Chance stopped, frozen! Only his eyes shifted, assessing the danger of the situation. The angle of the trajectory. The position of the shooter.

Instinctively, he pressed his body against an outside wall.

In the vacant building the shooter had already broken down the weapon, stowed it in the backpack, and raced down the stairs skipping every other tread. The clomping was loud. Loud enough for the rookie cop to hear it and move into the entry of the building. He stood there waiting to see who was about to show up: man, woman, teenager, homeless person? The shooter pounced onto the floor in front of the rookie and stopped instantly.

"Stop! Police!" The rookie yelled not four feet away, his right hand on his holstered service pistol. "What are you doing here? Put your hands up! Put your hands up! What are you doing here?"

The sniper hesitated. Maybe because the cop was just a kid. Still a boy, really. But the boy had looked at the face of the sniper. There was no choice.

Rapidly, as fast as a gun can be drawn, the experienced killer pulled the matte black pistol from the pouch of the sweatshirt. The sound was deafening. The fire from the barrel was an orange-red rocket blast. The bullet almost as fast as a laser. The first bullet punctured the rookie's body below the protective vest, just above the groin area. The boy went down, hand still on his holstered weapon. The shooter took a pace closer and put the gun to the rookie's forehead. The boy's eyes glanced up into the eyes of the killer above him. A moment later a bullet exploded from the barrel.

A restaurant worker who was emptying trash into a dumpster on the backside of the Hotel Embassy heard the shots and looked in that direction. He saw the hooded backpacker jogging away from the scene. The worker dialed

911. Within a minute, police sirens were heard from down the street coming from both directions.

Inside the hotel, at the lobby bar, Chaz put his drink to his lips and took a sip. He sat there alone, an empty bar stool next to him. Chance rushed up to the bar.

"Where's Nicole?"

"She said she left her purse in the van and she had to get it."

"Here I am," Nicole walked up holding a credit card for them both to see. "The drinks are on PIC–10," she said with a smile. But her words were almost drowned out by the wailing police sirens. They seemed to be right in the room. Chaz turned his head trying to pinpoint the sound.

"It's around back. Let's go!" Chance said urgently.

The three ran through the service door behind the bar, through a brightly-lit kitchen and out the back door. Two police cars, lights flashing, and four officers were already on the scene. One of the officers was kneeling over the rookie on the floor choking back tears, coughing out words. "We shouldn't have left him alone. Fuck! What idiots! How stupid! Now look! What do I tell his mother?" Another officer was on the radio reporting.

"My God, he's just a kid," Nicole said to Chance and Chaz. Then struggling to fulfill her role as a professional, she said to Chaz, "Better bring the van around. Let's get this on tape."

She turned to Chance, "How did you know right off that this was happening on this side of the hotel? Did you hear or see something?"

"You might say so, yeah. A bullet came whizzing through my hotel window five minutes ago. Thank God the sniper didn't know it was a mirror and not me!"

• • •

"I'm so sorry, Mr. Stoneman," the hotel manager said very apologetically standing in front of the mirror fragments on the floor. "Of course, you'll need another room. We'll arrange that as quickly as possible." The well-groomed man in the impeccable black suit was gracious to the point of being nauseating. "We'll assist you in gathering your clothes and accessories and we'll get them to your next room."

"I, ah, think I'm going to have to find different accommodations, Mr. Ogilsby. I'm sorry, I appreciate your hospitality, but under the circumstances…"

"Perhaps a suite, then. We want to do everything we can to make your stay with us as pleasant as possible. Even under the…circumstances."

"That's very kind of you, as I said, Mr. Ogilsby, but I think it would be safer for your other hotel guests, and you, as well, if I vacated. Don't you think?"

"Well, yes, I didn't' think of that." There was a slight pause. Ogilsby thought for a second. "Of course. Ahh, how soon can you…I mean, when would you be on your way?"

Having gathered his belongings, all fitting into a carry-on suitcase and military size duffle bag, Chance made his way to the lobby. Nicole was sitting in a comfy chair waiting for him. Chaz was waiting out front in the van.

"Well, that was a close call," Nicole said.

"Yeah, kind of nostalgic. Made me feel like old times," said Chance.

"I'll have to hear about those old times one day."

"We're going to need a lot more than one day. For right now, I need to find a nice safe place to bed down."

"This is New York." Nicole said, "No shortage of places to stay."

"I said a nice safe place to stay," Chance said emphasizing safe.

"The media is going to be all over this. You might not be safe anywhere."

"Well let's not tell the media about me almost getting shot," Chance said.

"You think Mr. Ogilsby can keep his mouth shut?" Nicole asked.

"He's the last person who would want anyone to know his hotel was shot at."

"I suppose you're right about that," Nicole agreed.

"And, as far as the police know, this was another Monday sniper shooting. No one knows except Ogilsby that the sniper was actually shooting at me! And Wertz is going to want to keep the shooting quiet, at least for today," Chance said.

"It's too late. Other reporters are already in back of the hotel.

"When this news breaks…" Chance started to say.

Nicole interjected, "*When* it breaks? It probably already broke."

"We're going to have our hands full outside the 64th Precinct," Chance cautioned.

"We already had our sniper shooting for this Monday. Do you think the sniper is through shooting people for today?" Nicole asked, somewhat snidely.

They started to walk out of the lobby. But Nicole stopped. "Hey, I have an idea," she said, "I know a place you could stay that no one would ever think of looking." Chance had the look of *Oh? Where?* He gave this look to Nikki.

"My place!" she said a little hopeful.

"Your place?"

"It's safe, just across the river from City Hall. And I might get to hear some of those long stories."

"You forgot one thing," Chance said.

"What's that?"

"It's also close to Pasquale's."

. . .

"Three days!" Cha-ley said when he picked up the phone.

"Three days, what?" Chance said back.

"It's been three days since you left home and I haven't heard from you. I guess things have been pretty good…up 'til now."

"You're right, Cha-ley. They tried to blow-up The Beaver."

"Well, tried is a lot better than did."

"You're going to have to come here, Cha-ley. I could use your help to watch over The Beaver and maybe do some other things, too."

"Should I bring the judge?" (a sawed-off shot gun)

"No, but you can bring Addie Mae with you. I think I might be able to use her, too."

"She'll be happy to hear that. She's been moping around here like somebody died."

"Well, not yet. So tell her to cheer up. And tell her to bring a few of the nicest dresses she has."

"Sounds like we're going to go to some parties."

"Yeah," Chance said sarcastically, "but not the kind of parties you're thinking of."

THIRTEEN

It was 4 P.M. The intersection and the streets outside the 64th Precinct were wall-to-wall protestors. But there was something different about this protest. There was a new addition to the rally. An unknown group was here. They were in front of the vacant building where the sniper had set up his shooting perch. The group called themselves The Innercity Soldiers. They had tables set up with stacks of printed propaganda held down by bricks on top.

TV news trucks were parked along Hester Street. One of them was the white PIC TV–10 van. Nicole Jensen, Chaz, camera at the ready, and Chance, who was wearing a large sunhat and sunglasses as a makeshift disguise, got out of the van and walked toward the crowd.

"Chaz, grab some of this," Nicole said as they walked past The Innercity Soldiers.

Chance was all eyes, looking everywhere at once. Just this morning the sniper had a perfect shot at him…but shot a mirror instead. Now, the killer would be pissed, incensed, crazed, determined to get a bead on Frank Stoneman again. Maybe right now. Chance looked up at the second-floor window of the vacant yellow brick building. He also looked for Chameleon, he would likely be at this protest. Teardrop is probably here too, Chance thought.

The crowd grew in size. The crowd grew in noise level. The crowd grew in anger. The news of the rookie's slaughter was out there. It spread like wildfire. And this crowd was smoldering. It wouldn't take long for it to burst into flames.

The Innercity Soldiers handed out red baseball caps to anyone with his or her hand out. The hats were embroidered with two big white words on the front. The script was hard to read from a distance. They handed out something else, too. Probably the most important thing to their organization. Applications to join their movement. The application had two mandatory requirements: 1. An email address. 2. A phone number. This was a group that knew how to muster troops for flash mobs and protests.

"Excuse me, sir!" Nicole called out to the 24-year-old black man in the red hat on the other side of the table. He was busy handing out hats and applications. "Excuse me, sir!" He looked at Nicole.

"Sir, where are you from?" She put a microphone to his face. The camera rolled.

"I'm right here."

"No, I mean, where's your organization from?"

"Everywhere. We're everywhere."

"This is the first time I've heard of your group, The Innercity Soldiers. Is this a new group?"

"Yes, but now the world will know that The Innercity Soldiers are here."

"But, ahh, who are the leaders? Who's in charge? Who put this together? I mean, it didn't just pop up today, did it?"

He didn't answer. So she pressed on. "Are you the leader?"

"Every Innercity Soldier is a leader."

"But is there a spokesman? A General? Who is that?"

"I gotta go. I'm busy right now, as you can see."

People – Asians, whites, blacks…all kinds of people – were crowding the tables picking up their free hats and applications. So many that Nicole and Chaz were being pushed aside.

Nicole spoke to the camera: "Looks like we'll be hearing more from this group as the protest gets underway."

There was a woman standing in the bed of a pickup truck parked directly in front of the police station. She spoke into a microphone attached to a small portable PA system, "Do you know who I am?"

Nicole, Chaz and the crowd turned their attention to her.

"Do you know who I am?" she repeated.

The crowd settled down.

"I'm the mother of Jamal Jones."

The crowd was silent.

"I'm the mother of the 21-year-old police officer who was shot in cold blood. Murdered."

The tears were streaming down her face. She wiped them away with a tissue.

"I'm a single mother. He was my only child. And do you know what I have left?"

She looked into the faces of the crowd.

"Nothin'," she said, barely holding back sobs.

You could hear a pin drop.

"And what am I goin' to do? What's the Mayor goin' to do? Nothin'. Whose gonna help me now?"

And then, from the loudspeakers across the street in front of the yellow brick building, came the words: "We're going to help you." It was the young man that Nicole had interviewed earlier. The man from The Innercity Soldiers. He was standing on a table with a microphone in hand. He was wearing a red hat.

"We're The Innercity Soldiers. And we're here to force the city government to do what it won't do." He raised his fist high into the air. The crowd went wild. The cheering was as loud as a football stadium. In unison, as if a living thing, the crowd turned and faced the man on the table. The crowd crushed toward the young man in the red hat.

Inside City Hall, Mayor Wertz and Commissioner Brix were watching the protest from many angles on six monitors. "We have to take some action right now," Brix urged.

"Careful," Wertz cautioned. Nevertheless, Brix was on his phone. "Sullivan?"

"Yes Sir, Commissioner." A uniformed officer answered in what looked like a command center inside the 64th Precinct.

"Sullivan, this could boil over at any minute. Get a couple of snipers on the roof, but have them keep a low profile. And beef up the teams outside every entry point to the station house."

"Will do! ASAP!"

The man in the red hat continued. "The problem is, the Mayor just tells you what's already happened. We're here to tell you what's *going* to happen!"

The crowd erupted again in wild enthusiasm. They were eager to hear what this leader, this new leader, had to tell them.

"Instead of talking about all this, we're here to *do* something about this."

There was cheering. Fists in the air. Red hats waving.

"We all came together here on these streets, in sight of the police station, where three of our city's men in blue were murdered. By who?"

From the crowd: "Yeah, who? Who? Who? Who?" The chant started and got louder.

"We're going to find out! And when we do we're going to tear him apart!"

The crowd cheered wildly.

"Now…now…we're here, on the streets. And guess what Mr. Mayor? We're not going anywhere! We're going to stay on these streets!"

Another unified uproar started with cheering and fists in the air.

"Until…" Red Hat continued, "until next Monday."

The crowd became silent. Waiting.

"We're going to occupy these streets until next Monday. And if we have one more policeman die…"

The group was silent.

"…the streets are not the only thing we will occupy!"

The crowd went ballistic. It was pandemonium. Fists pounded the air.

"Starting now! Right now! We're going to occupy that building." The young man in the red hat pointed to the yellow brick building behind him. Forty people from the crowd immediately stormed the chain-link fence pushing it down easily. They flooded into the building knocking down the rickety doors.

"My God!" the Commissioner said as he watched on the monitor, "we have to put a stop to this right now!" He grabbed his phone.

"Let them go! Let them go!" the Mayor insisted.

"What do you mean let them go? They're invading a crime scene, for God's sake!" Brix spat out the words.

"Crime scene? We've gone over that crime scene with a fine-tooth comb three times over. Besides, they're already inside. It's done. We'll do a lot more damage trying to get them out. Just leave it alone and let's see how it plays out."

The Commissioner put the phone down.

Red Hat didn't miss a beat. "We will occupy the streets tonight. You see that white truck down there?" He pointed to a large white box truck parked on Hester Street right next to the PIC TV–10 van. As he said this, the slated door in the back of the truck rolled up. "We have canopies to sleep under and blankets to put over ourselves."

The crowd could not believe their eyes and ears. The cheers of approval erupted again. Who is this guy, many asked. And so did Chance. This guy, he thought, didn't sound like a New Yorker. He didn't have the accent. No, he was from somewhere else. Where? Maybe California? No, not the West Coast. Louisiana? No, not the deep South. Maybe D.C.? Yeah, could be D.C.

The crowd gathered quickly at the back of the truck. Stacks and stacks of folded canopy material and dozens of aluminum posts and struts were handed out. Dozens of plastic pails were filled with hundreds of pounds of sand to be used to anchor the canopies without destroying the streets and sidewalks. The Innercity Soldiers were acting like…like an army. They had materials, logistics, a plan and…soldiers. This was no little-league operation. This was a machine. A well-funded machine. *By whom?* Chance thought. *From where?* Chance thought. *For what purpose?* Chance thought. *And…what will happen next?*

Nicole Jensen was on camera, moving fast. Chaz could hardly keep up. The camera was hot from almost non-stop taping. The batteries were draining faster than usual. But this was the story of the year. And she was there. She managed, somehow, to get back to the spokesman for The Innercity Soldiers. The young man in the red hat.

"Sir, tell me something," she said.

"I'm busy right now."

"Please, what is your name?"

"You don't need to hear my name. You need to hear my message."

"Who organized all of this? Where is your headquarters?"

"Right here."

Growing frustrated, Nicole thought she would try a different tack.

"Your hats! They're red."

"Very observant," he said sarcastically handing out more red hats.

"But, why are your hats red?"

He paused then said, "They're red because red symbolizes blood."

Nicole asked, "So the red hats symbolize the blood that African Americans have shed for so long?"

"Not just African Americans, but everyone who has ever shed blood for freedom, fighting for the rights of us all. All the soldiers fighting in wars, the Code Talkers, Native Americans who were on the front lines, the Tuskegee Airmen, African Americans who fought for civil rights, and even the police who are here today fighting a war on the streets. It's the blood that has been shed by all who join together for the freedom of all. And that's a lot of blood."

Nicole was speechless. Stunned. She didn't expect this young man to be so eloquent. So passionate. So right.

"Oh, just one more question. The words on the front of your hat say *Believe In…* what does that mean?"

"Well…what do *you* believe in?"

It looked like an art festival at the intersection of Grand Street and Hester Street. White canopies were set up on both streets for one block north, south, east and west.

"You want to just let this circus go on?" Commissioner Brix said to the Mayor in disbelief.

"That's right. How long do you think this is going to go on?" The mayor asked.

Brix countered, "They'll need food, water, medical…bathrooms, for God's sake. They'll be shitting and pissing everywhere!"

"Good thinking. Let's bring in a bunch of portable toilets and water."

Brix cocked his head to the side a little. His mouth opened a little. "Are you crazy? You want to make this a picnic for them? Oh, great idea, boss. Great idea!"

"I want to defuse the bomb, that's what I want to do, Bill. I want them to think the city has a heart and understands and is listening to them. That's what I want."

"Yeah, and you want to get re-elected this November. That's what you want. No offense Ed, but geez!"

"If I don't get re-elected you might be out of a good paying job, too. Surprise!"

"This could be a huge mistake, Ed."

"And it could be a stroke of genius. Let's see."

Police set up barricades and detour signs re-routing traffic around the closed streets. Flatbed trucks delivered portable toilets and set them up on all four ends of the encampment. A police officer stood at the back of an open van rationing out a bottle of water to anyone wanting one.

Dusk was descending fast upon The Innercity Soldiers' occupation. Stomachs were growling for food. There were no chairs to rest weary legs. Fatigue was setting in. Then it started to rain. Many protesters left for a hot meal at home and their televisions. They could keep tabs on the protest from their living rooms, get the kids fed and get ready for work the next morning.

A couple of TV crew trucks were pulling away from the curb.

"Things are winding down. Looks like we can wrap it up for now," Nicole said to Chance and Chaz.

"It's been a long, tiring day for everyone," Chance added.

"Especially for you. It's not every day you get shot at!"

"Yeah, another step forward and I would have been on the floor with the broken pieces of mirror."

"I bet you could use a drink. And some food. We didn't have lunch today. Again!"

"No lunch is getting to be a habit around here," Chance said.

"Tell you what," Nicole said, "Chaz has to get home to his family, but first he has to drop off the footage at the studio, so he can drop us off, too."

"Sounds like a plan," Chance said.

The van pulled away from the curb and left The Innercity Soldiers behind. At least for tonight.

• • •

The waiter put two goblets of wine on the tablecloth in front Nikki and Chance. The waiter announced, "Lino says the wine is on him tonight."

"Please tell Lino thank you," Chance said. "And tell him he could not have picked a better night for it. Here's to Lino." Chance and Nicole clinked their glasses together.

"I had a feeling we'd end up here at Pasquale's tonight," Chance said.

"I was hoping," Nikki added.

"There's nothing quite like the smell of garlic in your hair in the morning," Chance quipped.

"Don't you take a shower at night?" Nikki questioned.

"Well, you're getting kind of personal," Chance said playfully.

"Wine has a way of doing that," Nikki said just as playfully.

"Hey, personal is good if it's personal with the right person."

"Well, so far, so good," Nikki said.

Chance hesitated, looked at Nikki and said, "I'm glad to hear that."

"I'm glad to say it."

Things were warming up fast between them. They talked about the events of the day, the shooting, The Innercity Soldiers. And before they knew it, the waiter set their dinners before them.

"I'm starving!" they said simultaneously, which made them both laugh. They picked up their forks and dove into the steaming plates of melted mozzarella atop breaded chicken breasts. It was just what they needed. It went down easy. The wine went down even easier. They ordered a second glass. As they felt the stress and tension of the day oozing out of them, the conversation grew softer. Warmer. More personal.

"So, ah, here comes the trite question," Chance ventured. "I apologize in advance. Where did you go to school?"

"This sounds like a date. Is this a date?" Nikki said in mock annoyance.

"Do you want it to be?"

"Ahh…" Nikki deliberately drew out the pondering thought. But then said, "Sure! Why not? I haven't had a date in a while."

"I don't believe that for one minute!"

"It's true."

Chance cocked his head disbelieving.

Nikki said, "Do you know what kind of guys I get?"

Blank stare from Chance.

Nicole continued, "All they talk about is themselves."

Blank stare from Chance.

"Lawyers who talk about the 'big' cases they've won. Doctors who talk about how much they pay in malpractice insurance. CPA's who tell me they'll do my taxes for free."

Blank stare from Chance.

"Now," Nicole said flatly, "tell me about yourself."

Chance's face was mild amusement. "Is that a trick question?"

Blank stare from Nicole.

"Do you really think I'm going to talk about me when you hate guys who talk about themselves?"

"I didn't say I hated them."

"Well…where are they now? In the outbox."

"You don't want to end up in the outbox?" Nicole said, smiling, feeling she was one up on Chance.

There was a longer than normal pause in the conversation.

"Bolingbrook," Nicole finally said.

"Bolingbrook?"

"Bolingbrook College. Boston. School of Journalism, where I went to school." She sipped the rest of her wine. The waiter filled her glass immediately. Chance's, too.

"Isn't that one of the top schools for journalism?"

Nicole shook her head. "When I told my Dad I wanted to get into this business he said, 'Well, you might as well do it right. Pick the best school and that's where you'll go.' Fortunately, I got in."

"And you're lucky your Dad could send you. That's an expensive school from what I've heard."

"Very!" Nicole said. "Dad sold off some of the ranch property so I could go."

"A big ranch?"

"About six hundred acres, but four hundred of that is leased from the BLM. I lived with my aunt in Boston while I went to school, so that helped a lot."

"Must have been a big change for a girl from Wyoming."

"Scary at first. But there are a lot of really nice people in Boston. I made a lot of really great friends."

"Your name. Jensen. That's…"

"Danish."

"So your blonde hair is…natural?" Chance said, wondering if he should not have said it.

"Like sunshine, my Mom used to say."

"And your eyes, like the sky," Chance added.

"You're sweet, thank you."

Nikki told him more. "My Great Grandfather came from Copenhagen around 1850 through New York and then Utah. Eventually my Dad found his way to Wyoming, met a western girl, bought a ranch and here I am."

"An only child?"

"Yep. Just me."

"Me, too. See, we have something in common," Chance said. "Tell me about your Mom."

"She passed away last year."

"Oh, sorry."

"Yeah. The pain is still deep. Worse for my father, though. They were as much in love at the end as they were in the beginning. You could just tell." Nikki's eyes got misty.

"Looks like we have something in common there, too," Chance said.

"How so?" Nikki questioned.

"I lost my Mom, too. She died a little less than four years ago. I didn't get to see her before she...passed."

They were both quiet for a few seconds.

"How about your Dad? Where is he now?" Nikki asked.

"My Dad died when I was young. Went off on his job and never came back. He died in an accident on the jobsite. I can still see him waving goodbye as he got into a taxi to the airport."

"I'm sorry to hear that," Nikki said.

Once again, they were both quiet for a few seconds.

Nikki offered some comfort: "It hurts for a long time, I know, but they're together now."

"They are," Chance confirmed.

By now, every morsel of food was gone from their plates, the last of the wine in their glasses was finished off and the bill was paid.

"We'd better get going before Lino throws us out of here," Nikki said.

It was still raining lightly as they hurried down the glossy sidewalk, Nikki holding a newspaper over her head and Chance carrying his carry-on and duffle bag. Three blocks later, the sky opened up. The last half-block was a run. Quick with the key and inside the door.

"It's really coming down!" Nikki said.

"I think a big storm is coming in," Chance said.

They climbed the carpeted stairs in the older three-story building and Nikki unlocked the wooden door to her second-floor apartment. A flick of the light switch revealed an amazingly cozy and inviting setting. The kind of warmth and glow you'd expect of a girl from Wyoming. A girl raised with deep love of family and friends, deep roots in her small hometown. Memories were everywhere – in frames, on antique tables, on shelves and walls. A small bouquet of fresh flowers brought color to the center of a round eighty-year-old claw-foot oak table surrounded by four antique bentwood chairs.

"That's a beautiful table," Chance complimented.

"My Grandfather's. Now mine."

"Lucky girl."

"Yes, I am."

On the side table was a pioneer's candelabra: three small intertwined deer antlers and three tall white candles in the middle of them. Chance looked at some of the photos next to the candles. One was of Nicole holding a .3006 big game rifle in front of a large bull elk lying on the ground, dead, its head propped up. She had just shot it.

"How many shots did it take to bring that bad boy down?" Chance asked.

"Just one. That's all a good hunter needs," Nikki said matter-of-factly.

Chance said softly, almost to himself, but loud enough for Nikki to hear, "Umm, I may have just caught my sniper."

Nikki looked at Chance in feigned scorn. "Very funny!"

"How about an after dinner drink?" Nicole offered. "To celebrate your still being alive. You dodged a bullet today, remember?"

"Sure. What do you have?"

"I have, ahh, brandy and…ahh, brandy. What'll it be?"

"I'm not sure. I think I'll have…ahh, brandy."

"Good. I think I'll have the same. But…" Nicole paused motioning with her head at the squarish, kind-of-modern light brown leather couch. "Before you sit on my new leather sofa with those wet clothes, you'd better get into some dry ones. If you want, you can change in my bathroom and just leave the wet clothes in the tub."

"Yes, boss," Chance said with military snap. Nicole poured the spirits and placed the glasses on the coffee table.

Chance walked out of the bathroom in his bare feet, wearing beige baggy pants and nothing else. Nikki looked up and blinked. Twice. For a long moment, she forgot to breathe. When she inhaled, she knew she had given herself away.

"Fresh outta clean shirts," Chance announced, smiling.

"Good thing there's a washer and dryer in the basement," Nikki said trying to look as cool as a tall summer drink.

Something caught Chance's eye on the side table next to the candles. It was the picture of a young Nicole sitting atop a large Palomino. He had to be seventeen hands high. A big one. "You ride?"

"Everyday! I *did*! What girl in Wyoming doesn't?"

Chance looked at Nikki and wondered how long it had been since she had something powerful between her legs. Nikki looked at Chance and wondered the same thing.

Then! A thunderclap shook the building! It shuddered. The lights flickered and everything went black.

Within three seconds Nikki had all the candles lit. The room took on a romantic glow.

Suddenly! A crack of thunder made Nikki jump!

"Scared?" Chance asked, knowing the answer.

"Nahh." Nikki said reflexively, but then added, "Well, maybe."

Chance moved toward her. Nicole stood motionless. Like a rabbit discovered in the brush.

Chance was against her.

She melted into him.

As the rain streaked down the windowpane, clothes fell to the floor. So did Chance and Nikki. Pulses of lightning splashed into the room in white-hot flashes. Chance was over her, bathed in the soft glow of the flickering candlelight, palms on the floor. Nikki's eyes were huge, pupils completely dilated, looking up at him in awe. "My God," she said. But Chance did not hear. Maybe she said it only in her mind. It had been a long while for Nicole, not giving herself to just anyone. Persisting, long resisting the urge to merely satiate her longing for a man. Now she felt herself giving totally.

Chance wondered if he had ever made love to a woman this beautiful. And so spontaneously. The fuse was lit. And he was packed with explosives.

Lightning flashed and pulsed like a strobe light seemingly in sync with their bodies.

Chance was behind her now, pulling her long blonde hair like the reins of a horse, riding bareback. She moaned with pleasure with each gentle push growing more forceful.

Thunder shook the house again. A moment later, brilliant light poured in. She was on top of Chance looking down on him. His strong arms gripped her hips, but she didn't need any help with her rhythmic motion. Her breasts were moving, swaying before him.

Then she thrust her head back. She arched her back. Her mouth opened slightly. The moan was soft at first. Then louder. Louder still.

Chance's body stiffened, legs rigid. His grip on her soft body tightened. A soft moan. Rhythmic moans. Louder. Louder still. One long gutteral moan. Their bodies tensed in unison. Tightened. In spasms. Pleasurable, involuntary, primitive shuddering.

A tremendous thunderous boom from the heavens shook the house again! A quick pulsating of white-hot lightning. And it was over.

The rain lightened.

Chance carried Nikki to the bed.

The storm relented.

And a deep sleep came over Nikki and Chance.

FOURTEEN

Tuesday Morning: Day Four

It was a bright sunlit morning on the roof at City Hall.

"This is where I found the first one." Andy pointed to a spot on the black tar. "I had just put the flag at half-staff when I looked down and saw it. Then I saw the other lovebird over there."

"They must have been shot somewhere else and placed up here. That would be my guess," Chance said, looking around.

"I don't know how anybody would get up here. I have the keys to the access door on my belt right here. And Patty has keys in her desk but I don't think anybody knows about that. No reason for them to."

"Well, the birds got up here somehow. If we knew how, maybe we could find out who."

"Do you want to know about the ball?" Andy asked.

"The ball?" Chance was clueless. "What ball?"

"The ball from the top of the flagpole." Andy reached inside a copious jacket pocket and pulled out the metal brass ball. It was in two pieces.

"No, I didn't know about this."

"Found 'em right about there," Andy said, pointing. "Kicked one with my foot."

"Did anyone have these checked out? Ballistics? Detectives?"

"Nahh."

"Why not?"

"Well, I guess the thinking was we had more than

enough to worry about at the time and these were just overlooked."

Chance took the two pieces from Andy and placed them together, trying to make the ball whole again. The split was ragged at the edges on both sides. The very bottom, the part that is threaded so it can be screwed onto the top of the pole, was split more evenly. When Chance pinched the two halves together he could look into the hole of the mounting section and still see threads. He held the ball in front of him and tried to picture the event. He looked up at the top of the flagpole.

"Have any duct tape, Andy?"

"I can get you some. Give me five minutes."

Chance said, "I'll take the flag down."

Within fifteen minutes, Chance was halfway up the flagpole. He was fifteen feet away from the top, looking up, shielding his eyes from the sun. He climbed higher. The pole swayed a bit as he reached twenty feet. Then twenty-five. Finally, thirty and he was at the top. Gripping the white pole in a one-armed bear hug, he reached into the large pocket of his cargo pants and pulled out the ball that he had taped tightly together. Now, very carefully, he took the ball and began to screw it back onto the top of the pole. It went on easily at first, but then it wouldn't budge. He had to get the ball fully seated and in the right position for what he was about to do next. He unscrewed it just a bit. He tried to screw it down again. *Easy now. Don't break it! The tape has to hold!* It went past the tough spot. He screwed it all the way down. He breathed a sigh of relief. Now, the goal was at hand. He could see where the bullet had entered and exited the ball. Chance ducked his head a bit and sited through the jagged hole. It was quite precise. Almost as precise as the aiming sites on a rifle. He could see the building where the shot came from.

Number 321.

• • •

There were rust stains running down the concrete from the number 321 on the side of the old eight-story building. Chance walked up the three stone slabs to the entry door. The door was locked, as is virtually every entry door in Manhattan. To the left of the door were doorbell buttons with name slots under each. He counted sixteen doorbells but only fifteen names, none of which he recognized.

When Chance called the manager's number, he heard a recording: "Leave a message."

• • •

The tiny white squares were reflecting in Chance's eyes as he tapped the keyboard. He was going through the newspaper archive again looking up news reports from twenty-two years ago, delving into case histories involving then District Attorney Wertz, policemen Sheamus O'Neill and Arthur Stevens. One case caught his attention more than the others. A murder case against a man named Angel Perez.

DISTRICT ATTORNEY BUILDING CASE AGAINST PEREZ

> New York, NY: The case against murder suspect Angel Perez continues in the court room today led by District

Attorney Edward Wertz. Even in the face of new DNA evidence produced by Wertz and testimony by police officers involved in the case, patrolmen Sheamus O'Neill and Arthur Stevens, Perez steadfastly maintains his innocence.

Perez is accused in the shooting death of Marvin Shmutter, a jeweler. Perez was a security guard at Shmutter's Jewelry Store, Divine Diamonds and Jewelry, on West 47th Street. On the evening of June 16, DA Wertz alleges Perez had a heated argument with Shmutter over wages owed. The argument ended in Shmutter's death from a handgun. Wertz argues that diamond rings and other jewelry, valued at more than seventy thousand dollars, was taken as a bogus armed robbery cover up. Neither the weapon or the jewelry have been recovered. Perez has not provided an alibi for the estimated time of the killing. DA Wertz says DNA evidence left behind in the ensuing

> violent scuffle is irrefutable
> proof that Perez is the killer.
> Closing arguments are
> expected today. Showing
> support, as in all previous court
> appearances, Perez's wife,
> Rosalina and their 11-year-old
> son, Antonio, are expected to
> be present.

A picture of Angel Perez appeared in the body of the report. A picture of Rosalina and her son, Antonio, sitting in the court room, appeared at the end of the column.

Chance printed the page and exited the archived files. Then, in the search bar, he entered New York State Division of Corporations. He entered Divine Diamonds and Jewelry. The page appeared.

> Entity type: Sub Chapter S
> Origination Date: October 17, 1986
> Status Inactive: July 30, 1994
> Corporate Directors: Marvin Shmutter
> Adel Shmutter
> Bertram Wertz

· · ·

The tires chirped on the pavement as the black sedan stopped short, inches away from the car stopped in front of it. Chance had just tapped Nikki's number on his phone when he looked and saw the car just on time.

"Hi," Nikki said, happy to see who was calling her.

"Good morning." Chance said.

"I was worried about you," she said. "I hadn't heard

from you and, I, ahh, well after last night, I…"

"No worries on my side, I thought last night was great. I hope you…I mean, I…" he said awkwardly.

"No worries on my side either. I think it was great, too."

"Listen," Chance said, "I have to cut you short. I just wanted to let you know I just dug up a lot of interesting stuff that could lead to something big. And it could be a big break for you, but I can't explain now and…" Chance was driving in bumper-to-bumper traffic. Gas pedal, brake pedal, gas pedal, brake pedal… "…and I have a million things to do before I see you at the protest later."

"Can I help with anything," Nikki offered.

"I don't think so. I'm running too fast. I have to go look at some files in the property room, get a print out of a legal form, design and print out a label for a water bottle, make a bunch of airline reservations, and get to the Skyport…all within two and a half hours. So I gotta run. See you at the protest."

"See 'ya there."

Cars were honking behind Chance. He punched the gas pedal.

・ ・ ・

"I'm sorry, sir, I know who you are but I need to see some written authorization before letting you enter the Property Room to examine evidence." The male clerk behind the counter adhered to the letter-of-the-law, as he should. So Chance presented his letter from the Mayor granting Frank Stoneman unfettered access as a Special Agent for the City of New York. The clerk read the letter, examined the embossed seal at the bottom, and handed it back to Chance.

"Marie-Elena will take you to the files and bring you what you need." Chance and his escort disappeared through a locked entry door.

"We meet again," Chance said to the short Hispanic woman with the soft eyes. The same property assistant who was in the room when he examined the bullet fragment. Marie-Elena just smiled and nodded. "I'd like to see everything you have on this case," he said, handing her a slip of paper. Marie-Elena's eyes grew large, indicating that there was a lot to see. And that's exactly what Chance wanted. In the examination room, he donned latex gloves as he opened one box after another. Marie-Elena left the room to retrieve more. There were hundreds of photographs, audiotapes, fabric samples, lab results...items that Chance could not even identify. But when he opened one particular plastic box, he paid exacting attention. It was just some pieces of yellow fabric, possibly a section of a shirt, that his research had pointed him to. This was the one box that Chance had come to see. All the rest meant nothing to him. But, his requests kept Marie-Elena busy. Busy enough for him to get what he needed.

When Marie-Elena came back with yet another box, Chance was standing.

"Thank you, Marie-Elena. I have run out of time and I have an appointment. I have to leave now. Thank you for your help." Marie-Elena escorted him to the front counter area and he left quickly.

· · ·

Chance's red and white floatplane sat motionless on the East River this unusually calm day. As Chance pulled the black sedan through the gate of the Skyport, two people sat near the dock waiting patiently. Chance got out of the car with open arms, ready for big hugs.

"Addie Mae! Cha-ley! How was your flight?"

"Early," said Addie Mae.

Cha-ley added, "The worst part was yesterday getting from home to Miami. It's not everybody who has to take a swamp buggy, an airboat and a bus to the airport. But today was good."

"Sorry I wasn't there to fly you guys out."

"No worries. We're here now, that's what matters," said Addie Mae.

"Well, I hate to break the news to Cha-ley, but you won't be sleeping in The Beaver tonight."

"Great! Sounds like I'll get to sleep in a comfy bed in a swanky hotel."

"You're right, Cha-ley, you will. Just not in *this* city. Your hotel is in Louisiana."

"Louisiana? What? Why didn't I go straight there then?"

"Because I have to give you this." Chance handed Cha-ley a large manila envelope. "It's fifteen thousand dollars in cash."

"Gee!" Cha-ley said, "And it's not even Christmas."

"And this." Chance handed Cha-ley a few pieces of letterhead-size paper and two bottles of water.

"Ahh, OK!" Cha-ley said as he took the items from Chance. "Is this 'cause I might get thirsty on the way to Louisiana?"

"No. These are for your trip to San Francisco."

"My trip…? San Fran…?" Cha-ley was puzzled.

"And, on your way back, a brief stop in Ohio. You should be back here by Thursday night."

"I should'a packed more underwear," Cha-ley said,

still puzzled.

"Your plane leaves in two hours."

"Hello! Goodbye!" Cha-ley said.

"And Addie Mae," Chance continued, "I booked a nice hotel for you. I'll take you to check in. Then, tonight, I need you to start worming your way into some protest groups and find out what's going on, what's planned, before it happens."

"You mean, I'm going undercover?" she said with hopeful wonderment.

"Well, yes, I guess that's what I mean."

"Cool! I just gotta figure out how to walk-the-walk and talk-the-talk."

Cha-ley chimed in, "Yeah, you'll be walkin' and talkin' and I'll be flyin' all over the country doing what, I have no idea!"

"No worries, Cha-ley. Let me explain the whole thing."

. . .

Chameleon arrived at the mobile-home-trailer he shared with Teardrop during their deadly mission. Teardrop was sitting at a table cleaning a pistol. Ammo was spilled on the table from the empty gun. Teardrop looked up at Chameleon and did a double-take.

"What the fuck?" Teardrop blurted out, "You startin' to copy me, dressed like that?" Chameleon was wearing a black tank top and khaki cargo pants. So was Teardrop.

Chameleon looked like he'd been caught red-handed. He had a tough time hiding lies. Teardrop, on the other hand, was always impossibly skeptical. Suspicious. Insecure. Interrogating.

"You know where I'm goin' today?" Teardrop asked with eyes that were drilling into Chameleon.

"Where 'ya goin'?"

"Where am I goin'? Where am I goin'?" Teardrop said with disgust. "You know exactly where I'm goin'! What I'm doin'! Who I'm meetin'! And what I'm gettin', don't you?"

"I don't know nothin'."

"You fuck! You lyin' bastard prick! You know! You know!" Teardrop loaded the gun in his hands. He stood up and pointed the gun at Chameleon.

"Tell me the truth, you lyin' fuck, or I'll kill you right now!"

"I don't know what you're talkin' about! You're crazy!"

"I'm crazy? I'm crazy? *You're* crazy! Didn't you think I'd find this?" Teardrop had a tiny piece of paper that he waved in front of Chameleon's face. "See?" Teardrop taunted. "This note! Says 2p time S tues black tank k pants. You're always write'n notes 'cause you forget shit. Like this one! The one you wrote and then dropped on the floor. Like an idiot!"

"I...I didn't...I got a call...I didn't ask for this. Not for nothin' but 'ya gotta admit..."

"Sit down!" Teardrop had the gun pointed at Chameleon's chest. "Sit there! Just sit down and shut up!" Chameleon sat down. His right eye was flitting this way and that. Down, up, right, left. His left eye didn't move.

Teardrop put the gun down on the table between himself and Chameleon.

Chameleon's right eye went to the gun. Teardrop walked around the back of Chameleon to get something off a shelf. Chameleon lurched for the gun.

• • •

Chance was still at the wheel of the car, actually enjoying the peace and solitude in bumper-to-bumper traffic on one of the many one-way streets.

He reached deep into his pants pocket and took out the blue cell phone. He pressed a few keys and soon found an app that provoked him. A recording app. He made a few keystrokes and was mesmerized.

He heard the recorded voices:

"It's time for you to step up."

"Ahh...step up?"

"Yes. Time for you to take over the operation. And I'll pay you a lot of money to do it."

"Ahh, take over? A lot of money?"

"Fifty thousand dollars."

"Fif...fifty...fifty thousand...ahh..."

"He's going to waste you. He's going to kill you and keep the money he was going to pay you. So you have to waste him. Now, you get to live, get fifty Gs and change Ameerica forever."

Chance cocked his head a little when he heard how this guy pronounced America, but the recording kept going.

The car behind him beeped long and loud and Chance zoomed forward for all of twelve feet and stopped again.

Chance listened to the recording again. And again. And again.

• • •

For some reason, it seemed especially busy in Times Square

this Tuesday afternoon. The huge digital clock behind the three-story neon billboard selling tight fitting jeans changed from 1:54 to 1:55.

He was already there. Standing at attention in his camo combat boots, khaki cargo pants, black tank top and thick white-framed sunglasses; lenses so dark they hid everything behind them. He held one hand behind him, possibly concealing something.

He waited. 1:58…then 1:59…then two o'clock.

From nowhere, a gray suit and red tie were suddenly in front of him. Big sunglasses and a mop of silver hair on top. He had a four-inch scar from his left ear toward his mouth. Under one arm, he carried a plain cardboard box about the size of a four-slice toaster.

"You know why I'm here?" is all he said.

"Ahh, you're going to give me some, ahh…bread."

"How many slices?"

"Fifty…fifty thousand."

Mr. Suit handed over the box.

"Here!" Mr. Tank Top held up a smaller cardboard box. "Give this to your…ahh, to your boss."

"A bomb?" Mr. Suit said, eyebrows raised in disbelief.

"Ahh…no bomb. A token of my appreciation for his…vision."

Mr. Suit took the box, turned, and faded into Times Square mayhem.

· · ·

Chance parked the car three blocks away and walked to the event. Then he began weaving his way through the thickening crowd of fairly docile protestors. There were twice as many as last night, most of them milling about wondering what would happen next. Much of the noise came from conversations, some soft spoken, some loud and vociferous. There were some radios playing rap music and hip-hop. There were some teenagers talking tough and even some small children running around underfoot. At this time of day, 4:00, the demonstration felt more like an arts and crafts fair…without the arts and crafts.

Addie Mae arrived by taxi, and she was a sight to behold. She was photographable in her full-length muumuu dress of orange, deep blue, turquoise and coral. There was a lot of material in her dress because it had to cover her two hundred-fifty or so lovable, huggable pounds. In her jet-black hair was a golden alstroemeria, pilfered from the hotel lobby bouquet. On her feet were her beaded Seminole moccasins that her grandmother made for her years ago. Conversation with Addie Mae was guaranteed.

As ready as Addie Mae was for conversation, the police were just as ready for confrontation. Last night's storm of thunder, lightning and rain had put a damper on the protest. But tonight was different. The weather had been beautiful all day. Now it was dead calm and getting hot. It seemed to be getting hotter by the hour. The demonstrators were growing bored. And they were growing in number. So were the police. There were police cars, lights flashing, at all detour points on the streets. There were emergency vehicles positioned at-the-ready at the end of each street in the large X pattern of the canopies and people. There were police on bicycles cruising around the periphery. There were even undercover cops sprinkled throughout the mob, antenna out for hidden weapons, or talk of looting, rioting or violence. Addie Mae had her antenna out, too. And she just might pick-up on things a lot faster than the cops. She sashayed her way, as best as she could sashay, up to Red Hat's right-hand-man. A large man, an African American man, handing out applications to join The Innercity Soldiers.

"Here you go, good lookin'! Today's the day you can become a soldier," the man said to Addie Mae.

"Do I have to wear a uniform?" Addie Mae asked with soulful eyes; Addie Mae had the softest, warmest eyes on the planet.

"Darlin', the uniform you're wearing is good enough for me."

"Well, maybe you could help me fill out this here application and answer some questions for me?"

"I'm here for you my beauty. Anything I can do to help." The man left his post just like that and stepped to the side to help Addie Mae. He wasn't about to let this recruit slip out of his hands.

· · ·

A red-ball sun sat on the tip of the Washington Monument. Dusk was on its way to D.C. A gray-haired man in a gray suit and red tie walked through an office of empty cubicles. He carried a plain cardboard box. He knocked on the open wooden door.

"That was quick," Cufflinks said.

"No traffic. No cops." He held out the offering to Cufflinks. "He wanted to give you a present for your...vision."

"Aha! He means my vision in putting him in charge. I used to think this guy with one eye was an idiot. But maybe he's not so stupid after all. How do we know it's not a bomb?"

"That's what I said. But it doesn't weigh anything.

Light as a feather. So it can't be much of a bomb."

"OK, thanks. Just leave it and I'll see you tomorrow."

Cufflinks just stared at the box for a few moments before curiosity got the better of him. He picked it up and placed it before him. He grabbed a small knife and slit the clear packing tape.

"Let's see what this fruitcake sent me," he said out loud to himself. Cufflinks opened the big flaps first. Then he unfolded the side flaps. Cufflinks' hand reached in and removed a wad of tissue paper. He didn't see anything inside the box at first, so he tilted the box toward him slightly and peered inside.

There, nestled in more tissue paper, like bird's eggs, were two human eyeballs! One was perfect, glassy, shiny. The other was fogged over, like a dead fish's eye, blood vessels hanging away from it in red strings!

An electric shock ran up Cufflinks' arms! He wanted to throw the box down, but he couldn't let go of it! His hands shook, trying to break the hold the box had on him! Finally, his hands threw the box down…as a deep guttural scream came from his contorted face! He pulled his body away from the box and fell back into his chair. The box spilled over and the two eyeballs rolled out on the desk. They stopped rolling…and they looked at him. A deadly stare. In honor of his…vision.

• • •

Nicole Jensen was in front of the camera. "It's been a surprisingly quiet day on these streets where demonstrators have established a kind of camp, sleeping under these canopies, cooking on barbecues and making it very clear to

the Mayor and the world that they're not going anywhere
until the New York Sniper is caught or killed. They've
issued a strong ultimatum: if there's another Monday
murder, the citizens of the 'City within the City' will take
matters into their own hands. The Innercity Soldiers are here
again, too. Many here just call them 'The Red Hats' because
of the bright red hats they wear and hand out to the crowd."
The video showed their tables in front of the yellow brick
building. People around them were wearing red hats. Nicole
continued: "They're calling for the occupation of the streets.
Their plan is to build an army of so-called 'soldiers'. Police
are hoping that emotions don't boil over in the sweltering
heat of the day."

Chance couldn't make his way through the throng all
the way to Nikki, but he did see her clearly from a block
away. Chance started scanning the crowd. Could he spot a
weapon in the crowd? Could he spot Chameleon? Could he
spot Teardrop? Could he spot the black barrel of a .50
caliber sniper rifle? It would certainly be pointed at him.
Would he see the sniper before the sniper saw him? Lots of
people. Lots of faces. All kinds of faces.

Chance's eyes were scanning from left to right,
combing through the crowd. Back and forth. *Wait! Go back!
What was that? Where is that face I just saw? It was just
there. Gone! There! There he is! Teardrop! Teardrop is at
the edge of the crowd! He's scanning the crowd himself.
Looking for what? For whom? Looking to communicate with
Chameleon, perhaps. He's not with The Innercity Soldiers.
Who the hell is this guy? Is he the sniper? Could be. Gotta
get a look at his shoes. Sneakers? Gotta move. Get closer.
Can't see his feet.*

Persistently moving through the slightly swaying
crowd reminded Chance of moving through the tall

sawgrass, years ago, in the river of grass, the Everglades. He progressed slowly, half-a-foot by half-a-foot, trying to not lose sight of Teardrop. *Damn it! He's moving,* Chance thought almost audibly. *Keep track. Maintain visual. So many people in the way. There he is! He's on the phone. He's moving and talking. The last time Teardrop was on the phone a building blew-up. Keep track! There! On the opposite side of the street! A guy looking toward Teardrop! He's on a phone, too!*

Then Chance spotted another suspicious looking guy on a phone. A three-way connection?

Chance, threading his way through the mass of people, was four rows behind Teardrop. Chance's height gave him away. Teardrop turned and looked directly at Chance. For the first time, Chance looked into the face of the man he had seen on video. Now live! Teardrop turned and moved quickly! Chance was after him, now two people between them. Chance looked down, head left, then right, trying to see around the bystanders. Finally, he saw Teardrop's feet. Not sneakers. Camo combat boots. Teardrop moved fast, pushing his way through the thick, almost impenetrable crowd. As soon as he went by, the crowd closed in behind him.

Chance was in a sea of voices. It was almost deafening.

Then! A bomb blast to his left!

A concussive boom that almost blew out his eardrums! A fiery explosion at the edge of the occupation! A huge ball of orange-red flame! A car hood flipped into the air! Canopies were flying, aluminum poles somersaulted into the crowd! Hundreds instantly cowered. Bodies and faces were in a freeze-frame looking in the direction of the blast!

. . .

The beige economy-size rental car was going forty-eight
miles per hour when it left the two-lane blacktop out in the
middle of nowhere and entered the dirt road, kicking up dust
behind it. Cha-ley was at the wheel squinting into a sun that
was low in the sky to the west. The clock on the dash said
4:55 Louisiana time. His flight didn't leave him much time
to get where he had to go. Thank God his destination was
only three minutes away now.

The simple painted white sign was held up by pipes
on either side of it, high enough to drive under. The letters
were black and peeling.

Tommy Crow Cemetery
Marquesses Parish
Louisiana Department of Corrections

Cha-ley turned into the driveway and spotted a very
small white clapboard building toward the center of the
twenty-some-odd-acre burial ground. As Cha-ley drove up, a
man closed the door of the little building behind him and
locked it with a key. The man was old, Cha-ley thought,
fitting for a man who watched over a graveyard. The old
man's face was weathered as much as the split boards on the
wooden landing and the three steps he was descending. He
walked carefully in his dull black dress shoes and baggy
black pants held up by polka-dot suspenders. He wore a
yellowed, wrinkled white dress shirt and a black bolo tie. His
Harry Truman era straw hat sat high on his head as he
jangled the keys to his rusty twenty-two-year-old pickup.

The old man had only one thing to say as Cha-ley
got out of the rental car.

"We're closed." The old man opened the creaky

door to his pickup.

"I, ahh, I'm sorry, I got here as fast as I could. I came here from very far away. If I could just talk with you for a minute I'd…"

"You already have. Come back tomorrow. Nine o'clock."

"Sir, I'm afraid I can't come back tomorrow."

"Then come back when you can. Or don't come back at all. Your choice."

"Sir, it's a matter of life and death."

The old man just stopped and looked at Cha-ley, like, 'you idiot'…and he said, "Just what do you think I do here all day?"

"Look, I just got off a plane from New York, I rented a car, drove as fast as I could, nothing to eat or drink, and I'm only asking for five minutes of your time. Please."

The old man looked at Cha-ley and thought for a few seconds. Maybe it was Cha-ley's British sounding accent. The old man closed his truck door.

"What in the hell is it you want that can't wait 'til tomorrow, for God's sake?"

"You have someone buried here named Angel Perez. Inmate number 999036. An inmate who died at the prison over there." Cha-ley's head motioned at the federal prison about a mile away, partially visible through an opening in the dense trees. "His body was never claimed by family so those prisoners get buried here, is that right?"

"Right. Now what in the hell is it that you want?"

"I need to get a DNA sample as soon as possible."

"You need to exhume the body?"

"Yes sir! I need to exhume the body and I have paperwork right here." Cha-ley handed a legal-size sheet to the old man who twisted his craggy, parched mouth as he scanned the page.

"And who signed this here document?"

"It's right on there at the bottom," Cha-ley said with his fingers crossed.

"Who the hell is Frank Stoneman?"

"Sir, it says under his name…"

"Special Agent. What the hell is a Special Agent? What does that mean? That doesn't say Coroner or M.E.! And besides, you need a list and approval of next of kin."

"Sir, there is no next of kin. No one to claim the body."

"Anyway, you can't get this done tonight, for God's sake. We're closed. Workers gone home. And that's where I'm goin', right now."

"Sir, I can make this worth your while."

The old man stopped. He gave Cha-ley a stare. Right in the eye. He munched his chewin' tobacco and spit on the ground. Cha-ley didn't know what this meant. Did it mean that Cha-ley would be locked up for trying to bribe a County, in this case Parish, official. Or would the old man get a shotgun out of his truck and shoot Cha-ley right now? This was the perfect place to do that.

Cha-ley looked back into the clammy eyes of the old man. Then decided to take another stab at it.

"We're desperate," Cha-ley said.

The old man hesitated. "How desperate?"

"About two thousand dollars desperate," Cha-ley ventured.

"That's not desperate enough," the old man countered.

"Three?" Cha-ley said.

The old man shook his head. "Not worth my time young man."

"Five then. Five thousand. Cash. Tonight. All I need is one tooth and I'll be on my way."

The old man thought. Then spit on the ground. Then said, "Five thousand, cash, before we break ground. Plus five hundred cash for each of my two guys."

"You got it. When can we get started?"

"Come back here at eight o'clock. It'll be dark by then."

"Eight o'clock," Cha-ley repeated, trying not to look overly disappointed. The old man patted his stomach and started to get into his truck.

"Sir," Cha-ley said.

The old man stopped and waited.

"Would you happen to have a pair of pliers?"

. . .

It was as if a freeze-frame of a video was released. Six hundred scared-to-death people turned and ran away from the bomb blast. Some were trampled underfoot. Children fell beneath the stampede. A pregnant woman tripped and fell down. Dozens of shoes dug into her back and forced her head against the pavement. Screams replaced the chanting. The car hood had fallen onto the stunned melee. It smashed the heads of three. Severed the arm of one. Smoke drifted over the crowd like a cloud-demon, choking the older folks who couldn't move fast enough.

Instead of running away from the blast, Chance tried to stand his ground and make his way toward the blast. The mass of people in front of him cleared out fast.

Then! A crash of glass! A store window was smashed! Looters scrambled into an appliance store! The manager and staff were helpless. They put up their hands in submission. Some in the crowd that ran away moments ago were now running in a different direction, carrying out window fans, room air conditioners, vacuum cleaners, even clothes washers and dryers.

Chance saw a police car engulfed in flames. An inferno. Some people were standing around it as if it were a campfire, just gawking, entranced by the flickering flames lighting up their faces. Sirens were heard and the trucks arrived, firemen sprayed foam on the carcass of the car being cremated, yelling at everyone to get back. Chance stood there, too. Tall, obvious, like a lighthouse in a storm, searching, scanning, peering for a sign of the hidden enemy.

· · ·

The headlight beams were bright cones penetrating the evening low-level fog that hung over the warm two-lane macadam road. The car dipped when the road turned to dirt. As soon as the car turned and drove under the white sign on the poles, the beams lit up the long dirt driveway that led to the little white building at the center of the cemetery. The graveyard looked different at night. The kind of place a living human had no place being after dark. Especially a graveyard filled with murderers, pedophiles and rapists. Spooky to say the least. Cha-ley strained his eyes to see what was ahead. In the headlights were three men, standing like ghosts, their feet and ankles invisible, fading into the fog rising from the ground. They stood dead-still, shoulder-to-shoulder staring straight into the headlights. It was the old man and two shorter men, one on either side of him. Cha-ley gulped as he drove the car slowly toward them. Very slowly. He muttered to himself. "Chance is not going to be happy if I don't get this tooth." He breathed hard. "He won't be happy if I get myself murdered, either."

The car stopped. Cha-ley waited. The three men waited. Finally, Cha-ley got out.

"These are my boys." The boys were about forty-five and fifty. They didn't know how to smile.

The old man laid out the palm of his hand in front of Cha-ley. He said nothing. Cha-ley laid a wad of cash in the open hand. The old man counted out the bills. But he did so very slowly. Painfully slowly. As if there was a problem. But then he said, "Let's get this over with." Cha-ley didn't know how to take that comment.

One of the men climbed up on a backhoe, the other grabbed a shovel. The old man walked and Cha-ley followed, seven rows down and two in from the driveway. That was the spot.

The grave marker was just a simple flat gray slab that could have been made of concrete. It was crudely engraved with *Angel Perez 999036 May 03, 1991*. The backhoe was already straddling the burial site, the mound long ago flattened by time. The single headlamp on the backhoe, splattered with mud and tinted with green mold, did little to illuminate the digging that was about to commence. The operator, pulling at the levers, had done this so many times he probably could have done his job in total darkness. Aside from the pitiful illumination, everything was black as ink. The backhoe's feet were out and secure on the ground. The bucket reached out, a metal hand on the end of a mechanical arm, and it dug deep into earth that hadn't been disturbed in nineteen years. The bucket swung to its right and deposited a square-yard of dirt on the driveway. Worms did a dance on top of the pile.

Another scoop came out of the hole. And another. And another. The excavation, now about three feet deep and six feet long, began to look like a grave. The bucket descended into the pit, pulled back, and a wretched scraping sound came from the hole. It almost sounded like someone calling out. The bucket was extracted. The backhoe motor was turned off, but the measly light was left on. The old man's other son grabbed his shovel and jumped into the hole, his boots making a hollow sound as they hit something buried in the ground. A casket, no doubt. The man started digging and throwing, digging and throwing, almost hitting Cha-ley in the face with the dirt that had a distinct foul smelling odor, all at once musty, moist and putrid. Old decaying fruit, Cha-ley thought. Until he thought better.

The man scraped the top of the coffin as best as he could and got out of the hole.

"Your turn," said the old man. "We're not going to mess with a dead body. If you want something, you're going to have to get to it. And you'd better get going, we ain't got all night."

Cha-ley just stood there not knowing exactly what to do next. The man with the shovel poked it at Cha-ley.

"Get the lid off, get what you want and get out," the old man said impatiently.

Cha-ley jumped on top of the casket in the black hole. He almost fell down when his feet hit. Then there was a shaft of light. One of the sons had a flashlight. It flashed into Cha-ley's eyes, making him blink and put up his arm. Cha-ley had a sinking feeling. They could kill him, keep the money and just cover him up. It would be the easiest thing in the world. No one the wiser. So what could Cha-ley do now…standing in a grave, standing on top of a coffin with a dead man inside it? What were his options?

Cha-ley started prying at a seam in the top of the casket. It was about halfway down and running across, a panel designed to be opened for viewing. The panel started to give a little. The latch on the side, buried in the moist earth, certainly would have rusted away by now. Cha-ley worked hard, sweat pouring from his face, droplets falling onto the casket like tears. Tears that were never shed for the dead man below.

Finally, the latch gave way. Rusty hinges creaked. The panel groaned and it opened. The flashlight beam, angled off to the side, now moved to the face of Angel Perez. Cha-ley's body flew back against the wall of dirt, clumps and crumbles of it falling into his hair and shirt. The face of the dead man was dark leathery skin pulled taught over the skull. Hair was long on his head and face. The eye sockets were empty. Lips and mouth were raked back, left and right, exposing huge teeth and a grotesque exaggerated ghoulish smile. It was hideous. Revolting. And the stench made Cha-ley gag and retch in spasms.

The old man spit on the ground. "Fer God's sake! Get 'er done or stay in the hole while we cover it up!" His two boys spit, too.

The old man threw something into the hellhole. It hit Cha-ley's foot. It was a pair of pliers. Cha-ley picked up the pliers and looked at Angel Perez. Cha-ley took a half a step forward and called out, "You wouldn't happen to have any gloves, would ya?"

The old man was pissed. "Willie, get the backhoe goin'. I had enough a this Yankee!" Hearing this Cha-ley laid into Mr. Perez. Cha-ley gritted his teeth, his own teeth, and tried to shove the pliers into the dead man's mouth. But Mr. Perez resisted. His mouth was clenched tighter than a tomb. Cha-ley heard the backhoe start up. He took the pliers and knocked two of the bottom teeth out and three of the top teeth. But they fell inside of the cadaver's mouth. As the backhoe bucket raised up, Cha-ley pried the dead man's mouth open, reached inside, and extracted the five teeth depositing them into his pants pocket.

No blood. No novocaine. No complaints from the patient. But a lot of torture for Cha-ley. Challenging any Olympic high jump record, Cha-ley vaulted out of the death pit. The bucket was already dumping a load on the open casket. And into Angel Perez's open mouth.

Cha-ley was dusting himself off and shaking the dirt out of his hair when two very bright flashlight beams struck him in the face.

Standing before him were two very big Marquesses Parish Police Officers.

. . .

Addie Mae was sprawled face down on the sidewalk in front of the yellow brick building. Chance was standing next to the burning police car when he spotted her. He was by her side in three seconds. She was dazed, breath knocked out of her, the flower in her hair gone. Chance lifted Addie Mae's head up off the cement and she sat upright now in an awkward position. With sirens sounding everywhere, swarms of looters yelling and rampaging, with the injured sobbing on the streets, Addie Mae looked up at Chance, vision a little blurred and out of focus. She heard nothing. Chance's mouth moved, "Are you alright?" But there was no sound. Silence, except for a strong ringing in her ears. She put her hands to her ears as if to comfort them, heal them, to no avail. Chance found a blown-over chair and helped Addie Mae into it.

Addie Mae looked around and began to cry.

• • •

"Whatcha doin? One of the Louisiana policemen asked Cha-ley, "Playin' in the dirt?"

Cha-ley just stood there.

The other officer had a lump of chewing tobacco between his lip and his gum. He spit out a long, brown, thick rope of saliva onto the ground at Cha-ley's feet.

"'Ya wanna play, you're gonna pay," he said. Then the other officer added, "Now, the question is how 'ya gonna pay? Don't matter to us, does it brother?" he said to the other officer.

"Nope. Don't matter to us. Matter to you, Hoss?" he said to Cha-ley.

Cha-ley didn't move a muscle. But his mind was going zero to sixty in three seconds. Cha-ley's heart was going the same rate of speed.

"He payin' you boys overtime?" the first officer asked the old man's sons.

They both nodded their heads.

"How much?" the other officer asked. One of them held up his hand, palm outward, fingers splayed open.

"Five hundred?" the first officer said. "Nice money for a little overtime."

The other officer said, "We're working overtime, too! And we got some dirt on our shoes…watchin' over this here sacred place…that should not be desecrated. For any reason, shape or form."

Cha-ley spoke feebly and choked out a few life saving words.

"I, ah, I could take care of the overtime. I'd be happy to."

"That'd be fine. That'd be fine. Wouldn't it

brother?"

"And appreciated," the other officer said. "I think the same pay these boys got should cover it."

"That should cover it for each of us," the first officer said.

Good thing Cha-ley had an extra grand in his pocket just in case the old man decided he wanted more. Cha-ley handed over the money.

"Got any more a that?" One of the officers asked.

Cha-ley pulled his pockets inside out. The dead man's teeth fell onto the dirt. "I'm down to five teeth."

• • •

Chance was with Addie Mae when Nikki and Chaz found them.

"Frank!"

"Nikki!" Chance said, thrilled to see her. "Are you and Chaz OK?"

They both nodded. "We didn't get much of the blast, thank God. But there are lots of people hurt bad."

Chance said, "Here's one! This is Addie Mae."

"Frank's told me a lot about you, Addie Mae."

"She can't hear you. The blast affected her hearing. At least for a while. I have to get her to a doctor."

"Two EMT busses are on the way," Nikki said.

"OK, thanks."

"Gotta go, Frank. I'm covering this live. I'll catch up with you later at my place."

"Be careful," Chance said.

"You, too."

Addie Mae had never worn makeup in her life. Ceremonial war paint, yes, but not lipstick, rouge and eyeliner. Until tonight. She wanted to do a good job as an undercover agent for Chance. And she did. But now her lipstick was smeared and her mascara had run down her face. She felt wozzy. But she was feeling a little better now with Chance at her side. She tried to speak, still unable to hear anything. Her words came out a bit slurred but understandable.

"They're here. The Outsiders are here," she said.

"The Outsiders?" Chance repeated.

She read his lips. "Yes, the ones from out of town. The ones who want to destroy the city," she said slowly.

"Do you know who they are?" Chance asked.

She shook her head no.

"Do you know what they're planning?"

"I…don't…understand."

"Do you know what…" suddenly, an EMT team appeared over them.

"Can we help anyone here?"

"Yes! Yes!" Chance said, "She can't hear. The blast hurt her eardrums."

The man and woman medics bent down close to Addie Mae and Chance moved aside to give them room.

Chance looked around the war zone. A lot of noxious smoke was drifting across the street in front of the 64th Precinct. Shards and tiny bits of window glass littered the sidewalk in front of stores. A dozen people were lying on the pavement, EMT teams at their sides administering first aid. A blanket covered a body near the burning car where the bomb exploded. A couple of people were on gurneys, rolling toward ambulances. Police had a half-dozen looters in plastic zip ties, leading them toward the station house. The canopies were crumpled in piles of white, like snow banks on the black street. Children were crying, some shoeless, some with cuts on their faces. This wasn't America. This was a place that Chance had never been to. The city where he was born. A city he didn't recognize tonight. What happened here tonight, what had been happening in this city for months, was breaking hearts across America. And from what Chance knew, this was just the beginning.

"She should be OK in a day or so." It was the male EMT. "Her eardrums were not punctured so her hearing will come back to normal. My EMT partner gave her something to calm her nerves and treat her ears."

"Thanks a lot. I really appreciate what you guys are doing."

"Just part of the job. Glad we could help. She's one of the lucky ones."

Chance crouched down and spoke to Addie Mae. "You," he pointed to her, "had better spend the night," he put the palms of his hands together next to his face, "with us," he pointed to himself and Nikki reporting on the other side of the street. Addie Mae's eyes filled up and she grabbed Chance's hand. She was thankful. Chance was thankful, too.

· · ·

Addie Mae was sound asleep on the brown leather sofa in Nikki's living room. Chance had just pulled the cover up to her chin when he heard the key turn in the lock. Nikki looked exhausted.

"Is she OK?" Nikki asked quietly.

"Yeah, she'll be fine in a day or so. How about you?" he asked.

"Beat. You must be beat too. We were all almost killed today. We're all very lucky," Nikki said.

"Yes, we are. Let's go to bed."

"No hanky-panky. I'm too tired," Nikki said.

"I wouldn't think of it," Chance said."

FIFTEEN

Wednesday Morning: Day Five

The early morning light barely illuminated the room. The cell phone next to Chance's head rang with a lion's roar. It was 5:40.

"I was wondering when I'd hear from you," Chance said, groggy from only six hours of sleep.

"I don't have much time to talk, they're boarding my flight to Frisco."

"How'd it go last night? Did you get what we need?"

"Yeah, I got it. But it was like pulling teeth. Gotta run! Talk with you later.

CLICK

Nicole was just coming out of the bathroom, dressed and ready for work.

"Up and at'em, cowboy," Nikki said to Chance, up on one elbow in bed as he put down his phone on the side table. "I have to edit footage at the studio and get to a press conference at City Hall at ten."

"Breakfast?" he asked.

"I'll grab something on the way to work."

"OK, but let's check on Addie Mae before you leave," Chance suggested.

Nikki walked into the living room putting on an earring as she walked. Chance threw on a pair of pants and was by Addie Mae's side in a flash.

"I hate to wake her," Chance said softly.

"I'm already awake," Addie Mae said, slowly opening her sleepy eyes.

Chance and Nikki smiled, "You can hear?" Chance said, surprised.

"Thank the Lord!" Addie Mae confirmed. "Miracles do happen, especially for those of us who…believe!"

"Amen!" Chance added.

Nikki had a big smile on her face. But then her face turned a little sour. A little concerned. And she asked Addie Mae, "Just when did your hearing come back?"

Chance and Nikki looked at each other.

Addie Mae just smiled.

• • •

Tom Elliott knocked lightly on the wooden door and walked up to Mayor Wertz's desk. The Mayor was reading some papers and hurriedly scratching out lines of copy with a marker.

"Mr. Mayor, did you see the hiring report and budget that you asked me and Knickerbocker to work on? I left it right there on your desk?"

"Forget that for now. Here's the script you gave me for the ten o'clock press conference. Make sure the Commissioner and other speakers have it so we don't make fools of ourselves." Wertz handed the papers to Elliott.

"But…Ed…you crossed out half the copy."

"That's right, that's right. I should have crossed out more. But, as you can see, I added copy on the sides. Get it retyped ASAP."

Elliott quickly read some of the revises.

"Ed, I know you don't want to escalate this thing but…"

"But nothing. This isn't your call. You're not the Mayor. You don't have to go out there and talk."

"I'm trying to protect you, Ed. Some of these things you've added…well, they're just not factual. If some people dig even a little bit, they'll dispute these things about us being prepared, everything that took place, that there were fewer injuries than there actually were, that you stopped things that didn't actually happen and…"

"You say if some people dig into this. You mean, like who?"

"Like reporters, for one."

"And one specifically? Like your little friend, Jensen? Is that like who? If she knows what's good for her, she'll back off. She was good for a while, but she's getting cocky again."

"Well, she's one, yeah, but it could be…"

"Jensen! She thinks she knows everything. Causin' trouble for me, for the city, just to help herself."

"Mr. Mayor, I…"

"Listen, Tom, I've been doing this longer than you've been alive. I know when to speak and when to shut up. I know when to give details and when not to. And you…"

"But Ed, they'll get you on transparency."

"Transparency? Transparency?" the Mayor was shouting, "Transparency only means something if people can see! But they're blind! They can't see what I'm trying to do here to survive. To calm things down. To get past this. And apparently you don't see it either."

"I'm only trying to…"

"Exactly what is it that you're trying to do Elliott? Exactly what? You only have this position because of me! Me! You weren't elected. Except for one vote. Mine! Now get this done. And fast!"

. . .

Chance removed the large framed picture from the living room wall and moved a table and chair to the side. He was dressed now and ready to start his work day. A day of organizing information, analyzing facts, connecting the dots and boiling things down. If he is going to catch this sniper before Monday he has to know who the sniper is today. He ripped an 18 x 24 inch sheet of paper from a drawing pad and taped it high and centered on the wall. This was the beginning of his 'Wall of Justice'. With a black marker, he wrote the word WHO? on the sheet. Below that, he taped a lineup of sheets from left to right. He wrote words on each: HATES? on the first, BENEFITS? on the second, HAS PHYSICAL ABILITY? on the third, and HAS INSIDE INFO? on the fourth. Then he started another row below that one. UNUSUAL ASPECTS/EVIDENCE on one, MAP on another, BACKUP on the third.

This make-shift crime-sleuthing organizational aid was not the historically accepted and expected one you might see in police departments or in murder-mystery movies. Chance was completely aware of the Five W Method: who, what, where, when and why, with origins dating back to Cicero in Rome around 106 BC. Chance was also aware of the Means, Motive, Opportunity work sheet. But Chance preferred a less formulaic approach. A simpler format. Ironic for a math genius comfortable with more complex systems and theories.

"Gotta go now." It was Addie Mae.

"Feeling better?" Chance asked.

"Lots. My hearing is only about fifty-percent but getting better every minute now."

"Where are you off to?"

"I have to go to my hotel and get gussied up. I didn't have a chance to tell you, I have a meeting to go to. Undercover."

"So yesterday was a bad day, but a good day," Chance asked.

"Yes. That guy…I should call him dude, I have to get into character. That dude, the big guy with The Red Hats, he took a shine to me and told me they are meeting today to talk about what happened and what happens next. This guy mentioned a second group, too. Said he would fill me in when I see him. But I don't know what happened to him after the bomb went off. Could be dead for all I know."

"Let's hope he shows up," Chance said.

"Let's hope! So I'd better look good and talk good."

"Maybe the second group is The Outsiders?"

"I hope to find out."

"Be careful. Call me if you get into a tough spot," Chance said.

"Oh, don't you worry. You'll be the first one to know."

As soon as Addie Mae closed the door behind her, Chance walked to the sheet of paper on the wall that said ABILITY?

He wrote in the name Nicole Jensen.

• • •

The telephone rang and Nicole answered. "To what do I owe this displeasure?"

"Very funny," Tom Elliott said. "You won't think it's so funny when I tell you what the Mayor had to say about you."

"Oh, is that right? I'm sure it's nothing I haven't

heard before from that ungrateful ass."

"It's not just you that turns his stomach. Now I'm on his shit list, too."

"That's impossible."

"Well, tell me if this qualifies me." As Elliott droned on, Nicole's eyebrows raised and she pursed her lips.

• • •

Cha-ley stepped off the trolley car at the top of the hill and stood directly in front of Bayfront Jewlers – Custom Jewelry, Diamonds and Dreams. He was dressed in a suit, tie and dress shoes, all rented from a nearby wedding/event clothing rental store. He carried a briefcase purchased that morning at a discount store. Summoning up all the confidence he could, Cha-ley walked into Bayfront Jewelers.

"Welcome to Bayfront Jewelers! How can I help you?"

"Greetings!" Cha-ley said with a perky tone and friendly smile, "I'd like a minute with the owner, if you don't mind."

"Well, it's your lucky day. I'm the owner."

"Perfect! This may be your lucky day, too," Cha-ley said with his British intoned Kiwi accent.

"Why is that?"

"I'm Maximilian Talbot from Unique Marketing Concepts. We're testing a new product before we launch it with ad campaigns." Cha-ley set his briefcase on the jewelry case, removed two clear plastic bottles of water and placed them on the countertop.

"The product is called Sparkling Diamond Water." Cha-ley showed the owner the label on one of the bottles.

"We'd like you to taste-test our Sparkling Diamond

Water against Brand X. Cha-ley showed the other bottle.

"We'll pay you one hundred dollars cash right now just for taking a sip or two from each and giving us your opinion. I'll video record this taste-test on my phone. Other jewelers will be queried as well. If you are chosen by our advertising agency, in about three weeks, you'll receive five thousand dollars and an appearance on a national TV commercial. A very good way to showcase your jewelry store."

The jewelry store owner raised his eyebrows and said, "That's all I have to do? Taste the water and give you my comments?"

"That's all. Just takes a few minutes."

"Let's do it then!"

Cha-ley removed the caps on both bottles and made sure the labels faced outward from the owner so the cell phone would see them clearly. Cha-ley fussed over this a bit, twisting the bottles left and right to get the right angle.

"Should I put my jacket on or comb my hair?" the owner asked.

"Not necessary at this time. This is just a…screen test, if you will. We'll be back with a camera crew and stylist to make sure you look really good in the shot." The owner stroked at his hair to smooth it out.

"OK then!" Cha-ley stood back a bit, appraised the composition on his cell phone and said, "standby…get ready…and…action!"

The owner took a sip of the Brand X water, swished it around in his mouth and swallowed.

"This Brand X," he said, showing the label to the camera, "kind of OK. Ordinary. What you might expect from, well, a bottle of water. An ordinary bottle of water." He put Brand X down, picked up the other bottle and twirled it so Cha-ley could read the label. "Now, I'll try," he read the label, "Sparkling Diamond Water." He sipped from the bottle, swallowed a bit and paused. He repeated his actions to add some drama. "Sparkling Diamond Water." He showed the label to the camera, "It has a...clarity, ahh, a brilliance, a sparkle and clean, clear taste. It's the best water I've ever tasted." He didn't know that the water from both bottles was exactly the same. He smiled broadly at the camera.

"How was that?" he asked.

"Marvelous!" exclaimed Cha-ley. "I shouldn't tell you this, but you are the best so far. You're a natural."

"Three weeks?"

"I beg your pardon, three weeks?" Cha-ley asked, perplexed.

"Until you decide. Three weeks," the owner said.

"Oh, yes, of course, three weeks. Or even less. I see no need to hesitate when we know we have the winner."

"Great! I'm available anytime."

"So...here is your one hundred dollars cash."

"Thank you."

"But first, I'm required to have you recap the bottles and place them inside these two plastic bags just in case they leak. Now, just one more thing, just fill out this form and sign the bottom. Sign here and print your name here."

As the owner signed the form, Cha-ley placed the bags inside his briefcase. He picked up the signed form and looked at the bottom.

"Well, thank you Mr...ahh...Mr. Bertram Wertz. Our authorities will be contacting you."

• • •

Nicole Jensen excused herself as she squeezed past a few

reporters already seated in the third row. Mayor Wertz was just approaching the podium. "Ahumm, ahumm," is the sound he made as he cleared his throat before speaking. "Good morning. We are here to address the events of yesterday that started with a peaceful demonstration but ended with some corrective action by our police and EMTs. About six hundred peaceful demonstrators were gathered last night in front of the 64th Precinct on an especially hot summer night. Our police department was very well prepared for the demonstration and did an excellent job of handling the large assembly. Unfortunately, a police car was set on fire and some bystanders were injured. The Fire Department quickly put out the blaze. EMT personnel tended to those injured and the streets emptied quickly with only a few demonstrators lingering for a few hours. There was some limited looting which was controlled and ended without incident. We are investigating all violent and other criminal activity and will quickly bring the violators to justice. We are expecting this to be the end of unruly demonstrations and are anticipating peaceful days ahead. The city has had more than enough unrest. It's time for peace. We'll take a few questions."

Eight hands were raised.

"OK, you, there in the back." It was one of the major network reporters.

"Mr. Mayor, how many people were injured when the police car was on fire?"

"Three."

Another reporter shouted, "One died!" It was Nicole Jensen who said this in a calm voice. The room started to buzz. Mayor Wertz glowered at Nicole Jensen.

Someone said. "Is that right, Mayor? Was a person killed? How? Did they die in the fire?"

"Yes," the Mayor responded matter-of-factly.

"It was a bomb!" It was Nicole Jensen again.
Wertz's eyes could kill. The room lit up with loud murmurs.

"Mr. Mayor, is she right? Was it a bomb?" The other reporter asked.

"We're investigating if it was a bomb or if the gas tank exploded," Ed Wertz said.

Nicole spoke up again: "The hood flew off the car when the bomb exploded. Gas tanks are in the back." She was not to be silenced.

The Mayor growled out, "Ms. Jensen, a press conference is where *you* ask the questions and *we* give the answers. That's all the questions we have time for." The Mayor walked off in an obvious huff.

The Mayor walked briskly to his office. Commissioner Brix was a pace behind. Neither noticed Tom Elliott behind them, following at some distance. In his office, Wertz turned to Brix and said, "We need to do something about that bitch! She's gone too far this time. She doesn't learn."

Then Brix suggested, "Take her off the press list. Ban her from any pressers. Make a personal call to her boss, Eric Jacoby."

"Eric Jacoby?" Wertz scowled. "What's Jacoby going to do? Fire her?"

"At least we'll be rid of her."

"Yeah, until she gets a job at another station. No, we need to get *rid* of her."

Brix stared at Wertz. Silent. Wertz started up again. "And we may as well get rid of that asshole, what's his name, Frank, too. They're probably in cahoots, thinking they're going to shag us for at least a million."

It was then that the team of Wertz and Brix noticed

Tom Elliott standing in the doorway. In a half-second the
doorway was empty.

Wertz made an upset stomach face and said sotto
voce, "Looks like we'd better get rid of that asshole, too."

"What do you suggest, Ed?"

"What do I suggest? This is your department, not
mine. This isn't your first rodeo. Be creative. All I know is
we need to get rid of her, them, once and for all. I've had
enough."

"Ed, I've always gone way over the line for you. But
this is a line I won't cross. You're on your own with this
one."

. . .

Ask anyone and they will tell you it would be impossible for
Addie Mae to look more beautiful than she did yesterday.
Until today! Addie Mae carried her two hundred fifty or so
pounds very well. Today her dress was even more colorful
than the day before. Her hair, glossy black, fell around her
shoulders as straight as an arrow since her Seminole birth.
But it was her face and smile and personality that made
Addie Mae beautiful to anyone who met her. As natural as a
warm summer morning. The hat she was wearing today
didn't hurt either. And, of course, she wore her beaded
moccasins proudly.

"This is it," the taxi driver announced.

"This is it?" Addie Mae wanted confirmation.

"This is it," he said with finality.

Addie Mae looked up at a twelve-story low-income
tenement building. What gave her pause before she exited
the taxi was that she felt just slightly overdressed for the
occasion.

"Yo, Mama! Spank me!" This was one of the more courteous comments from the men sitting on the sidewalk benches leading to the building. And this was one long sidewalk.

"*Smaackk!*" The sounds of big wet kisses came from another gentleman. "Hurt me, baby, hurt me!" was another gesture of appreciation for this fine-looking woman. To be sure, there were numerous other expressions of gratitude and recognition bestowed upon Addie Mae before she reached the entrance to the decrepit building.

Passing a mother pushing a stroller with twins while breast feeding her baby, Addie Mae entered the foul-smelling closet-size elevator and pushed the button for the sixth floor. It groaned, it lurched and took forever to rise to the level she requested. Stepping over dried vomit on the hall floor, she found number 605, took a deep breath, and knocked on the insipid green door.

In the peephole she could see an eyeball looking at her. The door opened swiftly.

"Hi!" The deep voice of the big African American man said. It was the big dude she had met at the Innercity Soldiers' table during the demonstration. He was happy to see her. Addie Mae let out a big sigh of relief, hoping later that her relief was not too obvious.

"Hi! Good to see you again," she said.

"Likewise, yeah, likewise."

Addie Mae said, "I'm sorry but I don't think I ever got your name."

"Glaad, my name's Glaad, like, 'Glad to see you' but with two a's."

Addie Mae seemed happy with this reintroduction.

"And you are…Annie?"

"Addie Mae."

"Right, right," Glaad repeated a lot.

"It's good to see you could make it. I think you'll like the group. Come on in."

The surprisingly pleasant living room was filled with people, all African Americans, both male and female. There was even a baby and a toddler present.

A hush came over the lively conversation when Addie Mae made her entrance. Glaad officiated. "Everybody, this is Addie Mae." Various hello's, hi's, and friendly welcomes came from everyone there. Glaad added, "I spent a lot of time talking with Addie Mae at the rally and…"

"Yeah, we noticed that," someone called out and the group laughed together.

"…and she wants to learn more about us and maybe help us."

"We need all the help we can get so we're happy to see you, Addie Mae." It was the young spokesman of The Innercity Soldiers she saw at the protest. He looked a bit different today in this family setting surrounded by smiling faces. Addie Mae got the feeling that these were good people. But there was a definite contradiction between what she saw and felt at the street protest and what she saw and felt now. She waited for clarity and truth to show itself.

Glaad continued, pointing with the open palm of his hand, "This is our fearless leader, Jadon Daniels." Jadon nodded in recognition.

"And his wife, Ayana, *his* fearless leader." Everyone chuckled and Ayana said, "Yeah, right!"

"You'll get to know everyone else during the meeting. One of the men got up from his seat and offered it to Addie Mae, which she accepted. The man sat on the floor.

"So, Addie Mae, is that your first and last name or

just your first name?" Jadon asked respectfully.

"Addie Mae Cypress. Everyone calls me Addie Mae."

"Cypress. Is that…?"

"Seminole Indian. From the Florida Everglades."

"Wow! Cool!" Jadon added. "I bet there's a lot of history there, huh?"

"Yes, there is. My ancestors go back to the 1700s, when they were forced deep into the Everglades by the white man's expansion from the north. We fought wars that killed many of our people but we are the only Indian tribe that never surrendered."

"My God! That sounds like us!" Jadon said. That started a chatter in the room. He continued, "Well, we are especially glad you're here. Maybe we can learn something from you," Jadon said with surprising modesty.

Addie Mae just smiled, but then said, "I don't want to interfere with your meeting, but I do have some questions if you don't mind?"

"Not at all. What are your questions?"

"The red hats you gave out at the protest, and the canopies, they must be expensive. How do you…?"

"How can we afford to pay for them?"

"Well, yes."

"Ayana is in charge of our fundraising. She does a great job of convincing people that we are worth contributing to. The company that does the hats for us gives us a really low price. Some of the canopies were donated and some were bought online cheap. A friend lets us use his big truck. And every one of us pays what you might call dues. It's actually our own contribution to the cause."

"In that case, I want to make a donation before I leave today," Addie Mae said.

"That would be appreciated, thank you. What else are you wondering about?"

"Well, I'd like to know what the Innercity Soldiers are all about. *Really* about. What is your goal? What do you want to accomplish?"

"The Innercity Soldiers, what a lot of people call 'The Red Hats', we want to bring everyone together. We, everyone in this room, everyone who wants to be part of what we're trying to do, wants to eliminate what separates us. To get our points across so we can all, blacks and whites, Asians and Hispanics, get past the issues that separate us. That would make life better for all of us."

Jadon paused to think for a moment. The room was silent. "Now, you might think from our name that The Innercity Soldiers are about war. Violence. Arming up. Hurting people. Rioting. Looting. Taking over. But The Innercity Soldiers are not about weapons. The Innercity Soldiers are about peace. Peaceful protest. Peaceful pressure. Peaceful power. And we're growing. We now have over three hundred and twenty members. We're adding more and more every day, thanks to our friend and yours, Glaad. He's in charge of signups. As you can see for yourself, Addie Mae, he's very good at it."

The room smiled and agreed with head-nods and comments.

Jadon added, "Now, another group, the one we should all be afraid of, is The Outsiders. The agitators. The professional race baiters. They're not out to help us. They're not here to bring us all together. They're not about civil rights. They're not from here, they're from out of town. They're bussed in. They're hired guns. That is where most of the riots and hatred come from. They turn us all against each other. They hate America. And they're out to destroy it.

Without America, there won't be anything left for the blacks, whites, Asians, Hispanics…anybody. When we all realize that, then you'll see us accept that we're all in this together."

No one said a word for a few seconds. They all thought about the profound words from Jadon.

Then one person in the room started clapping.

Then everyone joined in. Hands coming together for this young leader.

A man whose first name means: *God Is Heard*.

And whose sur name means: *God Is My Judge*.

· · ·

The red type crawling across the TV screen said:

NEWS UPDATE: RIOTING SUBSIDES

The woman on the screen was one of the well-known national network news anchors.

"Protestors appear to be taking the night off in New York City after last night's rioting, looting and bomb blast that left police and protestors licking their wounds. But is this the calm before the storm? Rumors on the streets say that the peaceful occupation of the streets by The Innercity Soldiers, also known as The Red Hats, will be back in full swing tomorrow. In other news…"

· · ·

"Don't tell me! You're at an airport again." Chance spoke into his phone, standing in front of his Wall of Justice.

"Driving there. But you know that. You planned my itinerary," Cha-ley replied.

"And your plane leaves in exactly forty-eight minutes."

"Very good, math genius. I've been running since I left New York."

"What do you mean? You had all that time on planes to catch your breath."

"That's the only time I had a chance to sleep."

"How'd it go with the water taste-test?"

"Sparkling," Cha-ley said with his usual Kiwi style sarcastic humor.

"Give me a call from Ohio."

"Aye, aye Captain."

CLICK

Chance turned back to his wall and began to study it. He only had one entry so far, the name Nicole Jensen on the sheet that said ABILITY. She was a good shot. He added Commissioner Brix, a trained marksman. He entered Bill Spencer in Ballistics plus his assistants, John and Pete. They know more about the weapon and The Blender Blade Bullet than anyone. He wrote the name Robert Knickerbocker. He works out, strong enough to lift a heavy weapon. He wrote the words Rogue Policeman. But he added the words 'Not Likely'.

Chance ran his finger down the list from top to bottom and shook his head. It seemed like he was nowhere.

Chance stood back and stared at the wall. An artist evaluating his painting. He went to the sheet of paper labeled HATES? In smaller letters he stroked in Sheamus O'Neill, then Arthur Stevens.

He stood in front of the sheet that said WHO BENEFITS? He thought for a moment. Then wrote…Wertz (if Wertz solves the problem that he created, he's a hero and wins reelection). Then he wrote…Innercity Soldiers (they make a name for themselves). Then he wrote…The Media. Then smaller, next to Media, he wrote…Nicole.

He stood back again, his hand to his mouth.

On the UNUSUAL ASPECTS/EVIDENCE sheet he stroked in the words Sneaker Print, Bullet Fragment: 4AP, Lovebirds, Blender Blade Bullet, Special Made Rifle, City Owned Vacant Buildings, Top of Flag Post.

He took three steps back. His eyes scanned all the sheets. He sighed.

Then he removed a stack of paper from the coffee table, went to the MAP sheet on the wall and dropped the stack on the floor under that sheet. He wrote in Sniper Locations, Protest Locations, Evidence Locations.

Without hesitation, he went to the BACKUP sheet. He taped up crime scene photos, statements, forensic reports and old newspaper articles about Mayor Wertz, Sheamus O'Neill and the cases they worked on together.

He stepped back, looked, and scratched his head. "Nowhere," he said out loud to himself.

He walked into the kitchen and poured himself a cup of coffee. He sat on the couch, sipping, engrossed by his Wall of Justice. Waiting. Waiting for the answer to come.

Chance sat there for twenty-two minutes. His coffee was gone. Drained. As was he.

He looked over at his laptop. In moments he was looking at the Mayor's City Hall staff. Bio's with pictures. He started pressing keys and printing portraits; the Mayor, Patty Bromstad, Police Commissioner Brix, Deputy Chief Wilcox, FDNY Battalion Chief Neal Waters, Tom Elliott, Phil Constantine, Robert Knickerbocker, Bill Spencer in Ballistics, Dean DiAmico of the Counter Terrorism Task Force.

Chance took a fresh sheet, wrote the words PLAYERS on it and taped it toward the bottom of the Wall of Justice. Then he taped a picture of each person's face from left to right. It made quite a show. A valiant effort. But where did it get him?

Time for another cup of coffee. Time for the couch again. And time for Chance to utter the same hollow word to himself again…

"Nothing."

Chance's gaze was broken by his phone. A call from Addie Mae.

"Good news or bad news," he said.

"Both," Addie Mae said and went on, "I had a good meeting today. The Innercity Soldiers see themselves as a peaceful power. The uniter. Bringing us all together. The real threat is from The Outsiders. They will do anything to destroy unity, the police, the Government. They hate America. They are here. Expect the city to have big problems starting tomorrow. That's all I know."

"That's a lot," Chance said. "You did a good job!"

"Thanks. Hey, I'm kind of tired after yesterday and today. If you have no objection, I'm going to bed early tonight."

"You did great! Get some rest. You deserve it. Thanks!"

In her hotel room, Addie Mae turned to Glaad and said, "See, I didn't lie!"

The room was silent. Chance just sat motionless. Still. The only thing that moved were his eyes. They studied the entire Wall of Justice, top to bottom, side to side. He focused on each picture, one-by-one, lingering on each face hoping one of them would speak to him. Tell him a story. Give him a clue. Maybe he would see something in someone's eyes. Their mouth. Their hair. Something. Anything that would telegraph a message.

Chance sat there for almost a half hour in a trance like state, the pictures burning into his eyes, until keys jangled and Nicole came through the door. She didn't even say 'Hello.' All she said was "Am I exhausted! Running around all day! How 'bout you?"

"Exhausted. Been sitting all day."

"Have you?"

"Well, yeah, sort of."

"Oh, I see!" She noticed her wall, which had become his wall.

"Redecorating?"

"Sorry, Nikki, I should have asked first. But it's all on with tape that doesn't take the paint off with it."

Nikki looked at Chance as if he had been a bad boy.

"Dinner?" he asked.

"I just want to take a shower. Like now," she responded. "Dinner, maybe later," she said.

"Sounds good," he said.

Nikki started the water running, wriggled out of her work clothes and left them in a heap on the bathroom floor. A palm-up test for temperature and she disappeared behind the glass shower door.

About one minute later, Chance walked through the same shower door.

"What took you so long?" Nikki asked.

SIXTEEN

Thursday Morning: Day Six

The room was dark and quiet. Nikki was curled up on the bed on her right side facing away from Chance. The clock read 4:10. Chance was sleeping on his back, mouth slightly open. He was deep in the REM zone, eyeballs moving beneath the lids. The eye movement became more rapid.

As if reacting to a starter's pistol, Chance bolted up in bed, an instant sit up, eyes wide open! He saw something. Something that had been 'cooking' in his subconscious mind all night. The little boy in the picture. The picture from the newspaper of the family sitting in the court room twenty-two years ago. Little Antonio Perez.

Chance's feet hit the floor, a big oversized shirt whipped over his body and he hurried to the Wall of Justice. He clicked on the side table lamp! He struggled, blinking to clear his eyes of sleep. His eyes telescoped to the little boy in the newspaper article. Almost directly below the boy's courtroom picture, was the head shot of Robert Knickerbocker.

Chance ripped both pictures off the wall, the boy in one hand, the man in the other. He placed them both on the table beneath the lampshade. Then he grabbed a pen and circled three beauty marks, dark moles, on the young boy's face. One above his right eye, one on his middle right cheek and one on the left side of his mouth.

He held the marked picture up with his left hand against the white shade. He held up the picture of Robert Knickerbocker with his right hand…

The beauty marks all matched perfectly!

It was the same person!

Robert Knickerbocker is Antonio Perez!

Chance turned suddenly as if jerked by invisible strings. He scanned the wall, his eyes coming to the UNIQUE ASPECTS/EVIDENCE sheet. There it was. The enlarged picture that abruptly came to mind. It was the cell phone shot he took of the bullet fragment with 4AP scratched into the bottom.

Within seconds, Chance tore all the sheets off the wall except for the one with the word WHO? on the top. Below that one, he placed the pictures of young Antonio, Knickerbocker, and the blowup of the bullet fragment.

He wrote under the bullet 4 Angel Perez

"Can't sleep?" Nikki said in her bathrobe.

"I think I may have found the sniper," Chance said with a resolute look on his face followed by just a hint of a smile.

"Look!" He showed Nikki the pictures and pointed out the beauty marks.

"Knickerbocker?" she said, not believing.

"Knickerbocker," he said, confidently.

"But…why?"

"That's what I have to find out. This doesn't prove that he's the sniper, it only proves that he's the boy in the picture. The boy of the father who Ed Wertz sent to death row twenty-two years ago. So far, this is just circumstantial. It really doesn't prove anything. I have to know what happened between this picture and this picture. I have to connect a bunch of dots together to bring a strong case."

"How can I help?"

"Where will you be today?"

"There's a special update for media at City Hall at

ten."

Chance said, "I don't trust Wertz. I'll call you just before you go in. I'll be nearby."

"Thanks, that'll make me feel a lot better."

"Now, let me show you a few things." Nikki followed Chance into the bedroom. Next to his luggage was a khaki duffle bag. He put it on the bed and opened it.

"This is my tool box."

From the bag, he removed a spider-like set of ropes. There were three strands, each about eighteen-inches long and all joined at one end. A rock was tied at the other end of each rope.

"This is my bolo. You swing it over your head and throw it. It grabs the legs of deer to stop them in their tracks."

"Like a boomerang?"

"Sort of. But *this* is a boomerang." Chance removed a large black boomerang from his bag and laid it on the bed.

"Here's my spear gun. Can't live without it." He placed it on the bed.

"These are my knives. One for throwing, one for plunging, one for slicing, one for tearing, one for bone, one for scaling and filleting fish, one small one for hiding in a small place, one for cutting brush like a machete."

"My God! They look deadly!"

"Well, here's the deadliest weapon in my bag."

"It's just a…club," Nikki said.

"It's not *just* a club. It's made of the hardest wood on the planet. Burled ironwood. It has a bulging knob on one end. It has a no-slip texture on the shaft. It's balanced for throwing, striking, poking."

"I wouldn't want to get poked by that!" Nikki said with a grimace.

"And I have a few other tricks up my loin cloth, too."

"Yes, I've seen some of those tricks," she said.

Then Chance removed something else from the bag. Not a weapon. A necklace. He slipped it over his head.

"A necklace!" Nikki said.

"A *special* necklace. My good luck charm," Chance said.

"What are these?"

"These are diamondback rattlesnake fangs."

"Still poisonous?"

"The poison is dried up. But some residual venom may still be in there. Don't want to find out."

"Don't fall asleep on them."

"And these are rattlesnake tails. Not the best things to have when you want to sneak up on somebody." He shook them. *Chuuka chuuka chuuka.*

"And these are alligator teeth."

"My God, they're huge, how did you get them?"

"Well, that's a…" Nikki joined with Chance and it became a duet, … "long story."

"Now, I have a lot of research to do," he said.

"And I have to get to the studio early so I can get a few things done before I go to see Wertz. Maybe I should bring one of your knives with me."

"Not a good idea. I won't be far away."

With that, necklace around his neck, Chance went to work at his laptop.

Nikki went to work.

When Chance typed in the name Antonio Perez, every Antonio Perez in the world, or so it seemed, popped up on the screen. Except the one he was looking for.

The best place to start a search for a boy, Chance concluded, would probably be with the boy's mother, Rosalina Perez. *Where is Rosalina now? Did Rosalina work and if so, where? Did they move when Angel Perez was transferred to a Louisiana prison? What is Antonio's birth date? Did he go into the military? How did he learn about weapons? Computers? What was the Perez's address at the time of the sentencing?* Of course, all these questions could be answered quickly if anyone could get an injection of sodium pentothal into Robert Knickerbocker.

The hours went by fast and furious. Chance thought the keyboard would wear out before he finished. He took dozens of screen shots and pages of notes. By 7:30 A.M., he had gleaned information from death records, school yearbooks, the Riker's Island Correctional Facility, newspaper articles, court records, and legal judgments against a pedophile warden and a corrupt prison guard gang. Like a math problem, the elements started adding up.

• • •

The sun was just starting to peek over the top of the building in Ohio's central time zone as Cha-ley walked up to the large glass doors, briefcase in hand. In large gold-leaf letters glinting in the early light it said:

GLOBAL DNA DIAGNOSTICS CENTER
Independent State-of-the-Art DNA Testing
for the World

In the lobby, Cha-ley walked the thirty feet up to a curving mahogany reception desk. Just as he was about to introduce himself to the attractive brunette sitting there, he heard a voice behind him.

"Mr. Hastings?"

"Yes. Good morning. You must be Dr. Strand."

"Yours truly."

"Thanks for meeting me so early," Cha-ley said appreciatively.

"No problem at all, we work 24/7. I was expecting you. And since this is an extreme rush, we had better get started. What do you have for us?"

Cha-ley opened his briefcase on the reception desk and handed Dr. Strand the plastic bag containing the two water bottles. Then he removed a plastic bag containing a piece of yellow fabric. "We're looking for a match." Dr. Strand accepted the two samples without comment.

"And…" Cha-ley continued, "we are hoping that the DNA on the water bottles and fabric do not match these." Cha-ley handed over a plastic bag containing five human teeth.

"Anything else," Strand queried?

"Nope. That's it."

"Now, just to reiterate our expedited rush service, we're looking at approximately six hours and you're looking at double our normal charge."

"Yes, sir," Cha-ley said crisply, "and I have the cash with me and can pay up front."

"Excellent! In that case, we'll see if we can get this done in less than six hours."

"I'll wait," Cha-ley said. He took a seat. A comfortable seat.

· · ·

By 8:30 A.M., Chance was at City Hall walking up to Patty

Bromstad's desk.

"I knew I'd find you here early," he said.

"I get here an hour early and I leave an hour early 'cause I live in Jersey. One of the perks of working for the Mayor for so long."

"Hey, I've been trying to find Bob Knickerbocker's address everywhere, but I haven't been able to. Would you happen to have it?"

"Ahh, I think I might have written it down somewhere. Let me see." Patty began to rummage around in her desk drawers. He lives just across the park, you know."

"No, I didn't know," Chance said. "I'm just curious, why is his the only address I couldn't find in the emergency contact information file? All the other key executives are in there."

"Well, I don't know," Patty said, still looking. "When he started, he had a P.O. Box. I guess he never updated the file."

"That's kind of odd, dontcha think, since he's in charge of the Digital Department."

"You know what they say, the shoemaker's children never get their shoes fixed. Oh, here it is!" Patty found a notepad-size piece of paper with the address written large across it. "Speaking of the shoemaker, I should have filed this a long time ago."

Chance wrote the address on a fresh piece of paper. He really didn't have to write it down. He knew it by heart. It was 321.

"I'll tell Bob you were looking for him, Frank. Or you can tell him yourself, he usually gets here about nine after going to the gym by his apartment."

"No, no, that's OK. Bob did a favor for me and I, uh, I want to send him a gift card as a thank you. I want it to be a surprise. So…"

"Mums the word," she said holding her index finger up to her lips.

The clock over the security check-in point said 8:37. Outside, Chance strode down the steps and looked across the park. He saw a man jogging through a light rain toward the large fountain. Chance's telescopic vision zeroed in on the figure. It was Robert Knickerbocker. Chance jogged quickly to his right, in a wide circular pattern, trying to avoid Knickerbocker. Chance was in line with the fountain when Knickerbocker reached the far side of it and continued to City Hall.

Chance's jog turned into a run directly for 321. Knickerbocker bounced up the stairs two at a time and walked through security without even breathing hard.

Chance was in front of 321 standing in the light drizzle staring at the sidewalk, searching for something. He walked out to the curb and looked to his right toward the corner. He could see the sign for Silver's Super Gym. The entrance doors to 321 were up a few stone steps and inset a bit. There it was! Wet sneaker prints! The design Chance had been searching for. They matched the image in his memory. An exact layover print.

A human form flashed by Chance. A young man going to the front door. He had keys. He entered. And before the automatic door-closer-mechanism could latch the door, Chance grabbed the door and he was in!

Not eight feet past security, Knickerbocker heard his name called. "Hey, Bob!" It was Phil from the office next to his.

"Hey, Phil, what's up?"

"I hurt my back throwing a football with Mikey and it hurts like hell, right here. I don't know if I can work today. You exercise all the time so I thought you might have some advice on stretching or somethin'."

"Show me again where it hurts, exactly." Knickerbocker and Phil Constantine stood in the rotunda going through gyrations for a good ten minutes.

Chance was standing in a hallway at 321. He needed to know which apartment was Knickerbocker's. Having been a respected young math genius at NYU, it was easy for Chance to close his eyes and create a three-dimensional wire-grid display in his mind – based upon the visualized trajectory of the bullet when he looked through the hole in the ball at the top of the flagpole. He saw himself coming through the entry door downstairs, walking up the flights of stairs to the third floor, walking to the middle of the hall and standing still, facing the end of the hall. In his mind's-eye he was visually plotting the streets outside, the street corner, the park across the street...he could 'see' the direction of City Hall. He plotted the trajectory of the bullet from the flagpole to the perch of the sniper. With his eyes still closed, he backed up four paces and stopped. He turned to his left ninety-degrees. When he opened his eyes, he was looking at a wooden door. Number 302.

"Thanks, Bob," Phil said with one arm cranked around to the small of his back. "I'll try what you said and see how it goes."

"You should feel better in two weeks. If not, you'll have to go to a doctor."

"OK. I'm going home. See 'ya tomorrow."

Knickerbocker walked down the hall, turned right at the end and saw Patty Bromstad standing at some filing cabinets.

"Morning, Patty."

Patty closed the drawer to the file cabinet.

"Good morning, Bob."

Chance saw a space at the bottom of the door. Light was coming through it. He got down on his knees, put his head as close to the floor as he could, and tried to see into the room. A chair leg was blocking most of his view, so he dog-walked forward a foot. There, stacked in a corner, was a box marked AERONAUTICAL DRONE – Load Delivery Capable. And on top of that, an odd shaped box marked with a generic *Thank You! From your local pet shop!*

"Hey, if you want, I'll be happy to scan those files for you and save you some room in here," Bob Knickerbocker said to Patty.

"These are original signed documents the Mayor wants in their original form. But thanks anyway."

Knickerbocker looked down on Patty's desk and saw the paper with his address on it.

"Patty, uh, why do you have my address on your desk? Sending me something?"

"No, not me. But…"

"But what?"

Patty resisted. "I, I don't want to spoil the surprise. I promised to keep it a secret."

Knickerbocker's face showed that he was thinking hard. Fast. He said, "I'm going out of town. I won't be home. And people have had their mail stolen at my apartment building lately. So why don't you tell me and I can thank whoever it is before I leave town?"

"Well, it's…"

Knickerbocker was hanging on every second of her hesitation.

"It was…Frank Stoneman."

Robert Knickerbocker's eye's widened. His nostrils flared. His face turned red.

He turned, walked fast, and broke into a jog before he exited the building.

Chance, on all fours, nearly bumped into the worn black shoes and spindly legs. The old woman, ninety-four years of age, stood before him like a monument, even though she was only four-feet-eleven. Chance hauled his six-foot-five-inch frame up from the floor and towered over her. She wore a forty-year-old dark flowered dress and a white lace fringed apron. Her gray hair was in a bun and she had a dried-apple face. She held a cane in her right hand. Chance thought she was going to hit him with it. She was not happy.

"How did you get in here?" she snarled.

"I…ah...the door was…"

"Robert told me to watch out for people like you!" she growled. "What are you doing here?"

"I came to see Robert and I, ah, dropped my contact lens on the floor. I was looking for…"

"You'd better get going or…"

"Yes, ma'm, no problem. I'll come back when Robert's home."

"I'll tell him you were lookin' for him as soon as I see him."

"Thanks. Thank you. Very much," Chance was laying it on thick. He moved toward the staircase. The old woman opened her apartment door and shuffled inside.

Knickerbocker was jogging across the lawn of the park. The rain had stopped and the sun was peeking through dark clouds. From out of the blue, an airborne flying disc almost hit him in the face. At belt level, two dogs crashed together for the disc. Knickerbocker tumbled onto wet grass.

The old woman reached out for something on her round table covered with a yellowed-lace tablecloth. It was a picture of her face next to Knickerbocker's face, cheek-to-cheek, in front of a cake with a big red 94 on top and one big candle. They were both smiling. She opened the lid of a small white box that looked like a miniature grand piano. The music box played a song for her. She closed her eyes and smiled. The music stopped. The room was silent. She cocked her head and turned up her hearing aid. She hurried out the door, cane helping to steady her. Her eyes bore down on Chance, standing at the top of the stairs looking intently below. Coming up fast, at the second floor, was Robert Knickerbocker.

Chance was waiting to pounce. Knickerbocker was rising two steps at a time.

A screeching, crackling voice assaulted Chance's right ear. "Robert!" the old lady screamed, "Your friend is here!"

Knickerbocker stopped dead in his tracks. He turned and bolted for the front door. Chance's body took a slight involuntary movement back before launching himself toward the first stair-step down. The old lady thrust her cane between the vertical banister supports across his path. He tumbled ass-over-head down the steps sprawling flat on the landing, breath knocked out of him. Knickerbocker was out the door. Chance bounced up as if on a trampoline and sprinted down the stairs two and three steps at a time. The front door flew open, glass almost breaking, as Chance burst onto the sidewalk, head twisting, eyes searching frantically. To no avail. Nothing.

He noticed something on the street in the direction of City Hall. A manhole cover was removed, pushed to the side. He raced toward the hole. But ten feet away from it, a taxi drove right into it and stopped. Its front wheel was half swallowed.

"Shit!"

Chance ran to the front of the car, grabbed under the front bumper, and attempted to extricate the vehicle. A few people saw him try this impossible feat. They did nothing. But then, a young man was at Chance's side, helping. Then another man. And another. And yet another. The taxi driver gunned his engine. "Easy! Easy!" Chance advised. "Slow and steady."

The wheel grabbed the edge of the hole. The car slowly moved upward and backward.

"Thanks!" Chance said to his helpers just before jumping into the hole and climbing down a metal ladder.

All the helpers just looked into the hole and scratched their heads.

Twelve feet down, Chance's feet and ankles disappeared into a black-brown goop. The New York City Sewer System.

The open manhole cover allowed just enough light for Chance to see that a layer of water skin-coated the sludge. It was flowing slowly in one direction. Comparing both sides, left and right of the ladder, Chance could make out a slight difference on the surface to the left. There was a telltale swirl or trough, a disturbance on the surface. It was moving with the direction of the flow. North. So was

Knickerbocker. And now, so was Chance.

. . .

At 9:45, Nicole Jensen passed through security and walked down the hall to the Blue Room, the usual location of nearly all press conferences. The place was empty. The only footsteps that she heard were her own. It seemed eerie. She stopped mid-way, getting nervous. She grabbed her phone and called Chance. No answer. She bit her lip but continued on.

She walked through the open doors of the Blue Room and saw the usual setup of folding chairs. No one was at the podium. No cameras, no microphones. No one. Just her.

"Ms. Jensen." She turned. It was the Mayor.

"Your e-mail said ten o'clock," Nicole said. "Was the time changed?"

"No. The time is right."

Nicole gave him the curious cocked-head look of a puppy.

Wertz continued, "The update conference is just between you and me." Nicole's eyes moved past the shoulders of the Mayor to the doors and hall. There were two cops stationed to the left of the doors. And two more cops on the right.

The Mayor closed the doors.

They were alone in the Blue Room.

. . .

Chance left the circular spotlight from the manhole shaft and waded into the watery black tunnel. It was round, eight-feet in diameter, and lined with red brick mortared into place in the 1930s. Chance's fingertips tapped along the rough surface of the brick walls. About ten feet in, where the last vestiges of light from above faded to black, the walls seemed to move on both sides. Chance thought his eyes were playing tricks on him. As his eyes adjusted to the darkness, he could see a thousand cockroaches moving away from his right hand and another thousand retreating from his left hand. He trudged on regardless, thankful that the darkness quickly took away his sight. Like a blind man reading Braille.

• • •

"Is this another one of your tricks, Mr. Mayor?" Nicole questioned in disgust.

"My tricks?" The Mayor retorted, "My tricks? I don't play tricks or games, but you do. And they're stopping as of now. I've had it with your nonsense."

"Nonsense?"

The Mayor didn't break stride: "You deliberately undermine me! In fact, you undermine the entire city!"

"Listen, it's obvious you are not giving us all the facts, hiding things from the people and the press. Did you really think that would work? If I didn't call you out, others would have."

"Oh, but *you* had to be the one. We had an agreement that you would lighten up. Not be so aggressive. Let things lie. But…"

"Lie is the right word." Nicole spit out the words now. "That's the way you play the game. How you…"

"You're done! And so is that blonde boyfriend of yours."

"He's not my boyfriend, for God's sake!"

"And I intend to prove that you're in cahoots with him, a conspiracy to con me and the city out of millions of dollars!"

"What!"

"He's not going to catch anybody! And he and you share a million bucks! You're in shit so deep you'll never get out!"

. . .

Chance was in shit so deep he thought he'd never get out. Up to his knees now. Every ten feet or so, he would stop and listen intently. If it is possible to 'strain one's ears', he tried. Ten more heavy steps forward and he stopped again. This time he heard something faint. A sloshing. Rhythmic. Then…nothing. This wasn't the first time in Chance's life that he found himself in a mysterious, dangerous place in which he had no desire to be. He was literally thrown into the Everglades, the American jungle.* And he survived. Eventually, he even thrived. Here, the almost total silence, the total darkness, changed everything.

. . .

In the Blue Room, Wertz was spitting out venom and Nicole was doing her best to avoid the poison, but still stand her ground. Finally, Nicole blurted out, "We already know who the sniper is!"

Wertz stopped in mid-sentence and waited. Silent.

"Knickerbocker," she said flatly.

---

* To find out how Chance was literally thrown into the most impenetrable part of the vast Everglades, read SAVING AN INNOCENT MAN, the first of the SAVING SERIES of thrillers.

"Knickerbocker?" The Mayor was incredulous. "Knickerbocker?" he repeated. "Now I know I'm being conned! Holy shit! Knickerbocker!"

"Chance can prove it!"

"Then why hasn't he? Why hasn't he come to me and the Commissioner with evidence?"

"Because he's getting more evidence. Irrefutable evidence. If we speak too soon, we could lose Knickerbocker."

"And where is Frank now?"

A loud and rapid knocking on the door interrupted the boxing match.

The Mayor, pissed at the intrusion, swung the door open with force. "What is it?" His face was red and sweating.

"Mr. Mayor, I'm sorry." It was a police officer. "We're afraid you may be in danger. Two men went down a manhole at the other side of the park. They may be terrorists and they could get to City Hall through some old access tunnels."

Nicole and the Mayor looked at each other.

"What did they look like," the Mayor asked.

"One had dark hair and one had long blonde hair."

The Mayor and Nicole looked at each other again. Wertz picked up his phone and pushed a speed dial number. The name Brix popped on the screen.

"Yeah, what's up?"

"Meet me at the DEP (NYC Department of Environmental Protection) as soon as possible. We have two rats in the sewer."

. . .

Chance was slogging forward, faster now. The rhythmic
sloshing he heard must certainly be Knickerbocker. What
else could it be, he thought? But Chance now heard a
different sound. A chirping. Not a bird. Rats! These were not
your average house rats, or forest rats, or even jungle rats.
These were filthy, parasite and disease-ridden rats. They
weren't used to sharing their disgusting, putrid home with
humans. Chance could hear them, but he couldn't see them.
One jumped on his shoulder and shrieked in his ear. Chance
shrugged it off. Then another jumped on his chest, near his
neck. He brushed it away, hoping its filthy, germy nails
didn't break his skin.

Chance moved on, the thick sludge straining his
legs. His fingertips tapping the sloping brick wall.
Cockroaches running.

. . .

"This is Duncan Arroyo, Chief Engineer for the DEP."
Mayor Wertz did the introductions for Nicole, Brix and the
officer who had reported to the Mayor. Then the Mayor
reiterated the urgency of the meeting: "Duncan, as I told you
on the phone, there are two men who entered the sewer
system and we need to find them ASAP. We have reason to
believe that one of them may be the sniper and the other
could be Frank Stoneman, the Special Agent we hired to
catch the sniper. They got into a manhole by City Hall,
outside the park on Broadway. What can you do to help us?"

Duncan pressed a few keys on his keyboard and a
schematic of the sewer system appeared on his very large
screen. It was the entire system. A few more taps and the
screen isolated lower Manhattan. A few more taps and there
was the exact manhole on Broadway.

"So this is the point where they entered, right?" Duncan asked.

"Yes, that's it," the officer said.

Duncan continued: "So they could have gone north or south. Does anyone know which way they went?"

"One of the witnesses said he thought they went north."

"Is that for sure?"

"You know how eyewitnesses get confused," the officer responded.

"OK, let's assume they went this way. North," Duncan said. "How long have they been down there?"

The officer looked at his watch. "About forty-five minutes."

"OK, so if they did go this way, they would probably be around…here." Duncan enlarged the diagram and then pointed.

"That doesn't look very far from the manhole," the Commissioner said.

"Well, it isn't," Duncan responded, "but you have to remember it's pretty much pitch black down there and creepy. They won't be going fast. They can't see much. It takes about a half-hour to forty-five minutes for our eyes to adjust. After that it's amazing what the human eye can make out. Not like a cat's eyes, but surprisingly good."

"Even in no light at all?" Wertz asked.

"Well, let's say in very little light. The quick explanation is it depends on the cones and rods in the retina. The cones can only adjust so much, but the rods are much more sensitive. They take much longer to be receptive to little bits of light. It could take hours. But once they adjust, they can see quite a lot in almost total darkness."

At this very moment, eighteen feet below the

surface, Chance was starting to see faint dark shapes. A brick pattern under his right hand. A barely perceptible tunnel shape before him. And, unfortunately a few rat shapes to his sides and in front.

"And," Duncan continued "it's not totally dark everywhere down there. Some light comes in from storm drains."

"Storm drains are part of the sewers?" Nicole asked.

"Yes, we have a combined system. Rainwater from street drains can overflow into the sewers. Some light does penetrate into the sewers here and there. For example," Duncan pointed to a spot where two large pipes feed into the main one, "right here, where three pipes connect."

Chance was starting to see more and more as he plodded on. At first, he thought his eyes were adjusting surprisingly well. Then he saw the reason for his improving vision. The light filtering in from the outside at street level. He was just about to step into a much larger space, a sort of room, where two large pipes fed into the stream of sludge and waste he was in. The 'room' had a vaulted ceiling of intersecting brick arches reminiscent of an ancient church. Beautiful in its own way. But as he entered into this mysterious, totally unexpected place, the flow of effluent and floating objects increased. He saw things that turned his face ugly and almost made him gag. Small logs of feces floated by. Dead mice. A condom. A hypodermic syringe, needle sticking out ready to impale anything in its way. A live small baby turtle, the kind you buy for a buck at a pet shop, probably flushed down the toilet along with the six dead goldfish that drifted by. That was all bad enough, but Chance didn't expect to see a dismembered finger. And worse, various parts of a baby. A human baby. One perhaps just born. This reached deep into the heart and soul of tough man, bad-ass tracker Chance. He closed his eyes to give them a rest from such a painful sight. Or perhaps to offer a moment of peace and love for a child's life taken and disposed of in such a heinous, ungodly way. Chance took in a deep breath of the stinking, foul, putrid, germ-laden air.

"They should be right about here by now," Duncan said, pointing to the confluence of the three pipes. "There happens to be a storm drain right here."

"So they can see things?" Nicole asked hopefully.

"Yes. But maybe they don't want to. There's some pretty nasty stuff down there. Most of it, no one should see," Duncan said regretfully.

"Like?" Nicole asked innocently.

"Like…anything and everything people flush down toilets. Dead or alive. 1.3 billion gallons flow through our sewers every day. You can't even imagine what's down there."

"I've heard that there are alligators down there. Is that true?" Nicole asked.

Duncan looked at the Mayor, then spoke. "Well, that's something that has been reported and talked about as myth, legend, rumor, and tall-tales for years. In fact, since 1932. We don't talk about it much in this department."

"But," Nicole pressed, "just between us, is there any truth to it?"

Duncan paused, thought, and opened a file drawer on the side of his desk. He pulled out a sheaf of papers and photographs.

"Back in the 30s, there were many reports of people finding two-foot alligators in and around the system that existed back then. Here are some photos taken back in the day. Even with these pictures, and many others like these, the reports were disputed and accused of being faked. There's a long history of reports and people who debunk the reports. In July of 2013, a report said a live alligator was pulled from the sewer around Central Park. It was approximately eight feet long." Duncan produced a photo of the creature hanging, dead, from a tripod. "The report said they cut open its stomach and found the remains of rats and two dogs." Nicole's face was one of both amazement and incredulity at the same time. "But, here again, we don't know for sure if the picture was faked."

Nicole added, "I heard someone say that it's too cold in the winter for them. That they can't digest food if the outside temperature is below fifty-five degrees. So how is it possible for them to survive?"

Duncan explained, "Our combined system includes water mains, storm drains, sewer pipes, gas lines, and one hundred and five miles of steam pipes that deliver three-hundred and fifty-degree heat to eighteen hundred buildings. The steam system was started in 1882 and today it's the largest steam heating system in the world."

"My God, I didn't know that," the Commissioner admitted.

"You think that's big? We have over six thousand-eight hundred miles of sewer pipes."

"Wow, how do you manage all that?" Nicole asked.

"With more than six thousand department employees. I'm just one."

Chance turned his head away from the steady stream of horrific flotsam and set his gaze toward the opposite side of the main tunnel. He didn't see it at first because the tunnel faded into darkness at that point, about forty feet in the distance. But he saw a hint of a shape that provoked him to keep staring, waiting for his eyes to regain some of the ocular adaptation he lost due to the light from the storm drain. He persisted, albeit patiently. In a minute or so, he was more convinced of what was there. A man! Knickerbocker! His body pressed against the wall conforming to the curved shape of the tunnel, turned away to hide his profile.

"It doesn't have to be this way," Chance called out, his voice reverberating in the large round chamber.

There was only silence.

"It doesn't have to be this way, Antonio."

Hearing his real name made Knickerbocker turn his head toward Chance.

He said nothing.

"Yes, I know, Bob…Antonio. I know what happened to you and your family."

A ghostly voice came from the darkness. "You don't know anything!"

"I know what happened after Wertz sent your father, Angel, to death row."

"He destroyed my family! He destroyed me! So I had to destroy him!"

Chance shouted back, "By shooting innocent police officers? Is that the way you destroyed Wertz? Why didn't you just kill him?"

"Kill him? Kill him? You mean one shot to the head and it's over for him? Nice and quick?"

Chance just waited. Silent.

Knickerbocker spoke again. "Twenty-two years! Twenty-two years of a slow death! For me! Twenty-two years of torture! For me! Twenty-two years of no family! No father! No mother! No wife! No kids! And he gets one bullet to the head? No! No fucking way!"

Chance went slow. "Why did it have to be cops?"

"Wertz's family are the cops...the city. That's all he knows. That's all he wants. So I took it away. Those two white cops, the first two I took out, were the sons of the two cops who helped Wertz put an end to my father's life. And my mother's. And mine. So I took their's."

"OK, I get it. But why all the others? What did they have to do with anything?"

"Ever hear of Rikers Island? Ever hear of a warden named Titus Washington? They called him 'Tight Ass Washington'. Because that's what he liked. He liked me. Him and his gang of jailers. Wertz did that to me. They fucked me over alright. Now, after all these years, I get a chance to fuck Wertz!"

"So killing cops is your way of getting even? Your way to destroy Wertz?"

"You got it! At this point, I don't give a shit who goes down. How many die. Including you."

"Antonio, look, it doesn't have to end this way," Chance implored and continued, "your father wouldn't want..." Chance's sentence was broken by a sudden, loud, wet spray and hissing behind him. He turned quickly, recognizing an all too familiar face. A ten-foot alligator, mouth fully agape, was three feet away from him. He could see monstrous teeth dripping with the thick, brown, greasy sludge it wallowed in. Its eyes were firey-orange, satanic fury, burning with the flame of its demonic ancestry. This was raw primitive instinct preserved for over thirty million years.

Chance did not recoil from the greenish-black monster. That only infuriated the demon even more! Instead, Chance slowly removed his long-sleeved white shirt revealing a turquoise tank top underneath. His rattlesnake necklace was still around his neck. He hoped the beast noticed the two huge alligator teeth hanging there. A trophy from a fight with a gator almost twice as long as this one.

Chance knew that alligators have a biting force of almost three-thousand pounds per square inch. A lion or tiger has a mere one thousand PSI. But Chance also knew that an alligator, ironically, has almost no strength in *opening* its huge mouth. Chance draped his shirt around his shoulders leaving both hands free. He reached out above the gaping jaws with his right hand and taunted the enormous reptile. The gator raised its head a bit, targeting Chance's hand. Rapidly, Chance swung his left hand through the animals open mouth. The gator snapped its jaws closed with a thunderous chomp. Polluted water sprayed everywhere. Chance did the action again…right hand above the head of the gator, almost hypnotizing it, swinging his left hand through the open mouth. Again, the deadly maw clomped shut. This time, both of Chance's hands grabbed the behemoth's mouth and held it closed easily. Swiftly, Chance jumped onto the gator's back, held its jaws closed with one hand, and wrapped the shirt around the jaws with the other. Carefully, quickly, Chance tied the gator's mouth closed and let go like a rodeo star tying a steer.

"You're lucky I don't need any more teeth for my necklace!" Chance said to the monster. The alligator blinked a couple of times as if to say, 'What the hell just happened?'

Chance looked over to the other side of the tunnel. Knickerbocker was long gone.

"Duncan," Mayor Wertz said, apparently tiring of Nicole's curiosity, "I appreciate learning about nature and the history of the New York Sewer System, interesting stuff, but I have two people to catch." He glanced at Nicole who had her eyes furrowed in laser-beams on Wertz. The Mayor revised his words: "I mean we have two people to find and get out of the sewer before the wrong one goes missing." Nicole smiled with her mouth only.

Wertz rattled on: "So, here's what I'm asking, Duncan, where would I put a SWAT team, who don't know the sewer system, to go down and ferret out these guys?"

Duncan turned to the screen, "I would put a few, not too many 'cause they'll end up tripping over each other, say four in the team, moving south…and I would put them down a manhole here," he said pointing to a spot on the diagram about eight miles from City Hall. "I'd say around 86th Street on the Upper East Side. And I would also put a team of three around Wall Street going north. They'll move faster than the team of four."

"You think we need two teams, Duncan?" Wertz asked.

"I would, for safety's sake. If the two guys you're searching for turn and run back, you want another team to stop them, pinched between the two teams."

"Good thinking, Duncan. Wertz then turned to Commissioner Brix. How fast can we make this happen?"

"As soon as I make a call," Brix said.

"OK, good." The Mayor tugged on Brix's arm and pulled him to the other side of the room. Wertz spoke so only Brix could hear.

"Tell the teams if they should happen to shoot the wrong guy, or both guys, they will not be held responsible."

Brix's face was expressionless.

Chance was moving more quickly now, trying to close the gap between himself and Knickerbocker. Even for Chance's strong legs, it was an effort getting through the mire.

Chance took a step forward and a spout of water poured over his left shoulder. It felt warm and clean. It sprang from the mortared seams in the brick wall. Another step and another spout of water. This one on his head and face. He held up his hands and rinsed them off.

Two steps further and he felt something hot on his face. So hot, he ducked down away from it. Steam, emanating from a crack in the wall.

Forty soggy paces downstream, he stopped to listen for any sign of Knickerbocker. Total silence. Knickerbocker could be waiting in ambush in the darkness ahead. Being an expert tracker, Chance knew how to move exceptionally quietly. But concern for a madman lurking ahead, in the dark, encouraged him to perfect his skills to a higher level. He moved on.

One of New York City's finest, from the NYPD Special Operations Unit, had one foot in the manhole on East 86th Street. He was wearing a helmet with a headlamp, a night vision scope, gas mask, rubber gloves and rubber waders, the kind fly fishermen wear. He also carried a black M4 Commando automatic rifle. All the things that Chance and Knickerbocker wished they had right now. The officer descended into the hole. Three officers followed. They said nothing as they began their mission to the south. At Wall Street, three other officers climbed down the metal ladder one-by-one, plunging into a pit of hell. They moved north.

There was black slime and glop hanging from Chance's legs as he brought them up and out of the muck. He could see it because the tunnel had become less dark. There was a storm drain ahead permitting just a bit of light to filter down onto the putrid shallow river. The brick wall had changed to concrete. And the tunnel ahead was of a larger diameter. Just ahead where the tunnel became larger, the smelly flow became a small waterfall. Chance was thankful he hadn't taken a spill into the deeper glop ahead. More good news: there was a narrow wooden walkway to his right. No railing, just boards secured to the wall just above the surface of the flow. Chance looked down to the boards to assure his footing and discovered crucial evidence: footprints.

The NYPD "A" Team heading south were single file, rooting ahead like pigs snorting out truffles. All four had their headlamps on, beams of light pointing in four different directions, never staying in one spot for more than a second. The ever-moving shafts of light were catching cockroaches, spiders and rats in their beams, blinding the dark-adapted critters, causing them to run and bump into each other like wind-up toys. With all the high-tech equipment, the teams made fast progress on their dedicated and restrictive route. They would surely be on target shortly.

Chance trudged on, his soggy sneakers spitting and emitting a squishing sound with each step. Knickerbocker could probably hear this right now, Chance thought. Chance stopped to listen. He thought he heard something in the distance. Was it the boardwalk making noise under the weight of Knickerbocker? Was it Knickerbocker's office dress shoes? Or was it rats? No telling. Except, as Chance moved forward, the faint sounds grew louder.

The three men in the Special Operations Unit were moving north from their Wall Street start point. They were

making good progress. With a good hour head start for
Chance and Knickerbocker, the odds were good that the
other team headed south would encounter them first. This
gave the team headed north an added degree of confidence,
so they moved quicker than the other team. It didn't take
them long to bypass the City Hall location where
Knickerbocker and Chance entered the sewer. The manhole
cover was open when they got there and some patrolmen
were above them voicing their support as if it were a 5K run.
The encouragement propelled them even faster. Cockroaches
ran in all directions on the rounded walls. Rats, blinded by
the headlights, careened into each other as they tried to
escape the one-eyed monsters invading their dark home.

Then, the lead team member saw some light ahead.
It was the same spot that Knickerbocker and Chance had
come upon earlier. The spot where the two intersecting tubes
fed into the main one. The spot that looked like an arching
brick cathedral. The spot where the alligator attacked
Chance.

That very same gator was still there, lurking in his
lair. But it was hard at work wriggling its huge head, rubbing
its toothy snout on the rough brick walls, slowly nudging,
coaxing, slipping the white shirt from its jaws. The shirt was
almost off when it turned its head in the direction of the
thrashing and beams of light coming its way.

The three men looked like troopers from another
planet as they entered the great room and marveled at the
unexpected. Their headlight beams darted everywhere. The
three beams roamed over the brick ceiling and walls.

Then they heard it! The hissing roar that sounded
like a steam pipe had just busted in front of them. All three
light beams instantly converged on one spot. The gator's
raging eyes looked huge and mad. Its teeth were as long as

bowling pins. Its mouth could bite off one whole leg with
one chomp. And once it got hold of you, it would not let go.
No matter what. The three brave men shrieked in horror
almost simultaneously! Three orange-yellow flames shot out
of three rifle barrels. The concussion from the blast loosened
mortar chunks and dust that fell on the men from above,
terrorizing them even more. The sound inside the domed
brick tomb was deafening. The men would not be able to
hear for a week. The sound-waves, confined to the relatively
tiny space traveled north as a shockwave. Knickerbocker
stopped dead in his tracks. Chance froze. And the four brave
souls who were headed south, ready for war, started walking
backwards.

Knickerbocker was moving fast now. But Chance
was moving faster. The gap was closing.

Knickerbocker looked backward a few times but saw
nothing. From out of nowhere, something bumped his right
arm. He jumped back. That's when he saw little slits of light,
five of them, as if light were seeping around a door. An
arched door. He reached out cautiously to see what bumped
his arm. His fingertips met rough metal. It was a wheel. Like
a small steering wheel. It was a door. The kind you see on
submarines between compartments. A hatch. Could this be
his escape hatch? He grabbed the wheel with both hands. He
tried turning it. It wouldn't budge. He could now hear the
squishing of Chance's sneakers. He tugged at the wheel of
the hatch. Nothing! He looked to his right. He could barely
make out a shape, maybe fifty paces away.

He bore down on the rusty metal with all the muscle
power he had in him. He strained with all his might as
Chance took another step.

Then…the wheel reluctantly gave way. Very slowly

at first, then faster, smoother. Knickerbocker spun the wheel furiously and the metal hatch sprung open, almost knocking him into the filthy stream.

Chance saw the light blast into the dark sewer tunnel.

Knickerbocker swung the door to his side and peered into the space now revealed to him: the subway!

There was a ladder on the left leading down to the tracks. Knickerbocker jumped on it like a monkey and descended rung-by-rung, hand-over-hand. Eight feet down, he heard the train coming. Then he saw it, moving out of the station, just starting to gather speed. As it passed just under him and to his right side, Knickerbocker leapt on to the roof and flattened himself immediately.

Chance was at the hatch. A gun-shot blast from his left filled the tunnel with earsplitting sound! Then another! One bullet pinged off the metal hatch just above his head. Another ricocheted off the door and struck the top of the tunnel. Chance was through the opening in an instant! Scrambling down the ladder to see the taillights of the train blurring by. He also noticed a dark shape on the top of the train. Knickerbocker. He jumped between the tracks and sprinted toward the train disappearing in front of him. He sprinted harder, sucking in as much air as possible, legs moving like pistons, arms acting like counterbalancing weights on a powerful machine. But still no sign of the train ahead. Just tracks disappearing into a big black hole.

Then he saw them. The red taillights stopped ahead at a station. He ran even faster. Harder. The passengers on the platform entered the train. Then a last second straggler. The doors slid shut.

Chance was running as if his life depended on it.

Knickerbocker looked back and saw Chance. The

train started to move. Chance poured it on. The back of the train was ten feet away, its electric motors spinning up. Eight feet away. The steel wheels on the steel tracks started to sing.

Five feet. Three. Within reach now, fingertips stretching out, upper body lunging forward like an Olympic runner stretching his body for the three-tenths-of-a-second photo finish. Then…contact!

Fingers reached out and wrapped themselves around a metal grab-hold. But Chance's feet were barely able to keep up. The toes of his shoes started to catch on each railroad tie. He was stumbling. Tripping. Suddenly, he had both hands on the grab-bar, hanging on with Herculean effort. In one Olympic broad jump leap, Chance's feet were on the coupling. He was riding the train!

Chance stayed put on the coupling, safely gripping the grab-bar. Knickerbocker couldn't see him and didn't know if he had caught up to the train. Anyone in his right mind would have assumed Chance didn't make it and was left behind. This was what Chance was betting on. If Knickerbocker thought he was safe for a while on a fast moving train, he would ride that train as far out of town as possible. All he had to do was slide his body to the opposite side of where the passengers were waiting in the station and not move. He wouldn't be seen.

The train pulled into 68th Street, the IRT Line. Chance peeked around the side of the train looking for anyone running. Anyone who looked like Knickerbocker. He didn't see anyone like that. The doors closed. The train left the station.

Chance crouched down on the coupling, catching his breath. Knickerbocker did the same lying on the roof of the train car. Every once in a while, Knickerbocker would look back and check. He felt pretty darn smug right now.

The train slowed. It came into the station, white subway tiles reflecting a bright array of fluorescent lights. 77th Street. Chance remained hidden but he was vigilant, checking again from the back of the train. Knickerbocker had not left his crow's nest.

The doors closed once again and the train built its momentum.

As luck would have it, a curious 10-year-old boy, a passenger on the last seat of the last car, fascinated by his journey down the tracks through the tunnel, looked out the back window and rolled his eyeballs to the bottom of their sockets. He started screaming bloody murder! He had spotted Chance!

In seconds, eight more eyeballs were bearing down on Chance. He looked up at them like a rat with his leg in a trap. A middle-age man bolted from the window to summon authorities, no doubt.

Chance had no choice. He had to climb. The grab-bar he was holding onto was repeated up the right side of the car. There were eight rungs making a ladder to the top. His head popped up cresting the roof of the carriage. He managed a low crawl on his belly to the middle of the car. That's when Knickerbocker saw him.

The train pulled into the 86th Street station. There were two dozen people waiting on the platform. As the train approached, many moved closer to the edge. There were no police in sight.

Before the train came to a complete stop, Knickerbocker slid off the roof at the front of the train and dropped to the platform like a circus acrobat. People screamed and ran from the intruder.

Chance dropped to the platform at the rear of the train. It was an invasion, some thought. Many passengers inside the train, seeing the two men leap down, remained inside, praying it would leave the station quickly. The people on the outside didn't know which way to run. A couple of them jumped to the tracks of the train going in the opposite direction rather than face certain death from the two terrorists.

Knickerbocker had the advantage. The steps leading to the street were on his side. He ran up the staircase as if it were flat ground. Chance was not so fortunate. Some of the people on the platform got in his way, not knowing if they should scurry left or right. Chance dodged around a half-dozen and was twenty-seconds behind his quarry.

Knickerbocker sprang out onto the street, a weasel popping out of a hole. He stopped in a freeze-frame, looked left, looked right, then took off straight ahead. He raced across Fifth Avenue toward thick trees. Central Park.

Chance bounded onto the street, eyes searching frantically everywhere at once. He caught sight of a head with dark hair disappearing quickly behind a knoll across the street. He dashed across the avenue to glimpse a dark-haired man rocketing toward the reservoir. Chance tried to keep his eyes on Knickerbocker, but he disappeared behind a dense stand of fat trees and bushes.

Chance rushed to the spot where he last saw Knickerbocker. His head swiveled, scanning like radar. He walked closer to the water, and there, at the edge, a sloshy footprint was embossed in the mud. He was in here all right. But this was a big reservoir. It was man-made but looked natural with mature trees, bushes and lawn surrounding it. The side that sat hard against Fifth Avenue was straight, but the rest of it was a pleasant, meandering amoeba shape and quite circular. It was large, reaching nearly across the entire width of the park all the way to Eighth Avenue, about a half-mile away.

The deepest part of this body of water was more than forty feet. It contained one million gallons. It looked so natural that it was home to hundreds of resident and migratory waterfowl. And right now, it provided cover for a different type of bird. He was out there all right.

The bird hunt was about to begin.

Fifty ducks were dipping below the surface. A gaggle of geese was cruising across the reservoir. Colonies of gulls were darting in the air and making water landings by the score. Somewhere in this jumble of aquatic flyers, floating, bobbing, paddling and diving in the water, a different kind of animal was breaking the surface.

Chance hid behind a thick-trunked tree. Peeking out, he scanned the reservoir from left to right over-and-over, waiting for his eyes and brain to identify the shape that didn't fit in. A rounded shape, like a boulder.

Is that him? Chance thought, eyes settling on a rounded form toward the middle. A change of focus in his eyes brought the image into much higher definition. *Yes! It's him!* His head was twisting, turning, surveying the water and the shoreline. Not spotting Chance, Knickerbocker started to feel secure. Chance stripped off his turquoise tank top but left his good luck necklace on. Knickerbocker treaded water very well, barely rippling the surface. He was calm, hardly moving, tricking a smattering of birds to venture within twenty feet. Knickerbocker exhaled deeply, closed his eyes briefly and allowed himself a moment to relax his intense surveillance of the surroundings. For a moment he could put his antennae away. He could allow himself this short respite.

Forty feet below, Chance stalked his prey above like a Great White. The seven-inch wide, seventeen-inch long red streak of thin skin on his back was covered with tiny bubbles

containing life supporting oxygen absorbed from the water
(H2O: two parts hydrogen and one part oxygen).
Knickerbocker had no idea that Chance possessed the
unbelievable ability to, essentially, breathe underwater
through a crude process of osmosis.*

Looking up from the bottom, Chance could see
Knickerbocker's legs moving back and forth, arms moving
side-to-side, in the cloudy water backlit by a strong sun.
Chance was vertical, close to the muddy bottom, measuring
the timing of Knickerbocker's movements. When
Knickerbocker's legs scissored past each other, Chance
launched himself straight up and grabbed Knickerbocker's
legs in a vice grip. A shark attack from forty feet down.

Knickerbocker hardly had time to gasp. Water
sucked in when he did. He choked and coughed as he went
down, hands slapping the water like a seal. The last strands
of his dark hair disappeared in the swirl. A small eddy
appeared on the surface. All was quiet above. All was a
tumult below.

Chance pulled him down and crawled up on his
body, getting Knickerbocker in a hammerlock.
Knickerbocker thrashed and bucked trying to shake Chance
off. But Chance was welded to his opponent, matching his
every undulation, thwarting every attempt at an elbow jab,
head butt, ankle kick and bite. Their position went from
vertical to horizontal, thrashing violently against the muddy
bottom, crashing against sunken logs sending clouds of
muck into the water. Sub-surface visibility was deteriorating
rapidly in the fast enveloping fog. Knickerbocker only had
two minutes, maybe three, before losing consciousness.

---

* To find out how Chance acquired this unbelievable ability, read
SAVING AN INNOCENT MAN, the first of the SAVING SERIES of
thrillers.

Chance had unlimited time. All Chance had to do was hold his catch long enough for him to either submit or wait for the inevitable.

Something caught Chance's eye, He turned his head slightly to the left and looked up. In an instant, Chance released Knickerbocker and darted away and upward, leaving Knickerbocker struggling with himself in the murk below.

The woman above Chance was going down for the third time. She tried valiantly to stay at the surface, but could not. A small boy, perhaps eight, was dog-paddling next to her. Chance could clearly see the bottom of the wooden rowboat as he shot upward to help her and the boy. Chance burst from the water like a Trident Missile.

"It's OK! I have you! Just relax and try to float on your back," Chance said reassuringly.

She kept flailing. Chance got behind her to perform a cross-chest-carry rescue maneuver, but she was panicked and flung her arms forcefully at him. He had to act quickly. He grabbed her long hair and pulled her onto her back toward him. He thrust his left arm across her body and started to swim backward to calm her down. "Are you OK?" Chance asked the boy.

"Yeah, ah, I learned to swim in school. But my Mom can't swim. I tried to save her." The woman was calm now realizing she was out of danger.

"Let's all get back into the boat," Chance said. He swam the woman over to the rowboat. "Now, hold onto the side of the boat." She clutched Chance's forearm. "It's OK, I'm right here. It won't sink. You're OK, as long as you hold on."

She reluctantly grabbed hold of the gunwale with her one hand, then the other.

"Jamie, Jamie, are you OK?" she called out.

"Yeah, Mom. I tried to save you."

She started crying.

Chance got into the boat easily, put his hand out for the boy and with one pull he yanked the boy into the boat.

"Jamie, sit on the other side of the boat to balance it and I'll pull your Mom in." Jamie did and Chance grabbed the woman under each arm and pulled hard. She belly-flopped into the boat like a big tuna. Not a pretty sight, but she was in and safe. Chance picked up an orange life jacket and held it in front of her with a look of *Do you know what this is?*

She said: "I was trying to adjust the straps and I sat on the side of the boat and then, plop!"

Chance adjusted the straps for her. "Here, try this." She did and it fit. "Now, let's get this boat to shore," he said. "You guys have had enough excitement for today." He grabbed the oars, pivoted the boat and headed for shore. He also headed for the lone swimmer stroking frantically in the same direction. Throughout the rescue, Chance never lost sight of his quarry. He pulled on the oars mightily. Any harder and he would have snapped them. The bow rose up. The wake behind the boat deepened. And mother and son hugged each other all the way in.

Knickerbocker was splashing, scrambling up the submerged embankment at the shoreline. Chance and his crew were fifty yards away. He turned his head frequently now, trying to keep eyes on Knickerbocker. Rowing the boat, he had his bare back to Knickerbocker the entire time. But it was the quickest way to get there.

Knickerbocker was already past the jogging path that surrounded the lake, already past the bridle path and just about to cross the 85th Street traverse, a two-lane street connecting Eighth Avenue on the west side to Fifth Avenue on the east. The biggest danger for Knickerbocker, once he got there, would be getting hit by a taxi.

The bow of the rowboat hit the shoreline and plowed up four inches of mud. Chance jumped out and hit the ground running.

"Hey! Thanks! Who are you?" the woman and the boy shouted. All they heard was the pounding of his feet.

Chance still had Knickerbocker in his sights but he was far behind. Knickerbocker, in the race of his life, glanced over his left shoulder. His face said it all. Could he outrun this machine chasing him?

There was an older man on a bicycle coming in Knickerbocker's direction. With one sharp shove, the man was on the lawn next to the paved trail and Knickerbocker was on the bike headed south. The labyrinth of city streets was only about a mile-and-a-quarter away, and that was the objective. Knickerbocker pedaled like a frenzied cyclist in a *Tour de Central Park*.

Chance's legs were pumping, too. Almost as fast as they did in the subway.

Knickerbocker had already blurred past the basketball courts on his right, past the ball fields and was approaching the Alexander Hamilton Statue on his left. He eyed the back of The Museum of Modern Art to his left, thinking he could easily find a hiding place. But he wanted to get more separation between himself and the missile behind him. It was just then, looking at the back of the museum, that a dog walker decided to cross in front of him! Knickerbocker had no time to react! The dog walker screamed! And five dogs, from Yorkshire to Saint Bernard, pissed on the spot and their eyeballs nearly fell out of their sockets. The bicycle hit the five leashes like a runner breaking a finish tape. The dog walker, the five dogs, the bicycle, and the man who had the best view of all, Knickerbocker, were all hurled fifteen feet in a tangled, howling, screaming heap of flying fur and four-letter words. Knickerbocker could not care less. He even ignored his smashed shoulder. He grabbed the bike, ran with it, and jumped onto the seat like a cowboy mounting a horse. Only to grimace at the pain between his legs when his soft parts met the hard seat.

Chance, knowing he couldn't compete with a bicycle, saw his only opportunity to travel faster than running. A kid with a skateboard. The 15-year-old carrying his board under his arm didn't know what happened. In a flash, his board was under this long-haired, bare-chested six-foot-five New York City wacko. All the kid could do was yell, "Hey!" Chance and his board were gone, rolling fast downhill on the paved path.

Chance's right leg was going so fast his hair was swept back. The wheels started to smoke and wobble. If he crashed now, he would need an ambulance. There was Knickerbocker up ahead, jumping on a bicycle. A pile of crying dogs and a woman giving him the finger were on the side of the trail when Chance went sizzling past.

Knickerbocker sped past the ancient obelisk known as Cleopatra's Needle on his left and then came upon the pedestrian underpass at the 79th Street traverse. The opening was beautiful white stone carved in a spade shape. But no time to stop and appreciate the artistry. Pedal!

Chance was in hot pursuit. But a skateboard was no match for a fast bike. Especially when trying to get through grass and soft turf. Chance had to find a better way. And there it was! One of the famous horse and carriage rides, parked in front of him. He hopped off the skateboard, jumped aboard the carriage, and grabbed the reins. One glance was all it took for the carriage driver to jump off. Next to jump were the two young lovers in the backseat. Chance looked like a deranged wild man; a bare-chested muscle-man with soaking-wet-tight pants, long stringy hair, a necklace of rattlesnake tails, fangs and feathers and long white gator teeth. And to top it all off, he literally smelled like shit! Tourists never moved so fast. And neither did Chance. "Giddy up!" he commanded with a smack of the reins. The horse did an equine wheelie, and they were off. The sound of the thundering hooves, the rattle of the big spoked wheels, axles and old springs, the huffing and snorting of the steed at full speed and the wild man bouncing madly on top made onlookers stop and stare dumbfounded. One man said to his wife, "They must be making a movie!"

Knickerbocker was rocking the bike side-to-side, punching the pedals, punishing his rear end in his flight for life. He barreled along in back of the Loeb Boat House, under Terrace Drive, and he sped by the bronze Statue of Balto, the legendary Alaskan sled dog. He studied it intently knowing he had angered the Dog-Gods and they would put a hex on him.

Chance, horse and carriage, rambled, bounced and shook over manicured lawns, over stone curbs, squeezed through tight pedestrian underpasses and careened over paved bicycle paths nearly running over women pushing baby carriages, old ladies in wheelchairs and little girls holding Daddy's hand. But no one died. No one was even injured. It was a spectacle to behold. A bit of the old west come to Central Park.

Things changed at the 65th Street traverse. This was a busy two-lane road that was more like a mini-highway. When Knickerbocker came upon it, he stopped the bike with

a side-skid. At that particular location, the street was below
him. He was at the edge of a six-foot-high stone wall. On the
other side, was a mirror image of the wall at his feet. On top
of the wall on the opposite side was an eight-foot high chain-
link fence spotted with white signs that said NO
TRESPASSING - DANGER. Knickerbocker only thought
"Escape!" He dropped the bike, dropped down to the road,
fended off oncoming cars and clambered up the opposite
stone wall. Without hesitation, he crawled up the chain-link
fence like a spider.

Chance came to the same spot within a half-minute
of Knickerbocker. He yanked his chariot to a skidding halt
and dashed to the edge of the wall. He saw Knickerbocker
jump to the ground on the other side of the fence.

Dozens of cars were now stopped below, bumper-to-
bumper, probably due to Knickerbocker disrupting the flow
of traffic. Chance leaped from the edge of the stone wall to
the roof of a yellow taxi, to the roof of a limousine and to the
wall on the other side. He was over the fence like a squirrel
and jumped to the soft earth below. There were trees. Lots
and lots of trees. A visual block for a three-story building not
thirty paces up an incline. There he was! Knickerbocker!
Climbing on a ladder affixed to the outside of a green stucco
wall. The kind of attached exterior ladder that takes you to
the roof. Knickerbocker was almost to the top, thirty-five
feet above, when Chance reached the bottom. Two rungs at a
time, hand-over-hand, foot-over-foot, Chance climbed like a
firefighter determined to save souls.

At the top, Chance saw Knickerbocker standing,
facing him, about fifteen feet away on the roof. But it wasn't
a roof. Not a normal roof. It was as if they were both
standing on a rocky mountain ledge of stone and boulders.

Knickerbocker and Chance both stood there without

speaking. Facing each other. Breathing hard. Knickerbocker could have taken a run at Chance, knocking him off the thirty-five-foot-tall wall. And Chance could have taken a run at Knickerbocker, knocking him off the man-made mountain, a jagged cliff of rocky outcroppings.

The two men were gladiators with no shields and no swords. This would be a battle of strength, skill and wits. And something else. Common sense.

"Like I said, Antonio, it doesn't have to be this way."

"Fuck you, Frank!"

"We don't have a lot of time. We've both been through enough. Why don't we make it easy on both of us?"

"How did you figure it out Frank? Just tell me that before we end this, one way or another."

"Well, you're not going to believe this, but it was a picture of you in the courtroom twenty-two years ago."

"I was just a boy then."

"Well, Antonio, it's a long story. And we don't have time for long stories."

Knickerbocker took a step to his left. Then another. Chance took two steps forward.

"I'm giving you a limited time offer, Antonio. Let's end this now."

In a blur, Knickerbocker bolted to his left. He didn't see the stream of gushing water, six feet away, coming out of a hole in the man-made mountain. And he didn't notice the bright green algae and moss beneath the rushing water that fell to a sparkling pool far below. When his foot hit the moss and algae, it was as if he stepped on ice. His leg flew out from under him. His head went back. He hit his spine against the jagged edge of the cliff and he fell about thirty feet, impacting a concrete ledge next to an oval pool.

Chance stood at the edge of the cliff looking down. Knickerbocker landed on his back, all four limbs splayed out. He moved his right arm and left leg. From a dark opening in the painted concrete mountain, the two six-hundred-pound grizzly bears, residents of the Central Park Zoo, emerged from their dens. They were immediately fixated on the supine body in their habitat. They sniffed. They snorted. They huffed. Then they rushed to the unexpected treat that had fallen from the sky. As Chance gazed down, he could hear the bloodcurdling screams. He could see the spectators, protected behind glass walls, cover their children's eyes and turn their own heads away.

At this very moment, Cha-ley was leaving a message for Chance.

BEEEEP

"Chance, great news! DNA proves that Angel Perez was innocent."

SEVENTEEN

The red type flashing on the screen said: BREAKING NOW: A PIC TV–10 EXCLUSIVE

The music sounded urgent.

"This is Nicole Jensen interrupting your regularly scheduled programming with a PIC TV–10 exclusive. The New York City sniper is dead. After a nearly day-long chase through the bowels of the New York City sewer system, the IRT Subway and a madcap chase through Central Park, the killer was confronted at Central Park Zoo where his life ended just minutes ago. Tracking the madman every step of the way was freelance Special Agent, Frank Stoneman, who finally brought the sniper to justice. More details will be announced at a press conference tomorrow morning by Mayor Wertz and Commissioner Brix at City Hall. For PIC TV–10, the first to bring you this breaking news, I'm Nicole Jensen."

· · ·

Chance was prone on the bed, face smushed into the pillow, body splayed out like a marionette with no strings attached. He was dead to the world after the harrowing day yesterday that drew him into the stench of the sewers, the screeching of the subway, the chase through Central Park and the death on 'Mount Grizzly'. But his eyes started to move beneath their lids when the undercurrent of chatter and clinking plates reached through his subconscious state.

In the other room, Nikki was arranging four place

settings at the table, Addie Mae was making a pot of freshly ground coffee, and Cha-ley was mixing up a potent pitcher of Mimosas. A big pan was already on the gas stove ready to be filled with all the ingredients for asparagus and Gouda omelets as soon as Chance woke from his well-deserved slumber. Which was right about now.

As soon as Chance walked in, wearing jeans and a white shirt with the sleeves rolled up, the awaiting trio bid him good morning with applause. They were proud of him. It was obvious to all that Chance was as humble as he was capable.

"You guys are too nice! Thank you."

"Here's to you, Chance!"

"Here's to all of us," Chance said.

The Mimosas went down easy. The fixin's went into the omelet pan. The four sat down to a bountiful breakfast brimming with warm conversation.

Between the hot buttered croissants and steaming coffee, Cha-ley regaled the table with his tales from the graveyard and the 'sting' in San Francisco. Addie Mae told of the cat-calls at the tenement building and the meeting with well-intentioned African Americans who didn't quite know how to channel their frustration and anger. And Nikki recounted the Mayor's continual threats and efforts to tamp down her enthusiasm and truthful reporting of events. Then Chance 'held court' as he related his colorful story of sloshing through the sewer system, the subway thrill ride, the horse and buggy chase through the park and bringing the Monday Morning Sniper to justice with a little help from some furry friends. The three were enraptured. "But," Chance said, "this story is far from over. I was hired to come here to get Knickerbocker. Mission accomplished. But there's more killing this city than the sniper. Knickerbocker lit a flame that is turning into a bonfire that can engulf this entire city. But we can help turn things around. We would have to do the impossible in just two days. If you're up for it, I'll explain what I have in mind."

. . .

The Blue Room at City Hall was overflowing with people and excitement. TV, radio and newspaper reporters were at the ready. Television cameras lined the back wall. Photographers sat on the floor up front. City officials, influential movers and shakers and avid citizens filled the middle. Most of them were aware of Nicole's breaking story last night. Nevertheless, the room was abuzz with lively anticipation of the details and timing of the capture.

The Mayor walked up to the podium. The room quieted down.

"Good morning, everyone," the Mayor began.

"Today is a great day. The day we've all been waiting for. This morning I am very pleased to announce, and confirm, that the sniper that has terrorized our fine city for weeks, and viciously taken the lives of so many of New York's finest, has finally been brought to justice."

The room erupted in raucous cheers and enthusiastic applause. When the ovation died down, the Mayor continued.

"Shortly, Commissioner Brix will present the details of the events that led to the capture, and ultimately the death, of the sniper and a timeline of the events. But first, there are many people to thank. First, we have to thank our brave men and women in blue who have had the courage to come to work every day regardless of the threat they faced."

A short standing ovation followed that recognition.

"We want to thank the FBI for their support throughout this ordeal."

Seated applause.

"We want to thank our forensic investigators, our people in ballistics, our amazing fire department, our detectives, our Special Investigations Unit, our Terrorism Task Force and so many others who contributed to the day-of-reckoning for the killer of so many good, innocent people."

More seated applause.

"But the one person who we owe the most gratitude to is our Special Agent, Frank Stoneman."

People rose from their seats and applauded loudly. They craned their necks looking for Frank, but didn't see him.

"Unfortunately, Frank is not here today."

Some disappointment was heard from the crowd.

"Frank, for all his unbelievable talent, bravery, intelligence and inner and outward strength is a humble, modest man who shuns the spotlight preferring to let it shine on others. This, after a grueling, nearly five-hour non-stop chase through about four miles of sewer tunnels, almost two miles on the top of a subway car and an exhausting one-and-a-half-mile chase through Central Park. Frank Stoneman not only identified the killer, he confronted him at his home, and tracked him doggedly until the killer fell into the grizzly bear exhibit where he finally succumbed to injuries sustained."

More seated applause.

"Adding much valued confirmation to the killer's identification, the NYPD obtained a warrant to enter the killer's premises where they found a specially handmade .50 caliber sniper rifle and unique, specially made ammunition." A picture of the rifle appeared on a screen. "Our Ballistics

Lab has identified it as the exact weapon and bullet used in the majority of the sniper attacks."

"So, Frank Stoneman," the Mayor said looking directly into the cameras at the back of the room, "here's to you as we symbolically raise a toast of thanks!" The Mayor held up an invisible glass of cheer as everyone in the room stood up and turned to the camera. Some raised invisible glasses, some women blew kisses, some men put their hands over their hearts and police officers in the room saluted.

"Thank you, Frank!" the Mayor said proudly.

"Thank you, Frank!" the room said in unison. They sat back down in their seats.

"Now, the hard part. The disappointing part. The identity of the gunman."

The Mayor paused, the room grew silent. Somber. "The gunman, unfortunately, is someone many of us knew."

You could have heard a pin drop.

"Robert Knickerbocker, our own Director of Digital Communications."

The room went into shock. Hands went to faces. Eyes opened wide in disbelief. Cell phones came out of pockets and purses, thumbs dancing over keypads. Cameras focused in on the screen showing a picture of Knickerbocker.

The Mayor let the audience absorb the impact of the bombshell before he continued.

"Apparently, Knickerbocker sat there amongst us for years, planning, gathering confidential information, deceiving us, until finally unleashing the heinous and devastating blow to our police department, to innocent families, to our city." The Mayor paused for a moment.

"And now, Commissioner Brix will give you more details and answer your questions."

"But Mayor, one question, please." It was Nicole Jensen, of course.

"Didn't Knickerbocker work directly for you? On a daily basis?"

"I just said that," the Mayor answered, annoyed.

"And wasn't he one of your Deputy Mayors, appointed by you?"

"You said one question. You got your one answer." Wertz actually sneered at her.

"Here's Brix," he said into the microphone.

• • •

The small Cape Cod style house looked like a set for a feel-good-movie. It was fringed with a classic white fence and huge sunflowers lording over the front yard.

Chance walked onto the Colonial-blue painted porch and knocked on the oak door. It opened. A man stood there with a silent questioning face.

Chance said, "Sheamus O'Neill?"

• • •

The black cell phone made the sound of a jackhammer on the oil-spotted wooden shelf next to a bag of ammonium nitrate.

Teardrop answered.

"You calling to thank me for the gift?"

Cufflinks was on the other end.

"I'm calling to thank you for getting rid of that dirt bag. But you didn't have to send me his eyes, for Christ's sake."

"You have a short memory, you lyin' fuck! I was the

one you wanted shafted."

Cufflinks fired back. "The better man won out! That's what I was after! Only the strong survive! You survived. I'm happy with that. And you should be overjoyed."

"Yeah, sure!" Teardrop was not impressed.

"Let's put all that petty bullshit behind us, we have bigger things to worry about and it looks like we're in this together. So let's get on with it and take this to the next level."

"I need money," Teardrop demanded.

"You just got fifty thousand, remember?"

"I changed the plan. I need a lot more."

"You changed the plan? I have news for you! You're not the one who changes the plan! I am!"

"You called me in to do a job. Let me do it. Or I'll walk."

There was silence for a few seconds.

"What's your reason for changing the plan?"

"Because this has gotten bigger than we thought it would. We're gettin' worldwide attention. So we need to make a worldwide statement. One the world has never seen. And will never forget."

There was a few seconds of silence again.

"How much do you need?"

"Three hundred and thirty-one thousand."

"Three hundred and…are you out of your mind?"

"Not a penny less."

"So that's three hundred thirty-one thousand *minus* the fifty you just got!"

"No! It's plus the fifty."

"So, what's this, a fifty-thousand-dollar penalty?"

"Yeah, you might say so. For trying to waste me!"

There was a slight pause in the conversation.

"I'll send you three hundred tomorrow."

"You'll send me three hundred and thirty-one thousand. You send me three hundred and you'll never see me or the money again. You send me the three-thirty-one and you'll get your mission accomplished. Not one dollar less."

Cufflinks cooled his jets for a moment. Thinking.

"Tell you what," Cufflinks ventured, "I'll send you three hundred now, and if, and only if you can get the mission finished by Sunday night, I'll send you an additional fifty. After it's done, you keep whatever you don't spend. How's that?"

"Why by Sunday night?"

"I have a meeting on Monday morning, and this would help me a lot at that meeting. It's worth more to have this in my back pocket."

Now Teardrop was the one cooling his jets.

Teardrop spoke: "Tomorrow. Special courier. Times Square. Two o'clock."

"Cufflinks responded: "OK…but…"

"But what?" Teardrop snarled.

"This had better be pretty fucking spectacular!"

. . .

"Get them the hell outta here. The party's over. Clear them out this afternoon."

Mayor Wertz was looking at a TV picture from a surveillance camera mounted on the 64th Street Precinct. The protestors were still occupying the streets.

"Just a few days ago you told me to bring them water and portable toilets," Commissioner Brix reminded the

Mayor.

"A few days ago we had a cop killer on our hands. Now he's dead. There's no reason for them to be there. Get rid of them."

"Ed, did you notice that there seems to be more of those white canopies now than there were before?"

The Mayor examined the screen. He pressed the arrow-right key on the keyboard and the camera on the building panned.

Brix added, "And there are more people out there than there were before."

"Yeah, but what's their fuckin' problem now?" the Mayor asked, frustrated.

"Well…*you* are, Ed. The problem you face now is…you! They want to know why you didn't see this coming. You saw Knickerbocker every day. You hired him, for Christ's sake!"

"I had no fuckin' idea and you know that!"

"Haven't you watched the news today? Too busy celebrating? It's all over the TV."

"It's that fucking two-faced bitch, Jensen. I told you to get rid of her!"

"It's not Jensen, or should I say, not only Jensen. Here, look for yourself."

Brix turned on one the three televisions in the room. A black-and-white cartoon came on. A cat hitting a rat over the head with a club. Brix switched the channel. A female reporter was speaking, "…but the Press Secretary, Tom Elliott, insisted that the Mayor's office had no idea that Robert Knickerbocker was killing police officers right under their noses." She played a clip of Elliott with a microphone to his face. Elliott spoke. "Not a hint. Not the tiniest suspicion."

The reporter asked: "Were there any tell-tale signs? Did he read internet sights on bombs, guns…anything at all that would have made people stop and think?"

"Nothing that I saw or heard. I worked closely with him for almost four years and there was nothing that made me suspicious."

"Didn't the Mayor hire Knickerbocker?"

"Yes."

"And did he check his background first?"

"I can't answer for the Mayor."

"Well, don't you think the Mayor needs to answer some questions? The people in the city want answers. Just look out on the streets."

Brix changed the channel. Now it was Nicole Jensen moving through the protestors, the occupiers. There she was, cameraman following, now stopping to talk with a middle-age woman under a canopy.

"And why are you here protesting today when the sniper was killed yesterday?" Nicole asked her.

"This isn't about the sniper. Not anymore. This is about the other killer."

"The other killer? What other killer?"

"The Mayor. Mayor Wertz."

"Mayor Wertz?"

"Yeah. He's a killer, too. Don't kid yourself. There's more to this. It ain't that simple. Like, the Mayor wants us to think he don't know nothin'. He knew somethin'!"

The crowd around Nicole became energized. Perhaps because of the media attention. Perhaps because they could hear the accusations being hurled at the Mayor. Another woman, an older one, pushed her way in front of Nicole.

"Yeah, she got that right. Maybe we should get

Frank to get the Mayor!" The crowd around Nicole picked up on that line. They started chanting: "Frank, get the Mayor, Frank, get the Mayor, Frank, get the Mayor…"

• • •

Chance, Addie Mae and Cha-ley sat in three different spots in Nicole's apartment. Nicole was there, too, her face on the television reporting from the occupation in front of the 64th Street Precinct. The sound on the TV was low because Chance, Addie Mae and Cha-ley were all talking on cell phones. Chance's plan was starting to come together.

"Hello, this is Hunter."

"Mr. Janus?"

"Yes, this is Hunter Janus." The 68-year-old Hunter Janus was standing in front of a 1936 Ford hot rod. The hood was up. He had a wrench in his hand.

"Mr. Janus this is Frank Stoneman. And I…"

"Frank Stoneman. Are you the guy I heard about on the TV? About the sniper in New York?"

"Ahh, yes, I am. Well, Mr. Janus…"

"Why aren't you there? This is your big day, man!"

"Well, because speaking with you on the phone is more important right now. I have a huge favor to ask of you."

"Ah huh."

"If I have my facts right, you were one of a number of African American astronauts to go into space."

"Yes, that's right. But I'm retired. I work on hot rods now. What do you need with an old astronaut?"

Cha-ley was sitting next to Chance, phone to his ear. "Dr. Chao?" Cha-ley asked.

"Yes. This is Dr. Chao. How can I help you?" Dr. Ken Chao was standing in front of a backlit x-ray screen. He had a stethoscope around his neck. He was a distinguished looking middle-age Chinese American.

"Dr. Chao, this is Charles Hastings," Cha-ley said in his Kiwi accent. "Thanks for taking my call. After I explained our needs to your secretary, she thought it would be OK if we spoke briefly."

"Yes. She told me about your call. How can I help?"

The pro-football player was in full uniform, helmet under his arm, towel around his neck, just about to start his afternoon of field practice with his team and coach.

"Make this quick, I gotta go!"

"Mr. Fernandez, this is Addie Mae Cypress."

. . .

The occupation grew by fifty-percent. Cardboard and blank poster board arrived somehow along with paint and markers. Somebody was handing out sticks and duct tape. Creativity flourished and sentiments were hoisted high over heads.

THE WERTZ MAYOR IN AMERICA

WERTZ IS BEHIND IT

Jadon, Glaad and a platoon of helpers were handing out red hats by the dozens. The occupation was increasing exponentially. As the sun went down, the noise level went up. Raucous now.

Many waited for the young leader of the Red Hats to speak his mind. To bring them a new perspective. There was a whole new dynamic tonight.

"This is Nicole Jensen reporting to you from the occupation on the Lower East Side. Even though the sniper that had wreaked havoc upon the city has been killed, the protestors continue. Protestors want answers from City Hall, because the sniper was, for years, one of them. Charges of conspiracy, collusion, blindness, ambivalence, negligence, duplicity are all being hurled at the Mayor. So far, the protest has been peaceful, but now, we're getting word of two more demonstrations gathering outside the Stock Exchange and another at Grand Central Station."

"Let's go now to PIC TV–10 reporter, Julie Madras on Wall Street."

The screen cut to Julie. "Nicole, bottles were just thrown at store windows across the street from where I'm standing but they either missed or bounced off. Police have had a light presence here, so far, since no one expected this demonstration to take place here tonight, apparently prompted by a social media flash-mob call-to-action."

CRASH!

"Oh, there it is, a store window smashed. It looks like it was smashed by a trash receptacle thrown through the window. Let's see if we can get a closer look." The young female reporter forced her way through the mob. The cameraman followed her and aimed the camera at a tobacco shop. Looters were already running out through the broken window with their booty – anything they could smoke or sell – arms full of cigarette cartons, boxes of expensive cigars, hand-carved humidors, credit card machines, walnut shelves, even a couple of lamps.

Then, another smash of glass a few doors down. The mob shifted like a school of fish.

The young reporter was in front of the camera again. "At this point, I'm going to toss this over to Jose Camarata at Grand Central. Jose?"

"Hey, Julie. Look behind me, you can see two

hundred, perhaps three-hundred people gathering in the main concourse at Grand Central Station. Police are standing around the perimeter but have let the protestors stand in the middle, yelling and shaking their signs at the hundreds of commuters making their way to trains, many of them on their way home from work. So far, no outburst of violence...but the night is young, for PIC TV–10, this is Jose Camarata."

Wertz turned cold. "Get the SWAT teams ready at all three of those locations. Send an equal number of officers as there are protestors. If the mob builds in number, we build in number. If they want to fight, we fight. If they want to destroy, we'll destroy them. If they want to kill, we'll kill. I'll show them what the worst Mayor in America can do!"

The street was teaming with protestors. Over their heads, the black-and-white street sign said Wall Street. And above the sign, a firey object trailing sparks came whistling by in an arc from right to left. The Molotov Cocktail smashed against the brass doors and burst into flames, fire washing down the door. Then another, hurled on a higher trajectory, smashed into the four words engraved into the light-colored stone: NEW YORK STOCK EXCHANGE.

A twelve-foot pole rose up from the crowd, possibly three selfie sticks taped together. At the end of the pole was a rag on fire. It rose up and ignited the American flag hanging from a flag pole at a forty-five-degree angle from the building.

The world's largest stock exchange, with listed capitalization of its companies at approximately nineteen trillion dollars, was under attack.

Police and fire truck sirens were wailing.

Inside Grand Central, a sign was hanging from the balcony over the portal to tracks 21–11. The sign said:
GET WERTZ OUT BEFORE WE GET OUT!

Some of the protestors started to move away from the main concourse gathering spot, causing the watchful police to become splintered, spreading their attention zone. A dozen protestors raced to the market, a large area of vendors with open tables and bins full of fresh fruits, spices, expensive chocolate, candies, artisan breads and cakes, coffee beans and cheeses. Within minutes much of these delicacies would be on the floor and in bags on their way out of the many exits.

On the Vanderbilt Avenue side of Grand Central, two of the heavy glass and metal entrance doors blew off their hinges injuring six passersby on the sidewalk.

Police and EMT sirens were screaming to the site.

The white canopies had spread to a nearby playground of basketball courts. Resident cars had given way to the occupation and found parking spaces elsewhere. The police were actually pushed back from their own front entrance, yielding to the protestors, forced to use rear and side entrances to their Precinct. Police cruisers, usually garaged in the below-building motor pool, were parked behind the precinct and used a back alley for ingress and egress. This seemed to be a sensible submission that promoted a mostly peaceful co-existence.

Until now.

Two civilian vehicles, one on either side of the two-block by two-block occupation exploded in eight-foot-high fireballs. Black smoke filled the night sky. It darkened the sodium vapor streetlights. It produced coughs and phlegm and spit from the mouths of dozens. The blasts injured fifteen.

Fire trucks, sirens blaring, were on their way to the scene.

EIGHTEEN

ALERT crawled across the TV screen. "Our newsroom has just learned that the National Guard has been ordered to help patrol and protect the streets of New York City following a night of violence."

The picture on the screen showed Guard troops from around the State climbing into the backs of large khaki-colored canvas-topped trucks, leaving their armories for Manhattan. "Nine hundred Guardsmen are being deployed immediately and will hit the streets at three main areas…the Stock Exchange, Grand Central Station and the 64th Police Precinct in the Lower East Side."

The screen cut to the three locations.

"The occupation of the streets that has lasted more than three days has grown. The Guard troops will assist police in traffic control, surveillance, safety measures and relieving overworked police and fire personal with some routine chores. What's the reason for the looting, fires and destruction? Protestors say 'To get rid of the Mayor'. Hopefully the standoff will soon come to an end."

The footage showed boots hitting the pavement, Guardsmen lining up in platoon formations on the streets of New York.

· · ·

Mr. Hunter Janus was wearing an astronaut suit, helmet cradled in his right arm, standing in front of a green wall.

Chance, Nicole and Ramon were sitting at the

editing console looking at Mr. Janus on a small monitor. On a monitor next to that one was a picture of a star field against black. The stars drifted slowly through the dark sky. With one keystroke the stars appeared as a backdrop behind the astronaut.

"Looking good, Hunter," Chance called out.

"I haven't worn this suit in more than thirty years. I'm surprised I still fit into it," Janus said.

"OK, now, say your line for a sound check, Mr. Janus," Ramon requested.

Addie Mae was on the football field standing in front of Osvaldo Fernandez, New York's popular tight end. Addie Mae handed Mr. Fernandez a script to look over as a freelance cameraman mounted the camera on his shoulder.

"I'm ready," Fernandez said confidently.

Dr. Ken Chao was wearing a white lab coat, stethoscope around his neck, as he stood in front of a green wall. Chance, Nicole and Ramon were at the editing controls once again. Ramon hit the editing key and an operating room appeared behind the famed neurosurgeon.

"Is the script OK with you, Dr. Chao?" Chance asked respectfully.

"Just what the doctor ordered," the Doctor said with a boyish smile.

The very tall, very thin, pro-basketball player was on the practice court with his team. He had the ball. He threw and made a perfect basket. The coach blew the whistle.

"Curtis Smith?" Cha-ley asked.

"That be me!" the giant said to little Cha-ley.

"I'm Cha-ley Hastings."

The R&B Band was on the stage for a sound check. There were four black musicians and two white playing behind the good looking African American man whaling on his guitar. His fingers danced across the fret board. Three big chords and the band killed it to a blistering crescendo.

"d'Andre?"

"Wassup?"

"I'm Addie Mae Cypress."

"Yeah, cool! Let's do it!"

• • •

Tom Elliott was in his office at City Hall looking at his computer screen checking tweets.

One tweet said: "It's only a matter of time chopped liver Wertz."

Another: "Don't sit in front of any windows, Mayor."

Elliott looked out his window at the gathering rabble.

• • •

They stood with their backs against the wall of the building, facing the protestors. The Guardsmen were stationed in front of 11 Wall Street every twenty feet. Each man held a black M-15 assault rifle, standard issue for army and other US military personnel. But these were not men from the regular army. These were 'Weekend Warriors'. Reservists. Soldiers who only see duty when they clean the latrine at the local armory. These are appliance delivery drivers, florists, A/C repairmen, waiters, lawyers, accountants and local auto parts counter clerks. Lucky for them that the angry, hungry, tired, pissed-off protestors didn't know that this barely-courageous band of sometime-soldiers standing before them had no bullets in their weapons. Not after the Scranton Commission's ruling on the Kent State Massacre and the Jackson State Killings.

In spite of the Guard presence, the power was with the people.

On the main concourse of Grand Central, the soldiers with the impotent arms had shepherded the militant mob to the outside, to the sidewalks and the streets.

The middle fingers in faces, the curses that assaulted ears, the sight of asses mooning the weary warriors would continue into the afternoon and into the night.

The occupation outside the 64th Precinct had grown even larger. It now extended two blocks to the north and two blocks to the south of the precinct and two blocks to the west. To the east, protestors, transients and the homeless had invaded the three and a half-acre Seward Park. It was becoming a tent city, although closed tents, not canopies, had been banned in the city since the Occupation-Of-Wall-Street in the fall of 2011. As the occupation grew, so did police and National Guard presence around them. They were just waiting for the next shoe to drop. To obey the Mayor's orders.

. . .

"That's a rap," Ramon said, getting up from his editing console. Chance and Nicole stood, too, joining Cha-ley and Addie Mae who had been sitting in chairs behind them.

"Looks good, thanks everyone," Chance said.

"I can't wait to see it on TV," Cha-ley chimed in.

"Me, too," said Addie Mae.

"We'll all see it soon," Nicole said. "We're sending it out to the stations right now. I'm sure they'll want to get it on the air as soon as possible."

"Fan-tastic!" Cha-ley said. "I'll watch it from my hotel room. Now that the killer's been killed, I don't have to camp out in The Beaver!"

"That's right," Chance agreed. "I think The Beaver is safe for tonight. You've earned a nice comfy bed!"

"My pillow is calling me right now."

Addie Mae broke in, "And I have plans tonight, too, if that's OK?"

"That's fine Addie Mae," Chance agreed. "You've worked hard, too. Take the night off and enjoy yourself. You deserve it. May I ask…"

Addie Mae knew what he was asking. "Ahh…that big, good looking man who introduced me to The Innercity Soldiers. He's very nice. He asked me out to dinner. So, I'm happy I'm able to accept."

"Absolutely! But he'd better be a gentleman or me and Cha-ley will…" Chance made a fist and a mock angry face, then smiled.

"I'm sure he'll be just the kind of gentleman I want him to be."

Nicole smiled at Addie Mae knowingly.

Addie Mae smiled shyly back.

Addie Mae and Cha-ley prepared to leave. Addie Mae picked up her purse and Cha-ley picked up his cell phone from the console.

"Hey, guys, before you leave, I have a seven o'clock meeting with the Mayor in the morning, but let's plan on getting together right after that, OK?" Chance said.

"Aye aye, captain," Cha-ley saluted.

"Just give me a call and I'll be wherever you want me," Addie Mae added.

"OK, have a good night, guys." Chance turned to Nicole and said, "Great job. I think we deserve something special tonight. A special night on the town."

"I have a slight headache," Nikki said.

"Does that mean, not tonight, I have a headache?"

"I said *slight* headache."

. . .

The business-like middle-age man with the rich, deep voice looked into the camera and said: "…and there's been a different kind of shooting in New York City today. One that this reporter is happy to tell you about. It's the shooting of a television commercial aimed at helping the inner city and the underprivileged. Take a look."

The TV screen cut to astronaut Hunter Janus in his space suit standing in front of the slowly moving star field. It said his name under him and the words: One of the first African American Astronauts.

Mr. Janus spoke to the viewers at home: "I grew up in the ghetto. And look how far I've come."

The picture on the screen changed to Dr. Chao standing in an operating room. Superimposed under him was: Dr. Ken Chao – world famous neurosurgeon.

"In the New York City neighborhood where I grew up, I needed a lot of help. Now, I'm helping lots of others."

The screen changed to tight end Osvaldo Fernandez.

"When I was growing up, I didn't have any goals. Now, I run for one every day."

The screen cut to d'Andre, popular R&B musician.

"On the streets I was known for some pretty bad (bleep). Now, I'm famous for somethin' I'm proud of."

The screen showed basketball legend Curtis Smith.

"When I was growing up, I couldn't even afford a basketball. Now, I give away a thousand of 'em a year."

The screen showed a beautiful young African American woman in a sexy flowing dress standing on stage. There were six beautiful African American women behind her. All of them stood in front of microphones. World-famous singer Banica. She spoke in a soft, deep, sultry tone.

"When I was a young girl, I was afraid to say anything in my neighborhood. Now, my voice is heard around the world."

The screen cut back to astronaut Janus. "These outstanding people are here to help you. If you're living in one of New York's inner cities, if you need a hand up, whether you're African American, white, Asian or Hispanic or any other ancestry, if you're male or female, of any age, sign up for life improving programs in science, music, sports, medicine...and more to come. Only two hundred spaces are available in each, so call or go online now. Introducing UP!"

A logo appeared. Janus pointed his finger toward the stars.

"It doesn't matter where you are now, the sky is the limit." A shooting star arced over Hunter Janus' shoulder, "Start going UP! today."

The news anchor continued, "And who is the brainchild behind all this? Well, the creator wants to remain anonymous. But our sources tell us it's Frank Stoneman, the Special Agent who caught the New York sniper."

. . .

"Another glass of wine," Glaad asked Addie Mae with big eyes and a toothy grin.

Addie Mae giggled her answer, "I've already had two! That's very sweet of you, but no thank you."

"I think I've had enough, too," Glaad said slugging the last inch of beer in his glass. They both had empty plates in front of them. The waiter removed them.

The sound of trumpets came from Glaad's shirt pocket. "I just better look to see...oh, oh!"

"What's the matter? Is something wrong?" Addie Mae asked with some concern.

"It's marked urgent." But Glaad was reluctant to answer right now.

"Well, then answer it!"

"Yes?" Glaad said seriously into the phone. He was quiet. Listening intently. Eyes flashing to Addie Mae. Her eyes lasered on his. Waiting.

"Hey...thanks. I owe you one, bro. Yeah, thanks."

Addie Mae said, "It's none of my business but..."

Glaad leaned his head forward and spoke sotto voce. "My friend knows where they are."

"Who is they?"

"Glaad leaned his head forward even more, "The Outsiders!"

Addie Mae's eyebrows went up as her eyes widened. "And where is that?" she asked.

"Not far from this restaurant. In an old warehouse in the meat packing district."

"Are you familiar with that area?"

"Yeah. I run a Hi-Lo for a meat distributor on 14th Street. The warehouse is just south of Ganesvoort in a small alley."

"Well?" Addie Mae said, matter-of-factly.

"Well, what?" Glaad said with no clue.

"Well, let's go have a look. Maybe take a picture for Ch…Frank."

"What about dessert?" Glaad asked.

"Dessert comes later."

The taxi stopped across the street and down the block from the rusty two-story metal building. Even the gabled roof was corrugated metal. The building had big windows on each side, but they were raised high off the ground about ten or twelve feet up. There were lights on inside. The building had two oversized roll-up garage doors in front. There was an alley about ten feet wide on either side. In the left alley was a dilapidated van with flat tires. It had probably sat there, idle, for ten years. The rear of it faced the street. And mounted on the back was an aluminum ladder, still relatively shiny, that gave handy access to a large luggage rack on its roof. In the darkness of the alley, Glaad and Addie Mae approached the van avoiding tin cans, discarded lumber and various debris.

"You first," Glaad said in a whisper.

"No way! I'm wearing a dress!"

Glaad carefully climbed the ladder hoping it wouldn't fall off the van under his weight. When he was on top, Addie Mae followed. The windowsill of the building was just barely above their eye level. They both leaned into the building and stretched their heavy bodies like big cats as best as they could. Their foreheads and their eyes peered over the rusty sill. What they saw inside the building made their eyes big. On the left, there were two rows of long tables, probably folding tables, put end to end. Each row was about sixteen feet long. On the tables, it looked like they were constructing bombs. There were wires connecting cell phones to off-white colored bricks about a foot long. And there was some kind of copper colored cylindrical device on top of the bricks. It looked like they were set up to make at least a dozen bombs but there were only two of the whitish bricks on the table.

There was an array of weapons: AK-47's, two grenade launchers, two rocket launchers, and at least a dozen black pistols with dozens of magazines.

On the right side of the room were two black vans facing the street. A man opened the back doors of the vans, went to the tables and picked up two short, fat looking rifles: grenade launchers. He put one in the back of each van. In the middle of the room were about a dozen men sitting in as many chairs, all facing a huge dry erase board, the kind of board the military would use for instructing before a big offensive attack. On the board, at the top, were the words The USA Group. An acronym for the secret Underground Subversive Attack group. The group Jadon calls The Outsiders.

Below the letters there was a crude drawing. Something tall, vertical, like a building.

"My God! It's the Statue of Liberty!" Addie Mae whispered to Glaad, "do you think…"

"Shhh," Glaad cautioned.

A man was at the board, writing on it. It was a man with a black teardrop tattoo under his eye. He stroked in the words SHE WILL FALL INTO HER WATERY GRAVE!

Then he wrote smaller words below that. Addie Mae and Glaad pushed themselves away from the wall. But before she did, Addie Mae snapped one quick picture with her cell phone. In a hurry, she turned the phone off and plunged it between her ample breasts.

When Addie Mae pushed away from the wall, she took a step backward to the middle of the roof of the van. The roof buckled loudly, the metal pushing in with a *PLONG*! sound. Addie Mae's face was silent alarm.

"Don't worry," Glaad comforted. "Sounds like a late truck delivery on the street." Glaad and Addie Mae wasted no time climbing down from the roof of the van. Addie Mae went first. Glaad was right behind her. Fortunately, the ladder held. But, unfortunately, as they turned to leave, there were six men blocking their exit. Glaad turned to look behind them. There were four more.

In the shadows of the alley, the situation looked grim. Frightening. Deadly.

It was.

NINETEEN

The assembly outside City Hall was turning into a swarm.
Homemade signs were twirling and shaking above heads.

IMPEACH WERTZ

WERTZ DESERTS US

Police arrived on foot, on bicycles, on horseback.
They stayed at the periphery. For now.

• • •

Inside the metal building, Addie Mae and Glaad sat on chairs
next to the dry erase board. Their hands were fastened
behind the backrests. Their ankles were zip tied to the front
legs of the chairs. They sat silent as mice with a cat in the
room. Behind them they could hear Teardrop having a fit.
He was throwing things down on a workbench in a rage.

"That fucking Walii! I'll kill him, I swear!"

"If you don't, one of us will," another man said.

Teardrop spit out the words, "This was going to be
perfect. The whole mission in the dark, over by 7 A.M. Now,
we won't even get going until 7 A.M.!"

"A lot of people are going to die today because of
him," the other man added.

"All he had to do was get the C-4 and get back here
by 4 A.M. But no, he's probably banging that bitch of his in
Newark!" Teardrop was super pissed.

"He's fuckin' her and fuckin' us at the same time."
It was a different man that spoke this time.

"Well, I'm not giving up my bonus 'cause of that

scumbag." Teardrop said. "We'll have to revise the plan so we don't go down because of him! Where's he now?"

"Not sure. On his way, I guess," one of the other men said.

"Well when he gets here, we should have a little party. A goodbye party!" Teardrop said.

"What time do we leave?" One of the men asked.

"Let's plan on seven. Ms. Liberty lays down at nine."

. . .

In his hotel room, Cha-ley walked out of the bathroom in boxer shorts that looked two-sizes too big. In keeping with Cha-ley's loving good nature, they had big red hearts over a white background.

The news was on TV, and as luck would have it, there was the TV spot that Cha-ley had a hand in making.

He dug into the pocket of his pants lying on the bed, retrieved his cell phone and turned it off for the night. He plopped onto the bed, exhausted. Sleep came in seconds.

. . .

In the alley close to the NYSE, a man dressed in total black, wearing a black ski mask, stepped out of the back doors of a black van and aimed the grenade launcher in a steep trajectory. He pulled the trigger. A projectile about the size of a ping-pong ball blasted from the large diameter barrel and flew toward the Stock Exchange. It smashed through an upper window sending glass fragments to the protestors on the street. The pulsating light from the fire it started could be seen from below.

The black van drove north on Park Avenue as fast as the fastest taxi. When it got within a block of 42nd Street, the sliding panel door on the side opened. The courtesy light was disabled, so it remained dark inside. The man looking out was dressed in total black, wearing a black ski mask, and had a strange bulky looking short-barreled rifle at his side. When the van was broadside Grand Central Station, the man raised the grenade launcher to his shoulder. The van never stopped. The man fired the weapon. The projectile flew in a long arc and penetrated an upper window. It fell to the floor near the center of the main concourse and burst into flames.

The man wearing black from head to toe was crouched down on the black tar roof. He aimed the grenade launcher at the three-story building across the street. The incendiary left the barrel and crash-landed on the roof of the 64th Precinct. The fire was immediate.

. . .

"I have to go to the bathroom," Addie Mae called out.

She was ignored. She waited.

Louder: "I have to go to the bathroom!"

Nothing.

She screamed, "I have to go to the fucking bathroom, or I'll shit and piss right here!"

The guard who was supposed to be watching over Addie Mae and Glaad woke up when Teardrop whopped him in the head.

"They're awake and you're asleep! Maybe I should tie you up with them, stupid! Untie her and let her go do her business." His head motioned to a tiny restroom opposite the dry erase board. The man cut the zip ties with a long black knife. Addie Mae got up stiffly and shuffled to the rest room. The man lingered behind staying a distance away. With the door closed, Addie Mae reached deep between her breasts and pulled out her phone. Just then, one of the big rollup garage doors filled the warehouse with noise as it opened. The noise masked any sound the phone would have made. But the phone made almost no sound at all as it started up.

As fast as she could, Addie Mae sent the one picture she took through the warehouse window to Chance's phone. All she typed into the subject line was 9:00 A.M. She shut the phone down. God forbid it should ring! She breathed a big sigh of relief. Then took a pee.

The rusty '96 pickup truck drove in and the big rollup door descended. Addie Mae left the bathroom and the guard took her back to her chair next to Glaad. The zip ties went on, just as before.

Walii got out of his truck, opened the passenger door and carried a large cardboard box containing a dozen off-white bricks of C-4. The box went on the explosives table.

"Hey, man, I'm really sorry it took so long," Walii said.

"Yeah, me too," Teardrop said standing about ten feet in front of him. "You were supposed to be back by four so we could have this done in the dark, but now…"

"I had a problem with the truck in Newark and…"

"You mean you had a problem with your bitch in Newark! Don't fuckin' lie, you piece a shit!" Teardrop took a step closer. Walii took a step back. He didn't see or hear the man behind him with the three-foot-long steel crow bar. He didn't see or hear the man wind up for a swing at his head. But he did feel the impact.

Two men picked up the body from the floor and

disposed of it. While two men went to the explosives table and finished the assembly of the bombs with the just-delivered C-4.

Teardrop addressed the gang. "Here's what we'll do. After the C-4 is all put in position around the base of the Statue, you guys take the boat to one of the old, unused docks on the Jersey side. They're close. It'll only take a few minutes to get there. Then spread out in the neighborhood for a few days. Maybe a week. I'll have the chopper pick me up at the top of the Statue, then fly a few feet over the water and drop me off behind some big old empty buildings on Ellis Island.* I'll hide in one of them with the rats. When it's safe, I'll mix in with the tourists who visit the island and take the ferry back to the city. I'll call each one of you when I think it's safe. Got it?"

"Got it," most of them said.

"Sounds like a plan," one said.

Teardrop continued, "This will give enough time for the news and police helicopters to get there. Just in time to show the world the Statue coming down…with these two assholes on top!" He motioned to Addie Mae and Glaad. Their eyes were filled with terror.

---

* Ellis Island covers more than twenty-seven acres. The south side has many large derelict buildings. Nearly all the buildings are closed to the public, although limited hard-hat tours of the historic hospital began in 2014.

TWENTY

The hands of the security checkpoint clock were at seven.
A strong morning sun was streaming into the rotunda at City
Hall when Chance walked through. The door to the Mayor's
office was open and Chance could see that Brix was trying to
get going, but the Mayor had more to say. His fist was in the
air. His face was rabid. "Crush 'em, hear me? I don't care
what the media says! Crush 'em!"

"Then we need more help. Serious help." Brix
stressed.

"I already made a call to the Governor for more
troops, but it's Sunday. I doubt they could be here until
tonight, if we're lucky."

"That's when we'll need them. It's usually quiet in
the mornings. The fires are still burning but under control.
But tonight, all hell could break loose."

"Then get your men ready. We put an end to this
tonight!" With that, Brix walked out and Chance walked in.

"I don't have your check ready yet. I suppose that's
why you wanted to meet this morning. I imagine you can't
wait to get back home."

"I decided to stay a few days. So, anytime before I
leave would be fine."

"Too bad you missed the press conference yesterday.
We all toasted you, symbolically."

"I heard. Thanks." Chance closed the door and
turned to Wertz. Wertz walked over to the chair behind his
desk.

"It's time, Ed."

Wertz, hand on his chair, looked at Chance inquisitively.

"It's over," Chance said to Wertz. "I know all about it. Marvin Shmutter. Your brother, Bertram. The whole thing."

Wertz sat down and ran his right hand over his thinning hair. "I don't know what you're talking about! And neither do you. So if you know what's…"

"Angel Perez," Chance said coldly. Wertz's eyes were quiet rage. They drilled into Chance.

Chance pressed on. "Sheamus O'Neill. Arthur Stevens. The jewelry store."

Wertz's face was red, blood pressure rising. "You can't prove anything! I have DNA evidence that proves…"

"So do I," Chance said calmly. Wertz's face was controlled anger and confusion combined. He was starting to sweat.

"I exhumed the body, Ed."

Wertz's eyes narrowed. "To do that, you'd have to steal DNA evidence from our Property Department. You're going to fucking jail!"

Chance retorted: "The DNA evidence you had, the DNA you planted, is right where it was. You took your brother's DNA samples and labeled them Angel Perez so they'd match the DNA found at the scene."

Wertz was pale now. In a cold sweat. The veins in his neck and forehead were pulsating. His hand was trembling as he reached for the top right drawer of his desk. He pulled the drawer out slowly. In the reflection from a shiny chrome vase behind Wertz, Chance could see a stainless steel revolver in the drawer.

"I wouldn't do that," Chance warned, "I'll be on you before you can even get your hand on it."

Wertz closed the drawer and glared at Chance. Strangely, Wertz's eyes began to fill.

"Twenty-two years ago, Ed. That's when it all started. That's when *you* created the New York cop killer. That's when *you* created Robert Knickerbocker."

"Robert Knickerbocker? What does Knickerbocker have to do with Angel Perez? It doesn't make any sense to me. And it won't to anyone else, either."

"You don't know?" Chance asked. Wertz's face was blank.

"Robert Knickerbocker is Antonio Perez, Angel's son." Wertz's mouth went a little slack. He blinked.

"After you and your henchmen sent Angel to death row, the lives of the Perez family were destroyed. Rosalina Perez, Angel's wife, started drinking. She became an alcoholic. She died in a car crash three years after Angel went to prison. Fourteen-year-old Antonio ran away to a life on the streets. He was homeless for a couple of years, with no family, no relatives in this country. He did what he had to do. B and E, armed robbery, gang member, drug addict…and hit man."

Wertz just sat there listening. His eyes diverted to the floor, the ceiling, the walls, as if the scenes of young Antonio's life were being projected there.

Chance continued. "At barely eighteen, Antonio ended up at Riker's Island, one of the world's largest correctional institutions. Infamous for its neglect and abuse of prisoners. The world's largest penal colony, as it's called. Devil's Island had nothing on Rikers. Just the kind of place a kid barely over seventeen could be saved, don't you think?"

Chance paused for it all to sink in. Wertz was stoic.

"But that's not the worst of it," Chance emphasized. "Young Antonio was in 'The Program'." Chance used his fingers to make quote marks in the air. "Young boys in The Program got favors from a radical, roving pack of guards, organized by a warped warden, Titus Washington, who fancied…young meat." Chance paused again. Wertz's eyes flashed at Chance, then away. He sat there tapping his fingertips on the desk, wondering how fast he could get to his gun. His eyes drifted to the drawer.

• • •

Cha-ley was brushing his teeth when he started up his phone for the day. An email alert made him look at the screen. He stopped brushing, toothbrush still in his mouth, when he realized it wasn't his phone. "I picked up Chance's phone by mistake! Holy shit!" White foam spilled out of his mouth. He spit it in the sink, grabbed his pants and shirt and stuffed his feet into his shoes.

Cha-ley was frantically threading his way through the mob outside City Hall as fast as he could. There were fewer protestors than last night, but still over a hundred. He finally got up to security, huffing and puffing. The Guard looked at him suspiciously. The Guard called for a backup officer. This would not go as fast as Cha-ley wanted.

• • •

Wertz's face was blank as Chance continued. "He bummed around for years and got a job at a survivalist magazine. He learned a lot in his seven years there. He wrote articles on guns, ammo, bombs, survival gear and martial arts. He became the magazine's computer guy who put the magazine together every month."

Chance paused for just a moment.

"By the time he got to you, all he needed was a name."

Wertz finally spoke: "So he picked Robert Knickerbocker."

"That's right. He fit right in," Chance said.

"He fooled me! Why didn't he just kill me? It would have been a lot easier," Wertz said.

"He didn't want your death to be easy. Or quick. He wanted it to be a slow death. Like his own. He wanted to ruin your life, everything you wanted and worked for. Just like you ruined his. You took everything away from him. Somewhere along the line, he dedicated his life, what was left of it, to taking yours. Slowly. Painfully. He killed the sons of O'Neill and Stevens. So that score was settled. He took the lives of police officers, so the Rikers score was settled. He took the people of your city and turned them against you. But he had no idea that sending his father to death row was to protect your own brother. He died not knowing the truth."

"He's my brother, for God's sake!"

"Your brother's a murderer. And so are you."

"You'll never get away with this!"

"That's not what Sheamus O'Neill thinks. He's willing to testify that he and Stevens helped you with lies, planted evidence and the DNA switch." Wertz looked up at Chance, his mind working overtime. His eyes moving rapidly from right to left a few times. Then he just stared straight ahead without focus. His shoulders dropped. He sat back in his chair. He let out a long sigh.

Just then…the door burst open. Cha-ley was sweating. "I'm sorry. I took your phone last night by mistake. Look…" he handed the phone to Chance. "You got this from Addie Mae." Chance looked at the image on the screen.

"That's all she sent? Just that?" Chance asked.

"Yes, that's all." It was a picture of the big dry erase board at the warehouse. Chance studied the picture. He read all the words.

"We gotta go!" Chance said urgently to Cha-ley.

"We'll finish this tomorrow morning," Chance said to Wertz. "You have a lot to think about between now and then." Chance leaned on Wertz's desk with both arms, his eyes penetrating into Wertz's eyes. "If you run, I'll find you," Chance said fiercely. "And when I find you, you'll wish you had stayed here." Chance's face and voice meant every word of what he said. He looked intently into Wertz's eyes to let it sink in.

"Let's go!" Chance said to Cha-ley. And they were gone.

Wertz was left alone, motionless, in his big fancy office, staring into nothingness.

TWENTY-ONE

"How'd it go with the Mayor," Nicole asked into the phone.

"So far, so good. We have something more important to do right now. I can't talk, but do me a favor," Chance said.

"Sure, what do you need?"

"My toolbox. Can you pick it up from your place and bring it to the occupation?"

"Yeah. I'm at the studio, so no problem."

"And call Jadon and tell him to be there, too. We need all hands on-deck. This is an emergency!"

"I will. Right away. Should I bring my film crew, too?"

"Only if you want the biggest scoop on national TV!"

. . .

The two big rollup doors of the metal building opened. Two black vans pulled out. Inside the first one, Glaad and Addie Mae sat, zip tied. Teardrop was driving. Teardrop's phone rang.

"Yeah?"

"You on your way?" Cufflinks asked.

"We're rollin', finally."

"What did you do with Walii?"

"We didn't want to make a bloody mess so we knocked him out and stuffed him in a big metal garbage can, then filled it with water."

"He could have ruined our entire mission," Cufflinks said, pissed."

"Tell me about it. Instead of doing this in the dark, we're gonna be with the tourists. Now a lot more people are going to die. Hey, I don't give a shit as long as we all make it out. I had to change the plan a little. You might not hear from me for a while. Gotta go, there's a police car behind me."

CLICK

Addie Mae and Glaad had heard what Teardrop said on the phone call. They could see out the heavily tinted back windows and out the windshield. They watched hopefully…but the police car drove by the van and vanished up ahead.

They sank.

• • •

There was a stuttering static sound from the loud speakers at the occupation outside the 64th Precinct. Chance came onto the makeshift stage and walked up to the microphone without hesitation. Cha-ley and Jadon followed and stood behind him.

"Listen up, everybody! Listen up! Please! Gather round! Come to the stage and gather round." Chance's urgent plea was heard in every part of the occupation. Every person heard his voice. "We need your help! The city needs your help! America needs your help!"

It was still morning. Most protestors had spent the night in their homes. But this was a hardy bunch. About seventy-five of them came up to the stage.

Nicole was at the back of the buzzing throng of protestors standing in front of the stage.

Chance's words were heavy. "This may be the most important day in any of our lives. And we have to act fast!"

The faces in the crowd were confused, but curious. More protestors came and joined in.

Chance continued. "The Outsiders who came to this protest and to the protest at Wall Street and at Grand Central…you know who I'm talking about…the agitators, the ones who try to convince us all to hate each other, to not trust each other, they're not just here for the protests. They're here to destroy our city! Our country! They have weapons, bombs and a plan!"

There was a murmur starting to spread in the crowd. One man yelled out, "What are you doing here? Sounds like you're talking hate right now!"

More protestors joined the crowd, now numbering over one hundred.

Chance forged ahead. "Right now, as we are all standing here, The Outsiders are on their way to destroy the Statue of Liberty!"

The crowd lit up with shock and doubt at what Chance was telling them. Some mocking him in disbelief. The voices grew louder. The crowd became a choppy sea of emotions, distrust, anger and frustration. Chance's voice was strong, firm, convinced. "The National Guard is not prepared for anything like this. The police will just go there and negotiate. We don't have time for negotiations. We have to do this ourselves! Right now! Right this minute! We have to do this for our families, our city, our country! We have to go and stop them! Are you with me?" Chance yelled into the microphone.

There was a sudden, thunderous "Yeah!" that rose up from the crowd. More than half of them wore the red hats and they waved them over their heads.

The roar was so loud, so spirited, so filled with emotion, it was as if the energy rolled across our nation at that very moment. And maybe it did. In a Kansas wheat field, an old farmer on his tractor heard the wind blow through the fields of grain. For some reason, he looked to the east for a moment, as if he heard something else on the wind.

Chance yelled into the mic again: "Are you with me?"

An even bigger, more enthusiastic "Yeah!" thundered from the hoard, now numbering over one hundred and eighty.

In Seattle, a middle-age ad man on the twenty-first floor looked out his office window and stared to the east at a rising sun. He could swear he heard something.

"Are you with me?" Chance was at the top of his voice. His most inspiring. The sea of faces cheered wildly and waved their red hats. They chanted "USA, USA, USA, USA…"

"Now…this is important…no women or children." The women didn't like that. They moaned and complained.

"Sorry 'bout that, but that's the way it has to be. Take care of things here. We'll be back as soon as we can. The bad guys are already on their way. So get there any way you can…taxi, bicycle, run, walk, but get there. Go to Jadon's Facebook page for any last minute news or instructions so we're all coordinated."

"ARE YOU READY?"

The response was ear crushing.

"YEAH!!!"

"LET'S ROLL!" Chance screamed.

• • •

The Red Hats were streaming through the congested streets on foot. They piled into taxis, they flooded subway platforms, they squeezed into crowded trains. The Red Hats were threading their way through city streets on bicycles, hanging off the backs of garbage trucks and flashing cash in front of regular citizens for a lift, only to pile in eight linebacker-sized guys.

Chaz was driving the white PIC-10 van south on West Street, but he wasn't alone. Nicole was in the right seat. And the rest of the van was jammed, shoulder-to-shoulder, hip-to-hip, with twelve other BFFs.

. . .

The surface of the Hudson River reflected clouds at 7:15 this Sunday morning. It was a flat-calm day. Pier 25 stuck out into the river for 360-feet, the longest of any pier in the Hudson River Park System. It offered citizens an eighteen-hole mini-golf course, a playground for kids, free tours of a 173-foot historic steam powered ship, beach volleyball and moorings for small boats.

It was packed with people today, like every fair summer weekend.

In stark contrast to this popular and beautiful place was the location Teardrop chose as the embarkation point for his team's voyage to Liberty Island – The New York City Department Sanitation pier, less than a mile and a half to the north. There would be hardly anyone there on a Sunday. And employees that were there would have very little interest in two innocuous vans pulling in and parking way in the back next to the trash transfer barge dock.

Revealing itself, as it came around the 20,000 square foot trash collection building, was a 38-foot cabin cruiser fishing boat. It would be there only three minutes. Just enough time to pick up twelve 'fishermen', all in navy blue T-shirts. The 'It's a Blast Fishing Club'. That's what it said on the backs of the shirts, anyway. And along for the ride was bound and gagged Addie Mae and Glaad. They were hustled into the cabin, out of sight.

The 'fishing boat' left promptly. With no one the wiser.

. . .

The city bus just passed a street sign that said CANAL ST. The nine Red Hats all checked Jadon's Facebook page.

MARINA JUST N OF BATT PK

. . .

The fishing boat cut a polluted off-white wave across the dirty-green harbor water. It was fast, even with the sixteen aboard. Liberty Island quickly grew in size. At the island, the boat slowed to idle speed but banged hard against the pilings of the dock on the west side of the island. This is where the ferry docks and lets hundreds of tourists off for their visit to the Statue. This is where the large, on-dock pavilion is located, a welcome center of sorts. And this is where the Park Service security guards greet tourists and point them in the right direction. Today, the guards were surprised by an impromptu visit from fishermen who either lost their way or had some kind of mechanical difficulty or a medical emergency.

"Help us! Help us! Please!" one of the fishermen called out to the guards on the dock. "He's had a heart attack."

Four security guards quickly assembled at the edge of the dock. Eight of the fishermen got off of the boat and scrambled onto the dock as the victim was being hoisted up for medical aide.

Eight fishermen, four guards, four flashing knives to throats and it was all over silently. Expeditiously. Heinously.

The remaining four 'fishermen' poured out of the cabin, along with Addie Mae and Glaad. When they were assembled on the dock, Teardrop said, "There are more of them at the Statue. Pick up your fishing poles and let's get this done. We're behind schedule." They moved quickly. Each man knew his pre-determined position on the island. Teardrop was moving, too, gun pointing at the backs of Addie Mae and Glaad. They walked toward the base of the Statue. They couldn't move as quickly as the others because the ankles of Glaad were tethered together so he could walk but couldn't kick. The same for Addie Mae. But the trio made good progress across the lawn and they were soon at the base of the Statue.

"Can I help you, gentlemen?" said one of the two men inside a long white tent at the base of the Statue, eager to help in any way.

"One of our guys in the fishing club is having a heart attack and we need your help right away!"

The two ambassadors came forward for a better look. And under the cover of the tent, away from the sight of other park attendants, their lives ended. Other attendants would soon greet the fishermen with smiles, too.

Inside, the fishermen's feet hammered against the two hundred and fifteen metal steps just to get to the top of the stone pedestal – a total of one hundred and fifty-four feet from the ground to the foot of the Statue – where the explosives would be placed in key spots to efficiently and effectively bring down Lady Liberty.

Teardrop and his two hostages had to travel much higher. An additional one hundred and fifty-one feet from Lady Liberty's heel to the torch. But Teardrop had discovered something to make the agonizing climb a lot easier and faster. A tiny emergency rescue elevator adjacent to the double spiral staircase. It could barely fit three people. Just big enough if they squeezed in. They squeezed in. The lift, the only one of its kind in the world, designed and built specifically for the Statue of Liberty, was an elongated rectangular shape of almost total glass. The three pressed in and the door closed. Teardrop had barely enough room to keep his gun trained on his captives. They could have easily bumped the barrel of the gun in a different direction. With certain death awaiting them at the top, was there anything to lose?

. . .

The big prop of The Beaver spun into action thrusting rivulets and chop onto the East River. A big puff of smoke added to the city's air pollution. Cha-ley pushed the float plane away from the dock, climbed up from the pontoon, and got into the right seat next to Chance. The Beaver pivoted and aimed for open water.

. . .

Teardrop did not take his eyes off of Glaad and Addie Mae inside the cramped little elevator. And Glaad had his eyes glued to the gun in Teardrop's hand. Halfway up, something got into Teardrop's nose - dust, pollen, the scent of cologne, perfume, sweaty body odor...whatever it was, Teardrop wrinkled his nose and closed his eyes for just a fraction of a second. The barrel of the gun dropped just a little. And Glaad made his move! He jerked his body in front of Teardrop pushing the gun toward the front of the elevator. The gun fired in a loud blast shattering the side wall near Addie Mae. With no hesitation, Glaad, taller and bigger than Teardrop, thrust his head violently forward aiming a powerful head-butt at the forehead of his captor. It was a battering-ram force. And perfectly aimed. But Teardrop moved his head to the side lightning fast and Glaad smashed his own head into the tempered glass elevator wall. Glaad pulled back, woozy, dumbed-down, blinking, the cuts on his forehead matching the cracks in the hard glass wall. Little bits of glass fell to the floor from his head.

Teardrop put the gun to Glaad's neck.

• • •

The band of Red Hats invaded the marina like a swarm of locusts. They alighted on small open bay boats, skiffs and dinghies. They yanked on rope starters, pulling outboards to life. They leapt onto twenty and thirty-foot sport boats, reaching under instrument panels to hotwire them into deep-throated roars. They jumped onto jet skis like cowboys and twisted throttles to high revs. Before any sleepy, Sunday morning onlookers could react, the armada was on its way out of safe harbor, sailing off to war in our own country.

• • •

The elevator reached the crown – its last stop. Teardrop backed out, followed by a still-stunned Glaad and a whimpering Addie Mae. Two of Teardrop's men, breathing hard from the climb up the stairs, arrived at the same spot. They each held a gun. Teardrop put his hand on a ladder close to his left side. "I'll go up first," Teardrop said to his men. "You two stay here at the bottom until these two pigs are at the top." He started his climb. Glaad and Addie Mae followed, Addie Mae first this time. The ladder rose through a vertical tunnel – the arm of the Statue. It wasn't easy for Glaad and Addie Mae to climb forty feet with their wrists tied and ankles tethered. But they did.

. . .

Nicole was having the time of her life. Literally. She was on one of the boats speeding across the harbor, toward Liberty Island, filming the entire flotilla. Jadon was driving one of the sport boats. Nicole could picture him storming the beach at Normandy. Nicole had her microphone out in the wind, recording the ambient sounds of an all-out vigilante attack. Chaz had his camera on his shoulder. Nicole started speaking, yelling into her mic now, hair flying wildly, making journalistic history.

. . .

Teardrop pushed the hatch open and it fell back on the decking. Sunlight poured into the dark arm. Teardrop helped Addie Mae struggle with all her might to wriggle up and off the ladder. She was shocked, dizzy, looking way down from the small platform where she stood. She was scared to death, drawing in a deep breath and not letting it out. She pressed her back against the five-foot-tall verdigris copper cylinder in the center of the platform. She felt heat behind her head. She glanced upward and she was momentarily blinded. It was the twenty-four-karat gold- plated flame of the torch reflecting the sun three hundred and five feet above the ground. Glaad was next, not doing much better than Addie Mae, perhaps because of the self-inflicted battering his brain received on the elevator. Dried blood ran down his cheeks. Teardrop yanked him to his feet. He, too, seeing the precipice at his toes, drew in a deep breath upon standing, wobbly. One little stumble in the wrong direction and he'd fall the equivalent of a twenty-two-story building.

"Get over there, against the railing, over there! Move!" Teardrop motioned with his gun and Addie Mae and Glaad slowly, ever so slowly, shuffled to the railing and faced the backside of the flame.

"Now," Teardrop announced, "I'm going to reach behind you and fasten your hands to the railing. You first, big man. If you try anything again, she goes off to the ground. And then you die, too. Remember, I can shoot a lot faster than you can move."

Teardrop took something out of his pocket. Zip ties. In a few seconds, Addie Mae was tied to the railing, also.

"Now, at least you can die with this bullshit symbol of freedom. You'll go down in history. Literally! Ha, ha, ha, ha! Ha, ha, ha, ha! You pigs!"

Teardrop heard something. A helicopter. He saw it coming to the Statue from New Jersey. It was low but rose up fast. He could see the man crouched in the large opening behind the pilot. Teardrop waved.

The helicopter rose up about fifteen feet above the flame and hovered there, stabilized. The man in the open hatch, dressed in black, pushed something from the opening. It was hanging on a rope. It was a cardboard box about three-cubic feet in size. It descended to the platform behind the flame, to Addie Mae's right side. Teardrop guided it

downwards into position. The man in the chopper sped up
the winch that had lowered the box, but instead of reeling in
the rope, it was faster for him to run the rope out and drop it
on the platform next to the box.

He quickly moved to a second winch that was
already prepared for the next drop. It wasn't a box, but a
combination generator/blower.

Again, Teardrop guided it into position near the box.
And again, the man at the winch ran the rope off the spool
and dropped it on the platform. The chopper moved off a bit
and hovered over the crown.

Teardrop wasted no time getting to the box and the
generator/blower.

He unpacked the contents and threw the empty box
over the side. There was a folded American flag on top and a
propane torch. He put these to his side. Then he unraveled
the plastic, flesh-colored material. It almost appeared to be
an airbed or waterbed. Then he went to the blower. He
hooked up the hose, the size of a vacuum hose, to a port
connection on the material. The material was still folded in
some places, part of it hanging over the railing. Teardrop
worked hard. Rapidly. Intently. He started up the generator
that powered the blower and the balloon started to fill.

The helicopter was rock-steady, hovering about
fifteen feet above and to the back of Lady Liberty's head.
The chopper was broadside, its front toward the torch, its tail
toward the tablet that Lady Liberty holds in her left arm.
There was something attached to the skids on either side of
the chopper. On the side facing the front of the Statue was
what appeared to be a long white tube about eight inches in
diameter and twenty-four feet long. On the skid toward the
rear of the Statue, was what looked like a plain aluminum
tube about two inches square and about sixteen-feet long.

The white tube on the left skid and the aluminum tube on the right skid were connected by a strap on each end.

The aluminum tube at the rear of the Statue's head was first. Using ropes, the man in the open hatch lowered the tube until it was in line with the back of the Lady Liberty's neck. As the chopper inched its way sideways, toward the front of the Statue, the aluminum tube caught on the copper 'hairline' at the back and held the tube in place. Then the man started lowering the long white tube in front of the Statue's face. As the tube descended, the ropes that were connected to the aluminum tube made a yoke that strapped over the shoulders of Lady Liberty. These shoulder straps held the long white tube in place, in a perfect horizontal, about ten feet below Lady Liberty's face. The tube extended all the way from her right armpit to her left shoulder. The man in the chopper just had one more thing to do. Release the twenty-four-foot long tube of rolled up white fabric, like a roll of carpeting, and let it fall, draping over the front of the Statue.

. . .

The floats of The Beaver lifted off the surface of the East River and the plane was in the air. The plane climbed quickly, but only to six hundred feet, more than enough altitude to clear the middle of the Brooklyn Bridge which was now under them.

In moments, Chance could see Governor's Island off his left wing. Cha-ley could see the Staten Island Ferry Terminal and Battery Park off to his right. And straight ahead, the Statue of Liberty. They would be there in minutes. Below them, Chance and Cha-ley saw what looked like a regatta. No, an armada of boats. A dozen of them. All sizes.

All streaking across the harbor. All headed to Liberty Island. And all on board were wearing red hats. A happy sight.

But, up ahead, as the Statue grew closer and larger, was a picture that no American could ever imagine. A sign hanging across the chest of Lady Liberty. A white sign with only two words on it. Blue letters on the top and red letters on the bottom. A sick, disgusting, red, white and blue sadistic joke. In big block letters, the sign said:

FUCK

AMERICA

As they flew closer, less than a hundred feet over the Statue, Chance and Cha-ley could see that there was something big in front of the torch held high over the welcoming harbor. It was a kind of blowup or balloon, a promotional advertising inflatable, five feet wide and twelve feet tall. But this advertising inflatable had a sinister message. It reached from the platform to beyond the top of the flame. It was a blowup of a giant human hand giving the middle finger to America. Literally.

Chance and Cha-ley were speechless. Until they saw Addie Mae and Glaad at the railing.

"My God," Cha-ley said in disbelief. "It's Addie Mae! They have her."

"Not for long, Cha-ley, not for long."

The Beaver passed over Addie Mae and Glaad with a deep-throated, authoritative roar and turned into a steep sixty-degree bank spiraling down to the water. Addie Mae's eyes widened, her face opened up, when she saw The Beaver overhead.

I knew he'd come, she thought to herself with her mouth still silenced by the silver duct tape. *I knew it!* Addie Mae's chin quivered. Her eyes filled. And tears ran down her cheeks.

Teardrop looked up and saw The Beaver fly over. "Sightseers!" he grumped. "I hope you took pictures, you assholes!"

Teardrop's men were busy inside the Statue looking at their phones. On the screens were diagrams showing them where the explosives should go and details on how to handle, place, position and mold the C-4 around struts, supports, pillars and posts. Each man had his own assignment. Each man studied his designated plan intently, methodically. So much so that they did not see or hear The Beaver land and set an anchor behind the cover of mature trees on the east side of the island.

Standing on one of the floats, Chance stripped off his white shirt, reached into his 'toolbox' and extracted his good luck charm. His rattlesnake fang/alligator tooth necklace. He put it on over his gray tank top. Chance slid into the water. Cha-ley handed him the toolbox duffle bag. Chance held it over his head. Cha-ley slid into the water and they both made their way to the stone seawall that offered lots of handholds to get them over the top.

The two men who had helped Teardrop at the ladder inside the Statue earlier were now assigned as watchmen. A perfect place to watch was from the stone parapet just below the copper base of the Statue. It encircled the Statue and the men would patrol its narrow walkway. But before they started their observation duty, they decided to share some cocaine just to heighten their senses. While they did, Chance and Cha-ley ran the relatively short distance to the stone foundation and pedestal. Scaling the walls here was somewhat easy and safe.

The lookouts had their elbows on the top of the parapet wall looking out at the skyline of the city. They still had their blue fishing club T-shirts on. Every one of the 'fishermen' did.

"I was there that day," one said to the other.

"What day?"

"The day the towers came down on 911. Right there." He pointed.

"Did you have anything to do with it?"

"No, but I wish I did."

As soon as he uttered that wish, a fast-spinning boomerang whomped him in his left temple. He dropped in place, a horizontal gash to his head penetrating deeply into his skull.

The other lookout, totally puzzled as to why his buddy dropped to the floor, was stunned at first. Until he saw Chance to his left. He turned to his right and started to run. He stopped running when the bolo Chance launched at his ankles brought him down hard against the stone floor smashing all his front teeth and flattening his nose to nothingness. Blood shot out of his eyes. He seemed to go to sleep.

• • •

The armada landed, albeit somewhat crudely. Some boats slammed sideways against pilings, splintering fiberglass, jet skis plowed straight in knocking riders off as the watercraft kept going under the dock, and some skiffs and dinghies mimicked a demolition derby. While not exercising military precision, the landing was carried out, nonetheless.

The Red Hats scoured all vessels for any and all possible defensive weapons. Soon, in the hands of the warriors were short wooden clubs, boat hooks on aluminum poles, gaffs…even fishing nets on the ends of poles. And, of course, there were more than a few fillet knives among the cache.

With remarkable pre-agreed silence, the one-hundred and seventeen-member Red Hat Stealth Force stormed the Statue. Except for the dull thunder of two hundred and thirty-four feet, it was a silent storm. They ran upstairs, they scaled walls and they climbed metal steps two at a time.

· · ·

Atop the torch platform, Teardrop's eyes were pulled away from his concentrated work. He shot to his feet as if his legs were springs. He looked down at the ground below. His nostrils flared, his mouth turned to a dog's snarl, teeth bared, eyes rabid. He grabbed the railing with both hands in a tight grip. The Red Hats were streaming across the lawns and walks, disappearing into the Statue like cockroaches under a baseboard.

Teardrop bent his body over the railing to get a better vantage point. He stepped one foot closer to the hatch opening. He spread his feet for better balance.

In a blur, a hand snapped out of the opening as fast as a rattlesnake striking. Chance had a vice-like grip on Teardrop's ankle. Teardrop kicked wildly to shake loose but couldn't. Chance twisted Teardrop's foot. Teardrop lost his balance and went down on the platform, wriggling in spasms.

Chance climbed up out of the hole with his free hand, never letting go of Teardrop's ankle. As Teardrop went down and Chance rose up, Teardrop's leg was twisted high in the air almost breaking his ankle and knee bones. But Teardrop rolled his whole body on its side, to ease the excruciating pain.

Chance shrugged his toolbox duffel off his shoulder and it dropped to the side of the hatch opening. With his rattlesnake necklace around his neck, he lorded over Teardrop. Chance was finally mano-a-mano with the man he had spotted out of masses of protestors in the news footage. He was, finally, eye-to-eye with the man he chased through the crowds at City Hall Plaza. Chance couldn't help a hint of a smile as he looked down on the squirming vermin at his feet.

Chance had no time to even look at Addie Mae and Glaad. But he knew they were there. He didn't survive in the Glades for almost two years without having outstanding peripheral vision. Right now, eyes had to be on his opponent. His very capable, very devious, very strong opponent.

Teardrop, in a flash, grabbed the propane bottle from the platform, pressed the instant-on trigger and a blue-white flame hissed out of the nozzle. In one fluid motion, Teardrop did a sit-up, lunged forward and the three-inch long super-hot blue flame was searing Chance's wrist and forearm. Chance had no good choice at the moment. He let go.

• • •

The man in the navy blue T-shirt was bent over a major support inside the Statue. He was referring to his cell phone schematic and carefully patting and molding the plasticized explosive around the support. No worries about patting too hard, you can drop C-4 off a cliff and it won't explode. It can only be exploded by a detonating device delivering intense heat and a shock wave. He was busy patting the C-4 cake when a gaffer's hook, the size fishermen use to pull in eight-hundred-pound marlin, impaled his shoulder and his body was yanked violently backward.

A heavy I-beam strut ran diagonally downward across the Statue's cavity from twenty feet above to the floor. The man in the blue shirt worked intently. Quietly. He was especially quiet after being struck in the head by the short wooden club.

But things didn't remain quiet for long. A man in a blue shirt, standing on an upper level of the spiral staircase, unleashed a barrage of automatic fire from an AK-47. A full-fledged bona fide machine gun. The rat-a-tat sound was loud and terrifying. Smoke wafted in the air. The smell of Independence Day fireworks permeated every nook and cranny. And it was an alarm bell for every blue shirt in the Statue.

But, miraculously, Jadon held something in his hand that could save them from a man firing a machine gun. Something he had pilfered from the boat that got him and his soldiers to the Island. A flare-gun.

Jadon had never fired a flare gun before, but he could see it was loaded with one big fat red flare. He aimed it at the blue T-shirt firing on his men. Bullets were ricocheting wildly off metal struts, posts and beams. Sparks were flying everywhere as if kids had Fourth of July sparklers. Jadon pulled the big curved trigger of the clunky flare gun. The flare left the large bore barrel, arched slightly across the interior of the Statue, and struck the man in the face burning a hole in his cheek the size of a coffee cup. His shirt caught on fire. It looked like the sun had come out inside Lady Liberty.

· · ·

Teardrop rotated his body like a top on the platform and popped to his feet in a ninja position in one gymnast-perfect move. He reached behind to the lumbar region of his back and extracted his six-shot stainless 9mm snub nose from a leather holster tucked inside his waistband.

When Chance saw where his hand was going, he leaped to the other side of the hatch opening and lifted up the hatch as a shield against the bullets that began flying at him. Lucky for Chance, the same three-inch-thick wooden platform and hatch that had been there since the day the Statue was erected in 1886, old heartwood oak, stopped every shot. All five. And then...*click-click-click* was the sound from the gun. *What happened to the sixth round?* Teardrop thought. He forgot that he fired one in the elevator.

Before Teardrop could reload, Chance slammed the hatch shut and in a literal second was hurtling at Teardrop.

Chance snatched the propane torch from the deck by the brass nozzle and swung the yellow metal bottle at the gun in a hard-driving golf swing. Teardrop's thumb was between the gun and the bottle. It became a crushed stump. Blood spattered across the 'Up Yours!' finger balloon. The gun left Teardrop's hand and did a two-and-a-half back flip off the boards. It dug deep into the lawn far below, barrel first.

Teardrop kicked between Chance's legs. Chance blocked him. Teardrop tried to stomp on Chance's feet in a kind of traditional Russian dance. He missed. Teardrop charged at Chance like a Rocky Mountain Big Horn Sheep during rutting season. When Teardrop buried his head in Chance's rippled six-pack, Chance, still holding the yellow propane bottle, hammered a pile driver blow to the small of Teardrop's back. The bull went down. And when he did, he pulled a razor-sharp hunting knife from a sheath strapped to his calf under his pant leg. He tried to plunge it deep into Chance's leg above the knee. But Chance blocked most of the blow and it only made a two-inch puncture. Bloody painful, nonetheless.

. . .

As the team of twenty or so Red Hats tossed their catch of fishermen out the door of the Statue, Nicole and Chaz shot footage of each and every one for the record. "What's your name?" Nicole would ask. They would scowl. They would spit. They would not answer. But at least she could show their faces on TV when this was all over. Then fifteen or twenty Red Hats would usher them down to the dock. After tying them up with fishing line, the captives would be thrown to the deck of one of the boats. There were four of them on the deck already, backs against the gunwale walls. As a gesture of thoughtfulness, the explosives that each of the fishermen was planting in the Statue was nestled right between their legs. Ten Red Hats guarded the 'prison boat'.

. . .

Chance looked down at the blood seeping from his leg. He looked up and saw a shiny blade dripping his blood. The burning slice in his thigh made him wince and blink. Teardrop backed off, knelt down on his knees and grabbed for his backpack. He pulled the big flap open and Chance could easily see what was inside. Teardrop pulled the bomb out with both hands. He reached in again and pulled out a black cell phone. All he had to do was press one number. Chance dove at the phone. They wrestled furiously until the phone was knocked out of Teardrop's hands. It slid across the platform toward the feet of Addie Mae and Glaad. Eight eyes drilled into it as it spun and stopped.

• • •

"That way, they went that way, toward the Statue!" The small, wirey man, with hair only on the sides of his head, was irate.

"They stole ten, maybe twelve boats," a big man with a beer-belly blurted out.

"And two wave runners!" a short, older woman with darkly-tanned crepey skin added.

The eight shabby-chic people on the dock were all trying to make their verbal contributions at the same time to the two police officers trying their best to understand exactly what, when and why all this happened.

"Sarge," one of the officers said into his shoulder microphone, "we've got a problem."

• • •

Thirteen men in blue T-shirts were strewn about the deck of the twenty-eight-foot fishing boat, all of them bound hand-and-foot with hefty monofilament. And each of them had explosives between their legs.

There were sixteen people on board the rental boat when it left the Sanitation Department Pier four hours ago: the boat driver, a dozen 'fishermen', Teardrop, Addie Mae and Glaad. Now, three of them were on top of the Statue of Liberty at this very moment: one fighting for his life with Chance and two praying for their lives as they watched the battle that would tell the story.

Cha-ley untied the lines from the dock, hopped

aboard the prison boat, and reached under the instrument panel. The engine roared to life. He pushed off from the dock with his thirteen swarthy captives at his feet and steered the boat away from the island. At a good two thousand feet off the island, Cha-ley cut the engine, opened a forward locker, and threw the anchor from the bow. He waited until the anchor line was taut. Then he looked down at the men sprawled before him and called out in his best pirate voice: "I best be on me way, mateys!" With a flourish, Cha-ley dove into the water and swam to the island.

"Holy shit!" One of the captives exclaimed looking at the bomb between his legs. "I gotta get the fuck outta here!" He went wild, thrashing, wriggling, bumping, thrusting his body up and down, banging against the other men until he was vertical, upright against the gunwale of the boat. The other men, silent, just looked at him. He looked at them. He didn't say a word. He just fell off backwards into the water with his hands and feet bound tightly. He could only attempt to move his body like a porpoise in the water. The men could hear him gasping. Gurgling. Choking. Until they didn't hear him anymore.

One of the men lying on the deck of the boat had an idea.

"If we can pull the wires out of the C-4, it can't explode!" he said.

There was silence for a moment.

Then, all at once, the twelve men became a wriggling, frantic mass of movement.

Like a can of worms.

• • •

Fifty-four Red Hats combed through the inside of the Statue

looking for any explosives they might have missed. They
searched and searched, often getting in each other's way.
There was one red hat for every twenty-five square feet of
floor space. They looked everywhere, behind every beam
and support, every strap and post. They hoped they wouldn't
find a missing bomb the hard way.

• • •

The black phone stopped spinning close to Glaad's feet. He
stared at the phone as if it were a rat or snake, just eyeing it.
All four people on the platform were paralyzed at that
moment. Everyone knew that Glaad's ankles were tethered
together to prevent him from kicking. But…the phone was
just close enough that Glaad could cock his ankle and give
the phone a good sideways whack. His foot was the hockey
stick that sent it back to the other side of the platform. It
stopped just before the 'middle finger' blowup.
        Teardrop's head snapped upward. He saw something
above the heads of Addie Mae and Glaad. Suddenly their
clothes and hair were blown by a turbulent wind. It was
Teardrop's rescue chopper. The man in the open hatch
unrolled a rope ladder that reached to the railing. Teardrop
bolted for the ladder. He managed to grab the bottom rung.
Then he jammed his left foot into Glaad's hip and climbed
up onto the railing. The man in the hatch was coaching him.
The pilot was fixated on him. They were ready to pull away.
Chance grabbed Teardrop's legs, getting them in a bear hug.
Chance was being pulled up by the chopper, but he would
not let go of Teardrop's legs. Chance wrapped his own legs
around the railing and pulled backwards on Teardrop's body
with all his might. The chopper swayed slightly away from
the Statue. Teardrop and Chance were stretched out

over…nothing! Nothing but air between them and the ground! A three-hundred-foot drop! The view downward was dizzying. Nauseating. Frightening. Both men would die. Just one more inch by the chopper and they would free-fall to their deaths. The Red Hats looking up from the lawn below were frozen. Unable to move or call out. Only to gasp. Nicole put her hands to her face. Chaz kept shooting, the camera almost completely vertical.

Teardrop and Chance were hanging there, a human rope only connected to life by Teardrop's fingertips and Chance's legs…and now just his feet.

One of Teardrop's hands gave way! He was holding on by one hand! The chopper pilot adjusted the cyclic control and the helicopter nudged back closer to the Statue. Teardrop regained his second hand on the ladder. Chance regained his leg-hold on the railing. They were both again over the platform. With his face showing the enormous strain, Chance closed his eyes and gave one last, massive tug on Teardrop and they both fell to the wooden deck.

Teardrop, on top of Chance, dashed for the black phone by the balloon.

Chance was up, but not running for Teardrop. Instead he ran for the bomb. He put it back inside the backpack and took it with him. Chance grabbed something from his toolbox duffle bag. A four-foot French pro-level spear gun. As he had done a thousand times before, he pulled back the four surgical rubber bands and cocked the gun, similar to a cross bow.

Teardrop was almost at the phone. He was frantic. His hand reached out for the phone, but his foot was in front of his hand. He kicked the phone under the balloon!

Chance rushed closer to the chopper. And with a perfect underhand toss, he hurled the backpack into the open hatch of the helicopter. Before it even flew through the opening, Chance raised his spear gun and, *whoosh!* The stainless steel, super-sharp spear easily pierced the plastic pilot-side window of the chopper and plunged deep into the pilot's left shoulder. The chopper immediately dove off to the right. Teardrop, head under the balloon, grabbed the phone and pressed the button. In one beautifully executed fireworks extravaganza, the chopper, about two thousand feet away to the back right of the Statue, and the prison boat, about two thousand feet to the front left of the Statue, exploded simultaneously. The chopper was now a huge neon fireball in the sky. Large, broken pieces of it fell heavy into the water below it, the hot metal releasing clouds of steam. The separated rotor blades spun downward in swirls and sliced into the surface.

The prison boat exploded sending ripples radiating in all directions. A cloud of fire and smoke rose up as high as the Statue. Cha-ley was blown down on the lawn below the Statue, but was unhurt. The concussion blew hard against Addie Mae and Glaad and caused Chance to take a step back from the blast.

Teardrop couldn't believe what just happened. He couldn't even blow himself up! His men, his rescue chopper, his place in history, all taken away. By his own hand. He threw the phone at Chance, bent down and grabbed the knife he used to stab Chance earlier. He came at Chance slashing like a machine gone berserk. He was determined to strike some part, any part of Chance. Chance's eyes could hardly follow the whirling blade. It was a blur, so fast it made sonic wave sounds as it cut the air. It glinted in the sun like a strobe. Teardrop came closer and closer.

Chance bent down and reached into his duffle bag toolbox, his war chest. The most deadly weapon in the bag was in his hands. The ironwood club with the big burled knob at the business end. The kind of club African warriors have used for centuries. It was in front of him now, between his chest and the spinning, rotating, jabbing, flashing blade of the bloody hunting knife.

Chance's eyes locked on the blade like a laser. His brain worked like a computer, processing tiny bits of information. His mathematical mind made a million calculations. The green light in his head lit. Chance hammered the club down as if he were driving a nail. The knife thrust into the wooden deck, point first, straight up. Teardrop foolishly bent to retrieve it. It wouldn't pull out.

Chance took his club and poked the bulbous end straight into the face of Teardrop. Blood let instantly from his nose and lips. He snarled and his teeth were bright red, dripping like a vampire. Chance, sensing what might happen next, backed up. He could feel the metal railing against his back.

Teardrop, enraged, possessed by primitive impulses, by a demonic evil, charged at Chance full force. He would knock Chance off the platform. He would take Chance with himself over the edge. He would grab hold and not let go. Taking both to their death.

Teardrop hit Chance like a locomotive. But a nano-second before total impact, Chance lifted his knee between Teardrop's legs. Chance kicked high toward his own chin.

Chance turned his club horizontal, a barrier across his abdomen. When Teardrop hit, Chance mashed the club just below Teardrop's ribcage and lifted the club up like a bar. A rising bar, over his own head.

Teardrop rose into the air above Chance as if he had sprung off a diving board. Free-falling in the air, he started to somersault. His head went down and his legs came up behind him. He was completely upside down three hundred feet above the ground. He continued to spin forward so his head came around and up again. A little more spin and his body was flat, horizontal over Lady Liberty's crown. The seven spikes of the crown, that represent the seven continents, jutted out and up.

Teardrop was belly-flopping fast! You could see it coming! You could envision the trajectory! As if it were fate, destined to happen, Teardrop was skewered by the center spike of the crown of Lady Liberty. *A fait accompli.*

Teardrop was motionless. Speared like a marshmallow on a stick. He hung there, lifeless, a ragdoll, high above the crowd, the city, America, on a spike just above the eyes of Lady Liberty. As if she took her 'pound of flesh'.

The crowd below went wild with glee! Justice!

Chance extracted the knife that was stuck in the wooden deck. He dashed to Addie Mae and Glaad and gently removed the duct tape over their mouths. He cut them loose from the railing. They clung to each other for half a minute before moving to the railing at the front of the Statue. They waved, signaling that they were all OK. Below them, a sight they'll never forget. One hundred and seventeen Red Hats were gathered together. And now they released a cheer that rose up to the top of the Statue. An enormously loud, wonderful, heart-warming cheer that filled the eyes of Chance and brought tears to the eyes of Addie Mae and Glaad. And tears to the eyes of Nicole. Chaz just kept shooting.

With the knife, Chance went to the 'middle finger' balloon and sliced it from top to bottom as far as he could reach. The balloon collapsed and hung over the side of the platform.

The crowd below cheered wildly!

Then Chance had something else to do. He went to his bag, took out two more small knives and stuck them all into his waistband. He explained his plan to Addie Mae and Glaad. He took the ropes that had been dropped by the chopper, tied them together and made two loops – one small loop at the very bottom and a larger loop about three feet up. He gathered the rest of the rope together and handed it to Addie Mae and Glaad. Then he climbed over the railing. He inserted his foot in the small bottom loop. Then he pulled the larger loop up to his waist. His two helpers lowered him down the outside of the forty-two-foot arm of the Statue.

The crowd watched in wonder and fear as Chance performed an unexpected circus-like act high above them. He made his way slowly and carefully down the copper arm all the way to the horizontal bar that held up the sign that hung in front of the Statue.

He carefully straddled the bar, which was actually made of wood. He had one leg on the inside, pressed against the Statue for balance, and one leg on the outside. Pushing down with his arms, he scooted his bottom along the wooden bar until he got to the spot he wanted…right above the letter 'U'. With one of his knives, he pried off the staples above the 'U'. He sliced this way and that and pulled the white fabric together so the 'U' became a crude 'O'. He stabbed his small knife into the wood to hold the letter in place.

He then inched his way over to the letter 'K', popping out some staples along the way. Again, he made long cuts along the fabric. Down on the right side and along the bottom of the letter. Then he tugged hard and pulled on the fabric, almost falling off, until he could fold the fabric over on itself so the letter 'C' was covered up. Then he cut the top of the 'K' until it became a somewhat recognizable

'R'.

When he was finished, he pushed with his arms and moved his butt backward along the board. As he climbed back up the rope, the throng below erupted in the largest cheer yet. The police chopper flying to the Statue had the best view of all. The news chopper following would, too.

Chance had changed the sign from:

FUCK AMERICA

to

FOR AMERICA

"I think we just witnessed a miracle," the police-pilot said to the co-pilot.

With the help of Addie Mae and Glaad, Chance made his way safely back to the platform.

The one hundred and seventeen Red Hats were applauding and cheering wildly!

Then, when Chance picked up the American flag, the one that Teardrop was going to burn, the crowd grew silent. They all just looked up, coming to the realization of what just happened. One hundred and seventeen faces, eyes gazing upward, were fixed on a sign that said FOR AMERICA. And on a symbol of freedom and liberty for all Americans, no matter what color, race, religion, or anything.

Bring us your tired, your weary...the inscription said.

The faces, the silence, the eyes of the Red Hats said it all without saying a word.

But then, there was a voice. One voice. A voice in the crowd started singing...low at first.

"God Bless America, land that I love..."

A few more voices joined in...

"Stand beside her, and guide her..."

Chance took the ropes at his feet and threaded one

end through the grommets of the flag.

More voices joined in, "Through the night with the light from above."

Chance tossed the rope over the flame at the top of the torch and pulled on the rope. The American flag rose up. It was flying.

Everyone was singing, "From the mountains, to the prairies, to the oceans, white with foam…"

The wind picked up. The flag was full. It waved over the Statue of Liberty. It waved high above New York City. It waved high above America.

They all sang: "God bless America, my home sweet home."

Tears were flowing down faces. The words were felt in every soul.

"God bless America, my home sweet home!"

In one spontaneous, unexplainable, unanimous gesture, all one hundred and seventeen red hats were tossed into the air in an exuberant act of thankfulness.

Thankful to be an American.

Today of all days.

TWENTY-TWO

A 'lion's roar' alarm came from the cell phone on the table next to the bed. Nikki was in a tidy 'S' curve on her side. Chance was sprawled all over the rest of the bed. He reached out and shut off the alarm.

Without turning her head, Nikki said, "What time is it?"

"Seven," Chance answered, also without moving.

"Don't you think you deserve to sleep in this morning?" Nikki moaned.

"Yes, I do. But I have a busy day ahead."

Nikki said, "Oh, you must be talking about the Mayor." Nikki was still only moving her mouth.

" 'Fraid so," Chance said.

"Can't he wait?" she asked.

"I hope he did wait. He might not be there. Cha-ley's going with me. I told him to meet me at City Hall at eight. I want to get there early and wait for Wertz. If he shows up."

"Good thing we…celebrated last night, then," Nikki concluded.

"Let's hope the day goes well so there's another reason to celebrate tonight," Chance said.

"Do we need a reason?" Nikki turned her head and smiled warmly at Chance.

• • •

It was five minutes after eight when Chance and Cha-ley walked away from the security checkpoint at City Hall. It seemed like an especially long walk down to the Mayor's office that morning. As they turned the corner, Patty Bromstad was already at her desk.

"Looks like you're a celebrity," Patty said to Chance.

"No one asked for my autograph on the way here," Chance said with a humble smile.

The Mayor's door was closed.

"Have you seen the Mayor?" Chance asked.

"He's...he's in his office," she said, sounding worried.

"Is something wrong, Patty?"

"His door is never closed in the morning. Too much for us to get done. And it's locked. It's never locked. It was closed when I left last night, too. Something's not right."

"How do you know he's in there?"

"He made a call. I could see his line was lit up. It was a long call, too. Not like him in the morning."

"Well, I'm afraid I have some unpleasant things to talk to the Mayor about. I'm sorry if it doesn't turn out very well," Chance cautioned.

"I...I suspected it wouldn't be a good day today. I think I know a little too much." Patty looked down at the rug on the floor. Chance and Cha-ley made believe they didn't hear what Patty had said.

Chance turned and knocked on the wooden door. No response.

He knocked again.

Inside the Mayor's office, a shot glass sat on the edge of his desk. It was empty. A whiskey bottle sat next to the glass. It was half-full.

The Mayor sat there, in his chair, studying an unframed photo on his desk. It was a picture of himself standing next to his brother, Bert. They were smiling, during happier times.

Edward Wertz pivoted slightly in his chair. He pulled out the top right drawer of his desk. The one with the stainless revolver in it.

Chance knocked on the door again. Harder, this time.

BAAANG!!! The unmistakable sound of a gunshot. The sound of a gun falling to the floor. The deafening silence that followed.

Patty's hands went to her face. Tears came to her eyes. She was sobbing.

Chance said to Cha-ley, "We'd better get a hold of Brix."

• • •

A policeman stood on either side of the door of the charming Cape Cod with the white picket fence as two detectives led Sheamus O'Neill out in handcuffs to the waiting police car.

• • •

Arthur Stevens, hands behind his back, walked down the cement steps in front of his red brick home, escorted by detectives and two policemen.

• • •

Two detectives walked into Bayfront Jewelers in San Francisco.

"Are you Bertram Wertz?" one of them asked the smiling man behind the jewelry case.

"Yes! Are you the guys from the bottled water

promotion?"

• • •

A stack of NYCritic Newspapers were thrown from the delivery truck to the sidewalk at the corner newsstand. The headline:

MORE MONDAY MADNESS!
Mayor Kills Himself at City Hall!

TWENTY-THREE

The podium was set up in front of the stone steps outside
City Hall. Six microphones were there to capture the words
that would be said there this morning. And what a glorious
day it was. The weather was perfect.

All the network TV reporters were there, with their
camera crews, sound guys, photographers…there were radio
talk show hosts, newspaper reporters…and, of course, local
PIC TV–10 reporter…journalist, Nicole Jensen.

"After weeks of doom and gloom, death and
destruction, it's time for celebration in New York City. The
Monday Murders are over. The sniper that terrorized our city
is gone and the Statue of Liberty is still standing, thanks to
the man who will be honored here today. As you can see,
Chaz, if you'll turn the camera around, there are more than a
thousand people here this morning on the plaza and
stretching into the park all the way to Broadway. All here to
show respect and gratitude for the man who, in one week,
removed a deadly threat to our police officers and citizens,
brought justice to City Hall, and unity to our neighborhoods.
Presiding over today's event will be Deputy Mayor and
Press Secretary, Tom Elliott. The event is about to begin.
Let's watch!"

A stream of men and women from City Hall,
perhaps thirty or forty, began to fill the steps standing behind
the podium. They were all there: Police Commissioner Brix,
local FBI Branch Director Bill Murphy, FDNY Battalion
Chief Neal Waters, Psychiatrist Gloria Mahaffey, M.E. Dr.
Grinell, Bill Spencer from Ballistics, Detective Julio Morales

and Patty Bromstad. And last, but not least, Andy
Cartwright.

Next to walk out and take their places closest to the
podium were Jadon Daniels, Glaad Reynolds, Bill
Wilkinson, the Governor of Florida, Cha-ley and Addie Mae.

Next was Tom Elliott, Deputy Mayor and Press
Secretary.

And finally, Frank Stoneman...Chance.

The sea of thrilled citizens erupted into applause.
Two thousand hands clapped enthusiastically, loudly,
together. The crowd was a mix of black and white faces,
Hispanic, Asian and East Indian. The multi-ethnic faces of a
world city.

Tom Elliott stood at the microphone, but the
applause refused to die down. He waited. He put his hands
up to calm things down so he could proceed. It took a while.
But finally...

"Good morning! Good morning, everyone! We are
here this morning, all of us, to say thank you to a man, a
'Miracle Man', who has done more for our city in such a
short time than anyone I can remember in recent history. Mr.
Frank Stoneman."

The crowd erupted in vigorous appreciation.

"To do what Frank did was truly astonishing. He
brought to justice a madman, a killer, hiding in plain sight,
eluding all of us for years."

The crowd applauded.

"He uncovered corruption, crime and murder, lies
and deception at the very top of our city government, which
would never have been discovered if not for Frank."

Applause again.

"He created and started the UP! Program to help our
challenged innercity and underprivileged neighbors to get a

hand up and improve their lives for themselves and their families!"

Louder applause now.

"And he, with a little help from his friends, saved the Statue of Liberty from total destruction."

Wild applause from everyone!

"The Statue that, since 1886, has been America's proud symbol of liberty and freedom for all who seek it and for our great country. I have to add that Frank Stoneman himself is also our strong symbol for liberty and freedom. We're all proud of him."

Long, wild applause.

"And here's the man himself, Frank Stoneman!"

Then came an ovation few have ever seen or heard. Thunderous applause. Then a hypnotic chant… "Frank, Frank, Frank, Frank…" It went on for a long time. Deservedly so.

Chance, at the microphone, patted the air with his hands to quiet the crowd down. He had more than a few words to say.

"Thank you! Thank you! …Thank you! Thank you, very much! Thank you! There is someone who needs to be up here with the rest of us." Chance was looking around in the crowd. Then he saw her.

"Nicole Jensen! Nicole, come up here!"

Nicole was holding her microphone. She awkwardly handed it to Chaz and made her way to the stairs and stood beside Addie Mae.

"These people…" Chance put his arm out, palm up, "these people deserve as much credit as I do, if not more."

The audience didn't quite believe him, thinking him overly humble.

"But they're not the only ones. You see the people

right there," Chance was pointing into the gathering, "all those people with the red hats. They are amazing people, too!"

Applause again.

"First, let me tell you a little about Nicole Jensen." Nicole had no idea what Chance was going to say, and instead of her confident on-air personae, she was feeling a little shy right now.

"Nicole Jensen is the person who got me here in the first place. It was Nicole who brought me to the attention of…the city government. She pushed and pushed and finally got them to agree. With some helpful reinforcement from the Governor of the State of Florida, Bill Wilkinson." Chance pointed to the Governor.

Applause.

"It was Nicole Jensen who stood up courageously to the unscrupulous Mayor Wertz to bring truth and integrity to journalism here in the city, against his objections and threats."

Enthusiastic applause.

"It was Nicole Jensen, and Chaz her cameraman, who risked their lives to film and record history in the making in the Statue of Liberty raid and rescue."

Big applause again.

"And thanks go to this man." Chance pointed to Cha-ley.

"Charles Hastings, a man of many talents. He single-handedly crossed the nation, coast-to-coast, risking life and limb to gather evidence that allowed us to open a case of murder, lies and deception that led to the destruction of a good immigrant family and the creation of the killer we know as the sniper. And…Cha-ley, as we call him, was part of the invasion of Liberty Island that saved the Statue."

Long, warm, appreciative applause.

"But the courage doesn't stop there. This woman, Addie Mae Cypress, and this man, Glaad Reynolds, are two amazingly brave, tenacious, determined people who found and actually went to the location of a group calling themselves The USA Group. Secretly that stands for The Underground Subversive Attack Group. It's who we were calling The Outsiders. A group of professional agitators that are funded by extremists who fan the flames of hatred and encourage riots, looting, and destruction of our inner cities. But this group went far beyond riots and looting. These people wanted to destroy the best ideas and symbols of American freedom and democracy. Dangerous dudes, to be sure. But these two incredible people, Addie Mae and Glaad, who were captured and held hostage and then tied up to the top of the Statue, intended to be part of the destruction of the Statue…they remained steadfast, patriotic and true. Ready to die for America. An American Indian woman and an African American man."

The applause was overwhelming.

"And our thanks go to this young man, Jadon Daniels, the new generation of black pride and potential."

Applause.

"And to the men and women wearing the red hats. Jadon calls them The Innercity Soldiers. And soldiers, they are. Soldiers for good. Soldiers for freedom. Soldiers for their people. Soldiers for America. There were one hundred and seventeen of them, who, on an instant's notice, raced to the Statue of Liberty to save her. These are the men who put their own lives second and America first. Without flinching, without hesitation, they took Liberty Island by storm. Ignoring the constant danger from guns, knives and bombs that would have ended their lives in an instant. Their bravery, their unwavering commitment and dedication to their families, their city, to their country, was tested and proven that day. I'm proud of each and every one of them. And I know you are, too."

The biggest ovation yet was for these heroes.

"And just one more thing about the Red Hats. It's about their…red hats! On the front of the hat it says…Believe In…" Chance held up one of the hats and pointed to the words. "I asked Jadon what this means. Why it's on the front of the hat? He said because it's important to believe in…yourself. Believe in…the future. Believe in hard work. Believe in a better life. Believe in your husband…your wife. Believe in your children. That you can be a better father or mother. Believe in your church. Your community. Your city. Believe in America. And the American dream. When you 'believe', you have hope. And when you have hope, you have one of the most important things in life. So…Jadon…we believe in *you*!"

Chance waited and waited for the enthusiastic applause to die down. When it did: "So…in closing, I'd like to say, you are *all* great people…African Americans, whites, Hispanics, Asians…the great melting pot…*you* are what makes America great! Trust each other! Help each other! Listen to each other! If you do, your neighborhood, your city, your country will be better than ever! Thank you! God bless New York City and God bless America!"

On cue, from the loudspeakers on the sides of the steps, the song God Bless America was playing. The citizens of New York City left City Hall Plaza singing.

TWENTY-FOUR

The light from the candle flickered through the glass of wine sending red reflections dancing across the white tablecloth at Pasquale's.

Chance and Nikki picked up their glasses for a toast.

"Well, here's to you, Chance. You did it. And more."

"That's the first time you called me Chance."

"Well, of course. You're not Frank anymore, are you?"

"No. No, I'm not. Never really was."

"I bet you're glad it's over," she said.

"Parts of it, yes. Parts of it, no," he replied.

"How about this part," Nikki ventured.

"This part?"

Nikki cocked her head, waiting.

"This part," he continued, "was the best part."

She smiled.

"Well. It was for me, too. But…" she trailed off.

"But?" Chance said.

"But now, I suppose you're going home."

Chance paused before answering. "Well, I do miss Coralina."

"I knew there had to be another woman!"

Chance smiled smugly. "Coralina is my fishing boat. It's a Greek word. It means 'from the coral of the sea'."

"Ahh." Nikki was obviously relieved a bit. "So," she continued, "the spear gun is not merely a weapon used to take down nasty criminals?"

"Mostly nasty Grouper."

"You love your way of life, don't you Chance?"

"Yes. More than I ever thought I would. Do you love yours?"

Nikki hesitated, "Less than I thought I would. But it's getting better. You helped me see that."

"Gee, everyone's giving me credit for all kinds of things today."

"You deserve it."

"And so do you. You're a great reporter," he said, teasing.

"Journalist!" Nikki corrected, with mock admonishment.

"Journalist," Chance repeated, smiling.

He continued: "And you have a bright future here in New York. I'm sure of it."

"So…?" Nikki was fishing.

"So?" Chance was not biting.

"So, I guess this is goodbye," Nikki said with an unhappy face.

"Not a good bye, but not a bad bye. Just…a bye. A bye for now."

Nikki was looking sad. Downright sad. She was fighting to stop her eyes from filling up.

"Look," Chance said softly, warmly, "we're both young. You put your heart and soul into this unbelievably challenging, stimulating career. Not to mention the money your father put into your education getting you here. You're destined to do great things. It's in your nature. And one thing I've learned about nature, you let it take its course."

A tear ran down Nikki's cheek. *Damn it!* she thought, *I didn't want to cry. And I'm supposed to be so tough. Damn it!* She dragged some strength up from somewhere and said, "Well, being a country girl from Wyoming, I know a thing or two about nature. And I know that a country girl's nature means getting her ass down to the Everglades for a boat ride on Coralina."

"Let's plan on it, for sure," Chance said.

"Promise?"

"Promise."

Nikki was afraid to ask this: "When do you leave?"

Chance was afraid to answer: "In the morning."

Nikki sighed, then said, "We'd better make the most of tonight, then."

Chance smiled and said, "Promise?"

Nikki answered, "Promise." She reached out and grabbed his hand.

TWENTY-FIVE

Two Months Later…

The music had an urgent, ticker-tape kind of sound. The red type crawling across the bottom of the screen said: BREAKING NEWS NOW. At the top of the screen it said UNN – Urgent News Network. The off-camera voice announced: "This is UNN…the nation's #1 News Network with America's most popular news anchor, Nicole Jensen."

Nicole, sitting at a large, modern desk, turned to the camera and said, "Hi everyone, I'm Nicole Jensen with Urgent News Now."

. . .

The big sign on the lime green wall said:
THE CHANGE WE NEED!
THE MAYOR WE NEED! TOM ELLIOTT!

Tom Elliott had the sleeves of his white dress shirt rolled up, his tie was loose and he was talking on the phone. It was one of a dozen phones manned by a dozen fast-talking, excited young people in the storefront of Elliott Election Headquarters.

"I'll be there!" Tom said into the phone. "Any rally is a good rally."

. . .

Palm trees reached high into the deep blue sky as The Beaver and the Coralina floated languidly at the dock. The sea was an especially vibrant mix of blues and turquoise today. Chance walked down the hall in his beautiful home onto the flagstone patio to the outdoor kitchen and dining area. He sat down at the big dining table where Cha-ley and Addie Mae were already seated. There were big oval plates in front of each of them, occupied by grilled mangrove snapper so big the heads and tails hung off the sides of the plates.

The seventy-inch flat-screen TV mounted on the wall under the eaves was showing UNN, of course. On the screen, at the bottom, it said RACE FOR THE WHITEHOUSE from Washington DC.

On the screen was a podium on a stage with eight American flags behind it. At the podium was a woman motioning with her hands and raising her arms as she spoke.

"Can't hear her," Cha-ley said grabbing the remote. Her voice got louder.

"…and it is my incredible honor and distinct pleasure to introduce to you, the next President of the United States, Damian Erring!"

Cufflinks stepped up to the podium.

"My fellow Ameericans…"

Chance's ears perked up.

"I am here today, at this campaign rally, to tell you how we are going to change Ameerica forever."

Chance put his fork down, got up, and went inside the house. He came back holding a blue cell phone. He tapped the screen a couple of times and he heard the recording.

"…because you will be the one to change Ameerica forever." It was Cufflinks speaking to Chameleon. Chance had Chameleon's phone. The phone he picked up off the ground at the rally when he bumped into Chameleon. The cell phone he had deliberately held onto all this time, hoping it would someday, somehow, lead to the man behind The USA Group – The Underground Subversive Attack Group. The man who pronounced America...Ameerica.

Chance looked up at the TV screen. He listened carefully. He looked at Mr. Damien Erring's lips.

"Are you ready to help me change Ameerica forever?" Mr. Erring asked again.

Chance turned to his two best friends. "Addie Mae, pack a lunch. Cha-ley, get The Beaver ready. Looks like I'm going to Washington, DC."

Cha-ley gave The Beaver a shove and it pivoted away from the dock. From the open window, Chance yelled, "I love you guys!"

Addie Mae yelled, "Love you, too! Love you, too!"

Cha-ley yelled, "Call if you need us!"

"Oh, I will," said Chance, "I will."

The Beaver rose from the water, banked to the left and straightened its wings as it climbed. Addie Mae and Cha-ley waved goodbye from the dock. The plane dipped its wings left and right to 'wave' goodbye, too.

The Beaver flew over the fronds of the palm trees and headed north. To another adventure.

To be continued...

The Journey...

I hope you enjoyed reading *Saving New York* as much as I enjoyed writing it. I learned a lot researching the hundreds of facts and figures that, I hope, made this book a rich reading experience for you. For any author, writing a book is a journey. I'd like to share some interesting things I picked up along the way that didn't make it into the pages of my story.

• **There's a top-secret room under Grand Central Station**. It's called M-42. It's not on any blueprint or plan. Its exact location is classified. During World War II, a person could be shot on sight just for entering. Its existence was only acknowledged in the 1980's.

 • **During WWI German spies blew up an ammo dump near the Statue of Liberty**. It was in New Jersey, only a four-minute boat ride from Lady Liberty. One thousand tons of war ammunition was ready for distribution to the front lines when it exploded on July 30, 1916. The blast nearly ripped the arm off the Statue and it blew out thousands of windows in Manhattan. The arm and torch have been closed to visitors ever since.

• **Two wine cellars are built into the Brooklyn Bridge**. One on each side. They were rented to wine merchants as early as 1876, seven years before the bridge opened. Eventually, the rent was as much as five thousand dollars a year for the Manhattan side and five hundred dollars a year for the Brooklyn side.

• **Thin skin** – the copper 'skin' on the Stature of Liberty is equal to the thickness of two pennies.

• **Wired** – the Brooklyn Bridge, a marvel of steel wire suspension, was designed by John A. Roebling. He just happened to own a steel wire factory.

• **Design & Build** – the Statue of Liberty was designed by French sculptor Frederic Bartholdi. It was built by Gustave Eiffel. Yes, that Eiffel.

• **No body** – when the Statue of Liberty arrived in the U.S. from France, there were no funds to build a pedestal. Between 1876 and 1882, the head of the Statue was on display on the streets of New York City. The arm and torch were on display in Philadelphia.

• **Castle Clinton** – named for NYC Mayor DeWitt Clinton, this is now the departure point for the Statue of Liberty tours. But between 1855 and 1890, before there was an Ellis Island, it was an entry point for more than eight thousand immigrants. I'm sure you've heard of some of them: Mother Cabrini, William Fox (Twentieth Century Fox), Harry Houdini (Erich Weisz), Joseph Pulitzer, Nikola Tesla and Frederic Trump, grandfather of Donald Trump, our 45th President.

• **The real dirt** – between 1860 and 1873, ten million cartloads of sub-par dirt and rocks were removed from Central Park. Then, 18,500 cubic yards of good soil were brought in from New Jersey. This was soil deemed good enough to transplant over four million trees, shrubs and plants.

• **Manhattan was once the Capital of America** – it

happened between January 11, 1785 and December 5, 1790.

• **What's in a name?** When I write a book, I create a world of interesting characters. There are more than seventy-three named characters in this book alone. I believe character names should be as interesting as the characters themselves. The names should have some kind of memorable connection to the dimension and personality of the character – historical, occupational, psychological, ethnic, religious…something! This makes it more fun for you, the reader, and involves you in more than just the next clue.

    For example:

• Robert Knickerbocker – a name carefully selected by Antonio Perez to "fit in" to New York City culture. Robert 'Bob' is a traditionally trusted and 'good guy' first name. In the sixteen-hundreds, Dutch settlers came to 'New Amsterdam' wearing their traditional style of pants called Knickerbockers. What we now refer to as 'knickers'. Not coincidently, New York City's favorite basketball team is called "The Knicks".

• Duncan Arroyo, Chief Engineer for the NYC Department of Environmental Protection (sewers) – Duncan comes from the Gaelic word for brown warrior (that seems appropriate for a sewer manager) and Arroyo derives from a Spanish word for water course or irrigation channel.

• Jadon Daniels, leader of The Innercity Soldiers (The Red Hats) – Jadon is of Hebrew origin and means *God is heard*. Daniels means *God is my judge*.

• Chance – to truly understand the meaning of this name, a name chosen by Chance himself, read my book *Saving an*

Innocent Man. It will deepen your understanding and sweeten your connection with every book in the SAVING SERIES and explain how a man called Chance was born.

Thank you for reading *Saving New York*.
Please go to RobertWrightThrillers.com for highlights of my current books and novels to come.

A thriller that bites with mystery and suspense!

SAVING
AN
INNOCENT MAN

He's running for his life.
From a thousand bullets...
and a thousand teeth!

ROBERT E. B. WRIGHT

The book that started it all!

SAVING AN INNOCENT MAN
He's running for his life.
From a thousand bullets...and a thousand teeth!

A small plane crashes violently in the most isolated part of
the vast Everglades. The lone survivor is in a bloody heap
next to the dead pilot. An EMT and chopper pilot/cop are on
their way.

Not to rescue him.

To kill him.

Four and half million in cash can make murderers out of
honest men. All they have to do is find the suitcase full of
money and leave him there to die. What they don't know is
that this poor guy was in the wrong place at the wrong time.
He has no idea where the money is. But he does hear their
plan.

Knowing for certain his life will come to a horrifying
end, he manages a surprise move and is able to make an
agonizing escape into the jungle. It's a chance he has to take,
even if it means facing death from alligators or poisonous
snakes, starvation, dehydration, exhaustion or disease.

But the chase is just beginning.

Naples, Florida Police Officer: *"I've imagined getting
my hands on big money for a long time..."*

Chicago Detective, Tony DiSantis: *"If we don't get
him, the rednecks will."*

Miami Detective, Craig Mulhulland: *"DiSantis should
do what he does best. Stay in Chicago."*

Glades Redneck: *"Lock & load."*

Beautiful young Indian girl: *"The tribe wants you to stay."*

Beautiful blonde who dropped her bath towel: *"You're an animal."*

Chicago crime boss, Joey Esposito: *"The old man wants his money. Cabish?"*

Central American mercenary: *"Burn him!"*

A thriller that roars with mystery and suspense!

SAVING KENYA

Who is this man called Chance?
And why is the President of Kenya desperate for his help?

Another Novel Thriller from

ROBERT E. B. WRIGHT

Let the thrills continue!
SAVING KENYA
**Who is this man called Chance?
And why is the President of Kenya
desperate for his help?**

Newly-elected President of Kenya, Victor Mutuma, is at the pinnacle of his life. It wasn't easy getting to the top. Now it's up to Mutuma to take his country to the next level. To take his hard-won success and create a legacy of achievement that would last a century.

But something is in his way. The explosive increase in the poaching of Kenya's treasure trove of wildlife. The animals millions of tourists come to Kenya to see. A single rhinoceros horn can bring $340,000 on the Black Market. A leopard pelt, $35,000. A Cape buffalo head, $30,000. Ounce-for-ounce, poached parts sell for more than cocaine or heroin. It's a nineteen billion dollar-a year-business of ruthless international crime syndicates equipped with night vision scopes, high-tech weapons, drones, helicopters and armies of savage killers. They're not just slaughtering endangered species and tens of thousands of animals, they're murdering hundreds of Rangers trying to protect the animals. They're killing the tourism industry of Kenya. And they'll kill anyone who tries to stop them.

Mutuma declares war on the poachers.

The syndicate declares war on him.

They'll stop at nothing. Not assassination. Not the kidnapping of his son. And not the man Mutuma brings in to fight them.

A man called Chance.

Chance revels in the nature of Kenya. It reminds him of his beloved Everglades. Bucolic in a way. But the upheaval is about to start.

Chance has never seen a woman like Nefertari Mahmoud, obvious mistress of President Mutuma. And she has never seen a man like Chance.

Chance has his hands full in more ways than one.

From the squalid poacher tent camps in the African bush to a sex-nest penthouse in Dubai…from a billionaire's luxury yacht moored in the Persian Gulf to the filthy smuggler ships steaming to China and Asia…Chance is climbing on top of dead bodies, both human and animal.

To save a boy.

To save a country. .

To save a continent.

Will he have to sacrifice his own life to do it?

Acknowledgments

My thanks go out to a few people who graciously volunteered to read advance copies of this book. Thank you to Linda Gavit, Ian Harrison, Lindy Leftwich and Sharon Matt.

Thanks also go to Lindy Leftwich and Jed Leftwich at Hilton Graphics for their talent, skill and patience crafting the cover concept into an exciting visual.

And thanks to my wife, Valerie Cardarelli-Wright, for her uncanny editing prowess and unending patience evaluating continuity, accurate time lines and story logistics. Valerie should also be recognized for the herculean task of typing the entire manuscript of 105,410 words (from a transcribing machine). Valerie also contributed mightily to cover design, book interior design and all digital formatting. With her myriad talents and unwavering dedication to the project, Valerie made this a better book than I wrote.

About the Author

Robert E. B. Wright was born in New York City with a fitting last name. It means maker (shipwright, cartwright, playwright). And that's exactly what Robert has been doing since he could hold a pencil. Making. Creating. Writing.

For many years, Robert had the good fortune to be Vice President/Creative Director at some of the largest advertising agencies in the world making award-winning ads and TV commercials. His travels have taken him to many continents…from the tops of snowcapped mountains to the dark depths of the ocean…from the vast Everglades to the jungles of Africa and South America. As Robert says, "If you're gonna write a thriller, it helps to live a thrilling life." Robert does. He's an accomplished pilot, scuba diver, skier and musician.

Robert and his wife, Valerie, divide their time between an authentic, hand-hewn log cabin in the high mountains of the Western Rockies and a beach house on a tropical ocean…as well as exploring the worldwide locations described in the Saving Series of novels.

Visit the author's official website at RobertWrightThrillers.com and sign on for unexpected adventures and breathtaking thrills! Join the journey to exotic places, heart-stopping dangers and "Aha" moments at every twist and turn along the way.

Made in the USA
Middletown, DE
28 December 2019